Russell James

was described by Ian Rankin as 'The Godfather of British Noir'. He is a British crime writer known for his hard-hitting, low-life thrillers. When he started writing, James wrote counter to the spirit of the times (which wanted sex 'n' shopping and international conspiracy novels) and instead wrote hard-bitten, multi-layered underworld thrillers, rich on character and locale; the kind of books more common in America than the UK.

Named by *The Times* as 'something of a cult', James is a truly noir crime writer. There are no detectives in his books, and when the police do appear it is on the sidelines. Russell James concentrates on the criminals, their victims and the people caught up in what's going on – never more so than in this latest book. He was Chairman of the Crime Writers' Association for 2001-2002.

His website can be found at www.russelljames.co.uk

Russell James' Books Include:

PICK ANY TITLE (The Do-Not Press)
THE ANNEX (Five Star Mysteries)
PAINTING IN THE DARK (The Do-Not Press)
OH NO, NOT MY BABY (The Do-Not Press)
COUNT ME OUT (Serpent's Tail)
SLAUGHTER MUSIC (Allison & Busby)
PAYBACK (Gollancz)
DAYLIGHT (Gollancz)
UNDERGROUND (Gollancz)

No One Gets Hurt

a novel by
Russell James

First Published in Great Britain in 2003 by
The Do-Not Press Limited
16 The Woodlands
London SE13 6TY
www.thedonotpress.co.uk
email: NOGH@thedonotpress.co.uk

Copyright © 2003 by Russell James
The right of Russell James to be identified as the Author of this work has been asserted by him in accordance with the Copyright, Designs & Patents Act 1988.

B-format paperback: ISBN 1 904 316 07 7
Casebound edition: ISBN 1 904 316 06 9

British Library Cataloguing in Publication Data. A catalogue record for this book is available from the British Library.

All rights reserved. No part of this publication may be reproduced, transmitted or stored in a retrieval system, in any form or by any means without the express permission in writing of The Do-Not Press Limited having first been obtained.

This book is sold on the condition that it shall not, by way of trade or otherwise, be lent, resold or hired out or otherwise circulated without the publisher's prior consent in any form of binding or cover other than that in which it is published and without a similar condition being imposed on the subsequent purchaser.

1 3 5 7 9 10 8 6 4 2

Printed and bound in Great Britain by Biddles Limited

For Jim Driver,
one of the few pioneers still out there.

No One Gets Hurt

a novel by
Russell James

Imagine a story that unfurls from seven battered cans containing unequal lengths of film. Each can bears a label.

Reel One:	FOREPLAY
Reel Two:	WARM-UP
Reel Three:	BODILY CONTACT
Reel Four:	PENETRATION
Reel Five:	INTIMACY
Reel Six:	CLIMAX
Reel Seven:	PETIT MORT

Reel One:

FOREPLAY

- 1 -

THE PHONE STARTED ringing as Kirsty squeezed the car into a parking space. She cursed, peered through the back windscreen and eased the Clio closer to the van parked behind. She checked the front wing and pulled in close to the kerb. The phone kept on ringing and Kirsty glared at her handbag. Perhaps they'd stop.

She switched off the engine. She shouldn't have brought the phone – and she shouldn't answer it now, not while she was working. But she grabbed it, pressed the key.

'Kirsty Rice.'

'It's Zoë.'

Kirsty had thought it would be Ken. She had *hoped* it would be. She couldn't get used to the idea that he'd never call her again.

But it was Zoë. Kirsty said, 'I'm outside Neil Garvey's – and I'm late.'

She stared across the narrow street. Light was fading. Two shop windows were lit, another was boarded, but all the others were unlit. A ball of newspaper stirred by the wall.

'I'm sorry, Kirsty. I've got in too far.'

Kirsty grunted. Zoë hadn't yet learned that in this job you had to get in too far.

'I'm playing a part in the film.'

'Part?' Kirsty was watching the front door. Then she realised what Zoë meant. '*Acting* in it?'

'If you can call it acting—'

'What do they want you to do?'

Zoë's voice shivered. Maybe she was trying to laugh: 'I had to go with it, you know? I told them…'

'You're not—'

'Yes.'

Kirsty glanced at the clock on the dash. Zoë said, 'They want me to… I'm scared.'

Kirsty paused. 'Where's your camera?'

'In the bag. Set up.'

'Have you got much on film?'

'Not enough.'

Kirsty chewed her lip. 'It's too great a risk.'

'It's not… dangerous. I just don't want to do it.'

'Who would?' Kirsty's voice softened. 'Did you bring the bag out?'

'I left it in there. They've started now.'

'Zoë, you can walk away.'

'I can't.'

Kirsty glared through the windscreen. She shouldn't have let Zoë do this.

'They're calling for me.'

'Grab the bag and come out.'

'I can't fetch it without—'

'Get the bag. Run away.'

'Speak to you later. OK?'

'Zoë, look. They can't make you. Just tell them—'

But the line had gone dead.

*

Kirsty stared at the handset. She knew Zoë's number but it sounded as if Zoë had made the call secretly. It might be dangerous to phone back.

She left the phone primed on the passenger seat while she reached in the seat-well for her case. Zoë might phone straight back. Kirsty could wait two minutes. Christ, Zoë – she was too young. Inexperienced. More to fill time than anything, Kirsty unzipped the case and glanced inside. Gleaming equipment: several thousand pounds. Camera, tripod, audio pack, foldaway reflector, boom mike. Conventional stuff, compared to Zoë's.

But Kirsty was already late. Here she was, killing time, when for the last ten minutes she had been cursing London traffic, thrusting the Clio into any gap, edging forwards, jumping her turn. Now she sat and waited for Zoë who, bet your life, would not ring back.

Kirsty glanced in the mirror but hardly saw her face at all. Just as well: since Ken had left, she had stopped wearing make-up, stopped making the effort. Now what? She should call Neil Garvey, apologise for being late – but that would be ridiculous, outside his door. Besides, if she tied up the phone, Zoë wouldn't be able to get through. In the tiny car mirror Kirsty caught sight of her irritated expression: green eyes frowning, the freckles across her nose looking as if they'd been newly charged with blood – and her red hair hacked back to expose over-large ears. Everyone has some part of themself that they wish they didn't have. With Kirsty it was her ears: they'd been hidden before, but now that she'd had her hair styled into a contemporary Smart Businesswoman look her ears looked outrageous, she thought. A pixie's ears.

When her hair had been longer she had worn it scraped back or let down. Usually, and certainly when not working, she had let it hang loose around her face to hide her pixie ears from view. Not working? She was always working – and not only since Ken had left. She sniffed. It had nothing to do with him: she had always worked. She loved it. And this new short hairstyle went with her new lifestyle. Smart. Professional. A week ago she had come in one night and gone straight to bed leaving her old, uncut hair scraped formally back, and had woken the following morning with her skin stretched taut like a witch. She had looked thirty-five instead of – what was she? – twenty-five, no, twenty-six. Last week's birthday, spent alone. That was when she had treated herself to the haircut. From Kirsty to Kirsty, lots of love.

Ken had preferred her hair to hang loose. He said she seemed two different people – the icy professional and the softer feminine type he loved. Had he used the word 'loved'? Whatever. Ken had liked to run his fingers through her long flaming hair and pull back a hank to expose one of her silly ears. He liked to nibble on them. He actually liked—

No. Kirsty reached down, snapped off the phone, tossed it in the case. When she stepped out of the car she was a professional again.

*

Zoë had slipped the phone inside the pocket of her flowing green skirt. The costume, like most of the others, had been hired and didn't fit. The back was held with safety pins. It was an elaborate, mock-medieval dress with lace flounces at the breast, lace cupped sleeves and a tightly drawn waist. In her hand she held the tall wimple she'd wear for filming, but it was a ludicrous thing and kept falling off.

'Take your places, boys and girls.'

She would be Lady Eleanor, and as far as costumes went, hers was more serviceable than those worn by most girls. Two wore full-length ball gowns like her own but the younger ones had been given skimpier things to wear. The scene – and as far as Zoë could tell, practically the whole film – was set at a fancy dress ball at the eighteenth century Hell Fire Club. Most of the participants had come dressed for a Bacchanalian orgy. Some orgy: there were only a dozen people in the film. *Barely* a dozen, she thought wryly. Girls had one or both breasts exposed, Cassie was naked apart from a hat, another girl lay naked on a side table, while the men wore doublets and tights. One man was dressed as the Red Monk and another had the front of his tunic cut away to expose his best parts.

Although the rest of the cast were grinning and making bad jokes, Zoë was nervous. As she made her way to her chalk mark she saw a girl in a feather skirt kneel before the man in the cutaway tunic, cup his balls lightly in her hands and lower her face into his groin.

Cassie said, 'That should warm him up.' Cassie played Zoë's maid, and maids did not wear clothes.

Zoë whispered, 'We're not filming yet,' and Cassie laughed: 'Erecting the set.'

Zoë smiled, but her smile was strained. That girl in the feather skirt looked just a child. Her breasts weren't fully formed. But Zoë didn't say anything: she'd let things take their unnatural course.

Everyone was in place. She glanced to her right, to where her bag stood on the floor beneath a spotlight. A man appeared, adjusted the light, and as he did so he kicked the bag. He hardly noticed but the heavy pouch shifted on the floor and in its new position it pointed towards the back of the studio. Zoë flinched but couldn't go to it. She would have to wait for a break. There were bound to be breaks. Although she had never acted in a film she knew they were shot in hundreds of tiny takes. There would be plenty of opportunity to reset the bag.

'Here we go,' called the director. 'The party's in full swing. Mark and Peter come in, grab the maids and start having fun. Boris, are you ready now, dear? Very good. So, once everyone has started, we'll move in and shoot background. Give it some welly, dearies, and let's *all* have fun.'

'One take?' Zoë whispered.

Cassie laughed. 'It's only background, innit? Usually they do orgies in three or four long takes, then spend ages on the close-ups.'

*

Neil Garvey was about fifty, she reckoned, although his blond crew-cut made him look younger – from a distance. The way the hall light glinted on his hair, Kirsty wondered if it were dyed. He was fifty? It was dyed.

'No, no, you're not late.' His grey eyes held hers. He was a lean man. Black tee-shirt. Narrow hips. 'Only amateurs come early.' He smiled. 'Professionals come late.'

Very smooth, she thought. Yuk.

He led her into a sitting room come office: motel style furniture, a desk, video camera on a stand. Floodlamp and reflector. Kirsty glanced around the room. There was a still camera also; film posters on the wall: sci-fi, Alfred Hitchcock, Jean Harlow, James Dean. All repro, like the furniture, but tasteful. Quite safe. Reminded her of Ken's flat—

'Coffee? Soft drink? Somethin' stronger?'

'Coffee. Black.'

Neil Garvey moved into a small kitchen at the side. Kirsty placed her case beside an armchair but instead of sitting she stood beside it, looking around the room. Urban and urbane. Unthreatening. With Neil's video camera in the corner, the room looked like a film set, quickly assembled, anonymous, the backdrop to a scene.

'Look around the place. Feel free.'

He was still in the kitchen. She smelt coffee.

'You see?' he called airily, 'I've nothin' to hide.'

She matched his light tone: 'Now, don't disappoint me. I came specially.'

Watch it, she thought, he'll think you're flirting. She reached instinctively to smooth her wild red hair – but of course, it wasn't long now. It was shorn. She didn't need to adjust it: the new style sat as rigid and unyielding as a hat.

Garvey emerged from the kitchen, a coffee mug in each hand. 'Only you?' he asked as she took a coffee. 'No crew?'

'Tight budget.'

He snorted.

'Modern equipment,' she explained. 'Saves manpower.'

'More intimate.'

She looked away. He stayed close: 'In my day we took four or five crew on any shoot.'

She felt his closeness but did not move away. 'Expensive,' she said. 'Who were you with?'

He nodded across the room to her case: 'You wanna tape this?'

'Not yet.' She smiled. 'This is foreplay.'

He chuckled. 'That's how I work – just me and the... subject. No gaping crew. It builds confidence.'

'Puts the girl in the mood?'

Nick nudged her. 'Like you're doin' now? We're not so different.'

She drifted towards her case. 'Only in the stuff that we film.'

He remained in the centre of the bland room, holding his coffee in both hands. 'I do sex. What d'you do?'

'I do you.'

He smiled – with his eyes, to strengthen rapport. 'Everyone's fascinated by sex. The girls who pose for me, they *love* sex. That's why they do it.'

'Not for money?'

'Sure, the money. But they like attention as well.'

'It's the money.' She put down her coffee. She felt tired.

Garvey grinned. 'You'd be surprised. Anyway, in your film I'll show everything you want. It's my turn to reveal all, yeah? I'm being paid!'

When he put down his coffee he seemed comfortable, at ease. As he should be. At no time since she arrived had Kirsty felt under threat – but in the two weeks since Ken had left she had stopped feeling anything. She had become mechanical, a camera. She was shut in a studio with a man who made porn videos. He seemed open, frank and reassuring and she saw what it must be like for a nervous girl to come here: open, frank and reassuring. He'd put any girl at ease.

'I'm in your hands, Kirsty. Whatever you want.'

'What*ever* I want?'

'Anything.' He held her eyes again and smiled teasingly. 'I'm bombproof here. Some of my stuff may surprise you – but it'll look good on film. Anything risky you can cut.'

'You're happy with that?'

'It's your picture, isn't it? For *public* television.'

'And if it shows you in a bad light?'

Neil laughed. 'It's a living.'

*

Zoë felt his hands massage her breasts. Her lace bodice had been tossed aside, skirt thrown up, and the half naked man lay propped above her on one arm to give a clear view to the camera while he rubbed her revealed flesh. This wasn't real, it wasn't happening, she felt less aroused than at the doctor's. Zoë stared at his impassive face – fixed, plastic, a demon king. Only his eyes moved: he wore a mask. They all did. All the men wore animal masks. His was a wolf, she thought, a fox maybe – and he was saying something. Because of his mask and foreign accent she could hardly make it out: 'Pull my top down, off my shoulders.'

She raised her hands unquestioningly. She could feel his naked legs between her thighs. As she tugged feebly at his doublet she felt the man's hips begin to pound – but she was dry, she knew. 'I'm not ready yet.'

He chuckled, a hiss behind the mask: 'You are not the only one. Don't worry.'

She realised that although he pounded against her he was flaccid. He might look convincing but—

'Save your juice for the close-ups,' said the wolf man. 'But please bite my shoulder. Pretend you're enjoying this.'

He gave a wolf-like howl and lowered his face to her breasts. 'This bloody mask,' he said, his accent thickening. 'Whose stupid idea was this?'

Zoë chuckled involuntarily, suddenly struck by the absurdity. Here she was, dry as a scouring pad. There *he* was, thrusting against her with his loose bunch of grapes. All around them, couples on the floor were simulating—

'Is anyone really doing it?'

'Not if they have sense. Not yet. Ah, that's better – you look more like it now.'

Zoë let herself relax. Her initial panic seeped away. She chuckled again – and to join in the act she rolled her head and yelped as if in ecstasy.

'Much better,' the man said.

As she began nuzzling his throat Zoë felt him stiffen between her thighs. A curled banana in the bunch of loose grapes. Oh well, she thought, he's only human. He won't do anything, not yet. And she was human too: she was softening below.

A cameraman was picking his way between the couples, tracking from one tangle to the next, filling his viewfinder with shots of heaving flesh. Zoë saw a naked black girl straddle a half nude white man who wore a bear's head. The girl is pretending, Zoë thought – just sitting, doors closed. She saw the rampant Red Monk thrusting – convincingly, she thought – into a young white girl bent uncomfortably across the table: the young girl with half-formed breasts, now crushed against the table top. The young girl that Zoë had spoken to earlier but who had seemed numbed, spaced out, not really there.

The cameraman closed in on the Red Monk, moved to his side, and as he pressed the zoom lever Zoë realised that the Red Monk was not simulating: he and the girl were the climax to a tracking shot.

Zoë looked aside. She needed to reach her own camera, but she couldn't see the bag through the bright lights and close-packed bodies. Over there somewhere. Pointing off set.

*

Kirsty had the video camera snug against her shoulder while Neil busied himself on the floor loading his own camera as he spoke, as unfazed as an actor. 'People talk as if we snatch girls off the street, drug 'em, force 'em to take part in vicious films. Garbage. I mean, do I look like a white slave merchant?'

Kirsty shrugged behind her camera.

'The girls I use have never been in a movie – the only time they've been this close to a video camera is when their boyfriend nicked it. Most times, they're short of money, they live in a grotty little pad, and they come here – I mean, this place is not luxurious or anything but it's clean, trendy, and the first thing they see here is a film camera.' He smiled. 'Imagine you are one of these girls. You're hard up, maybe you've always dreamt of gettin' into films – or maybe you're on the game. No, scrap that. You're an amateur.'

He pushed his own camera away.

'One day you look in the paper and you see my little advert: '*You too can be a glamour model. Three hundred pounds a day. No experience needed.*' You think: three hundred quid. No experience needed.'

Aware that he was on film, Neil stood up and tinkered with his reflector.

'So you ask yourself, what does that really mean? Modelling. Glamour. Three hundred quid. You weren't born yesterday.'

He moved to a lamp and opened its shutter – although the lamp wasn't on: he was acting. 'Before you phone me you make a pact with yourself: how far are you prepared to go? This far, no further. Then you take a deep breath and call my number.'

He swivelled the lamp and pointed it at her camera. 'On the phone I don't sound unpleasant – just matter of fact. I ask a few easy questions, like: have you done this kind of work before? How old are you – how tall? What colour? What's your favourite music?' He grinned. 'It makes 'em laugh, that. Helps the girl relax. Then I find out what she really looks like'

'How?'

'Easy questions. I start with how old, how tall, would you call yourself slim? D'you have a boyfriend – how would *he* describe you? Somewhere around here she'll say something revealing – you know, she's a bit overweight, she has big tits, no tits, or she sometimes get spots. I ask if her hair colour's natural. Chatty stuff, so she can chat back.'

'How old d'you want her to be?'

'Thirty-five max – that's really max.'

'Down to?'

He nodded. 'No kids. I don't do kid stuff. Sixteen minimum. Preferably eighteen.'

'Fourteen?'

'Never happens. A fourteen year old does not phone my number – and if she does, she says she's sixteen. Seventeen maybe. Anyway, I ask her to come in so we can talk about it. I say, tell a friend that you're coming. You've nothin' to worry about.' He paused. 'Maybe she calls a friend, maybe not. She may not want to.'

'Don't they ask what kind of modelling?'

'Oh, they know.'

'But if they ask?'

'I tell 'em. No point pretendin' it's to model hats.'

Like an actor on set, Neil moved across to his low-slung settee. 'Honesty, that's the name of the game.' He sat down, his arm draped along the settee back. 'When they come in they're nervous, so I offer 'em coffee, soft drink, nothing hard.'

As he did me, she remembered. 'So a girl comes in, says she's sixteen—'

'But obviously she's not? Well, I still give her a coffee, but then I send her back home.'

'Always?'

'Sure. I mean, I don't ask for her birth certificate, but I run a straight business here, whatever you think. So. Let's assume the girl's old enough: I talk to her, and show her what's involved. She doesn't like it, she can leave. They don't usually, though.'

'And what *is* involved?'

Neil chuckled. 'Like I say, we don't model hats. Here's how I explain it: I show the girl some magazines, nothing kinky, but hot – the kind of stuff you see on the top shelf at the newsagents. I ask, are you OK with that?'

Kirsty zoomed out slowly to a full shot of Neil lounging complacently on his settee.

'Like I say, they're not stupid. They've seen these magazines – hey, their boyfriend probably reads 'em – and they know when they answer my ad that they'll have to take their clothes off. In fact, we may have touched on this when they first phoned: listen, they tell me, I won't do sex. Don't worry, I say, this is juicy but it is nothin' like that. So what is it, they ask – wondering about the word 'juicy', perhaps.' Neil sniggered. 'Skin shots, I say. Nude stuff. Are you OK with that? Just me, they ask, or with someone else?'

Neil gazed past the camera, straight into her eyes.

'Anyway, she comes round. We're chatting – in this very room. Here we are, a man and a woman, together alone. We've never met, and we're talking about sex. We're sittin' in this little warm room – intimate, that's the word – and we both know that at some point you are going to take your bra off and give me a good long look at your pretty young breasts. Then you're going to slip out of your panties so I can take my camera and move in close. When I gaze through my viewfinder I'll be so close you could smother me.' Neil still held Kirsty's eyes. 'You knew that before you arrived – or if you didn't then, you do now.'

He watched her. She said, 'Then you start filming?'

He spoke gently. 'No, I said I wouldn't film the girl today. Right? I said we'd talk about it, and I'd decide if she was... suitable.'

'Depending on what?'

'Photographs. I mean, often a girl comes in and she's a real dog – so I say no, thanks very much, you can go home. Otherwise we move on to photographs – because it's the only way to know if she's photogenic. Can she relax in front of the camera? It's better if they relax.'

'Essential, I'd have thought.' She was still filming him.

He smiled craftily. 'Not always. You've seen those Asian Babe shots? A lot of those girls are whores – you can tell, they're so professional – but the pictures men really like are when the Asian girl is not relaxed, when she's not happy – like doing this is not in her culture – but although she doesn't want to, she has agreed to show all she's got. They can be powerful, those shots.'

'Rape fantasy.'

'Don't go feminist on me, *please*. Where was I? Right, the photographs. Yeah, we shoot off a set, and through all this I am totally professional. 'Cos this is reassurance time, yeah? The girl has got her kit off, she's writhing about for me, doin' things that very possibly she has not done for anyone before – though she may have dreamt about it!' Neil laughed. 'But I do not come on to her. I do not... touch. Well, maybe I do touch a little, you know, to adjust things and move her into position – to see how she reacts. But I do not get involved. I stay professional. She appreciates that. We don't kid ourselves that what we're doin' is like popping down to the doctor: it *is* more personal than that. These are not medical photographs – although sometimes, you know... Anyway, that's what we do.'

Neil was still on the settee, his arm along the back. Kirsty encouraged his flow: 'You just take photographs?'

'*Still* photos. The girl probably expects video. God knows what she expects. But I only take still photos. I do not come on to her. I show that I like her but I don't *do* anything. This may be an anticlimax – who knows? – but it's kind of nice. The girl goes home feelin', hey, that was all right: I can *do* this, I can earn money and *enjoy* myself without gettin' hurt. Mind you—' Neil's grin broadened. 'She hasn't actually earned anything yet. Remember our agreement: I said we'd talk about it and I'd decide afterwards whether she was up for this or not. Hence the photographs. They're the test. They do not get paid for taking a test – but let's be fair, darlin': they don't pay me for auditionin' them neither. We both give our time for free.'

'Except you now have a pack of sexy photographs – which you could sell?'

'Come on, that would be a bit cheap, wouldn't it? I mean, I'd set all this up – the studio, the small ads, just to get some glam shots I didn't pay for? I'd have to be bottom of the pile to do that.'

'So what *do* you do?'

He paused briefly. 'I ask her to come back, so we can look at the photographs together.'

'And then?'

*

Between takes, the cast stood around drinking non-alcoholic fluids. The men wanted nothing that might diminish their performance, and like most of the cast they drank high energy fruit drinks from the can. Although she felt thirsty Zoë wasn't sure she'd keep the drink down. Cassie offered speed but Zoë declined.

The crew prepared for close-ups. No simulation this time. At the side of the set Zoë squatted beside her sports bag, unzipped the top, and from the upper chamber took out a plastic bottle filled with orange juice. She sipped, but the juice tasted sharp and the acid scoured her stomach. With a grimace she replaced the bottle in the small chamber above the false bottom of the bag. Then she zipped it up and adjusted the bag's angle so the hidden video camera pointed out again at the set. The next scene was on the sheepskin carpet, so she aimed the peep-hole at that.

She was too far away, but maybe she could get a general view of actors straining on the floor while the cameraman leant in towards their thighs. What really worked were her candid one-on-one shots – Zoë and the director; the actresses between takes; the skinny under-age girl shooting up. Zoë had caught the German stud with his packet of Viagra. And she had several off-set conversations: the director and cameraman, the cameraman and sound boy, the director and the under-age girl. She featured in a lot of Zoë's shots – because Zoë had concentrated on her. At some point Zoë was going to find out how old she really was. How she had got into this business. How she lived.

There was a delay again – it was like film-making anywhere: endless longeurs. A couple of men came in – not actors, since they were dressed in modern clothes – and they laughed and wasted time with the director by the wall. From the way he played along with them, they might be the backers for this film. One white, one black. Zoë considered turning her camera bag towards them but all three were at the far side of the studio, where the light was too dim.

And yet.

To catch a snatch of conversation between Gordon, who directed the film, and the men who paid for it was the kind of thing she had come here to do. Two lines of dialogue – the right dialogue – could be worth two hours of skin shots. And these were new faces: the money men.

Zoë picked up her bag and sauntered casually across the floor.

- 2 -

KIRSTY AND NEIL Garvey were in his kitchenette, looking for all the world like a domestic couple – she and Ken, for instance – fixing coffee or afternoon tea. Then the doorbell rang.

Kirsty watched him. Things had been too cosy. She had hoped her camera would expose Neil like a moth pinned to a board, but she couldn't capture him. He was too relaxed. As if he were running the show.

She knew the visitor was not accidental. 'That'll be Trisha,' he said. 'I asked her to drop by.'

He left the kitchenette. As he crossed the living room he dried his hands on a kitchen cloth and added, 'She thinks it's a great hoot you've come by.'

Kirsty drifted into the room, then suddenly scooped up her camera and switched it on. As Neil returned from the hall she had the camera pointed at the door. But he was still relaxed. 'This is Trisha. Meet Kirsty.'

The girl who followed him in wore a short red dress, white shoes, and a mass of bubbly blonde hair.

'Hi!' she said to the camera. 'Pleased to meet you.'

'My leading actress.'

Trisha grinned. 'I bet you say that to *all* the girls.'

'But I don't mean it with *them*.'

Trisha continued to camera: 'Hi, I'm Trisha, I'm twenty-two years old and I'm a porn actress. Being a porn star is something I never thought I'd do but it's funny how life turns out. I've been an actress for eighteen months and I can honestly say I've loved every minute of it.'

She smiled brightly and stuck out her hip.

Kirsty sighed. 'Have you rehearsed this?'

'It's really cool that you're making a film of us.' Trisha paused, smiled and began again: 'When I first got into porn films I was an innocent young girl. And I'm still innocent in my way.' She giggled fetchingly. 'I might not *look* innocent—' She adjusted her hip. 'But underneath I am still the same sweet little schoolgirl who dreams that one day when she grows up she's going to find a man who will stand by her and let her express herself. Actually, in the evenings, when I am soaping myself in the bath—'

'Oh, puh-lease!' snapped Kirsty, switching off her camera.

Trisha pouted and kept her eyes eagerly on the camera.

'This is not a promo video.'

'I was only trying to help.'

Trisha ran her hand through her hair, pushed up a great fluffy mound of it, and for some reason her action made Kirsty regret cutting her own hair. She felt cold around the neck.

Neil placed a hand on Trisha's shoulder. 'Kirsty doesn't want a piece to camera, Trish. She's come to film us going about our daily work.'

'Like, natural?' Trisha queried. 'I can be natural, can't I? They don't come more natural than me.'

Kirsty sniffed. 'Like you're a natural blonde?'

Trisha laughed. 'You can't wind me up. I work with experts. I work with the spitefullest, cattiest girls in the whole of Europe! Of course I'm a natural blonde – I'll show you.'

She flicked the front of her red dress open and stood instantly revealed in pink lace undies. 'I love the sound of Velcro, the way it rips.'

Placing her thumbs in her panties, she grinned at the camera. 'Natural blonde, right? Hello, boys. Snatch a glimpse of this.'

*

As Zoë crossed the floor she immediately felt conspicuous. The actors were chatting on set and this wasn't the kind of film that wasted money on a big crew. At the back of the studio were only Gordon and the two suits who had just come in. There was no practicable way Zoë could stand close to them – but she saw a small canvas chair and made straight for that. When she sat down she made sure she had her back to the men. She placed her sports bag on her lap and angled it so the camera peep-hole would point their way. Wherever the camera pointed, the directional mike pointed too. If Zoë could hear the conversation the mike should pick it up.

'—could buy a *bag* of 'em at Schiphol airport. Any day.'

'But they'd be stale,' Gordon said.

'Stale? You kiddin' me? I'll tell you what stale is—'
'Made twenty years ago. Thirty, some of them.'
'Where's the difference, bro?'
'This is fresh. It'll *look* fresh—'
'Poncing about in medieval costumes—'
'Eighteenth century—'
'It's a pantomime, bro. Now *listen* to me: are those masks supposed to be real?'
'It's a masqued ball—'
'That's *right*,' cut in a third voice. 'It's all balls.'
Zoë frowned. She was sitting with her back to them but she'd only seen one black man. Both sounded black. The first one continued: 'I want to see something makes this shit worth selling.'
'I'm doing that—'
'What, fancy *dress*? Girl shows her titties?'
'It'll get better—'
'Surely can't get no worse.'
'Give it a few minutes—'
'What's the name of that skinny babe?'
'The young one?'
'Looks like a child.'
'Emmaline. Probably Emma, but she spruced it up to be a movie star.'
'Hot damn,' drawled the visitor. 'Didn't they used to make porno flicks way back called Emmaline?'
'Emanuel,' said Gordon patiently. 'Not the same.'
'Well, I tell you, Gordon, that child, whatever her name, she's the best – who's that?'
'Which?'
'Hey, you!'
Zoë didn't realise they meant her till she felt a thump on her shoulder. When she turned it was the white man: 'You enjoyin' this conversation?'
'Pardon?'
'You *listenin'* to us, bitch?'
'I'm just—'
'What's your name?'
'Zoë.'
His companion appeared: 'They all the same, bro. They choose their names out the phone box.'

Zoë stared up at him. They both sounded black, though the first was as white as her. Both men were younger than she had realised. The white with the black voice seemed in charge. He was young but big, like an overgrown schoolboy, the playground bully. 'Out the phone book?' he queried.

'Phone *box*, bro – you know, they little cards on the wall? Miss Whiplash, Jamaican Beauty, Princess Pricktease, and now this – what you call yourself – Zoë?'

The young white man prodded her. 'Listen Zoë, you know what's good for you, you get out of that chair and get your backside away across the floor.'

'Get *on* your backside down on the floor,' laughed his friend. 'Oh man, I get horny standing here.'

The boss stared at her. 'Go.'

But as she stood up he asked, 'What you carryin' in that bag?'

'Just make-up. Orange juice.'

'Open up.'

Zoë didn't hesitate. She didn't want the bag too close to their eyes, so she dropped it to the floor, squatted over it and pulled back the zip. From the upper compartment she produced her plastic bottle of fresh orange juice, a paperback, a can of hairspray.

'What's that?' he asked.

She held up the can. He took it. Pointed it.

'You keep out my hair in future, bitch.'

He pressed the nozzle. A squirt of hair lacquer fogged her face. As she recoiled coughing, he said, 'We don't like nosy people.'

'Shoo, fly, shoo,' laughed his friend.

Her face streaming, Zoë was half way across the floor when the boss boy called after her: 'Zoë. *Zoë!* No, that *ain't* your name, is it.'

'Damn!' laughed the black.

As her vision cleared she saw the white boy toss the can across the littered studio.

'Catch,' he said.

- 3 -

TRISHA HAD GONE upstairs to get changed.

'Take a shot of her,' Neil muttered, pushing Kirsty into the hall, and Kirsty stood at the foot of the narrow stairs filming Trisha as she flounced up in bra and panties, her red dress slung across her shoulder. When she reached the top, Trisha turned and smiled seductively, tilting her head. Then she laughed and disappeared.

'Catch her before and after,' suggested Neil. 'When she comes down again you can film *me* filming her.' Kirsty followed him into the living room. 'Get me while I prepare.'

She switched on.

Neil gathered his camera and tripod and began carrying them to the hall. He was talking to the camera like a Film Studies lecturer: 'A classic shot for indoor video is up a flight of stairs. It's easier for amateur actors: stick 'em in the middle of the floor they stiffen up, but put 'em on a staircase and they can walk up, come down, run their fingers down the banister. And you have more angles – full on, from below, from above. Through the balusters.'

He had erected his camera at the foot and to one side. As he returned to the living room for his lamp, Kirsty trailed him with her camera.

'Lighting a staircase is tricky. But I've done this shot a million times. Floodlight at the top, supplementary below. Never forget your reflector.'

An educational video, she thought.

He grinned. 'As I say, you get nice angles on the stairs.' They were in the hall again, where he arranged his second lamp. 'My films are not all rumpty-tumpty, you know? I like some glamour, striptease. If a girl starts out naked there's nothin' for the audience to wait for. So I start the girl nicely dressed, then half dressed, then almost naked – but not quite. Eventually we get down to it.'

He peered up the stairs and called: 'You makin' the bed up there?'

'You can wait, Neil honey. You like to wait.'

He leant forward confidentially. 'She's fixing her make-up – spot the difference! Truth is, Trisha's excited you're here. It'll be her first appearance on terrestrial television.'

'One for the family?'

'They already know what Trisha does.'

'They don't care?'

'She earns more than her dad. —Come on, Trish!'

'On my way.'

Neil rolled his eyes. 'These teaser shots are important. We get to the nitty-gritty later – that's why men buy the films – but the build-up is important. Though we don't want hours and hours of it.' He ran his fingers through his crew-cut. 'Folk have been making films like this for forty years, and there's a rule of three: build-up, action, climax. These films are made to serve a purpose. When they watch 'em they're by themselves, so for them it's private. The film runs and the man does what a man has to do, if you understan' me. So he *wants* a build-up. Each of my films reaches its climax in about twenty minutes. That's as long as a man wants.'

Neil glanced curiously at Kirsty's camera. 'For your programme I'm not sure I should say this, but during that twenty minute sequence the film gets hotter, the man gets hotter, then whoosh! Both reach climax. Twenty minutes is about right.'

'Short video.'

'They get two or three climaxes in a film.'

Trisha called, 'I'm coming, ready or not.'

'Oh, I thought you'd gone to bed.'

Kirsty squeezed into the corner by the front door to frame a shot containing Neil filming from the bottom step as Trisha walked slowly down stairs. She had changed her pretty underwear for a stripper's thong and high-support bra, worn beneath a gossamer-thin housecoat open down the front.

Neil talked her down: 'Nice and easy – hold it. Push your hair back. That's nice. Give us your long cool look. Come on down. Stop. Smile – slowly. Now stick your tongue out. Lick your lips. That's nice. Yes. Push your housecoat off your hips. Give us your *meaningful* look, Trish. Right. Lovely. Now – and remember it's family television – run your hands down your body. That's it. No darlin', keep your panties on! Toss your head again. That's it. Come slowly down the stairs.'

As she descended the last few steps Neil moved round to crouch in front of her. 'Stop!' He turned to Kirsty. 'Here's where I either zoom right in or pan up.'

He scanned up Trisha's body to her face. 'Big smile now, darlin'. Gaze into the lens. Show you want me, Trish. Show that you want to get down and lick my parts.'

Trisha giggled. 'Your parts? So refined!'

'Family television, this. I could do Blue Peter, me.'

'So could I.' She giggled again. 'And his brother.' She almost tumbled into the hall. 'Come on. I'll show you something on the settee.'

Kirsty stayed in the doorway to film across the living room as Trisha draped herself decorously on the settee. 'So far, you haven't showed much. Sexy underwear. Glamour shots.'

'That's the foreplay,' Neil said. 'You haven't waited twenty minutes.'

*

Zoë is on hands and knees. Now that the moment has come it's so much easier than she expected – not only because other couples are similarly engaged but because her partner is a pro. Zoë has not seen behind his wolf mask but she can fantasise. He has a good body, she likes his accent, and his face is whatever she wants it to be. Crouched away from him on the floor allows her to be more detached, less intimate, in her own world of fantasy. Even when he slides efficiently between her thighs, when he thrusts surprisingly far inside, when he grabs her breasts and weighs them in his hands, Zoë could be pleasuring herself with a dildo. Not that she ever has—

'Oh!'

He thrusts harder. Zoë is aware of the cameraman at her side – but it doesn't freeze her, even if she *is* naked on hands and knees, serviced by a stranger in a wolf mask. Zoë's face is inches from a black girl's backside, and the girl sits astride a white man with a bear's head. If Zoë leans forward she can lick the black girl's spine. If she reaches sideways she can touch Cassie kneeling to a rampant Lion King. If she turns around she'll see the Red Monk licking that young white girl – and the whole experience is so unreal it can't *be* real.

The Wolf Man is real.

Zoë can't see the cameraman but she knows he must be almost as close to her haunches as is the Wolf Man – who exaggerates his thrusts, pushing into her but withdrawing slowly, almost entirely, to let the camera record the full length of his wet tool. Zoë's juices are flowing and she has thrown away her shame. The anonymity and nearness of other bodies makes her – yes, she admits it – excited and aroused. What she is doing is wicked, dirty – or is it? She can't be sure. Good sex means going to the edge, stimulating her body in secret ways, allowing herself to think about and to do things that normally are unthinkable. She has to go beyond the barrier. Sex *within* the barriers is barely sex at all.

And this *is* sex. Real sex. She isn't acting – any more than the Wolf Man is acting. As the camera hovers she feels the Wolf Man's thrusts push deeper, she feels his hard cock grow stronger, and amid the sighs and groans around her she can make out his own more urgent gasps. She senses his increased warmth, and to heighten his pleasure she reaches down between her legs and cups her fingers around his balls.

'Lovely,' says the cameraman. Both men enjoying it.

'I'm coming,' calls the Wolf Man. 'Wait for me, please.'

Who is he talking to? The cameraman, of course. The Wolf Man jerks inside her, she feels the spasm – and then suddenly, cruelly, he pulls out. His hot sperm splatters on her wrist.

'I like it,' declares the cameraman.

The Wolf Man's penis flops in her hand, warm and erect – yet already, she sees, diminishing. More sperm seeps onto her palm.

'Hold that,' commands the cameraman.

She squeezes the Wolf Man's penis.

'Not his cock. Don't lose the stuff.'

She misunderstood. The cameraman focuses on the sperm in Zoë's hand. She peers down between her legs to see the glistening droplets on palm and wrist. Carefully she brings her hand back through her legs, sits up slowly, waits for the cameraman to come to her front – then with exaggerated sensuality she smears the stickiness across her breasts.

'Nipples,' says the cameraman.

Zoë rubs what remained of the Wolf Man's essence onto each of her blushing nipples. She expects them to sparkle in the light but the effect is hardly noticeable. She raises her hand, spits on it, and smears spittle there instead. The cameraman remains in front of her.

'Hans,' he calls. Hans – is that the Wolf Man's name? Or perhaps the cameraman said Hands, because as he closes in on Zoë's breasts she feels her anonymous partner's hands come around her trunk to fondle them. Between finger and thumb the Wolf Man displays her bright red nipples and she, a fellow photographer, watches the cameraman zoom in.

*

Neil said, 'I've found some videos.' He held a carrier bag. 'To watch when you get home.'

'My twenty minute climax?' Kirsty took the bag.

Neil smiled knowingly. Trisha asked if she were in the videos.

'We're both in them.' He turned to Kirsty. 'Want to watch one now?'

She remained behind the camera as he chuckled. 'I do that trick in some films. You know: girl and boy watch a sexy video – or two girls watch it. Whatever. *We* watch the video with them, which is great because it lets me use bits from another film – and that gives the *first* climax. Watching the video turns them on, so they start playin' about on their own. Second climax! Then her friend comes in – girl or boyfriend, dependin' on whether the first two were straight or lesbo – and all three start playin' till bang! Third climax.'

Trisha laughed. 'Well, there's three of us here now.'

Neil glanced at Kirsty, who didn't move. 'No takers,' he said, stooping to the floor to insert a cassette in the machine. 'But you can film this, Kirsty. It's quite safe – well, the start is. We'll leave the sound off – the music's dreadful.'

Kirsty panned to the monitor as he continued. 'Remember those girls who answer my advertisements? After the photo session they come back to see the results.'

Trisha said, 'He's a lovely photographer.' She was full-length along the settee, hoping Kirsty would take a shot of her.

'We look at the photos and I tell her how great she looks. Some of the shots are... revealing, shall we say? But I stay cool. I want the girl to trust me again, like the first time.'

Trisha yawned. 'No reason not to.'

Kirsty swung round to put Trisha in frame. The blonde girl lay in her gaping housecoat like an opening shot for one of his movies. Trisha said, 'Even the first time, when Neil just takes photos, the girl knows what she's getting into.' She propped herself up – one for the male viewers. 'Most girls come *expecting* sex. I did when I came.'

'You weren't worried?'

Trisha threw her head back. 'Girls like sex too, you know.'

'With a stranger?'

Neil intervened. 'We're jumping ahead – don't get impatient, Kirsty, we haven't reached the climax yet. Nor has the girl. She's been here before and nothing happened – she feels confident. Relaxed.'

She turned her camera on him.

'Usually the girl is happy with my photos, so I tell her we can shoot another session *but*, I say, she'd earn more dosh from movies, if that's something she'd like to do.'

Trisha chuckled. 'Everyone wants to be in the movies.'

'While we're chatting and drinking coffee I show a video – like we're doin' now. She gets more relaxed.'

Kirsty checked that it was safe to include a shot of Garvey's monitor. It was. A girl in a nightie was dancing dreamily to an unheard soundtrack, twisting her body and pouting like a disco dancer.

Neil said, 'Tame, isn't it? All my films are tame.'

'Really?'

'You should see the real stuff. I'm just the entry level.'

Trisha laughed. He gave her a look.

'The point is, a girl has to *want* to make a video. She's new to this, maybe self-conscious, so to help her warm up I let her do what she's doing there.'

He pointed to the monitor. The girl on screen was still alone but her dance had become more lewd. She ran her hands across her breasts and between her legs.

'Are you telling her what to do?'

'I'm not even in the room.' He grinned again. 'This is still foreplay to build her confidence. That room is my upstairs studio—'

'His bedroom, actually.'

'No, not my bedroom, Trish – it's a bedroom *set*.'

'You sleep there.'

'Anyway, I say to the girl, look darlin', I know you're shy, so I'm gonna leave you on your own where you can pose in safety and be as sexy as you dare. You see? I don't hide nothin'. I make it absolutely clear there's a camera connected to this monitor down here. Yes, I tell her, I will be watchin' you. You won't see me but I'll see you. It's what professionals call a screen test.'

Trisha sighed.

Kirsty sighed as well. Holding the camera was tiring. Listening to these two discussing porn videos as if they were holiday snaps was tiring too. She felt a pull across her shoulder. She raised a hand to her new short hair.

Neil nodded at the monitor. 'She's auditioning. She knows that.'

Kirsty glanced at the monitor but didn't film it. The girl was on the bed now, nightie off, and what she was doing could not be shown on public television.

'You keep the audition videos afterwards?'

Neil shrugged. 'If she's a particularly hot looker I might hold onto it.'

He picked up the remote and changed the video to Fast Forward. Kirsty hardly glanced at the jerky nude. He said, 'Once the girl has warmed up and is really into it, I come back. And join in.'

Kirsty wavered with the camera. There on screen she saw a back view of Neil Garvey dressed in black tee-shirt and jeans, sitting on the bed with the nude girl. At Fast Forward, Kirsty couldn't tell how the girl was reacting to his presence, but she didn't seem uncomfortable. She wasn't covering her breasts.

Trisha spoke from the settee: 'I remember this girl. I was downstairs. They feel better if there's another woman around.'

From the corner of her eye Kirsty saw Neil close in on the girl. He was adjusting her pose. Was he? No. The real Neil beside her clicked back to Play: the girl was pulling off his tee-shirt.

Kirsty panned around to Trisha, who lay on the settee watching the video with a grin across her face. Neil stood in the centre of the room to watch himself perform.

To break the silence, Kirsty asked, 'Does this happen often?'

He mocked her: 'Do you come here often? Yes, I do. I come here very often.'

'They expect it,' Trisha said.

'Girls come here and... with a stranger?' Kirsty said feebly.

'I'm not a stranger. I'm their friend.'

On screen he had his jeans off. He and the girl were now both nude. They skipped foreplay, and almost immediately he and the girl were making love. If that was the word for it. Kirsty, Neil and Trisha watched in silence as Neil's backside thumped up and down. From this angle Neil reminded her of Ken — except that Ken had longer hair, of course, and was younger. But they had the same lean, wiry body. Not that she could really tell from the video. A man and a woman. Any man. Kirsty shook the thought away and focussed on Neil's face. 'Aren't you just taking the opportunity for free sex?'

He gazed boldly at her camera. 'We both are. What's wrong with that? She and I have a good time. She gets paid. I sell the movie. Later, some punter sits in his lonely room and watches the thing. Maybe he doesn't have as good a time as she and I did, but in the end there's no complaints. No one gets hurt.'

*

'You can't do that,' protests Zoë. 'It will hurt.'

'We have to,' he whispers. He says 'have' with a double F.

'I won't – I'm sorry.'

'You don't do anal?'

She and the Wolf Man are in a naked embrace. They look convincing but Zoë is clenched tight. From behind the camera the director queries the delay.

Wolf Man says, 'She will not do anal.'

'Oh, for Heaven's sake, dearie—'

'Not with that.' Zoë points to the plastic banana that the Wolf holds in his hand.

'It's no bigger than his own,' says Gordon crossly.

'I'll be gentle,' whispers Wolf.

Zoë is the centre of attention but there are limits to what she will do. 'I can't.'

Gordon tuts at her. 'I suppose you're new to this?'

'Fairly.'

'Amateurs! Anyone?'

There is a slight pause before the black girl says *she'll* do it. She glances at Zoë, still naked on the floor. 'You sure you're in the right business, hon?'

Zoë mutters 'Sorry' and scrambles to her feet. She tries to remember where her clothes are. Everyone is watching her. She wants to wrap her arms across her breasts.

Then Cassie appears with Zoë's medieval costume. 'You'll get cold.'

Cassie is around twenty, a streaky blonde.

Gratefully, Zoë slips the dress on and uses the safety pins to pull it tight. When she looks up, embarrassed, she sees that everyone has returned to what they were doing. Only Cassie remains. 'You OK?'

Zoë nods.

Cassie leans forward. 'His banana *was* greased, you know? But I never like 'em up *my* bum.'

'I made a fool of myself, didn't I?'

Cassie shrugs. 'Don't worry, they'll forget.'

Zoë watches the action on set. 'I wouldn't forget.'

Wolf Man is crouching beside the black girl. She has her knees against her chest and she thrusts her rump at him while he eases the banana in. The cameraman leans close, and is joined by several observers from the cast. The boss and his companion move in. The black girl squeals with every thrust – but she is faking it. She has done this trick before. And the banana is greased, as Cassie said. Zoë finds herself watching the Wolf Man. Five minutes ago she had been with him. She has never seen behind his wolf mask, yet they are a couple, in a way.

Cassie has gone.

Zoë sees the under-age girl sitting on her own, ignoring the scene on set. What's her name? Emily? No: 'Emmaline. How's it going?'

The girl wears a cheap leather coat draped around her shoulders but is naked underneath. She does not look up. When Zoë squats beside her, the pinned costume begins to slip. Zoë clutches at it. 'You're not enjoying this?'

The girl shrugs. Zoë adjusts the safety pins and says, 'Well, I've blown *my* ticket. I might as well go.' She hesitates. 'Coming?'

Emmaline stares at the floor. 'I'm on next,' she mutters.

'You don't have to do this.'

'Leave me alone.'

Zoë moistens her lips. 'Well, if you need a friend or anything…'

The girl does not react. Zoë rises awkwardly and wanders off to find her sports bag. On set they have wrapped the anal scene and are rearranging furniture. A wooden table is brought centre stage. The director comes to where Emmaline is sitting and helps her to her feet. She lets the jacket fall to the floor and follows him naked onto set, holding his hand like a child led to her bath.

At the table waits the Red Monk and the Lion King. Without a glance at either of them, Emmaline bends across the table. Zoë realises what is about to happen but is unsure whether to film it or to rush on set and drag the girl away. But it isn't an option. Where *is* her bag? She left it on the floor at the back of the studio, close to the boss boy and his friend. Have they noticed it? Zoë can see the bag on the floor. Her camera must still be running, filling its cassette with an unchanging view of the back wall. Maybe the mike has picked something up. Maybe the batteries have not gone flat. How long has it been running?

Zoë quickly collects the bag and just as she is about to switch off the hidden camera she remembers what is happening on set. She turns, saddened, and sees the Red Monk, his cape open, shafting Emmaline from behind. The cameraman hovers but this time there are fewer spectators. Perhaps Zoë is not the only one who feels uneasy. She edges towards the set where the Lion King is waiting, the boss boy and companion at his side.

Zoë raises her bag unnaturally high. Standing five yards off she holds the bag with its peep-hole aimed front. Suddenly the Red Monk flops away from the unmoving Emmaline and turns to Zoë. But he isn't looking at her. His cape trails behind him to expose his white naked front. Zoë keeps the camera on him, hoping the battery will last. He raises a placatory hand: 'It's gone, man. Give me a minute.'

But the director ignores him and hustles the Lion King on set. 'Straight in. This is a gang bang, remember.'

The Lion wakes up. As if dreaming of the savannah the Lion King shakes himself, then rushes into place and fumbles quickly at his groin. From behind his fierce mask comes a plaintive 'Not ready yet.'

'Cut!' snaps the director. 'For Heaven's sake, you people! Why can't I work with professionals?'

'Sorry, man, I didn't realise he'd finish so soon.'

'Hurry up. We haven't got all day.'

'Don't tell me to hurry, man. It slows me down.'

'Oh, forget it, I'll edit out the break. Wake me when you're ready.'

The boss boy intervenes: 'This man's ready. I been horny all night.'

Zoë turns towards him and watches in astonishment as the young white man rips off his suit and throws his clothes onto the floor. Stepping out of his CKs he asks, 'Who gonna lend me a face mask?'

Gordon shrugs. 'Two hundred years ago a naked man looked just the same as you do now.'

'With *this* hair style? No way. My face will *not* be in your film.'

His black friend laughs. 'Lot of women will recognise your cock, bro.'

Zoë glances at her former partner but he keeps his wolf mask on. The Bear holds out his own mask and the boy quickly fastens it. But he isn't absolutely ready. The black girl notices, and steps across to him: 'Hey man, give me that white willy, or you ain't never going to get it up.'

She reaches down for it. 'Hot damn!' he says, and tilts his bear head.

Emmaline mutters from the table, 'Hurry up. I'm freezing here.'

*

Neil and Kirsty have cracked a bottle of Chardonnay. But Kirsty never stops working: as Trisha and Neil sit at the table, she films sporadically. Several of Neil's videos lie scattered across the table and he fingers them as he speaks.

'I know the girls look amateur but that's the point. Realism – like this scene now.' He grins directly at the camera. 'Yes folks, your intrepid girl reporter is carrying a hand-held camera to get in close with me and Trish. I use one too. My film quality may look rough but I go for long takes – no cutaways, no editing – 'cos you wanna be sure that the couple you're watching is really doin' it. Nothing simulated. No fake orgasms. The real thing.'

'No one likes a fake orgasm,' Trisha agrees, sipping her wine.

Neil continues to the camera: 'Have you ever seen *Readers' Wives*? Great idea. The thing started as still photos, then switched to video. Ordinary women, no great lookers, in ordinary settings: their own bedrooms, the sitting room carpet, the settee.'

'Kitchen cabinet,' says Trisha. 'The chopping block. —Hey, there must be a joke in that somewhere.' She ponders but can't make it work.

Neil says, '*Readers' Wives* is exactly what they are – real women. Keen amateurs – emphasis on keen. A lot of men get turned on by that. Women send in pictures uninvited.'

Trisha says, 'Men send photos of their own wives.'

'The same with my videos. Every day I get letters from girls who want to make 'em. You may not want to believe it—'

'Women like sex too.'

'I do know this,' says Kirsty. Of course women liked sex. Until two weeks ago she had liked sex with Ken. She'd thought *he* liked sex with her.

Neil pours another glass of wine. 'I used to work with a guy who made these – well, *Readers' Wives* type videos. No-nonsense stuff but fun. You've heard of the *Ben Dover* movies? That's his name – Ben

Dover. Well, it was his name in the videos, so you can guess what they were about. Ben had this inexhaustible supply of everyday women who came to do the business for him. And when I ask him one day, 'Where do you advertise, what do you pay?' he tells me, 'I don't advertise, I don't pay. What I do,' he says, 'is I go out with my camera and a pocket full of business cards, and every time I see a likely looking girl I go straight up to her and ask if she wants to be in a video.' Just like that! OK, most women tell Ben to sod off, but some ask what kind of video and some say straight out they will.'

Neil raises a glass to Trisha: 'You did one of those videos, didn't you?'

Trisha giggles. She even blushes. 'I did not.'

But Neil chuckles. 'Yes, you did. Ben Dover.'

'No, I've been in some funny videos—'

'I'll say.'

'Seriously. What will people think? I'm not ashamed of the films I've made, but those *Ben Dover* films are naff.'

'You've *seen* 'em, then?'

'I'm a professional, aren't I? I have to keep up with what's going on.'

'They sell well, that's the point.'

Trisha sulks over her wine glass. Neil adds, 'They're cheap, simple, no mucking about. I mean, you don't get a *plot* or anythin' – but you do get the real thing.'

Trisha shrugs. 'Who needs a plot?'

*

A journalist is a witness; she does not get involved. Zoë quivers as the unresisting Emmaline stoops across the table to simulate gang rape from behind. Just a scene in a movie, you might say – if you weren't Emmaline. First had been the Red Monk, and they joked about him 'going off half cock'. Then the boss boy with his ridiculous fake black accent – jumping at the girl, shouting and cackling like a drunken schoolboy. Then his black companion joined in, the Red Monk's cape draped around his back. He was the first to make Emmaline cry out: something cruel about his thrusts. But by then Gordon was lining up his cast to make the gang rape more realistic. No sooner had the black boy pulled out than the Lion King stepped in. And now, while the Lion forces himself to climax, Zoë sees her Wolf Man next in line. Gordon stands right behind him, ready to push him forward when the Lion King is done. And as the men attack the unresponsive girl, Zoë fights to keep the sports bag steady beneath her arm.

The Lion King staggers back and the Wolf Man takes his place. The director laughs: 'Once more into the breach, dear friends!'

Zoë makes herself stand firm so she can film him from the rear. She stares at the back of the Wolf Man's head. He's as bad as any of them.

A thump in her back.

The bag yanked from her arms.

Zoë staggers, turns, and sees the boss boy clutching her bag across his chest. He has donned a gaping cloak. Before Zoë can move – either to grab her bag or run away – she feels her arms pinned from behind. 'What's in the bag?' the boy demands.

'I showed you,' she says weakly.

He stares at her, then unzips the bag and turns it upside down. As the contents fall to the floor she hears Gordon's weary call, 'Cut!'

A moment's silence. The boy is large and menacing. He glances at her juice and hair spray on the floor, then peers inside the bag. 'It's heavy, this.' He puts his hand in. 'How d'you get under the false bottom, bitch?'

Her mouth has dried. The man behind hisses in her ear: 'You better say something.'

The boy continues to feel inside. 'Is this sewn in or what?'

In a surprisingly calm voice, Zoë says, 'It's Velcro.'

He pulls at the lining but cannot open it. When he throws the bag to the floor it lands heavily. 'It's a camera, right?'

She nods. Everything is over. The boy stands beside the bag and the cape flaps about him like a dressing gown. 'Are you a cop?'

Zoë makes the worst mistake of her life: 'No, I'm a journalist.'

He nods, then speaks beyond her to the black man: 'Open the bag, Cornell.'

She is suddenly free. Not that she can run anywhere. It seems to her that the silent cast has melted away towards the edges of the studio. Only Zoë is in the light. The boss boy's helper – Cornell, is that his name? – stoops to her bag and begins tugging at the material. He is half dressed, his trousers on. Bare feet. Bare black chest.

The boss makes no attempt to hide his nakedness. He stares at Zoë as if she is a book he cannot read. But he doesn't say a word.

'Got you, baby,' calls Cornell from the floor. The Velcro rips.

Using both hands he brings out her hidden camera and lifts it towards his boss.

'Open it.'

Cornell frowns, finds the button, and ejects the cassette. He grins triumphantly. 'This ain't a film, bro. It won't turn black exposed to light.'

'You think that's funny, Cornell?'

The man looks down.

The white boy quickly kneels and picks up Zoë's can of hair spray. 'What's this, bitch – a micro camera?' He holds it out to her.

Zoë says, 'I think I should warn you that my company knows where I—'

He slaps her face. If anyone gasps she doesn't hear it. He may have cut her cheek with the metal canister. She glances around her. Could she run?

He shoots out a left jab, but instead of hitting her he grabs her medieval costume. It immediately falls loose. Cornell is on his feet now, at her side. Too late to run.

The boy squirts hair spray at her. Once he gets an idea he sticks to it. Zoë turns her head but before she can move she feels Cornell grab her by the arm. The boss sprays again.

Cornell yelps. 'Hey! You got me in the eyes, bro.'

'Could be a false bottom in this can.'

He sprays again. Cornell leans away from her. 'Damn!' he says. 'That's way too close.'

Zoë tries to shield herself with her free hand, but the stinging lacquer engulfs her head. She begins coughing. Her eyes stream. Though she can't see, she can sense the boss boy leaning closer: 'Who sent you?'

Giving her no time to answer, he slaps her face. She begins to cry. Her eyes sting, her mouth and nostrils are clogged with hair lacquer, and a pin from the loosened dress jabs in her back. The boss is shouting. She can hardly hear. Now he is shouting at Cornell.

She tries to open her eyes but they are sticky and filled with red. Cornell lets go her arm and pushes her to the ground. As she falls she bangs her knee but with her hands pressed against the floor she knows she will be safe there. They won't hit her while she is down.

As she kneels at the big boy's feet she feels him spraying her again. Her eyes are already closed, so she keeps them screwed up tight. She keeps her mouth clamped shut as well. She tries not to breathe.

'Cornell,' he says.

Then he sprays again. It has no effect now because she is encased in stinging glue. He is adding a layer on top. He keeps spraying till the can runs out.

'What's this film called, Cornell?'

'The hell do I know, bro?'

'It's called The Hell-Fire Club.'

She doesn't hear the click. She doesn't see the glint of the cigarette lighter, nor the first small flame on its cotton wick. She only feels a searing pain as her sticky hair catches fire.

Reel Two:

WARM-UP

- 4 -

At half-past six in the morning it is surprising how many people are about. Some like to get to work before the rush hour, some *are* working, some just coming home. The milk van glides along the street, larger vans make early deliveries, newsagents are open, and all the shift workers from the underground, buses, railway, food factories, hospitals and utilities emerge quietly into the innocent morning air. It's a good time for bicycles and dog walkers. Some say it's the best time of the day.

This morning a pale sun glints on the heavy brown waters of the Thames. There is traffic out there: three barges, two small motor boats and a launch. The tide has turned now, and as waters rise across the expanse of sticky mud between the river and its stone walls, flocks of grubby birds peck at scraps and deposits on the glistening slime.

Dog walkers, striding along solid pavements beside the river, look out beyond the mud to admire the channel of vigorous water which bisects the capital. They watch the way it swirls powerfully around the sturdy pillars beneath each bridge. Early walkers inhale a wet metallic smell, and at this spacious time of day they greet each other. They pause to look out across the Thames and occasionally glance down at the mud below.

When the man in the trilby first spotted it he couldn't be certain it was what he thought. His eyesight was no longer what it had been, and he had left his spectacles at home. While he leant across the round-topped stone wall and peered down at the mud he resisted the tug of his little terrier, too small to see over and unaware that there was anything of interest below. The dog was more interested in an approaching Scottie, smaller than the terrier but no less aggressive. The woman controlling it tightened the lead, and when it felt its pace checked the Scottie tried to scamper faster, its leathery footpads scratching at the ground. The terrier barked at it.

'Good morning!' said his owner.

The woman tugged the Scottie closer. He said, 'I think there's someone down there. I can't quite see.'

'Excuse me?'

The woman kept ten yards away. Both dogs growled.

He said, 'Down in the mud. Can't make it out.'

She stared at him. He added, 'I haven't got my glasses on. Could you take a look?'

The Scottie yapped and the terrier barked back.

'Well, I really don't—'

'Because I think it might be a body.'

She shortened the lead.

'Sorry to be a nuisance,' the man said.

The woman edged towards the river wall. She eyed the man warily, then peeped across. 'Oh, goodness.'

His terrier whined. 'It *is* a body? I thought it was.'

She nodded. The Scottie tried to scale the wall. She asked, 'Have you phoned the police?'

'No, I've just noticed it. You wouldn't have a phone on you?'

She had but wouldn't say so, because she didn't want to get involved. 'No, there must be a phone box somewhere.'

'I'd better stay here – keep an eye on it. Perhaps *you* could phone them?'

'*You* should phone them. You saw it first.'

'I don't like to wander off and leave it.'

She bent down to smack the Scottie. 'I don't think she's going anywhere.'

'It's a she, then, is it?'

The woman eyed him suspiciously. 'Of course it's a she.'

'I can't see without my glasses.'

She pulled her dog away from the wall. 'Well, you can't just stand here staring at it. And I've got things to do.'

She began to walk away.

'If you should happen to pass a phone box—'

'No,' she snapped. 'You found it. You must phone.'

He gazed reproachfully after her. 'But we're both witnesses.'

*

When the police arrived, the incoming tide had almost reached the body. The first two officers took a glum look at the oozing mud and called immediately for their Detective Inspector and paramedics. They waited twelve minutes, watching the waters slurp closer, dreading the moment when one of them would have to clamber down onto the mud, and while they waited they erected incident tape to hold back the first tiny group of spectators. They hoped the Marine Support Unit would arrive soon.

*

By the time the big river reaches Thames Ditton its character has changed. It has surged through the City beneath impressive bridges at the Tower, Blackfriars and Westminster, and has continued steadily past Lambeth, Vauxhall and Battersea. Beyond Wandsworth and Putney the murky waters become domesticated. A last outpost of industrialisation recurs at a loop in the river around Barn Elms Water Works and the Fulham Wharves, but by genteel Chiswick the river has become a water feature at the foot of neat green gardens. From Barnes, Mortlake and Richmond it flows ever more sweetly past Twickenham with its playing fields, to the watershed at Teddington where tidal water ends. At Kingston the vast parks of Hampton Court stretch along the banks, and opposite the grandeur of Hampton Court lie the quiet suburbs of Surbiton and Thames Ditton: fringes of Greater London where dockers and watermen are unknown. Noisy pleasure boats carry tourists and power majestically between irritating little rowing boats and pristine motor boats. Also in the water are small islands with willow trees. And there are bywaters. In some of those bywaters are moored houseboats – dark ramshackle crafts with peeling paint, vaguely resented by land-owning neighbours. On one of the houseboats lives Kirsty Rice.

Her boat is a little smaller than average and on rainy days seems to sit lower in the water. It is one of a colony of barely a dozen craft, and on rainy days each of the weather-beaten houseboats bobs against its mooring as if it wants to crawl ashore. But the inhabitants have become so used to living on water, so wedded to the river, that they would no more give up their way of life than a newt would choose to live on land. The boats leak, creak and are mildly insanitary. Ceilings are low. Yet the houseboats are as cosseting and cosy as floating nests.

A nest, thought Kirsty Rice, where a mother broods upon her eggs.

She sat at her pull-down breakfast table and stirred muesli with an antique spoon – one of her mother's spoons, Irish silver, handed down by her own mother decades before.

Mothers.

Kirsty stared at the muesli, lifeless in the bowl. Muesli was good for you. She put down the spoon, picked up a mug of coffee and drank instead. When she had woken that morning her first thought had been 'Day Five, and nothing yet.' Five days since her period should have begun.

But she couldn't be pregnant. She didn't *have* to be. A day or two late was not unusual. But five days: had that happened before? Perhaps not – though a few days did not prove anything.

Kirsty glanced at the wooden steps to the deck. Tucked behind them was a bulky cardboard box. It belonged to Ken, or the contents did. Spare clothes, a gaudy dressing gown, some books and computer magazines. But no washing things, no credit cards, nothing precious. Nothing he'd need to come back for. Nothing he would miss.

She was not pregnant.

Kirsty took a spoonful of muesli but didn't want it. The milk trickled down her throat and she was left with a wad of chewy cereal and dried fruit. Her stomach clenched.

She stood up and moved briskly around the cabin, collecting things for work. With Ken no longer there, Kirsty had allowed it to become more an office than a dwelling space: her PC had replaced the television, she had a second-hand video editing deck, two whiteboards, and seven small heaps of cardboard files. Post-it notes were stuck to the walls alongside cuttings from magazines and newspapers. It was as if she had allowed her office world to push her domestic life aside.

But she was young, she thought. Why not? She was a working girl. Her exciting job absorbed her every moment. She worked irregular hours but to some extent could *choose* her hours – and beside, she didn't want to reduce them: she didn't resent time spent at work.

She loved it. Her job was the most important thing in her life – much more important than moping about the houseboat, wondering why some wretched man had walked out on her. A man who used to run his fingers through her hair. She was glad that he had gone. She was glad she'd cut her hair. Now she could concentrate on the things that really mattered.

Briskly, she fitted a new battery in her video camera, then crammed the camera, spare battery and three blank cassettes into her travelling bag. She collected her notebook and her purse. When she had swallowed the last of the strong black coffee she left the mug beside the bowl of muesli on the pull-down table. They could wait till she came home.

*

Although the discovery of the body was not reported immediately on the News, the disruption to traffic was. As the rush hour reached its peak the closure of a main road along the Surrey Bank caused innumerable delays. Diversion signs directed traffic away from the affected route but gave no guidance as to which road one should take instead.

A hundred yards either side of where the body had been found, the road was sealed with wooden barriers. A further forty yards in from there, tapes were stretched across the road. Between the incident tapes and the wooden barriers stood half a dozen vehicles – one of which, an ambulance, held the recovered corpse, a woman Detective Inspector and the male police surgeon. But the two ignored the body. Inside the ambulance, out of sight, they had a furtive cup of tea.

The police surgeon sniffed. 'Not my job to say *how* she died.'

'But it *was* murder?'

'It was certainly suspicious, Jennifer.'

The surgeon smiled. He and DI Jennifer Gillett had worked together before. Beside them in the ambulance the girl's body lay on a bed beneath a sheet. The surgeon glanced at it. 'Most irregular, you know, bringing her in before I'd examined her.'

'You'd have been up to your shoulders in Thames water if we hadn't. Tide's coming in.' Gillett shrugged. 'And if we'd dumped her at the roadside we'd have had the press firing off their long-range cameras.'

'Your DCI wouldn't like that.'

Gillett sipped her tea. 'She wasn't drowned, then?'

'Can't be sure. But I don't think she'd even been in the water. The pathologist will confirm.' He put down his cup before her next question. 'Well, I've done here, Jennifer. Time for surgery.'

As he moved for the door, Gillett asked, 'The black and scorching – that's what killed her?'

The doctor paused before opening the ambulance door, 'As I say, it isn't my job to diagnose, but it looks like it. The shock alone might have killed her. But what we don't know is whether there were other contributory factors. You need the pathologist.'

They stepped out into morning light. A constable stood outside to stop unauthorised persons from climbing in. A few yards away, beside the river wall, they could see the Deputy Chief Inspector and his Scene of Crime Officers, all dressed like nuclear scientists in white paper overalls and overshoes, meticulously picking over the ground in an attempt to sift clues from city dirt and trash.

The DI led the doctor back to the tape. Out of earshot of her superior officer she said, 'We're just the warm-up before the stars arrive.'

'It was ever thus. I defer to the pathologist.'

'I to the DCI.'

Having reached the tape they turned back to glance at the white-shrouded officers. He said, 'A policeman's lot, Jennifer—'

'Is not well paid.'

Genteel jests for a gentle morning. The doctor ducked beneath the tape and made his way back to his car. His job was done. Like most police surgeons he was a family doctor, called in to establish not the cause of death but merely that death had occurred, and whether or not the circumstances looked suspicious.

Which they did. But as he drove through rush hour London, the doctor switched on his radio to help him forget the grisly corpse. What mattered now was whether or not he already had a backlog of patients at his morning surgery.

*

DarkAlley Films had bought two days of Neil Garvey's time. Two days, thought Kirsty, were quite enough. His easy manner was insidious: he behaved with her as he had with Trisha, as he behaved no doubt with every woman who visited his studio, as he behaved this morning with Melanie in her council flat – as if they each had been his lover: no, not his lover, Kirsty thought, just a person with whom he'd had sex. He'd had sex with Trisha, but were they lovers? What *was* a lover? Neil and Trisha had had sex in his videos, and from the way Trisha behaved around his house, they'd had sex at other times as well. Did that make them lovers? To them, sex seemed no more significant than sharing a cup of coffee.

Neil had had sex with this dark-haired Melanie, as he'd had sex with so many girls in his movies. There are men who keep a count of the women they have had – a kind of boasting, if only to themselves – but Garvey must long ago have stopped counting. Sex to him was part of work.

But to this young mother it was her way out. Melanie's Deptford flat was poorly built and had never been well maintained. She led Kirsty around its few run-down rooms. The two small bedrooms were drab and the living room was just that – the room where they all lived. A suspiciously smart television stood beside an equally impressive stereo and half-full CD rack. The armchairs looked as if they had been rescued from a skip – and didn't match – and the battered table was cluttered with food and magazines. Much of the remaining floor space was taken up by a rickety playpen, inside which was a little girl, about eighteen months – still in nappies by the smell. Her silence had been bought with a cup of orange juice and bag of sweets. The child's brother looked a year older. He wandered around with his thumb in his mouth, and with his other hand he clutched at his mother's skirt.

Melanie said, 'It costs too much to have child minders.'

She had black hair, a gypsy face, and before the kids she'd probably had an attractive figure. She was heavier now. As was her makeup. Knowing Kirsty was coming, she had put on a purple dancing dress.

She glanced at the video camera: 'Take a shot of what we have to put up with in the bathroom.'

If this were a different programme, the bathroom would have been star of the show. Its walls were black with damp and the grimy window hung crooked in its frame.

'Been bust forever,' Melanie explained.

She pointed to the ceiling. An ugly brown stain spread from one corner to the centre. In the corner where the stain was darkest, part of the plasterboard had crumbled away.

'When they pull the bath plug upstairs, some of the water leaks down here. But they have to wash themselves, don't they? It's not their fault.'

Kirsty shrugged hopelessly: it was not her subject. Back in the crowded living room the child in the playpen started grizzling.

'Oh precious! Did you wonder where Mummy had gone?'

Melanie picked up the child, sniffed, and told Kirsty she didn't think she'd want to film the next bit. 'I mean, this *is* dirty, know what I mean?'

She carried the child to the bathroom as Neil wandered back from the kitchen. He looked as at home in Melanie's flat as in his own place. He was carrying three coffees. 'She's a good girl, Melanie.'

'I can hear you,' Melanie called.

'So can the neighbours,' he muttered. 'Walls are thin.'

'You never filmed here?' Kirsty asked.

'You're joking. You're the first person who's ever wanted to do that.'

They glanced at the armchairs but didn't use them. As they listened to Melanie changing the baby, Kirsty put her camera on the floor. She sipped some coffee and her stomach clenched. She thought: phantom contraction.

I am not pregnant.

*

Melanie sat in an armchair, baby on her knee, the little boy sitting at her feet. Kirsty had closed in on her face. Shooting the girl with kiddies crawling over her did not seem right.

'I'm still young, and I've got my life ahead of me. —I've got a life behind me as well!' Melanie grinned defiantly. 'My kids have got a proper dad, you know – I was married to him and that. Too young, of course, like mum said. Parents have to be right sometimes, don't they? I'm a parent myself.'

The little girl reared up and began pinching Melanie's face. Kirsty pulled back a little. She couldn't exclude the kids entirely from her film.

'But he buggered off, of course, as men do.'

She grinned at Neil but he wasn't listening. He was sitting at her table, leafing through a magazine.

'He's supposed to pay me maintenance but I don't know if he ever does. I get my Giro from the CSA but you can't live on that. Anyway, I saw this ad in a window and I thought I might as well give it a try. Didn't think it could do no harm. Anyway, this bloke—' She broke off to speak directly to Kirsty: 'Neil, I mean. Can I mention Neil?

Right. Well, he was... a proper gentleman.' She laughed, and called to Neil: 'You hear that? Flattery. Professor Higgins, that's what you were!'

He looked up. 'My Bare Lady: I've done that film – twice!'

She chuckled. 'What I mean is when I answered Neil's ad I thought this has got to be about sex, yeah? I'm going to have to...' She nodded. 'But no, it was nothing like that. Well, not the first time.'

Melanie chuckled, then took a breath and stared directly at the camera. Kirsty zoomed in. 'Sex isn't such a big deal. It's not like you get raped or something. You just join in. Nothing nasty happens. No one gets hurt.'

'Did you enjoy it?'

'I enjoyed the money!' Melanie laughed. 'I mean, lots of women do sex for money. But they sit in a room and wait – they don't know who the hell will come wandering in. I'd never stoop to that, not me. This way, you've got time to get to know the bloke, and you can back out if you want to. But why bother? You're in a comfortable room. You can take your time about it. Like Neil says, the more you enjoy yourself the better it'll look on film. So you might as well enjoy it.'

'What did you earn?'

'Two or three hundred quid. Depends. For someone like me, that's good money. And it's only a start, isn't it? I mean, let's be honest – I want to be famous. No, don't laugh. There's lots of famous actresses started out in porno. Really famous. People front up famous actresses sometimes and try and blackmail 'em about those early movies – but *they* should worry, on a million dollars a film. Pay *me* a million – see if I give a monkey's what people said. No, I'm sorry, I don't care if it's straight or porno as long as it pays decent. I've got to feed the kids, haven't I? On top of that, what I want, what I really want, is to get famous and know that men like to look at me and give me things I want.'

- 5 -

A CUP OF tea can calm and fortify, coffee perks you up, and a shot of whisky is unwise before an autopsy. Since Harris had been conducting autopsies for fifteen years he felt there was nothing he hadn't seen, but he still prefaced each autopsy with a cup of tea. This morning's cuppa was shared with four interested parties: DCI Damon Wright, senior investigating officer; DI Jennifer Gillett, recently promoted from Detective Sergeant; Sergeant Ian Lawrence, police photographer; and Nigel Flint, mortuary technician.

They drank their tea in the mortuary office. The tea was so hot they had to blow on it, although a morning chill hung about the office, as if cold air crept in from next door.

'Still no clues to her identity?' Wright asked.

Jennifer Gillett had already checked. 'No reports of missing persons.'

'Early in the day.'

Harris put down his cup, the steam rising. 'No reason to wait.' He seemed irritable today.

Inspector Damon Wright savoured his tea; he had an asbestos throat. 'No hope of a visual identification?'

Gillett blew on her scalding tea. 'Unlikely. There's little left of her face.'

'Too badly burnt. Oh well. A druggie?'

'No needle scars. But it's a typical druggie death.'

'Vicious bastards. Still, we'll keep an open mind. Right, Mr Harris?'

The pathologist gave a tired smile. 'Oh, you want *my* opinion? I thought you two had already sussed it out.'

Wright placated him: 'We only saw what was obvious at the scene of crime. We need an expert now.'

Harris had conducted only a superficial examination at the crime scene. By the time he'd arrived the body had been moved, and he could infer nothing from its new position or environs. Thames water was lapping over the site and the corpse had been taken inside the ambulance. As for finding clues in the woman's clothing, they could forget it: she was practically naked. His first examination had had to take place inside the ambulance, where the body waited on a rubber bed. 'Bruising, of course, but you've moved her from pillar to post.' He had conducted on-site preliminaries: rigor, body temperature, recent wounds. He had waited while a forensic scientist tested for contact traces, but when these showed nothing unusual he had supervised the transfer to a zip-up body bag, and had returned to the mortuary in grumpy mood.

Jennifer Gillett put down her hot tea. 'I'm ready.'

Inside the mortuary the zipped-up body lay on a trolley by the working table. Nigel unzipped the bag, then he and Harris slid the dirty corpse onto the slab. While Nigel re-zipped the empty bag and placed it in storage for trace examination later, Sergeant Lawrence photographed the body. Normally the sergeant would take photographs as each piece of clothing was removed – a grisly striptease – but this body was already bare.

'Scraps of charred clothing remain adhered to the skin in places,' dictated Harris onto tape. 'Samples of this material, a kind of hessian perhaps, have been placed inside Bag A. The appearance of the cloth supports the view that the subject was severely burnt by fire. Superficial examination also suggests that at the time of burning the subject was not wearing underclothes, and the hessian-type material seems to have been all that she was wearing. The material could originally have been a heavy dress worn without underclothes or it may have been a dressing gown. But the material may have been nothing more than a wrapping put on the subject, alive or dead, before she caught fire.'

Gillett was interested that the pathologist concentrated more on the scraps of clothing than the body itself. Harris continued around the slab.

'The subject wears no jewellery. No rings on the fingers. No marks of rings having been removed. No immediately obvious tattoos, although the skin has not yet been cleaned. No scars, except a vaccination mark to the left upper arm. There are a number of small bruises, most of which appear to have been effected after the subject was dead.'

Harris then listed the bruises. Damon Wright glanced at Jennifer who had attended few autopsies before, but she didn't seem troubled.

She was studying the body as dispassionately as was Harris.

'The body is splattered and smeared with river mud. Although the mud probably comes from the riverside site where the body was found, samples from different parts from the body surface are being placed in Bags B through F.'

Nigel Flint diligently flaked off some mud samples. As each was bagged, Harris described the area of the body it had been taken from. As he continued his exterior inspection the two police officers grew bored. Jennifer wished she'd had time to finish her tea.

Eventually Harris and Flint started to bag fingernail scrapings. Before he could make a facial examination Harris asked Flint to bag samples of facial mud. Then he grumbled into his tape recorder that because the head was badly burnt he could take no samples of make-up, skin or surface blood. Flint washed the mud gently from her head. As he did so, Sergeant Lawrence moved in to photograph each stage. It was a delicate process. Slow.

Now came a more grisly stage: the girl had been badly burned, and her head had been at the seat of the fire. Flint had washed the mud away to reveal a crust of mud and black charred skin encasing reddish brown flesh and grey-white bone.

Harris searched for any hair. 'The complete absence of hair to the head means that its colour in life cannot yet be reported.' He left the head a moment to walk down beside the body. 'What remains of her pubic hair suggests that the subject would have had black or dark brown hair.' He returned to the head. 'Microscopic analysis of follicles in the scalp will determine the actual colour in due course.' He paused. 'Colour of eyes unknown.'

In the intervals when Harris wasn't speaking, the mortuary remained absolutely silent. All three police officers preferred to keep their eyes away from the blackened corpse, glancing back briefly – almost shyly – when Harris spoke. He was probing gently at where the woman's face would have been. 'I am unable to take samples of lipstick and make-up, and the charred state of the head means that I cannot ascertain whether the subject ever wore ear-rings or had her facial skin pierced in any similar way.' He probed again. 'The subject does appear to have a full set of teeth, which will be itemised later.'

The officers continued to avoid looking at her head. Flint and Harris worked on it and peeled away scraps of blackened husk, exposing more skull, until in a perverse way the exposed skull made the head seem more human. To Gillett, the streaks of red reminded her of *The Scream* by Edvard Munch.

*

As Kirsty and Neil Garvey were packing up they heard the front door open. Melanie was in the armchair with the baby, and she glanced up without interest. But the little boy seemed to grow tense.

The man who entered was in his early twenties, still showing a trace of teenage acne. His hair was very short, as if he had shaved it off two weeks ago and it had just started growing back. He looked at home and Kirsty noticed that he had let himself in. He didn't seem surprised that they were there. Perhaps his dull eyes were not surprised at anything.

'Still here, then?'

He stared at Kirsty. She wondered about her camera. No point hiding it away – he had already seen it.

Melanie greeted him from the armchair. 'You're early. But they're going now.'

Neil grinned easily. 'You must be Melanie's boyfriend. I'm Neil, by the way. Neil Garvey.'

'Yeah, I'm Gary.' He cocked his head. 'You could put me in your film – except I ain't got me make-up on!' He touched his cheek and grinned at Kirsty. 'You the director? No, *he's* the director. You're the cameraman.'

'My name's Kirsty.'

'We're going,' Neil said.

Gary stared at him. 'Are you the bloke who makes these films? I mean, it's all right: I know what she does and that.'

Melanie said, 'Gary doesn't mind.'

Kirsty pointed her camera at him. He shrugged happily. 'But I ain't taking my clothes off, mind – I'm not wearing sexy undies today!'

She left the film running. 'So you know about the films she makes?'

'Well, it's money, innit? Mel lets men see her tits. So what? I ain't bothered.'

Melanie said, 'They're not *your* tits.'

'You show more than tits.'

Kirsty broke in to ask if Gary had watched Melanie's films.

He grinned, then looked away. 'Yeah, me and Mel watched a

video. It's all right. I mean, it's all make-believe, innit?' He peered at Neil. 'You was in it, wasn't you?'

'Must have been my brother.'

Gary laughed. 'Your brother! No, Christ, I said I don't mind. It's like professional, innit? It's what she does. Someone has to do it. I mean, I'll watch a decent video like any man, and I reckon the girls are all like Mel, yeah? When the filming's over they go home to normal life. It don't mean nothing.'

'When you watch Melanie in a video—' Kirsty wasn't sure how much Gary had seen. 'When you watch Melanie with another man—'

'Like him?'

'Like my brother.'

'Your bleedin' brother!' Gary laughed.

Kirsty asked, 'You don't feel jealous?'

Gary's eyes flickered, but he stared straight at the camera. 'Well, it's a bit weird, you know? But I don't feel jealous. Why should I? I mean, I'm the bloke as really matters to her, aren't I?'

He glanced at Melanie for confirmation, but she was playing with the baby. 'If we had loads of money we wouldn't do it, obviously – but there's worse ways, ain't there?'

'How would *you* know?' Melanie asked. '*I* make the pictures.'

*

'Teeth,' explained Harris, 'can reveal a lot.'

He was probing inside the blackened mouth cavity, conducting a preliminary visual while his assistant Flint prepared wax to make a cast.

'Teeth are a unique identifier – and they usually survive a fire.' He bent closer so he could delve deeper. 'To destroy a set of teeth you'd need a far more intense heat than this woman was subjected to. Certainly the discolouration and loss of flesh indicates quite a savage fire – but a relatively short-lived one.' He smiled thinly. 'She just flared up.'

No one attempted to smile back. Jennifer Gillett asked, 'As if she was doused in a flammable liquid and set alight?'

'An accelerant, yes, that sort of thing.'

The pathologist used his pencil light to peer inside the mouth. 'Fire may damage the front teeth but not usually the back. The tongue acts as a heat sink.'

They nodded.

'Fortunately, any tell-tale fillings usually cluster at the back. Yes, she's had four. Wisdom teeth present but not yet emerged. Good. Puts her in her early twenties. So we now have size, age and race—'

'Race?'

'White feet. If she'd been in a worse fire it might have completely disguised her external skin pigment – even a blonde could look negroid. But we already know that this girl was white.' He was back inside the mouth. 'If we didn't, the amount of gum melanin would confirm her colouring. Teeth alone can give us race – because there are national styles in dentistry. Japan and Asia treat differently from each other. America stands out a mile. France, Italy, Germany – no, this girl's British, I would say. First prognosis, you understand?'

'British white female, aged twenty to twenty-five,' muttered Wright.

'She's had no significant operations. No body scars. She is not a drug injector. Ready with the mixture, Mr Flint?'

'Ready when you are,' Nigel purred.

Harris took the pot. 'We had one last week with perfect teeth. Not one of yours, Damon?'

Wright shook his head.

'Disappointing. Perfect teeth means no dentistry – no history. No dentistry means that either the subject was very young – which that one wasn't – or it could indicate that she recently arrived from the third world, where she was never able to afford dentistry.'

'Was that the case?'

Harris was pressing wax around her teeth. 'Presumably. She did have teeth missing, but none treated. Probably never *seen* a proper dentist – so there would be no records. Prostitute, I think. There were obvious signs.'

Gillett interrupted: 'This is *last* week's case?'

'Mhm, sorry, yes. Quite right. Concentrate on the matter in hand.' He eased out the wax dental impressions and handed them to Flint. 'We should get plenty of information from these for your missing person's report – even if, sadly, you can't have a photo of what she looked like.'

He stood back, smiled at them, and rubbed his hands together as if washing them. 'Time to poke about inside and find what she really died of. In cases of burning, the internal organs usually survive, certainly in a short-lived flash fire like this. Surprisingly resilient, the human body.'

He prowled around the blackened corpse on the table like a hunter sizing up his kill. 'She wasn't battered to death, nor stabbed, nor shot. I don't think she was strangled. No reason yet to believe she wasn't killed by fire, but we must eliminate all other possibilities. She could have been poisoned. Could have been suffocated. Who knows? We do know that around the time of death this woman was subjected to a sudden fierce burst of flame. If she was alive when that happened I doubt she would have survived it.'

He paused, watching Jennifer Gillett especially to see how well she would take the gruesome process. She looked pale but unconcerned.

Harris said, 'So we must confirm whether it was the fire or something else that killed her. Let's start with an analysis of stomach and bladder contents to give an idea of what she was up to in the last hours before she died. We've already taken vaginal and rectal swabs. We have hair and tissue samples, clippings, and some blood. Do you want any more external measurements or can I go ahead?'

They indicated he could. They didn't say anything. The only sound in the mortuary was of running water at the cleansing table.

'We'll remove the brain afterwards,' he said.

Harris took his knife and made a frontal incision from the middle of her neck in a straight line down her front between her sad and flattened breasts, across her abdomen and then all the way down to the dark triangle of her pubis.

She was dead, and she had now ceased to be a person.

- 6 -

'THAMES DITTON?' ASKED Kirsty. She glanced at Neil, but he was concentrating on the road and unaware of her reaction.

'Suburbia,' he grunted.

Kirsty watched him from the corner of her eye. Had he chosen Thames Ditton because she lived there? How could he know? London is made up of a hundred villages: the chance of his choosing her own by chance seemed remote, and yet... They had met in Southwark where Neil had his office, had gone to Deptford to meet Melanie, had called in at Catford where Trisha lived and were now driving to Kirsty's own village. Perhaps it wasn't surprising: each new village they visited increased the chance he would choose hers.

But she said, 'Thames Ditton doesn't sound your stamping ground.'

'Not all my girls come from the pits.'

'Melanie was all right.'

'Nice enough.' Neil was staring through the windscreen. 'But she's losing her looks. You must have noticed.'

'She seemed quite attractive.'

'If you like 'em plump. A girl wants to look good on camera she has to stay slim.'

'Melanie wants to be an actress.'

'They all say that.'

'Even nice ladies from Thames Ditton?'

He was driving her to meet Delia Blyth who he'd chosen specifically, he said, to contrast with the girls that Kirsty had met so far.

He said, 'Most girls do it for the money. Some for the kicks.'

'Like suburban housewives?'

'*Readers' Wives*. Think about it, Kirsty: the men who buy my videos don't all live in council flats. Far from it. Middle class men like to see middle class housewives taking their kit off – in a middle class sitting room. Turns 'em on.'

They were leaving the Kingston Bypass.

Kirsty asked, 'Don't they ever wonder what their own wives get up to when they're away?'

'No. They've no imagination.'

They passed a road sign to Thames Ditton. But while Kirsty lived on a boat moored adjacent to the area, the Thames Ditton that Neil was headed for was dry land. Where they were going had nothing to do with her.

*

As the freshly washed BMW approached the wrought iron gates, a sensor automatically picked up its radio signal and instructed the tall black gates to open. The BMW barely paused as it cruised into the protected yard. This small development of exclusive town houses stood flanked on one side by Turner's Dock and on each of the other sides by high brick walls. There were security cameras. Each house had its own integral garage, each opened by a sensor. Each garage and house had alarms.

High land and property prices meant the sacrifice of some convenience: the garages were small. Before driving into his own, Tony Iles asked his visitors to step out into the yard. Once inside the garage, he said, there wasn't room to open the car doors on both sides.

'I shouldn't have bought such a poncey motor.'

Craddock and Farrell got out and waited. It wasn't raining, but even if it had been, they would have stood patiently in the wet.

Tony squeezed his car into its kennel, worked his way out of the driving seat, closed the car door, and edged his way back to the yard. On the other side of his car, the passenger side, was a door leading from the garage into his house, but for Tony it was too much of a fag to squeeze around the BMW to reach it. Besides, his guests were waiting outside.

While he was lost inside the garage, Roy Farrell had muttered to Craddock that a cab would have been a damn sight easier, but Craddock reminded him that Tony liked his car. Roy sniffed. 'How many bottles did we get through?'

'Two. Plus the brandy.'

'And beers.'

'Beers don't count.'

Tony appeared. 'Am I missing something?'

'We were discussing the menu.'

'La-di-dah.'

Farrell and Craddock laughed politely.

Tony fitted his key. 'I do like oysters, though.'

'Aphrodisiac.'

'Not so I've noticed.'

The two men followed him into the hall. It wasn't a hall so much as a square of carpet at the foot of narrow stairs. A panel door led off to his long living room, where the two men waited uncomfortably while he stooped beside his drinks cabinet. 'Beer OK?'

'Brown ale for me,' Roy said quickly.

The room ran the length of the house and its rear window looked out across the refurbished Turner's Dock. Furnishings were cream and terracotta. There were no pictures on the walls but as Tony Iles often said: with a view like that, who needed pictures?

And he had a monster television.

'Sort yourself a video,' he said. The low bookshelf held videos and DVDs. 'Newest ones are on top. I just got 'em – pre-release.'

Farrell strolled across to the videos but Craddock glanced at his watch. 'I can't stay long. I need to check in at the office.'

Tony Iles was pouring beers. 'The office can wait.'

'Quarterly figures don't look good.'

Tony stared at him unmoved. 'They'll look the same tomorrow morning.'

'I like to strike while the iron's hot.'

Farrell selected a video. '*This* looks hot.'

As Roy tore off the shrink wrap Craddock said, 'I'll leave you to it. Thanks for lunch.'

Tony said, 'I've poured the beer now.' He held it out.

Craddock hesitated. 'Fifteen minutes, then.'

'Put a video on, Roy. Let's have a laugh.'

*

'The body of a young woman was recovered by police this morning on the banks of the Thames in Bermondsey. The woman has not yet been identified but is described as white, aged twenty to twenty-five, of medium height with dark hair. Before she was dumped on the muddy foreshore, the woman had been badly burnt, and police say she may have been set alight and burnt to death. The body appears to have been thrown onto the mud sometime between midnight and

6am and police have appealed for any witnesses or anyone with relevant information to contact them immediately.'

*

Becky Phelps was a bright girl but down on her luck. In the past six months her luck had been especially bad. First they had closed the factory where she worked. Then, because she had only worked there twenty months they said she wasn't due Redundancy. She got a job in a bread shop but that closed too. At the next job that she applied for they laughed and said, 'the last two places you worked at got shut down.' So she complained to the Job Shop and they told her she had an attitude problem and should go on a course.

She went on their course and while she was on it she missed another job – an excellent job for someone she'd previously worked for at the factory. But he said they didn't have another vacancy because it was only a small place, so she'd missed it. And the stupid course only lasted five days. Since that time there had been nothing Becky could apply for. On top of that, the Benefit people were now saying that if she didn't work soon they'd stop her money. Becky said she wanted to work but no one ever offered her anything. They told her she had an attitude problem and should go on a course.

Becky walked down the High Street, wearing her best short yellow coat. She liked to look smart. Looking smart, something might happen to you – with a bit of luck. But she didn't feel lucky at the moment. She wanted a decent pair of shoes, because the pair she had on was a bit run down and her other ones looked old fashioned. There was no point wearing an expensive coat if she was let down by her shoes. People notice shoes: they say a lot.

She couldn't afford a decent pair.

There was only one thing for it: she'd have to have a go on the Lottery. She could buy some tickets and wait or she could get some scratch cards and get an immediate result. You don't win as much on scratch cards but at least the results are fast. And although you don't win as much, you have a better chance. On the Lottery you have hardly any chance at all.

So she walked into the newsagents and handed that Indian bloke a fiver. Becky didn't want to scratch off the cards while the man was watching, so she went out onto the pavement. The sun was shining – a bit hazy but it was there.

Out in the daylight she could take her time. Savour the moment. She had splashed out a fiver, so she might as well enjoy herself. For a few seconds, Becky clutched the tickets in her hands and leant her back against the wall. She let the sun play on her face. She wouldn't say the sun was hot but it was pleasant, standing there.

Becky Phelps closed her eyes. She kept the tickets tightly gripped and imagined scratching one with a coin – seeing immediately that she'd won. How much would it be? A hundred pounds? A thousand?

Becky smiled in the weak sun and kept her eyes closed. You had to admit, it would be nice. A hundred pounds wasn't much but would buy a lovely pair of shoes. And ten thousand wasn't an *impossible* amount – not like millions on the Lottery, which no one she'd ever heard of had ever won. Though a million quid would be fantastic. Perhaps she should have bought one for the Lottery.

No. She opened her eyes and shook her head. She had a strategy. She looked at the scratch cards and licked her lips.

Becky reached in her handbag for her money. Not much there, of course – plenty of coins but not much paper. But it was a coin she needed. Pity she'd never had a lucky coin – one that as long as you used it only occasionally, when you really needed it, might help you win the jackpot. Since she didn't have a lucky coin she'd use a pound.

Use a pound to win a pound.

Becky looked along the road. No one watching. People shopping, wandering about – quite a lot of people, really, but this *was* the High Street. What would happen if she won? She imagined a great flashing neon sign: 'this week's winner is Becky Phelps!' Then she chuckled – it was only a scratch card. There wouldn't be a mega prize. She should have bought a Lottery ticket.

Don't let the moment fade.

Becky rubbed the first card with her coin.

Yes! She had won a prize. It was only 'Money Back Or Play Again' but it was a prize – and she had another four tickets left.

She rubbed the next one. No. Then the next.

Well. Two losers out of four was to be expected. She let the two useless cards fall from her hand and she gazed at the remaining pair. Could she *will* one of them to win? It sounds stupid but you never know. Becky took her winning 'Money Back' ticket and rubbed it gently against the last two, to see if some of its good luck could rub off.

Should she delay a minute, or rub them now? Do it now, of course – that's the point of a scratch card: it's instant. Find out instantly.

She rubbed a scratch card but didn't win. Then, as she stared at the last one, a funny thing happened: it seemed to shine a little, it seemed to grow. Even as she held it she could feel the ticket getting warmer. It couldn't be, could it? Yes, it could. This was the one. She took the card that had won already and placed it beside the one that she had left. It was like all those mystical magic things: if you try to check them scientifically they don't work. But if you leave out the science and trust in instincts, magic can come true. Everyone knows that. Except scientists. And those boring people who never take a chance.

Becky took a deep breath, then rubbed the silver ink off her scratch card. But she hadn't won. She kept staring. She couldn't believe it. She had known she'd won. How could all her instincts be wrong? That was really creepy.

It took twenty seconds – twenty long miserable blame-ridden seconds – before she realised. She *was* going to win: she would win on her last ticket. But not the ticket in her hand: 'Money Back Or Play Again'. If she went back into the newsagents she could either have the pound back – which was pointless – or take another ticket for free.

It was obvious, wasn't it? The one in her hand would buy the winning scratch card. —But she'd have to hurry. She'd have to run back inside the shop before another customer arrived, so she could buy the next one in the box.

The one with her name on it.

*

Thames Ditton is about half-way up the property ladder; half-way up the index of respectability. Half-way up is nowhere to aspire to – unless you start at the bottom. Had Delia Blyth started there? She'd never tell you. Certainly she had settled snugly in Thames Ditton, and for all her middle class trappings she looked as though she'd clawed up every rung. Her accent was shaky – too middle class, the kind of accent that in provincial towns still lingered from fifty years before. Her make-up was precise. The furniture in her house looked as if it had been desperately copied from back issues of *Homes and Gardens* and was so carefully arranged, the cushions so extravagantly plumped, that you couldn't believe her chairs had ever been sat upon.

But they had been. They had featured in Neil Garvey's films.

While Delia made a pot of tea, for which porcelain cups were arranged on a side table, Kirsty popped into the lavatory. It smelt of lavender. On the low-flush cistern stood a doll-like figure in a crinoline dress, inside which, Kirsty knew, would be a spare toilet roll. She smiled. Her mother had one. Her mother: Kirsty's smile faded. She must find a moment to buy a pregnancy test kit. If Ken had indeed made her pregnant – had walked out and left her pregnant – what would she do?

She went back into the living room. Delia would not permit herself to get pregnant. Her living room smelt of Pledge – and one of her pledges would be to remain childless. 'I indulge myself,' she said.

Kirsty started filming.

'Of course, the money's nice – though Neil doesn't pay anywhere near enough.' She smiled at him. 'But I indulge myself in the fantasy.'

She sat down gracefully on a plush unyielding sofa. 'I'm a housewife, I admit it, a bored housewife – but I don't think anyone would say I'm past it. I'm thirty-two, and let me tell you, there's plenty of life in this young lady yet. Oh yes. I like sex. I'm married – happily married, actually – but no honeymoon lasts forever, does it? My husband and I still have sex – of course we do, frequently – pretty good sex, actually. I encourage him to experiment.'

Delia giggled mischievously, her fingers to her lips. Watching her through the viewfinder Kirsty suddenly saw the woman's sex appeal: a middle class housewife talking dirty from her settee. Though she wasn't thirty-two.

'But he's away all day and I get bored. You want the truth? I was one of those *Readers' Wives* – you know what they are? It seemed harmless. It *was* harmless. I wore my sexy underwear – stuff my husband bought for me on a foreign business trip. Lacy slips. Sexy bras.'

Delia looked defiantly at the camera. Kirsty kept filming.

'And I took my own photographs, on delayed action. To be honest, I thought I looked very good. So I sent them off. There was no danger because my husband wouldn't read that sort of magazine.'

Quietly, Kirsty asked, 'How about his friends?'

'What about them? I meet very few of Jamie's friends, but if one did happen to see a copy of the magazine, so what? He'd see me in a new light, that's all.' She chuckled. 'Could be interesting. He'd see me in the magazine and think, "I know you, I could go for you", but where's the harm in that? I like men to look at me. I like sex.'

'Would you have sex with one of Jamie's friends?'

Delia shuddered prettily. 'Have you *seen* his friends? But I don't need to go for *them* – do I, Neil?'

He was at the side of the room, out of shot. Her eyes twinkled. 'Neil's feeling coy. Am I allowed to tell them, Neil?'

He nodded.

'*Readers' Wives* led on to video – which proves that I stood out. There are a lot of women in those magazines, plenty younger than me, but *I* was the one they asked to take a screen test. It was successful, of course, so I made a video – quite short. Nothing nasty. No real sex.'

Neil murmured, 'It was made by Ben somebody, wasn't it?'

She ignored that. 'It was a silly video, but it was a great help to my career. A stepping stone.'

She looked at Kirsty straight-faced, but then suddenly laughed. 'Career! Hark at me. I'm not a fool, you know, I'm not naïve. Oh no, I'm a little too wise for that. The fact is… well, these films are fantasy, male fantasy, but I should care – because the sex in them is great!'

If her confidence flickered it was only momentarily. She lifted her chin. But she did blush. 'You see, the men Neil uses in his films – well, to put it crudely, they're all studs. Women watch these movies too, you know, so the men have to be good looking, they have to have great bodies, and by golly, they have to perform!'

She glanced at Neil, as if for permission, but then leant closer to the camera. 'They've all got great long dicks!' She giggled like a schoolgirl. 'Well, I ask you – no, ask any bored housewife in her thirties: wouldn't *you* like some of that? Be honest, girls! There's nothing complicated, there are no consequences. The man won't call round afterwards and tell your husband. No one's going to know. It's just sex, you see. An afternoon's amusement and he's gone.'

Delia was animated. It was her chance to justify herself on film. 'What I say is that if a man wants to watch videos of people shagging, that's up to him. Men like to watch – but women like to touch!'

She paused to find the words to express her thoughts. 'I wouldn't tell my husband – that would be cruel. But if he finds out accidentally, it won't break us up. Oh no. He'll understand that what occurs in a film is just a game. It isn't love. It doesn't mean anything. No one gets hurt.'

*

At Turner's Dock the film they were watching was brand new, and had not been made by Neil Garvey. Or Ben Dover. Those films were tasters to the main meal, they were not the meat course. Time was when films like theirs, showing actual copulation, penetration shots, were at the edge. Men would gather in darkened rooms to watch them. But those films are available legitimately now in licensed sex shops. You watch them in your hotel bedroom.

Tony Iles couldn't be bothered with films like that. He, Craddock and Farrell were slumped in front of a lurid and largely plotless video of a seemingly real drug-induced orgy entitled *More Anal Nitrate*, in which supposedly unsuspecting London schoolgirls were dragged off the street to be sodomised by three actors and a donkey. The girls looked young, and at least two of them looked as if they had been jiggered with a date rape drug, roofie or GHB. They slumped unresistingly in whatever position they were pushed into and accepted whatever instrument was forced up their backsides. Quite why such a fiercely heterosexual trio as Iles, Farrell and Craddock *wanted* to watch a succession of anal sex scenes was a question no one asked. Craddock didn't want to be there anyway. He had given up glancing at his watch, but despite the graphic sex on screen he really would have preferred to be at the office, hunting down the shortfall in his quarterly returns. He agreed with Farrell's unfortunately timed remark: 'I've seen enough arse-holes. Let's see some tits and pretty faces.'

As if the cameraman had heard his plea, the shot switched to a close-up across a young girl's shoulder of a man's heavy face jammed hard against her cheek. The girl was expressionless, almost, although she winced at every thrust. She was a new one, another grabbed off the street—

'What the fuck is that?' called Tony Iles.

He yelled, 'Gimme the remote.'

Farrell tossed it to him. Craddock froze. The picture froze. Farrell would have frozen too if he had known. But Tony Iles boiled over. The screen of his monster television was filled with the two-shot of those faces. Farrell stared blankly: it meant nothing to him. It meant something to Craddock. And a damn sight more to Iles. He pressed Stop: 'Who made this? Where's the carton?'

Craddock fumbled for it. 'It won't tell you.'

'I'll check the titles.' Tony pressed Rewind.

'They use false names.'

Craddock held out the video case but Iles ignored it: 'No, the credits on the bloody video, at the start.'

Roy Farrell frowned.

Iles asked, 'Where did we get this film?'

'It's one of yours.'

Iles glared at the monitor. While the tape rewound, the TV had switched to a wildlife documentary. Daytime TV: animals in the wild.

Craddock stood up carefully. 'Maybe Roy and I should leave.'

Tony Iles spun on him. Someone who hadn't known the man might have said his eyes looked damp. But surely not – he must be angry. 'You saw that?'

Craddock nodded helplessly. 'What can I say?'

Tony looked at Roy, who looked away. 'And what did *you* think?'

'I don't know.'

'You don't know *what*?'

'Nothing. All I know is there were too many arse-holes in that film.'

Roy grinned, being a genius for getting it wrong. Iles shouted, 'You think it's funny?'

'What, you got religion or something? What?'

The Rewind stopped. The machine clunked but the TV still showed wild animals. Leopards and antelopes. Red meat. Tony pressed Play. 'We'll see who made this.'

Roy frowned at Craddock: what was going on?

Tony stared at the screen while a brief title sequence rolled by. But it was too quick: this wasn't the sort of film which named the executive producer's Best Boy.

Iles read off the screen: 'Van Cock Films. Oh, very funny. They made that up.'

Roy said, 'They always do.'

'We'll run a company search.' Iles turned to Craddock. 'That's your department.'

Craddock nodded. 'They won't be registered at Companies House.'

Roy chuckled. 'They won't even be British. Van Cock, that's a joke. They'll be Dutch – one of those Amsterdam units.'

'They filmed it *here*,' said Tony.

'Yeah, that street scene where they snatched the schoolgirls – that could've been London,' Roy agreed. 'Though it could've been Glasgow or—'

'It was London.'

'Right. You recognise the street?' Roy saw their faces but blundered on. He sang: 'I have often walked down this street before.'

Tony couldn't speak. Craddock spoke for him: 'Shut up, Roy. Tony recognised the actress.'

'Yeah, which one?' chuckled Roy. 'You've seen one arse, you've seen 'em all.'

Iles moved so fast he could have been on Fast Forward. He took a step, his arm shot out, and he grasped Roy's throat before the man stopped smiling. The speed of Tony's thrust took both men tumbling to the floor. When Roy hit the carpet he found Iles kneeling on his chest, his fingers round his throat.

Iles said, 'That young girl, Roy, when we stopped the film – that was my daughter.'

Roy pulled at Tony's fingers. He tried to say, 'You sure?'

Tony did not let go. With his other hand he back-handed Farrell's face. 'You think I don't know my own daughter?'

'Please, Tony...'

Roy's fingers scrabbling. Iles ignoring him. 'Craddock, find that company, right? And you—' He glared into Farrell's face. 'Go see the dealers. They tell you they don't know who made it, tell *them* I don't give a fuck – they know where they bought the things.'

He released his grip and stood up. Farrell rolled over but stayed on the floor, rubbing his throat.

Craddock said, 'I'll get straight onto it. Shall I take the video? — No.' He backed off nervously. 'I don't need the video.'

'No one sees this.' Tony looked down at Roy Farrell. 'What you hanging around down there for? Make every dealer give you every copy he's got. Send some people round all the dealers. I want every copy, seals unbroken.'

Farrell decided not to object. His throat hurt anyway.

Craddock was at the door. 'Anything else, Tony? I'm sorry about this.'

'*You're* sorry? Wait and see *these* guys feel sorry.'

Farrell was sitting now, trying to make amends: 'You want us to look out for your daughter, while we're at it?'

Tony's eyes were cold. 'You think I can't find my own daughter? With my fucking ex-wife – that's where my daughter is. I know that.'

Farrell stayed on the carpet. 'She hasn't moved away or nothing? I mean, she's definitely living there?'

'Of course she's living there. She's fourteen years old.'

- 7 -

EVERYONE SLIPS OCCASIONALLY. For the last hour an old rock tune had been repeating in her head: *The Girl Can't Help It, The Girl Can't Help It*. That simple, driving tune in which practically every line, certainly every second line, repeats *The Girl Can't Help It* was right for her.

Becky Phelps had binged on gambling. Her 'Money Back Or Play Again' card had bought a dud – but perhaps that was only to be expected: an evens card was not a winner. If she wanted a big-time winner she should buy a National Lottery ticket – but not from that poxy Indian newsagent. She had wasted six quid with him. A loser. The newsagent was a loser. No one ever won big-time there.

So Becky walked a hundred yards and invested a fiver at the garage. A fiver, she thought: hardly worth bothering. There are syndicates who bet on the Lottery every week and they invest *hundreds* of pounds every time. What chance did Becky have against *them*? Except that syndicates didn't always win – didn't usually win, come to think about it: most winners you heard about, most *big* winners, were just ordinary people like her. It was a people's lottery. So Becky spent a fiver on it.

When she looked in her purse she still had a rusty old pound coin. What could you do with that? She bought a one pound scratch card. It made sense, she thought: that pound was sitting there, all alone, telling her something. So she bought the scratch card and rubbed the ink off at the counter, but she didn't win anything. Nearly, though.

The man in the garage smiled: 'Could come up on your next ticket.'

But Becky wasn't daft. She walked out into the fresh air of the garage forecourt and stowed the five National Lottery tickets in her lucky compartment. As she slipped them inside her bag she was surprised to find a bunch of tickets already there. She frowned. Were they left from last week, unclaimed? She felt suddenly cold. She stood at the edge of the forecourt where it joined the pavement, and when she looked again she remembered that she had bought those five tickets yesterday. No, not five, there were ten. Had she really bought ten? She had fifteen now. Oh God – look: on one of those tickets she had chosen exactly the same numbers as on one she had just bought. Well, she would, of course she would: they were her lucky numbers. Becky smiled at the sun: if her lucky numbers came up – they had to some day, it stood to reason – then she'd win *twice*! Fancy that: two times five million. Fifteen quid wasn't much to invest – not when you could win *millions* of pounds, millions and millions. She could afford fifteen pounds.

As she continued down the High Street, Becky realised that fifteen pounds was hardly anything. Those syndicates invested *hundreds* of pounds, didn't they? If fifteen quid was all she spent, no one could say she was a gambler! Fifteen measly pounds. Plus what she spent on scratch cards. But scratch cards didn't count, because they were instant. You rubbed the card and you won or lost. You knew immediately. It wasn't a real investment where you planned your strategy and waited for results. Buying scratch cards was like buying sweets.

Everyone does that.

She grinned to herself: who was she trying to kid? She enjoyed gambling – though this wasn't gambling, it was fun. You need a bit of fun in life. You need a tingle. Why else – as if she didn't know – why else had she paused now outside the betting shop? She wasn't like *some* sad cases. Inside that betting shop she'd see really sad people – usually blokes, usually dressed in smelly clothes – who looked as if they'd been in the betting shop all day long. Hoping something came up.

Becky wasn't like them. Here she was, half-way through the afternoon and she hadn't even thought about the betting shop. By now, there'd be only a few races left – unless you bet on tomorrow's horses, but Becky didn't believe in that. Anything could happen. You had to place your bets on the actual day, when you knew exactly who was running, and what the weather was like. Anything else was silly – just taking a chance, no skill at all.

Becky pushed the door open. She'd place one bet – just one, because she couldn't afford several – then walk away. Well no, she wouldn't walk away immediately: she'd wait till the race was over. But she'd be strong today. While she waited she wouldn't bet on anything else. She'd try not to.

Becky stood inside the shop, in the comforting lack of air. A race commentary had been playing when she came in but she didn't listen. She hadn't bet on that race. She would take her time and read the remaining race cards very carefully: wait for a horse to leap out at her. One usually did. She would place her bet, wait and see what happened and then, whatever happened, she promised faithfully, she would collect her handbag and walk away.

Perhaps she could scrounge a cup of tea off her friend Melanie.

*

The duty officer rang Inspector Gillett.

'I heard you were still in the office, ma'am. We have a young lady here that I think you'd like to see. The Bermondsey riverside case.'

'A witness?'

'She claims to be. She says she has "evidence", and insists on speaking to the officer in charge.'

Jennifer's eyes glinted. 'Not a time-waster?'

'Don't think so, ma'am. She wants to talk confidentially.'

Jennifer was already reaching for her things. 'Don't they all?'

'The young lady looks distinctly scared, ma'am.'

'That's encouraging. I'm on my way.'

*

Kirsty said she had to get home. She and Neil were back at his Southwark base but she hadn't gone inside. Something in his tone suggested he had more in mind than an end-of-project review. Not that she couldn't have dealt with it: Neil took it for granted that practically every girl who walked through his door would have sex with him, so the chances were that he wouldn't press too strongly. Why make an effort for what he could get so easily?

As if he'd read her mind he said, 'No pressure.'

They both opened doors and climbed out. As she collected her video bag he spoke across the car roof: 'It was great workin' with you, Kirsty. Funny, isn't it, the way life goes? Two days in each other's pockets, then goodbye.'

'We may meet.'

'You've got my number. Call anytime.'

'Trisha said you say that to all the girls.'

'Ah, but I don't mean it with them.' Neil smiled. Light had faded in the grubby street. 'So now I just wait for my cheque?'

'Invoice us. You know the address.'

He smiled again. 'Let me know when the programme goes out.'

'I'll be in touch.'

She was walking away. Her thoughts had left him. She was mentally checking she'd gathered all her equipment. Hoping her car was where she had parked it. And creeping into her thoughts was the fact that she must look for a late-night chemist: she had to buy a pregnancy predictor.

*

Inspector Gillett shook her head. 'I'm not judging you.' She kept her voice soft. Encouraging. She was glad she had a woman PC in the room. Three women and no disturbing male presence would keep the atmosphere unthreatening. Cosy.

She said, 'You're perfectly entitled to make these movies.'

'Entitled, that's right.'

'It's not against the law.'

Cassie looked up. 'You sure of that?'

Jennifer smiled at her. 'Well, there is a line, but we'll assume you haven't crossed it.'

'I came voluntary.'

Jennifer nodded, waiting. Cassie's hair was streaked, like old stripped pine. She wore some lipstick, eyebrow pencil and the remains of yesterday's mascara. Her skin was practically unblemished – at nineteen she didn't need foundation. She looked tired.

'My mum don't know.'

'That you make these movies?'

'That I've come here.'

Cassie stared at the table. Jennifer pushed: 'About last night?'

Cassie swallowed. Jennifer watched. This was the moment, she knew, that Cassie would come out with it.

'It went too far. I mean, before... before the business, you know, it'd already gone too far.'

Gillett waited.

'In these movies, we have sex and that, you know? That's normal.' Cassie's gaze flickered, as if 'normal' was not the best word. 'But then... these others muscled in.'

'Others?'

'Right, the way it goes, like, we're all actors and we improvise. We have a script – a sort of script – but well, you make some parts up as you go along. A lot of it, really, the words and that.'

'These "others" you mentioned?'

'Yeah, they wasn't actors, know what I mean? They was only young but they seemed like... well, management.'

A pause. 'And?'

Cassie sighed. 'Well, these management or whatever joined in. They was...' Again she bit her lip. 'I mean, look, I might say something here that gets me in real trouble, you know? But I want to help you.'

'Who are you afraid of, Cassie?'

'Everyone.'

Silence. The tape hummed.

'Cassie, this is a confidential interview. No one will know you came.'

'Not yet they won't. But if this comes to trial...'

'We'll protect you.'

'Yeah.' Cassie looked at her fingernails. A child's hands, Gillett noticed. Cassie said, 'Look, this is murder, yeah? That girl in the river: it said on the News that she was burnt. Look, supposing, just supposing I've got evidence about it but, you know, if I tell you about it I've got to mix myself up in something else – not murder, nothing as bad as that – but you know, something that's still against the law?'

'We could work something.'

Cassie snorted. Her will was fading, Gillett knew. She was regretting having come. 'How serious, Cassie – drugs?'

'No, not drugs. That's nothing. Look, supposing one of us, one of us girls doing the picture, like, was under age? Supposing.'

'How far under age?'

'Fourteen. Or something. I don't know.'

Jennifer touched her hand. 'That's all right, then – you don't know. You *didn't* know, so you weren't responsible. You didn't commit a crime.'

'They raped her.'

The room fell silent, except for the tape machine.

'That was the start of it. These management types – boys, really – they joined in and – I mean, the girl was in the film, you know, and there *was* a rape scene but... these blokes did it for real.'

Cassie stopped again. Jennifer said softly, 'The murder victim was not fourteen.'

'Oh no, *she* was twenty-odd.'

'What happened?'

'She'd been filming it.'

'The cameraman?'

'No, no. She was like... an undercover journalist.'

Jennifer Gillett held her breath.

'She had this camera in a bag. And they found it. She'd filmed the whole rape business *and* these management blokes, and she had it in this bag, and they emptied it.'

Cassie paused and swallowed, but her mouth was dry. She sipped some tea.

'And she had this can of hair spray in the bag as well, and they sprayed it all over her – especially her head and, oh Christ, it was horrible... I mean, they emptied the whole can, you know? The whole bloody can. And then they set light to it. Set her hair alight. And... and all the rest of her burned as well. And well, it said on the telly, it said that this girl, this woman had been burned, and I thought, oh my God, it's *her*. 'Cos... 'Cos we saw her burned, like, burned to death.'

'We?'

'Yeah, the rest of us, the actors and... I suppose no one else has been and told you, like?'

'Not yet.'

'Not yet! No bloody chance. No way. I shouldn't have come here neither.'

'You're a brave girl, Cassie. You did what was right.'

'The bastards killed her. I mean, she was about twenty-two, twenty-three, right? Burned all round the head? Didn't have much clothes on?'

Jennifer nodded.

'Yeah, I knew it was her, soon as I heard it. I mean, I was waiting, wasn't I? And when they said it on the telly I said, that's Zoë, poor bleedin' cow.'

'Zoë – was that her name?'

'Course it was. She said so, anyway.'

'Could it have been a stage name?'

'She wasn't an actress. She was a journalist, wasn't she?'

'You're sure of that?'

'Of course I'm sure. It was me as got her in the film.'

- 8 -

TONY ILES RANG at eight o'clock in the morning: answerphone. Eight ten: answerphone. Eight twenty: get up, you bitch. Eight thirty she picked up the phone. Maybe she said something. Maybe she cleared her throat.

He said, 'Lisanne?'

'Ugh.'

'You still in bed?'

'For Christ's sake, Tony. Get off the phone.'

'I came round last night.'

'You want a date?'

'For Emma. She wasn't in.'

'So?'

'She's still living there, I hope?'

'What's the time?'

'Did you take her with you last night?'

'Christ, Tony, it's eight o'clock.'

'Eight thirty. Where'd you go?'

'I'm putting down the phone.'

'Let me speak to Emma.'

'She's asleep.'

'Eight thirty? Where were the pair of you last night?'

'I don't know. What's it to do with you?'

'I'm her father.'

'Yeah. Well, you get access, don't you? Talk to her then.'

'Put me on to her.'

'I'm not waking her. Get off the phone.'

'What d'you mean, you're not waking her – don't the girl go to school?'

'Christ, my head. Yeah, she's *gone* to school. Right? I don't know.'

'You're her mother. You got to know.'

'She's fourteen years old. She sorts herself.'

'And you don't even get out of bed?'

'Listen – God, why do I bother? Listen.' He could hear her sitting up in bed. 'Tony. I was out last night—'

'Where?'

'Clubbing. —And don't start bitching. It's my business what I do.'

'You take her?'

'Last night? No.'

'Sometimes?'

'Shit. Look, don't give me the third degree. 'Bye, Tony.'

'I want to speak to Emma.'

'At the weekend. I'm going now.'

'You'd better hear this.'

But Lisanne put down the phone.

*

At DarkAlley Films, Kirsty was in the editing suite. Although she had hours of video she had already noted the most promising pieces and she reviewed them first, indexing the sequences which had useful footage, and making a rough catalogue of her material. Several sequences looked certain to be used: Neil filming Trisha on the stairs; Neil showing off his wired bedroom and explaining how he used it as an audition suite; Neil boasting how he himself joined in; Melanie, young mother of two, with a shrugging boyfriend who knew what she did but didn't care; Delia, suburban housewife, posing lewdly on her immaculate settee.

Some of Neil's off-hand dismissive commentary could be used as voice-over, rather than have his smug face on screen too often. Even the exterior of his house-come-studio was a telling shot: although it identified the place it also emphasised the tacky, down at heel nature of that world. A glamorous film studio it was not.

Neither was DarkAlley. An exterior shot of *their* offices would show a drab anonymous plain-fronted building whose slab of multiple doorbells suggested a block of flats rather than offices. DarkAlley's interior was the same size as a flat. Housed on the wrong side of Victoria, the shared building revealed nothing of what lay inside. Once past the red front door a visitor would find an untidy but well-equipped set of offices, the walls covered with pinboards, posters, stills from past productions, framed citations and certificates, plus an assortment of business cards, post-it notes and takeaway menu cards.

There was a visitor now. Kirsty had heard the doorbell but she stayed in the editing suite. She wasn't expecting anybody. It wouldn't be for her. She was speeding through the Delia interview when Rosa came in.

Rosa Klein ran DarkAlley. A veteran journalist, she had expanded from freelance film-making to create this independent production company. All their work was documentary – an extension of Rosa's career – and the company worked jointly with other film-makers on large projects, although where possible it worked alone.

Rosa didn't know yet that Kirsty was pregnant. No one did, except Kirsty. Rosa said, 'I need you a minute.' She looked grim. One of the few women over forty who still smoked, Rosa had dark wiry hair, an attractively lined face, and a boyish figure that she attributed to the beneficial effects of nicotine.

Kirsty stopped the machine. Rosa glanced curiously at the frozen image of Delia sucking her thumb, and added, 'You'd better prepare yourself for a shock.'

*

Tony had no idea how the school schedule worked, so he decided not to wait till morning break. Did they still have such things – and if so, when? His daughter was fourteen. She wouldn't have playtime. But what did *he* know? He'd never taken an interest in school.

He rang her mobile. If she was in class she would have it switched off but if she was on a break, it might be on. Besides, he could always leave a message—

'Hi. This is Emmaline.'

'Emma*line*? Where did that come from?'

'Oh, hello, Dad.'

Her voice dropped. She sounded low. She had always been such a bubbly little thing.

'You changed your name?'

'I told you: Emma Iles sounds ugly. The words don't go together.'

'Sounds fine to me.'

'Emma Iles: two vowels. They don't slide easily.'

'Tony Iles: that's two vowels.'

'E is not a vowel – I mean, Y isn't.'

'I like it.'

She sighed – yawned, it sounded like. 'Why'd you phone, Dad?'

'Are you at school?'
Hesitation. Did he imagine it? 'Yes, of course I am.'
'I'm not interrupting class?'
'It's a free period – exam study.' She still sounded low.
'Are you on your own?'
'Sort of.'
'I got something to say to you.'
'That sounds bad.'
'It is.' He held the beat. 'I was watching a video.'
'Ye-es?'
'A video called *More Anal Nitrate*. Ring a bell?'
He heard her swallow and draw breath. 'Anal – you mean *amyl* nitrate?'
'You heard of it, then?'
'Well, it's a popper, isn't it? Don't worry, I don't use *poppers*, Dad,'
'I'm talking about the film.'
'What film?'
'*More Anal Nitrate*. You were in the damn thing, weren't you?'
Her voice dropped even quieter. 'Dunno what you mean. What film?'
'Don't give me this, Emma.' He made himself sound reasonable, like a father should. 'I saw it – what you did in it.' Silence. 'What they *did* to you. It was a porno video, Emma.'
'You've been watching porno films?'
'Look.' Still reasonable. Keep it reasonable. 'I'm not having a go at you—'
'Sounds like it.'
'I'm worried about you! Christ, Emma, that video. They were… You're fourteen years old.'
'So?' A small voice.
'Fourteen. Christ, you shouldn't be having *sex*—'
'I wasn't.'
'I *saw* it. You were—'
'Why were you watching porn videos? My own Dad. Christ, that's sick.'
He sighed. 'Someone showed it me, right? They recognised you. Anyone who knows you sees that film, they're gonna recognise you.'
'So that's it.'
'What?'

'You don't want people to recognise me – not because it's for *my* sake, but because I'm *your* daughter. You don't want your poncey friends sitting down to watch a video and going, 'Oh look, there's Tony's daughter!' You don't care about *me*, though—'

'Please—'

'Only what they think of *you*!'

'I saw you take it up the arse!'

He should not have said it. For a couple of moments neither of them spoke. Then she said, 'You're disgusting, you.'

'I saw the film.'

'You shouldn't watch them kind of films.'

'What happened, Emma? How did you get into this?'

'*You* should care.'

'I do care. Does your mother know—'

'Leave her out of this. Don't say anything to her.'

Placatory. Be placatory. 'All right, Emma, I promise. But I've got to see you. I'll come down to school for you—'

'No! You can't do that.'

'I've got to—'

'I'm not – I won't see you, Dad.'

'Come on, Emma.'

'No.'

Pause. 'You're not *at* school, are you?'

'I don't – want – to see you.'

'Emma—'

'No, Dad.'

'Where are you?'

*

Kirsty leant back against the desk, her hands against its angular edge. She had to hold herself upright; if she didn't prop herself up she would collapse. Her legs were trembling. Everyone in the room seemed to be staring at her. Rosa stood in front of her but to one side, her hand on Kirsty's arm as if to steady her. Janine was slumped on her typist's chair, white-faced, a starving waif. The two policewomen stood patiently, watching Kirsty. All women, she thought: there are no men here – yet this is men's business.

She forced herself to speak: 'Murdered?'

'It's a murder *investigation*. She was stripped naked, burned, dumped in the river – what would you call it?'

Kirsty stared at the woman. Strong, mid-thirties, sober clothes. *Plain* clothes. She was the inspector, hard as nails. That must be it: the inspector was playing tough, *shocking* the office with the brutality of language. Shocking them into saying something.

Rosa had her back to the police inspector. It would take more than language to disturb *her*. She asked Kirsty, 'Are you all right? Do you want to sit?'

Kirsty touched her hand. *Sit? I know I'm pregnant, but...* Rosa didn't look too good herself. The inspector said, 'Miss Rice, I believe you were working together on a film?'

Kirsty nodded. Her mouth was dry.

'On the sex industry?'

Kirsty nodded again.

'What one might call undercover journalism?'

Rosa spoke for Kirsty: 'We are specialists in covert filming – hidden microphones, disguised cameras, infiltration.' She smiled at the inspector. 'All legitimate, of course.'

'And this company you were investigating?'

'Companies. The industry. This was one programme in a series.'

'But the company that Miss Rand infiltrated?'

Miss Rand, she called her. She meant Zoë. Zoë was dead.

Rosa turned to Kirsty: 'You OK now?'

'I'll tell her.' Kirsty licked her lips. 'Zoë and I were investigating the practitioners – the companies that lure girls into sex films, as well as companies that make the films themselves. I had... I had the easy job.'

She swallowed. The inspector was waiting, not harrying.

'The company I worked on knew I was filming. We paid them, in fact. But Zoë...' Kirsty's voice stopped.

The inspector helped her out – gentle now they had started talking: 'She used a hidden camera. We know that. It seems that the camera may have been discovered—'

Kirsty groaned. Rosa said, 'Sit down.'

'I'll stand.'

'What we don't know,' explained Inspector Gillett, 'is the company she was investigating.'

'There's not much to tell. They use different names for different films, but there are bigger companies behind them. It's a tax dodge, mainly – it helps if one of their companies gets into trouble.'

'What kind of trouble?'

'Well, money – tax, of course – and debts and oh, any kind of trouble. We don't really know. It's the kind of thing Zoë was trying to find out.'

'And this particular company was called?'

Kirsty shrugged. 'It's a stupid name – but it's just an offshoot of the real company. It probably doesn't mean anything at all. Van Cock Films.'

'That much we knew,' said the inspector. 'But what's the real company? Where's it based?'

'I don't know.'

Gillett watched her.

Kirsty said, 'We're not the CID. We pick up what we can. We don't know everything.'

'Tell me what you do know.'

'How did *you* know about Van Cock Films?'

Gillett met her eyes but didn't answer.

Kirsty said, 'We started at the outside and gradually worked in. We contacted companies that advertise for so-called glamour models, where you can tell it's the sex industry.'

'You know a lot of those companies?'

'We're making a programme, inspector. It's not our job to rid the world of vice.'

Gillett nodded. 'So you said. And Miss Rand?'

'She was…' Kirsty closed her eyes. She felt a kick in her stomach, as if the baby had moved. But it was far too early for a baby to move. It was just that her whole body understood now that Zoë had been killed. She said, 'Zoë got herself a part in a Van Cock sex film. We'd been told they use under-age girls.'

'Shouldn't you have told the police?'

Kirsty looked up. 'You said you already knew about Van Cock.'

'We know about them now.'

'What *do* you know?'

'I'd rather hear what *you* know.'

Kirsty banished stubbornness from her eyes. The inspector wanted a one-way conversation, but there was little Kirsty could tell her, and nothing the inspector would give back. Yet Kirsty needed to know what the inspector knew. The inspector hadn't lost a good friend. The inspector hadn't worked on this story for three grubby months.

'I know less than you do,' she said.

She felt dizzy again, and clutched at the desk. But this time the dizziness was for a different reason, a reason she could barely let herself face. Guilt: when Zoë said she was frightened Kirsty had let her carry on. And there was something else: she didn't like to admit it but she should. Call her professional, call her a cold-hearted bitch, but because Zoë had been murdered, this routine story was about to become a scoop.

- 9 -

THE INSPECTOR HAD gone, leaving the woman constable to bag up Zoë's things. There wasn't much in her desk, although her four-drawer filing cabinet was stuffed with paper – little of which, as Rosa protested, had anything to do with the sex film project. But the police took everything.

While the constable bagged, Kirsty sat at her own PC and logged onto Zoë's computer files on the network. She didn't change or delete the files, she merely copied those that looked relevant. She copied Zoë's diary and address book, her files on Van Cock, Killporn.com, Eastendsex.com, Personal, Sundry and even Zoë's Finance file, in case it might have a useful invoice address. Kirsty sat as demurely as a typist while the constable worked. At some point the woman was going to realise about Zoë's PC files: she might simply copy them herself, or worse, she might remove or restrict the files so no one could access them. She might even freeze the network – though Rosa would fight like a devil over that. Even so. Kirsty copied files to her directory and made a Zip copy which she slipped into her handbag. She was doing nothing wrong, she told herself – anything the police might want was still on the machine. But she had a copy too.

Still at her PC, Kirsty skimmed the contents list to Zoë's folders, looking for any files which might stand out. Plenty of bedtime reading, she thought – but how much meat? She opened the address book and began working through the names, ignoring those she recognised and concentrating on those she did not. Less fruitful than she had hoped: she and Zoë had many names in common. They walked the same paths.

But not exactly the same.

*

He was described as 'Charming sleazeball' under the legend 'Van Cock Data'. Kirsty phoned from the editing suite, where she would not be overheard.

'Is that Luke Miller?'

'I have been called worse.'

'This is Kirsty Rice—'

'Sounds pretty. What can I do for you?'

He had a light, caressing voice. She said, 'I have to send a package to Van Cock Films, but I don't have your full address.'

'What address *do* you have?'

'Well, actually, I don't have *any*. It's on file somewhere, but...'

'What made you phone me?'

'You work for Van Cock.'

He didn't say anything. She continued in chatty vein: 'I work for a film company too – but not the same type of films!'

'Is that right?'

Luke Miller sounded pleasant – still that light attractive voice, but guarded now. She ploughed on. 'Soho Films. We owe Van Cock some money.'

'*Soho* Films?'

'If you could let me have your address?'

'Soho? Ho, ho.' He hadn't bought *that* one, she thought. 'Listen Kirsty, Van Cock is a brand. You're unlikely to owe it money.'

'Well, it's the group, of course, that we owe money to. The accounts department. Where would that be?'

'Hm.' He paused. 'You have an invoice from the accounts department? That should give you the address.'

'Well, yes, but I can't find it.'

'Yet you know how much the bill is for? You'd better wait for the reminder, I think. Who do you work for again?'

'Soho Films.'

'And who gave you my number?'

'You *are* Van Cock?'

'You tried that one, Kirsty – answering questions with questions. Who gave you my number?'

She hesitated. 'Zoë Rand.'

'Ah.' He went silent.

She couldn't let him ring off. 'I'd ask her myself but... she's not here.'

He hesitated. 'So you worked with Zoë?'

'I'm a friend.'

'They say friends are often the last to know.'

He waited again. There seemed little point in appealing to his better nature but she muttered, 'Can you help me? Please.'

Miller read her phone number back to her – just to show that he had it, she supposed – then said, 'I listen to the News too, you know.'

It was hopeless, but she carried on. 'So you heard about... what happened?'

'Nasty business. But seriously, Kirsty, I think you should leave this alone.'

'You're warning me off?'

'Advice from a friend, Miss Kirsty Rice.' He emphasised her name. Then repeated her phone number. 'You're new to me, Kirsty Rice.'

'All I want—'

'What happened to Zoë was terrible, don't you think? Truly terrible. Now, I know you're a journalist, but if I were you, Kirsty Rice, I'd stay away from this and let the police clear it up.'

*

She would be professional. She had never felt *more* professional. Or sad. Her friend had been murdered and Kirsty felt empty and cold – empty except for a tiny, almost invisible speck of new life. An embryo, perhaps three weeks old – no, four weeks. More than three, anyway: Ken had left two and a half weeks ago. An embryo, four weeks into a forty-week journey. That wasn't long, when you stopped to think about it: forty weeks to change from a tiny seed to an eight-pound baby, full of life. A new life being made *now* inside her, independent of what happened in the outside world – a parallel universe, a world of its own. Four weeks into its journey.

Kirsty picked up the phone. Another of Zoë's numbers: description – Actress.

'Yes, who's that?'

A character actress, thought Kirsty, with an older, smoky voice.

'Is that Cassie Nelson?'

'She's not here.'

Guarded, like Luke Miller. Less urbane.

'Do you know when Cassie will be back?'

'No.'

'I'd like to speak to her.'

'Who're you?'

'I'm Kirsty Rice – a friend of a friend.'

'You got a rank?'

'A rank?'

'Yeah. You're police.'

'No.' Kirsty frowned. Police again. 'I just wanted a chat.'

'She's gone away.'

'Are you Cassie's mum?'

A pause. 'Are you police?'

'No.'

'I'll tell her you rang.'

The phone went dead. Kirsty stared at the receiver, then put it down. Any decent reporter would call the woman straight back. Kirsty hadn't given her number, so Cassie's mother – if that's who she was – couldn't pass it on to Cassie. And the woman wouldn't have captured the number from her domestic phone – she wasn't Luke Miller, just Cassie's mum. Presumably. But both she and Luke Miller had been guarded. Both had mentioned police. Miller was guarded because he worked for Van Cock (what a ridiculous name, thought Kirsty) while the woman just sounded cautious. Was she cautious – or frightened? Cassie, an actress in Zoë's address book. Cassie, an actress who had 'gone away'. Cassie, whose mother feared the police.

Did Cassie work for Van Cock too? It seemed likely. Kirsty had followed the obvious leads from Zoë's address book but hadn't got far. Two nibbles. She may not have hooked anything, but there were fish in the water.

An idea occurred.

She strolled back into the main office, where the woman police officer was still sitting at Zoë's PC. It looked as if an idea had occurred to *her* as well. Calmly, Kirsty sat at her own machine and brought up the 'Full Find' program. She'd let the machine do the legwork. Let it scour Zoë's files looking for whatever keywords Kirsty typed in. Words like 'Cassie' and 'Miller' and first of all, the words 'Van Cock'.

*

Funny how it changed from day to day. Yesterday, Becky couldn't pass a single lottery outlet without popping inside to buy a ticket. Yesterday, she had nothing else to do. Yesterday, when Becky had called round for tea, her friend Mel had seemed tense – though there was nothing odd in that: Mel was often tense. Mel in a strop was best avoided. But this morning, when Mel phoned Becky, she didn't sound in a strop at all – she sounded tearful. Though there was a touch of steel in her voice. Typical Mel.

Becky strode along the High Street ignoring every lottery outlet, wondering what lay behind Mel's telephone call. Tearful but determined. She needed a friend. Becky smiled in the sunlight: she knew what was wrong with Mel – she could bet on it.

'It's Gary,' she said, and Mel nodded. Becky opened her arms. Melanie gave a sob and ran into her friend's embrace. It was hot in the room. The kid in the playpen took no notice but the two-year-old stood a yard away from Mel and Becky, staring up at his mother with his thumb in his mouth.

Melanie wasn't one to cry for long. She stepped back from Becky, blew her nose and said, 'That's that, then. I'm a rapid flush loo, me: quick burst and it's over.'

She blew her nose again, dabbed her eyes, then replaced the hankie inside her sleeve. Becky asked, 'Shall I make some tea?'

'That's all you ever think about.'

Mel was smiling now, the shower blown away. She followed Becky into the cramped kitchenette to tell the story. The toddler hung around at the door. It was hard to tell what the child understood, but they didn't pay him much attention.

Becky said, 'I never liked him much.'

She watched Mel warily. A risky statement.

But Mel laughed. 'Yeah, let's slag the bastard off. All men are bastards.'

'Especially Gary.'

Melanie exhaled so hard she might have just run up the stairs. 'And bloody Neil.'

'Who's this, then?'

'Oh, you don't know him.'

'Another man already?'

'It's nothing like that. Not exactly.'

Becky hooted. 'You dirty cow! What've you been up to?'

Melanie almost blushed. 'Come on, pour the tea.'

Becky poured with a flourish. 'Neil, eh? Sounds better than Gary. Did you *do* it with him?'

Melanie shook her head and grinned. 'You're so crude, you know? Straight to the crux.'

'We'll take that as a Yes, I think. What's he like in bed?'

'It wasn't like that.'

'But you've had it away with him?'

Melanie sipped her tea. Becky prodded further: 'Better looking than Gary?'

'Gary's all right. A good-looking bloke.'

Becky sensed the danger. 'Of course he is. I didn't mean that. I just hoped you'd found someone even more gorgeous.'

Melanie drank again, rolling the tea around her mouth like a professional tea-taster. 'Neil was strictly business.'

'You're joking!'

'Gary knows about him anyway.'

Becky put down her cup. 'Look, I don't want to sound thick or anything—'

'As if.'

'But if Neil was 'business' and Gary 'knows about him', I mean, have you been doing it for money, or what?'

Melanie winced. 'It's a bit more complicated.'

Becky wrapped her fingers round her cup, her eyes ablaze with interest. 'Go on, Mel, you can't stop now.'

'Well, I *have* stopped, haven't I? That's the point. Bloody Neil said I was past it.'

'*What?*'

'He scratched me off his list.'

'What list?'

Melanie gazed at her. 'Don't worry, I'm going to tell you. That's why I asked you round.' She grinned. 'But you'd better hold tight to that cup!'

*

It was too easy on the phone: he could chuckle, he could hedge, he could refuse to say anything. So Kirsty tackled Neil Garvey face to face.

If he was surprised to see her so soon he didn't show it. At the door he gave a confident grin and invited her in from the dingy street. When she followed him into the living room she couldn't fail to notice his big TV monitor, showing pictures of a girl – Asian, she looked – in Neil's audition room, the bedroom. She saw the red light on his video.

'A favourite tape?'

'Live performance. Up there now. I'm recording.' They watched a moment. 'Prettier than most. But inhibited.' He smiled at Kirsty. 'So far.'

Kirsty walked away from the screen. 'I hope I'm not interrupting?'

'Depends how long you want to stay. You haven't brought your camera?'

'Off the record.'

He tried to hold her gaze. 'Anything you like.' He glanced at the screen 'We could make a video.'

She laughed. 'You wish!'

'I do.'

The girl on screen was in her underclothes on his bed. She sat on the edge of the mattress and tested it for bounce.

Kirsty said, 'I didn't come here to make a video.'

Neil kept the warm tone: 'I can send her home if you like. We can... talk. Or whatever.'

He was coming on to her, she knew. He really thought he had a chance. She said, 'I only want two minutes.'

'I won't say the obvious.'

'Follow-up from yesterday.' She tried to sound businesslike. 'You don't distribute your films yourself? You just make them?'

He smirked. 'That's why I'm so poor, Kirsty. Distributors make the money, film makers don't.'

'You just get the pleasure.'

'But it's the poor wot gets the blame.'

He chuckled. She asked, 'Who are your distributors?'

He shrugged. 'Two or three different companies. There are plenty out there, but I've got regulars.'

'Such as?'

He shook his head. 'They wouldn't want me to give you their names. But it's not difficult to find out, Kirsty – buy some videos.'

'Do you ever sell to Van Cock?'

His face remained calm. 'Now, now. You're going to bounce names off me and work it out by a process of elimination? To tell the truth, Kirsty—'

'Why not?'

He grinned. 'I doubt they'd care. These aren't state secrets. They're not even criminals, these guys. The stuff we're dealin' with may not be to everyone's taste but it is legitimate.'

'So who *do* you sell to?'

He shook his head, amused. 'I'll pass on that one.'

'But I wouldn't be a million miles out, would I, if I said that Van Cock was one of your clients?'

He looked at her. 'I'm not sure I know that name.'

'They're in your line of business.'

'Why're you interested in Van Cock?'

'I'm raising them as an example.'

He chuckled. 'A fine example. What you might call a very upright company.' He switched his gaze back to the monitor. The Asian girl was back on her feet, still in her underclothes, still dancing to unheard music. Neil said, 'She don't know what she ought to do next.' He glanced at Kirsty. 'I'd better go pep her up.'

'Don't let me stop you.'

'You can, if you like.' He waited a moment. 'How about you sit down here a while and watch? It'd be an eye-opener.'

'No, thanks.'

'I don't mind, you know – I'm very broad-minded.'

'I bet.'

He leant towards her and for the first time, she smelt toothpaste: he'd spruced himself for the Asian girl. He said, 'You could watch me in action – see how you like it.'

'I'm off. Sorry.'

'Some other time.'

As she moved away she tried a 'last question at the door': 'OK, I'll contact Van Cock direct – d'you have their address?'

Neil stayed by his monitor. 'You're very interested in those people.'

She shrugged. 'It'll complete my story.' She smiled disarmingly. 'We must have their address on file. I just didn't want to trek back to the office.'

She smiled again. He smiled too. 'I'd love to help,' he said smoothly. 'But I can't.'

*

She had been all right at Neil's. She had been all right on the Underground. She was all right at the sandwich bar – but when she reached the DarkAlley offices and walked into that stunned, silent atmosphere she felt her legs weaken. Zoë was dead. The loss was palpable. Here in the office the policewoman had gone, but so had everything from Zoë's desk. Even her PC had disappeared.

Kirsty's face was mask-like. 'They didn't shut down the network?'

Janine sat ashen, an open bag of sandwiches on her desk. Her monitor was dead. 'They just took her PC.'

She and Kirsty stared at each other. 'Is Rosa here?'

'She needed a walk.'

To avoid further conversation Kirsty went into the editing suite. She opened her own sandwiches but they looked as inedible as the bag they came in. She moved the food to the edge of the desk: she'd get back to it later. She picked up a cassette but instead of slotting it into the deck she sat with it in her hand and stared dully at the blank screen. She was pregnant. She had known before she used the predictor – it only confirmed what she already knew. *She* was pregnant and Zoë was dead. One life ends; another begins. Babies – that's what sex should be about. Not this degrading muck.

She couldn't face the pictures. She'd had enough. Neil Garvey thought he was the acceptable face of the industry – pleasant, open, no pressure – opening the door and inviting her inside. No one gets hurt, they said – but people did. Right now, he would be screwing the Asian girl. And he had invited Kirsty to watch. But why be shocked? That's what Neil Garvey *did* – he filmed himself having sex with strangers, then sold the films for other strangers to watch.

How did Trisha feel? She behaved like his girlfriend – but she wasn't. Not really. She and Neil seemed familiar with each other because they *were* familiar; but every week Neil screwed a different woman, sampling them like new wine. How many had he sipped? Hundreds? Thousands? Hundreds and Thousands: those little chips of coloured sugar that people scatter on whipped cream. Each chip is brightly coloured but each one tastes the same. Indistinguishable. How many this week? The Asian girl. Delia, perhaps, in her suburban living room. Melanie in her council flat. Poor Melanie, who Neil said was past it. What would happen to her?

At least Melanie was alive.

*

Neil was on the phone. 'OK. Put me through to Rick.'

He wasn't sure they would connect him. He had spoken to Rick Miller occasionally, but only when Rick contacted *him*.

'Neil! How are you, son?'

'Fine, Rick, thanks. Look, I'm sorry to phone you—'

'Yes, I'm fine too. Thanks for asking.'

His voice purred in Neil's ear: that slight Hackney accent he was trying to lose.

Neil ignored the gibe. 'I was tryin' to get hold of Spencer but, well, you know Spencer – he's never in.'

'You try his mobile?'

'I don't have the number. Look, Rick, it's you that runs Van Cock, yeah?'

'Spencer does.'

'But...'

'What? You think my boy's not up to it?'

'No, no. But you're his dad, Rick. You know: don't talk to the monkey when—'

'He's a monkey. I'll pass that on to him, Neil.'

'No, a *joke*! Don't do that. Look, I'm sorry, Rick, but you know I've been doin' that documentary for Channel Four?'

'Yeah, Spencer told me – you know, that little *monkey* of mine?'

Neil sighed. 'It was easy money – and I could give 'em any old guff—'

'Channel Four? I thought it was some independent?'

'Commissioned by Channel Four.'

'DarkAlley Films, you said.'

'Did I?'

'Based in Victoria.'

Neil frowned. He didn't know Rick was interested. Rick said, 'Spencer ran a check on them – the little monkey! They seem kosher.'

Neil chuckled loudly. 'I'm glad somebody is.'

'I wasn't too keen on you doing this, Neil. Could be a set-up.'

'Oh, no—'

'Their way to investigate us. But you must have checked that out.'

'Yes—'

'Have they finished yet?'

'Yeah. It was just a girl – did the whole thing on her own.'

'I suppose you gave her satisfaction – in your own way?'

Neil chuckled eagerly. 'She wasn't on for that.'

'Shame. But you phoned for something, Neil? Don't let me waste your time.'

'Right. Look, the girl came back again today, askin' more questions.' There was silence on the phone. 'She asked about Van Cock.'

'Yeah?'

'I didn't say anythin'. I just stuck to what goes on at *my* place.'
'You mean she came back especially to ask about Van Cock?'
'It seemed like it.'
'She mention Spencer?'
'No.'
'How'd she hear about us?'
'You're not invisible, Rick. She could easily have got hold of a video.'
'What did you tell her about us?'
'Nothin' – that's the point.'
'Did she meet any of your actresses?'
'Yeah, but no one that's worked for Van Cock.'
'*Your* girls?'
'From the low-budget end.'
'We'd better have their names.'
Neil grimaced. 'Right. Look, Rick, it probably isn't anything.'
'So why did you ring?'
'I thought you should know.'
Rick paused. 'You know something, Neil? You should never have made this documentary.'

*

Tony Iles could be gentle when he wanted. He collected his daughter at the *Cutty Sark* by the Greenwich Maritime, then drove her to a nearby restaurant where he was known. A particular feature of the *Champignon Sauvage* was that it had cosy alcoves surrounded by thick white walls, where conversations could be kept private.

Tony was wearing a fresh blue suit, but with open shirt and no medallion. He might be single and of a certain age, but he no longer wore that medallion. Though he had the tan for it. Emma wore a yellow jogger top and jeans. They were clean, at least, and the jogger top bulked her out. She looked sixteen, more then fourteen – old enough not to be at school.

Tony gazed fondly across the table. There was his daughter, growing up before his eyes. Growing up *away* from his eyes. He had a sudden flash memory from the video – Emma naked, humped from behind. He wouldn't think about it. He mustn't. He was good at pushing things from his mind.

They skipped a starter to leave room for dessert. She hardly touched her main course, and although Tony normally had a great appetite, every time he looked at her for more than a moment he could hardly swallow his next mouthful. His little daughter sitting there. Christ! There had been a donkey in that film.

Emma said, 'I'm not really hungry. I'm watching my weight.'

'There's nothing to you.'

'Oh, this jogger top hides a lot. You should see me with no clothes on.'

Tony put down his fork.

She smiled sadly. 'I'm not anorexic, Dad. I'm just not used to big lunches.'

Tony fiddled with the fork. He was glad he hadn't watched the rest of that video – but he couldn't help sweating at the thought of that donkey. Surely she hadn't…

Emma looked up, his little girl. No, he thought, they would have used one of the older women, not Emma. She was too small.

She said, 'I'll save myself for afters.'

Tony sipped his wine. He had poured half a glass for Emma, but although she had added fizzy water she had hardly touched it. Yet if you looked at the bags around her eyes you'd think she was already a seasoned drinker.

He handed a menu across the table. 'Choose a dessert.'

'My just desserts.' She glanced at him guiltily. She had looked nervous since they met. 'You didn't bring me here just for a meal.'

'Can't a father treat his daughter? I mean, I don't see you that often—'

He felt a tear prick at his eye. Damn it! No one ever saw him cry. He concealed it by coughing into his napkin.

Emma looked concerned. 'Has something stuck in your throat, Dad?'

He grunted and drank some water. Then he wiped his face and dried his eye behind the napkin. He smiled shakily.

She bit her lip. 'I know you brought me here so you could have a go at me.'

'Did I?'

She raised her eyebrows. So arch. So young.

He asked, 'Have a go about what?'

'School perhaps. I miss a day sometimes.'

'Not that.'

Her face clammed up. 'Then what?'

He looked at her innocent little face. Was she doing drugs, he wondered. It would be easy to nag about that. But he said, 'You know what. I told you.'

'Oh, that.'

He moistened his lip. 'I don't want to start an argument.'

'That's what it looks like.' Her head was down.

'You're fourteen, Emma. No girl should ever make a film like that.'

'No one should watch one, then.'

'Don't fight me, Emma, I'm your Dad.'

She looked up once, then away.

'Emma, look, I saw that first scene in the film but I couldn't watch the rest of it, you know? So... Did they really do that to you or were you pretending?'

She wouldn't meet his eyes. 'I dunno what scene came first. I never saw the film.'

'Were you pretending or was it real?'

She was trembling. 'That's what you'd like, isn't it? It's all pretend. Your little girl's still a virgin and everything's a game. Well, life's not a game, Dad.'

She glared at him.

'What did I do wrong?' he asked.

'What did *you* do wrong? What's it to do with you?'

'Emma—'

'Emma*line*, if you don't mind. I'm different now.'

'I'm just trying to—'

'You don't control my life, Dad – not any more you don't. You're nothing to do with me, right? So get off my back!'

She leapt to her feet and would have run crying from the restaurant – but Tony was no placid businessman: he was out of his chair and around the table before Emma could escape the alcove. The girl beat her fists against him but Tony hugged her tight against his chest.

'That film was nothing,' she cried. 'Last night was worse.'

He didn't take it in.

'Oh, Daddy,' she sobbed. 'It was terrible.'

He patted her hair.

'There was things happened,' she said.

Tony stood in the alcove, his daughter in his arms. 'Who got you into this?'

*

Rick came to the phone. 'Tony Iles? A pleasure. How can I help?'

'We've got to meet.'

'Oh? What about?'

'It's personal.'

'Which means?'

'Personal.'

'Well. Let's fix a date.'

'We got to meet today.'

'I don't think—'

'You know who I am, Rick?'

A slight pause. 'I know who you are.'

'Good.'

'You wouldn't be threatening me?'

'Put it like this. If we don't meet today I'll burn your fucking house down with you inside it.'

'You serious?'

'Clerkenwell, isn't it – the Old Printing Works?'

'You've done your homework.'

'Believe it.'

'What would this meeting be about?'

'You run Van Cock Films?'

'It's one of our enterprises.'

'And you got two guys working with you called Spencer and Cornell?'

Rick hesitated. 'I don't think that's a secret.'

'Bring 'em with you.'

'Um… what have they done?'

'You don't know what happened last night?'

'Last night?'

'For fuck's sake! You do run Van Cock Films?'

'What happened?'

'Don't you know *nothing*? Ask Spencer and Cornell. Ask the police.'

'*What?*'

'That's why you and me have got to meet, Rick. And bring those bastards with you.'

Reel Three:
BODILY CONTACT

- 10 -

CLERKENWELL. THE SUN shines. In prettified areas we see dappled shade. Outside the bars and cafes around the Green are tables, chairs and parasols. The whole area is crowded – mostly young people, plus a few pretending to be young – and most of them have glasses in their hands. They throng the tables, sit on low walls, and stand in animated groups, laughing, gesticulating, jostling in the sun. By this time of day there ought to be room for everyone to sit down – it's past two o'clock, lunch hour is done, it is time for all these people to take their freshly-ironed deodorised shirt sleeves back to the offices they came from. But they're out here instead, spending money they have yet to earn.

There are local people too – not the middle-class immigrants who have colonised this old inner-city village, but true locals from flats and terraced housing which pre-date the new clean-brick developments, mews, crescents and avenues, the gutted and refurbished older properties – all of whose monetary values have been utterly transformed. Mills, warehouses and factories are housing units now, but the bright new conversions stand among unconverted dismal blocks. While expensively dressed office workers block the pavements, true locals slip by unnoticed. Sparkling pedestrian precincts stand beside urban tarmac. Sun frazzles grit.

On the exterior wall of one of the grimy unrefurbished blocks a legend is engraved in dark stone: *Clerkenwell Printing Works*.

Ground floor windows are boarded up. First floor windows are barred. The two floors above show no sign of life. Come by at night and you may see lights burning up there – you may even see the sweep of a car's headlights inside on the ground floor – but in daylight you'd see nothing. You wouldn't bother to look. There's nothing to look at.

Which is how Rick likes it.

Though you'd never realise, the third floor has been expensively converted. Originally a jumble of attic rooms, the space now forms a sprawling loft apartment. Colours are neutral, almost impersonal, but the imported furniture is of dark Dutch oak. On the walls, Rick has several abstracts – the kind which might have been bought wholesale by a hotel chain or which might each be worth a million pounds. Given the job, Clerkenwell's trendier interior designers might have left the floor timbers exposed, but they are cheap Victorian pine boards – stained, splintered, roughly fitted – and Rick Miller has had the whole floor thickly carpeted in pastel to help deaden the sound. Rick doesn't mind about noise; he is unaffected by it. When the rumble and clank of traffic rattles his windows Rick pays it no more attention than if a sparrow cheeped on his windowsill.

He told his son Luke to sit down. 'You've heard of Tony Iles? He wants to talk about Van Cock.'

'Does he want to buy the company?'

Luke had selected a sand-coloured armchair with sides so high he couldn't comfortably rest his forearms. Anyone who sat in it sat enclosed.

'He's angry about something.'

Luke raised an unconcerned brow. Rick stared at his son. Their resemblance wasn't obvious. Rick was a burly man, greying, while his son Luke was an elongated version of his father – at least six inches taller and with blond hair, not grey. They each had the same patrician nose.

Since Luke, tall as he was, couldn't drape his arms along the sides of the chair, he laced his fingers like an aesthete and rested his elbows on lean thighs. 'Tony Iles is angry with *us*?'

'He wants to talk to Spencer. Any idea why?'

Luke relaxed. A tête-à-tête with his father – Spencer excluded. It was a rare pleasure.

'So he's angry with Spencer?'

'And his idiot friend Cornell. You heard anything?'

'No.'

Rick paused a moment to lean against a heavy dark table which looked at least three centuries old. He seemed to be musing aloud. 'Could Spencer have been trespassing on his territory?'

'If Spencer has we all have. In what way?'

Rick shrugged and moved away from the table. 'Spencer can be foolhardy. I shouldn't tell you this.'

'I don't know my own brother? He's famous for it.'

'A good boy,' Rick insisted, moving behind Luke's armchair. 'The thing is... Spence enjoys the club scene.'

'Enjoys *going* to them,' Luke said airily. To keep track of Rick's movements he'd have to turn in his chair. But he'd learned to ignore his father's tricks.

Rick reappeared in front of him, looking worried. 'You think Spence wants to open his own club?'

Luke laughed. 'He hasn't time for that. He lives twenty-eight hours a day already.'

Rick lowered his voice as if there were anyone else to hear, as if his words could float from the third floor window to the narrow side street below. 'We've got a nice little business here—'

'Not so little!'

Rick brushed Luke aside. 'So what's this about? Iles doesn't make films and he's not on the internet. He doesn't run girls—'

'He's got girls in his clubs.'

Rick paused to stare at his son again. 'You think Iles wants to move into *our* business?'

Luke shrugged. 'You've agreed to meet him?'

Rick nodded. 'After I've spoken to Spence.'

'Best phone him.'

Rick continued to stare. 'I will, don't worry. But first, Luke, are you sure there's nothing I should know?'

'Phone Spencer.'

*

'What I want to know, Dad,' said Spencer on the phone, 'is how you got dragged into this business?'

'D'you call everyone 'Dad' nowadays, or just me?'

'*Qué?*'

'I'm fed up with this slang you and your friends use. 'Dad': what is that, the latest cool?'

'No way! They don't call people 'Dad' since the 1950s.'
'What happened, Spencer?'
'I wasn't born then – I don't know.'
'Last night – what happened?'
'Oh, I thought you were still—'
'Quit playing with me, Spencer. What happened?'
'Last night?'
Rick closed his eyes. Luke hid a smirk.
Spencer added, 'OK, last night. What?'
'I had Tony Iles on.'
'Iles?'
'Iles. Tony Iles. Runs half the clubs in London.'
'*North* London. So, Tony Iles – that's cool. What the man say?'
'He told me you fucked up.'
A slight pause. Spencer was offended. Luke smirked again.
'*I* did?'
'He said that if I was running Van Cock Films I'd already know what happened. What kind of fool does that make me look?'
'How that man Iles hear about this? Don't have *nothing* to do with him.'
'He thinks it does.'
'OK, Dad, listen. We were making a film, right?'
'That's what you do.'
'And some girl got herself hurt, yeah? It don't have nothing to do with him.'
'So why do we have to *meet* him today?'
Spencer exhaled. 'She was nothing—'
'Don't tell me that again. Iles is a hard man, Spencer, the kind you do not cross. He wants to see me – and you and Cornell. He wants to talk about what happened.'
'I don't know, man – this girl: no *way* she was one of his. She was a journalist.'
'A *journalist*?'
'That's *right*. She tricked her way onto the film. Had her own camera too. Hot damn! I had to hurt her, you know? Maybe I went a bit too far.'
'How far?'
Spencer chuckled. 'I got overheated.'
Luke nudged his father. 'Can I speak to him?'
Rick looked irritated. 'What's the point?'

Spencer was still talking as Luke took the phone and asked, 'This journalist—'

'Luke? Are you there? Who else?'

'Was this journalist—'

'*Who else is listening?*'

Luke winced and moved the handset away as if it might scald him. 'Just me and Dad. Now listen—'

'What you *doing* there, Luke?'

'Was this journalist called Zoë Rand, by any chance?'

'I should care.'

'The Zoë Rand that was found in the river this morning, dead?'

'Well, fancy.'

Luke knew Rick was watching him. 'The Zoë Rand who worked for DarkAlley Films?'

'What you saying?'

'The Zoë Rand whose colleague – another journalist – phoned me this morning? She had my number, God knows how. Is this the Zoë Rand we are talking about?'

Spencer was saying something smart as Rick snatched back the phone: 'What the hell is this *about*, Spencer?'

'Dad—'

'Shut up. I'm talking now. Listen. I'm going to meet this Tony Iles and find out why this bothers him.'

'Look, I'll—'

'Shut up. *I'll* meet him – you will not.'

'I can fight my own—'

'Shut up. When I do meet him, is there anything else – *anything* – I need to know?'

'Nothing. I—'

'Start thinking, Spencer. Then phone me back.'

Rick clicked off the phone. He turned to Luke. 'So you *did* know about this?'

Luke shook his head. 'It was on the News. They phoned me up.'

'Phoned you? Why you?'

'I met Zoë Rand. Once.'

Rick stood very still. 'Did you have anything to do with what happened to her last night?'

'I didn't know *Spencer* did till just now. The Rand girl tried to interview me a couple of weeks ago.'

'And?'

'And nothing. Zilch. Then I heard the News this morning. Then I got the phone call.'

'From the *News*?'

'From another journalist.' Luke thought a moment. 'Kirsty Rice. Mean anything?'

'She works for this DarkAlley mob?'

'You heard of them?'

'I've heard a sight too much.'

- 11 -

AFTER A TRAGEDY there is often a false sense of unreality. You feel lightness and detachment, as if you have been removed from the room to stare in through the window while it is being reorganised. A key piece missing, the structure changes. But like nerve cells, people are connected by a thousand invisible strings. At first, with one cell missing, you see the remaining ones shuffle about, rearrange themselves, stray tentatively into new space – then, as your vision alters, you notice the unconnected strings. They become visible. All those connections with nowhere to go – they dangle stupidly, groping in the void. And when you see your own strings trailing hopelessly towards the empty space she once inhabited, you suddenly realise that you have come back inside the room but it has been reorganised and you cannot change it. This is the world now. You'll have to get used to it.

Little separates life from death.

Zoë's desk had been stripped and raped. Where her PC used to stand was an empty space. There were no papers on the desk and none inside. It was a carcass.

Kirsty sat on the edge of her own desk. Janine mechanically typed a list into her word processor, her face set and concentrated. Rosa Klein stared from the window to the street below. If this were a movie you'd hear the ticking of a clock. But at DarkAlley Films the big office clock was an old railway chronometer. It sat silently through each full minute, waiting for the change. For fifty-nine silent seconds there was only the neat patter of Janine's fingers and the restless murmur of traffic below. No one had said a word since the chronometer last flipped over. They hadn't spoken in the minute before. Maybe not in the one before that. They didn't speak now.

Clunk. The minute ended.

Rosa turned from the window. 'Should we drop the story?'

Janine kept typing. Kirsty said, 'Not now.'

'It's not to die for.'

Kirsty wouldn't look at her. 'This is what we do, Rosa – we stick our noses into other people's business. We don't go away.'

Rosa was dark against the daylight. 'This is a decision time. We can pull out – with an unarguable excuse for our sponsors, or we can complete the programme, whatever it takes.'

'We'll finish it. How can you ask?'

'It's only one show in the series.'

Kirsty looked up. 'You were a war reporter for twenty years. You didn't pull out when someone died.'

'*Eighteen* years.'

'You've been there when people died.'

Rosa shrugged. 'That's in a battle zone. You expect it. But this is peacetime – we didn't volunteer for the front.'

'Zoë did.'

Rosa sighed. 'I've seen colleagues die. And I've seen how their colleagues behave afterwards. Professionals.'

'Am I going to like this?'

'They don't try to get revenge. They leave that to the soldiers.'

Kirsty snorted. 'Police?'

'When a war reporter dies, even hardened journalists feel the pain, but they don't pull out – and they don't pursue their own vendetta.' She stared at Kirsty. 'We're not trained for that. It's not what we do.'

Janine had stopped typing. She didn't look at the others, but was listening.

Kirsty muttered, 'I'll finish Zoë's film.'

'Don't take risks.'

'And if I come across a lead—'

'This is not a murder investigation.'

'Isn't it?'

Rosa moved in from the window. 'We'll leave that to the soldiers.'

Kirsty sighed. Rosa came to her and said, 'Maybe it's better if *I* take on this episode—'

'It's mine.'

'You're too involved.'

'Which is why I want to finish it. Just because you've been in war zones—' She caught Rosa's eye but blundered on. 'It doesn't mean you're the only one tough enough to…'

She broke off. Rosa said, 'Let's have coffee.'

'It's my story.'

Rosa smiled. She wouldn't push. Kirsty caught her eye again as the phone rang. But they let Janine answer it.

Rosa said, 'When the programme does go out, we'll dedicate it to Zoë Rand.'

Janine called Kirsty to the phone.

'Yes.' She didn't feel like saying more.

'Is that Kirsty Rice?'

She didn't recognise the voice. Didn't care much. Was it Melanie? Someone young.

'Can I help.'

'Oh, Miss Rice, you don't know me.'

Kirsty glanced across the room. Janine and Rosa were at the window.

'This is Cassie Nelson. You phoned my mum.'

Kirsty's brain felt duller than her eyes. 'Your mum?'

'You're Zoë's boss, aren't you?'

Kirsty's voice dried up. She couldn't even say Zoë's name.

Cassie said, 'Look, I'm sorry about what happened, but Zoë's dead. There's nothing we can do.'

'We?'

'You can't. I can't. We weren't responsible.'

'Who *was* responsible?'

Janine and Rosa had their backs to her. Rosa had her arm around Janine.

Cassie said, 'You shouldn't never have called my mum.'

'I was trying to get hold of *you*.'

'But my mum don't know anything.'

'Do *you* know?'

'Well…'

'If you know who killed her, Cassie, you have to tell someone.'

'I can't. I already did.'

'The police?'

'I shouldn't of.'

'Tell *me*, then.'

Rosa and Janine had turned to watch.

Cassie asked, 'How did you get my phone number?'

'It's on Zoë's file. How did you get ours?'

'Zoë told me who she was working for.'

'She told you my name?'

Rosa was moving to the switchboard.

'This film, right? You're making this programme—'

'Did you help Zoë?'

'Yeah.'

'Will you help *me*?'

'Get off my back.'

'Cassie, are you in trouble?'

Kirsty heard the girl's bitter laugh. Then: 'If they find out I phoned you...'

Kirsty was watching Rosa at the switchboard. 'Did you say you've spoken to the police?'

A pause. Cassie grunted. Kirsty asked, 'What did you tell them?'

'*My* business. That's why I'm phoning. Don't phone my mum.'

'Give me your number.'

'No. Don't call us ever again. Right?'

'One thing, Cassie – who did kill Zoë?'

Silence.

'Do you know?'

Cassie sighed. 'It was the management.' She cut the call.

Kirsty stared at the receiver. Rosa said, 'Here's the number she was calling from.'

'I'll call her back.'

'Sure. Try, anyway.'

Kirsty pressed Call-back and listened. She heard it ring. Rosa entered the same phone number on a PC, looked at the screen and said, 'It's not on the BT database.'

'Could it be ex-directory? A mobile?'

'Wrong dialling code. That's not a mobile number.'

Rosa stared glumly at the screen. Kirsty kept the handset to her ear. She could hear it ringing but knew that Cassie would never answer it.

Rosa said, 'I think it's a phone box.'

They waited a little more. Suddenly, to Kirsty's surprise, the phone was answered. A man's voice: 'Hullo,' he said. 'What number did you want? This is a phone box.'

Kirsty swore.

· 12 ·

EVENING. A WARM evening. Although light is fading, people with gardens linger among their flowers. People with balconies sit outside. People with neither, who live in cramped urban flats, keep a window open and gaze at the sinking sun. They *should* do – that's the dream. But in fact, at nearly nine o'clock on a Wednesday night, almost everyone sits in front of television and watches the vacuous build-up to the National Lottery draw. A quick song, some banter, a pair of co-presenters sparkling in suits, and a hyper audience shrieking at the fun. The synthetic party is watched by a huge and moribund TV audience, almost a quarter of the entire population: mums and dads, kids, aunts and uncles, babies who refuse to sleep, grandpas and grandmas, grandma alone, singles, couples, cats, dogs and budgerigars, high-life, low-life – even royalty, we're told. They view the draw from home or hospital, pub or factory, office or garden shed. And for the sake of all those huddled masses yearning to breathe free – but who can't get near a TV set – the winning numbers are repeated across every radio channel later on the News. And again at ten.

Mel and Becky watched from Melanie's flat.

'I could fancy him.'

'Get out, he's gay.'

'He's not.'

'Look at her, the silly cow.'

'If I had *her* money I'd never wear that.'

'Looks horrible.'

'More money than sense.'

'Are you all right now Gary's gone?'

'Never happier. My time's my own.'

'That's good.'

'Shut up and watch.'

'Shut up yourself.'

The two girls giggled and huddled together on Mel's settee. Becky had brought a giant bag of prawn cocktail crisps which they would share for the midweek draw. On the floor in front of her, Becky had laid out all her lottery tickets, all twenty-one of them. Mel kept both her tickets in her lap.

The first ball was rolled, showing number twelve.

'Yes!' cried Becky, leaning forward to grab those tickets with a number twelve.

Ball number: three.

Becky scrabbled through her tickets. 'Yes!' One of the Twelves also had a Three. She rummaged on the carpet for any other threes. There must be one somewhere.

Thirty-four.

'Shit.'

Mel smiled calmly and wrote the numbers down.

Forty-three.

'Oh, they've gone all high now.'

'There's always high ones.'

'It's not fair.'

'It's best to choose high numbers.'

Number forty-two.

'We've just had forty-*three*!'

'There's often two side by side.'

Forty-seven.

'That's ridiculous. No one could have guessed that. It's a fix.'

'Of course it isn't.'

'All these numbers in the forties. How come I never win?'

'You do sometimes.'

'What's the bonus ball?'

Forty-eight.

Becky threw her tickets on the floor. 'Bloody hell! They fixed that.'

'They didn't. You were watching.'

'It's a machine, innit? Technology. They can do anything with that.'

'Well, I had three come up,' said Melanie.

'I'm not playing again. It's stupid.'

'How many tickets have you got there?'

Betty gathered them up. 'I don't know. A dozen?'

'More like two dozen!'

'Don't be daft.'

'You're the one that's daft. You spend all your money on them.'

'What else am I supposed to do?'

Melanie said, 'I'll make some coffee.'

'I'll turn this rubbish off.'

Becky switched off the set and followed Mel to her kitchenette. 'Where's your microwave?'

'Gary took it.'

'You're well shot of him.'

'Yeah, it's peaceful now. Even the kids are sleeping.'

'Better off without the bugger.'

'Maybe.'

'Come on, Mel! Give yourself a break.'

Mel grinned. 'It's all right, Becky. Gary's toast. He's yesterday's newspaper.'

'He's last week's lottery ticket.'

Mel laughed aloud. 'His *balls* weren't good enough!'

Becky spooned some sugar in her cup. 'Balls is all they think about. Footballs. Cricket balls. Their own balls.'

'Cricket? You don't know Gary.'

'Football and sex.'

Mel watched Becky pour the coffee, then asked, 'Any sign of a job yet?'

'I'm looking. How about that film stuff *you* was doing – that's definitely finished, is it?'

'It never paid much.'

'Three hundred quid!' Becky was so vehement she spilled some coffee.

'Supposed to be. That's what they promised.'

'What *did* you get?'

'Two hundred tops. Two hundred a film.'

Becky blew on her coffee. 'Not to be sneezed at.'

'Better than a poke in the eye.'

'Or a poke in the—' Becky chuckled.

Mel said, 'I've got another idea now – but I need someone to come in with me.'

'Oh?' Becky put down her coffee.

'We could earn two hundred a day. Easy.'

'A day? In porno films?'

'No, not acting. We'd get two hundred each, clear of expenses.'

'I wish!'

'*Do* you?'

They stared at each other. Then Mel shrugged. 'If you're interested.'

*

'Charming sleazeball?' repeated Rosa Klein. 'Van Cock Films? I didn't know we were making a comedy series.'

She and Kirsty were in the *Cask and Glass*. The tiny pub was getting its second wind: office workers had gone home, the pre-theatre crowd had been and gone, and the first of the mid-evening trade were wandering in. But as yet it was still possible to hold a reasonably private conversation. Not that anyone would try to overhear: they were too busy listening to themselves.

'This is no comedy.'

Rosa sipped her drink in silence. She had shadows beneath her eyes.

Kirsty said, 'Zoë's notes don't say much.'

'We'll drink to her anyway.'

'Like a funeral.'

'Alcohol helps. It lets you talk.'

'Oh, talking helps?'

'More than *not* talking. Here's to Zoë.' Rosa raised her glass.

'Zoë. A wonderful friend.'

They drank a little. Kirsty took a breath and blew it out. Rosa lit a cigarette. 'It's been a while since someone died in the line of duty.'

'That's how you see it?'

'Forgive the military turn of phrase. You pick up their way of speaking.'

'Zoë said she was acting in one of their films.'

'Really acting?'

'In one of *those* films.'

Rosa shook her head. 'You know what they *do* in those films?'

'I've seen some.'

'How could Zoë actually… I suppose if she was just an extra—'

'They don't have extras – not in that sense.'

Rosa cupped her cigarette as if she needed its raw warmth. 'But to let some man – a succession of men—'

Kirsty reached across the table and touched her hand. 'Maybe it was gay sex – the luscious lesbian scene.' Rosa chuckled, despite herself. Kirsty continued: 'Don't think about it, Rosa. Don't let it get inside your head.'

Rosa took three quick drags without inhaling. She had a scrap of tobacco on her lip. 'We talk about sex as if that's what matters. The poor girl's dead.'

Kirsty took her hand again. 'We have to carry on.'

Rosa met her gaze. 'Isn't that what *I'm* supposed to say? Aren't I the hard-bitten one?'

'You're a softie.'

'I always was.'

Kirsty moved her glass. 'Did Zoë never mention anyone – Luke Miller, for instance?'

'No, she was out there on her own. I never heard his name until you told me. Charming sleazeball: he didn't say anything useful on the phone?'

'He closed up tight.'

'Find anything else on file?'

'Only... It did say, 'see notes with Ken'.'

The two women stared at each other. Rosa said, 'Ouch. You haven't spoken to him?'

'I suppose I'll have to.'

'*I'll* ask him, if that's easier.'

Kirsty chuckled mirthlessly. 'It *would* be easier, but I can't spend the rest of my life avoiding him.'

'A bit soon, though.'

'Life goes on.'

Kirsty winced, and this time it was Rosa who reached out for *her* hand. 'Let *me* speak to him.'

'I'm a big girl now. And it's my film, anyway.'

'It's *our* series.'

Kirsty left her hand there. 'Is Ken still working on that internet stuff?' she asked casually.

'Should have finished a week ago. Keeps finding more material.'

'Nature of the beast.'

'You're talking about the internet, I take it?'

Kirsty smiled. 'I tried to tap into his PC files but they're protected.'

'What d'you expect? He may have been your boyfriend – but you have to admit he's anally retentive.'

'He is not!'

Rosa laughed. 'You're defending him again!'

'Defending him? I could crucify the bastard.'

Rosa was still chuckling as she stubbed out her cigarette. 'That's the spirit. Sounds like you're ready for him now.'

*

When Cassie's mother answered the door she kept it on the chain. 'Yes?' She squinted into growing darkness: two men.

'Is Cassie in?'

'No. Who is it?'

'Gordon.'

'I don't know you.'

'I work with Cassie.'

'She isn't here.'

'Yes, she is,' smiled Gordon. 'She may be upset. Tell her Gordon is here.'

'Gordon who?'

'I'm a film director. She'll know who I am.'

The woman hesitated. 'She isn't here.'

When she tried to shut the door the other man pushed his hand against it. He looked little more than a boy but he was a big man, bigger than Gordon. He put his foot in the frame. 'You want I knock this down?'

The woman protested. But the man suddenly shot out his hand and grabbed the front of her dress. 'Call her down. Tell her Gordon wants a word.'

*

'Your mother,' Spencer declared, 'is the worst liar I ever saw. She couldn't lie straight in a bed.'

Cassie didn't know if she was meant to smile.

'Your mum acts like she is frightened. You know why?'

Cassie shook her head.

'I think you told her something, babe.'

'No.' Cassie couldn't stop shaking her head.

'OK, that's cool,' said Spencer, sympathetic as a snake. 'You came home upset, you wanted to tell someone and you thought, hey, I can talk to my old mum. That's what mums are for.'

'I didn't tell her.'

'Then why is she so scared?'

'Because you locked her in the bathroom.'

'No, babe, I locked her in the bathroom so she could shit herself in peace. I mean *before* I got here – why'd she have the chain on the front door?'

'We have to, living round here.'

'Relax, Cassie, everything is cool. But you did tell her, didn't you?'

'No.'

Cassie glanced at Gordon, as if *he* might help her. As if he would. But the director was standing by the window trying to look interested in the *TV Times*. Every now and then he would peer outside from behind the curtain.

'What did I tell you?' Spencer asked her. 'What did I tell every damn one of you people?'

'It was an accident.'

'Not that. More important than that.'

'Not to tell anybody.'

'That's right, babe. Not to breathe a mother-fucking word.'

'I didn't—'

Spencer thumped the table. 'That bitch was spying on us! Right? You want to go to jail?'

'No, I...' Cassie looked up at him. 'I didn't do anything. I was just acting in the film.'

'Accessory,' Spencer said. 'You're all accessories. But you already knew the girl, didn't you – this Zoë Rand?'

'No, I – well...' Cassie glanced at the director, but he was immersed in the *TV Times*. Spencer glanced at him too: 'What you tell me, Gordon baby?'

'I said it was Cassie brought the Rand girl in.'

Spencer's head jerked forward. Cassie flinched. 'Hot damn!' said Spencer softly. 'You knew her, Cassie – you knew what that bitch was.'

'No—'

'Listen, babe. You say No to me once more and I will break your little nose. Listen.' A weird smile settled on his face. 'Don't give me no more *Noes*, or else I'll have to break your little nose! It rhymes, yeah? How'd you *like* that?'

He stared at her, eyes glinting. Cassie said, 'I didn't know she was a journalist.'

'So why'd you bring her in?'

'She... she said she needed a job.' He waited. 'She seemed OK.'

Spencer thumped the table again, and the whole room rattled. 'A fucking journalist? You didn't know?'

'No—'

'Don't *say* that word to me! No noes. What did she pay you?'

'She didn't – I didn't know she was a journalist. I thought she was...'

'Some actress? Yeah, she was *some* actress.' Spencer studied her. 'You know the easiest thing – what makes sense? I killed the Rand girl – so I should just kill you!'

'Please, n... n... Please don't.'

'That girl was your friend?'

'No, I – Oh Christ.'

He put a hand up. 'I told you not to say no. Cassie, listen to me. She didn't pay you, she wasn't a friend of yours – so why the fuck you let her in?'

Cassie shook her head. Her face was wet. Spencer didn't know it, but Cassie's knickers were wet as well. 'I thought she needed a job.'

'And she wasn't a friend of yours?'

'N—' Her voice froze. 'She wasn't.'

Gordon looked up from his magazine. 'I saw them talking to each other on set.'

A sudden silence fell. Spencer let it hang.

Cassie broke it: 'Of *course* I spoke to her! I never said I didn't know her – I got her the job!'

She looked angry now, and Spencer smiled. 'That's better, babe – you speak your mind. Who else did you tell about this, apart from your old mum?'

'I didn't tell my mum.'

Spencer straightened as if to hit her, but Cassie said, 'All I told her was I was frightened. I said some bad shit went down.'

'You use that language to your mother? I'm ashamed of you.'

Cassie sighed with exasperation. Spencer said, 'Tell me about DarkAlley Films.' Her face went stiff. He said, 'You know, the company that bitch worked for.'

Cassie shook her head. 'I don't know anything about them.'

'Have they been in touch with you?'

'I never heard of them.'

'What did the cops say to you?'

'Cops?'

Cassie fought to keep her face still.

'You know, when you talked to them?'

'I never talked to them. I never said anything. I never saw no cops.'

He leant so close that their noses almost touched. 'No bastard goes near the fucking cops, right? You hear me?' She nodded. 'No one says *any*thing.'

Spencer stepped back. She didn't move. He continued to watch her, then said, 'I don't know about you, Cassie, I really don't.'

She didn't risk a reply.

He said, 'Maybe the cops will come ask you questions. What you going to say?'

'Nothing. I don't know anything.'

'That's right. Even if they tell you they *know* you were in the film, you'll keep your mouth shut. Yes, you do films sometimes, you'll say – but you don't know nothing about this business. *Capisce*?'

She nodded.

'Because if I hear a suggestion that you or anyone you've met has been *near* the cops, you know what I'm going to do to you?'

She nodded again. He raised a hand. 'I can see myself out, thanks.'

He began towards the door, and Gordon hurried to hold it open for him. Spencer paused inside the frame. 'Just remember, babe.' He looked at her. 'It's the fire next time.'

- 13 -

KIRSTY WAS AT home, putting off the phone call. She prowled around the houseboat reading junk mail, and when eventually she went to the galley to make some tea she found a cup she'd made when she first came in. She made a fresh one.

Then she cleared the table.

Drank the tea.

Then, although it was late, she went up on deck to take a breath of river air. The night was warm. Lights from riverside houses caught at wavelets in the river. From nearby boats she could smell other people's supper. She heard music and someone laughing. A breeze had crept along the river to stir leaves in the trees.

Life went on. Yet somewhere along the river Zoë's body had been dumped. Zoë, so young, had been brutally murdered by someone from the disgusting industry that DarkAlley was investigating. When Kirsty had first started on the project she had thought it tacky, exploitative – but only of people who had chosen to get involved. People might debase themselves but they did not deserve to die.

Zoë died. Zoë was dead. Presumably the police, in their dull but methodical way, would find out who had killed her. It shouldn't be difficult. They would track down this ridiculously named Van Cock Films, find which film Zoë had been investigating, and they'd identify the murderer. What kind of man would it be – one like Luke Miller? Had Kirsty spoken to Zoë's murderer?

On the phone Luke Miller had been relaxed. Confident. A charming sleazeball, said the notes. Could he charm his sleazy way out of this? He might; God knows he might. The police were so useless nowadays that they might not even bring the case to trial. Should it be left to the police? Would they get *anywhere*?

Zoë had been her friend. Kirsty could not stand back, a spectator, while the incompetent police bumbled around making routine enquiries. She had to meet these demons face to face.

She sat on the deck to phone from there. For a couple of minutes she gazed at other boats on the river and looked across at distant houses. There was a moon tonight.

She keyed the number, programmed in.

'Ken Lawrence. Hi.'

Same voice. Perky. But it was the tone of voice Ken kept for strangers, when nothing showed on his phone ID. He must have deleted her from memory.

'It's Kirsty.'

'Oh hi! Yes.' Ken was thinking, changing gear. 'How are you keeping?'

'You?'

'Well, I'm up to my eyes in work, you know? Same old project, won't go away! But... I'm trying to fit in a little recreation. Yes, life is good – and *you're* OK?'

'Mm. I'm sitting out on deck.'

'Well, that's great. I'm glad to hear it. Isn't the weather gorgeous? I went to a ballet last night and it was so nice we were able to walk home—'

'A ballet? You?'

'Yes, I'm becoming a regular balletophile – what? – oh, sorry: balletomane. A fan, anyway.'

'Is someone with you?'

He hesitated. She could picture him trying to keep the smile on his face. But he had to answer. 'Yes, Marion trained for ballet, actually.'

'Oh, *Marion*. Has she been with you long?'

'You must meet her. Perhaps we'll have a drink sometime?'

'Did you hear about Zoë?'

'No?'

'She's dead.'

'Zoë... from the office?'

'She was murdered.'

'Wow.'

That should shut him up. Kirsty looked along the deck at the quivering lights on the river. She had ruined his evening. Perhaps he'd talk it over at length with Marion and ruin *her* evening too.

'You know she was working undercover on that Van Cock company?'

'Well, yes. Did somebody...'

'Weren't you working on them too?'

'Me?'

'Zoë left a note on file. Said you had all the details.'

'I... Van what?'

'Cock, darling. Their kind of joke. There's a man called Luke Miller – Zoë called him a 'charming sleazeball'. But she also said, 'see notes with Ken'.'

'Luke Miller? Wait a minute. I'd need to look at my files.'

'Can you do that now?'

'It's nine o'clock, Kirsty. Gone nine.'

'You must have them there in your flat. That's where you work.'

'Yes, but—'

'Does Luke Miller know you have a file on him?'

It sounded for a moment as if the line was breaking up, but Ken was clearing his throat. He asked, 'Do the police think Luke had something to do with Zoë's murder?'

'How would I know what the police think?'

He put his hand across the mouthpiece to say something Kirsty couldn't hear. Explaining things to Marion. Explaining why he had used the dread word 'murder'.

Ken came back. 'Look, this isn't a very convenient time just now.'

'Is Marion showing you her ballet positions? The Nutcracker, perhaps?'

'I'll catch you in the office tomorrow—'

'Suddenly you're working office hours? What happened to your independent free-wheeling spirit?'

'I'm busy now.'

'Are you serious about her?'

'Who?'

'Marion, Ken, who else? Because unless she's a passing fancy she'll have to get used to you working all hours. That's who you are. Or is she a one-night stand?'

'No way!'

'I'm sure she'll understand.'

She heard him put his hand across the phone again. This time she could half make out his words: something about an urgent job. Something about looking on his PC. She couldn't hear Marion. She didn't want to.

Ken said, 'I'll phone you back.'

'You can come over if you like.'

Immediately she'd said the words she regretted them. But she blundered on: 'You left some things here anyway. And... No, forget it.'

'Hey, hey,' he said, and paused. Maybe he looked at Marion, maybe he didn't. 'D'you really think Luke's family could be involved in this?'

'Family?'

'His brother, you know? Was *he* on file?'

'What brother?'

'Look... Maybe you're right. Maybe we'd better meet.'

'Tonight?' she breathed.

'All right,' he said. 'Check.' He was back to his perky voice, the one for business contacts. 'I'll consult my files, then we could meet up at the office. Say a couple of hours or so. Maybe three.'

'The office?'

'Yes.' He sounded brisk now. Businesslike. His act for Marion. 'I'll meet you at the Thames Ditton office. If that's OK?'

Thames Ditton. Bastard.

- 14 -

Night falls on Clerkenwell. In the prettified areas, warm house-lights glow through clean and fashionably uncurtained windows. Outside darkened bars and cafes near the Green the tables, chairs and parasols are put away. The last few revellers go home, and nearby, an old red bus hesitates as if it no longer recognises the transformed area, then it slinks away. Traffic is lighter now, even on Farringdon Road. All that is left are a few cars, the occasional taxi, and one or two anonymous trucks and vans.

Fifty yards from the Clerkenwell Printing Works, two BMWs glide to a halt. Although this is not one of the area's smarter streets, the lighting is enough to ensure that anyone watching will see the cars. They might not notice the unmarked transit van which parked a few minutes ago in a quieter street out back. The van looks empty, no sign of life – although a passer-by might hear a muffled murmur inside.

The two BMWs make no attempt at concealment. Tony Iles and Roy Farrell get out of the first car and walk to the second, parked behind. Four men fill it.

The passenger window opens and Tony leans inside. 'You all set?'

'Yeah. Dave called. He's round the back.'

'I know.'

'He found a parking space, at least.'

'Me and Roy are going in now. Don't fall asleep.'

'Keep in touch.'

'Listen for my pager.'

In the street it is so quiet that the two men don't bother to look before they cross.

*

Rick has left the outside of the building untouched. The boarded windows suggest that the Works is derelict and the heavy wooden doors have settled on their hinges, but in the recess at the side is a small entry-phone. Tony presses the bright square button, and Roy stands with his back to the door to stare out across the street. Little to see, apart from two BMWs parked along the road.

The machine speaks: 'Yeah?'

'Tony Iles.'

'And who's your friend?'

'Let us in.'

There must have been a camera somewhere but Tony didn't look for it. He heard a step behind the door, a clunk as the door unlocked – but when it swung open, barely a sound: no scrape, no rusty hinge.

The door opened onto the dingy, ill-lit, unfurnished ground floor. Several cars were parked, and a van. Apart from the man inside there was no other sign of life. He was a big man, though. He took a shrewd look at Roy, then concentrated on Iles.

'Rick says why not bring your cars inside? They'll be safer in.'

'They're OK out.'

The dusty concrete floor and smell of motor fumes suggested that the ground floor was used solely as a car park. At some previous time the floor had been partitioned but those internal walls had been ripped out.

'Rick asks if you're carrying.'

'You want a look?'

'Rules of the house.'

The big man checked inside their jackets, then in their waist bands at the back. He checked their ankles. 'Your friends out in the car?'

'Yeah, they're carrying.'

'They stay in the car?'

'If nothing goes wrong.'

They followed the man between parked cars across the floor to an old industrial lift against the rear wall. The three men stepped onto its metal platform and the big man pulled an iron trellis across. Then he pressed the Up button and the machinery shuddered into life. He asked, 'How will your friends know if something does go wrong?'

'It won't.'

They only went one floor. The lift clanked to a halt on a floor that looked as if it hadn't changed since the Victorian era – though Victorians would have kept it cleaner. And they'd have had gas light instead of the few unshaded lamps hanging on wires draped from the ceiling. On this floor most of the partitioned offices had been left, but they were not illuminated. The only lamps hung in the open space beside the lift.

As it arrived, Tony saw a heavy well-dressed man facing them, and two young black men to his side, sitting on metal chairs turned backwards. Although he couldn't see guns behind the chair backs Iles guessed the men would have them. There was no one else. No other furniture.

Tony and Roy came off the lift onto the scruffy open floor. The big man stepped off after them and Tony said, 'I don't like people behind my back.'

In front of him, the white man nodded and the doorkeeper walked away. Tony glanced around the derelict interior. 'Nice place you got.'

'Convenient.'

'You Rick Miller?'

'You're Tony Iles.' Rick's eyes shifted to Tony's side.

'Roy Farrell.'

They looked at each other. 'So,' said Tony. 'Thanks for the drink.'

Rick smiled perfunctorily. 'Oh, this was a social call? Forgive me.'

Tony Iles turned to the big man who had admitted them: 'You felt me down, right?' The man nodded warily. 'So you know I'm clean.' Tony raised an empty hand, then slid it inside his jacket. Everyone watched him except Farrell. When Tony's hand reappeared it held a tiny pager. He pressed a button. 'See this?'

Roy Farrell chuckled. 'They're slow, these guys.'

The doorkeeper growled.

Tony said, 'I've just paged my friends outside. Now they're waiting for the next call – tells 'em how much I am enjoying myself.' He replaced the pager in his pocket. 'Just in case you had other ideas.'

'See this?' said Farrell, his voice an echo of his boss. All eyes went to him. From his inside jacket pocket he slowly drew out a pack of cigarettes. 'Could've been anything,' he remarked. 'Still *might* be something.'

He tapped out a cigarette and lit it. They watched his lighter as if it were a bomb. Farrell smiled, flicked off the lighter, then slipped it and the cigarettes back inside his jacket.

Rick sighed. 'You two a double act or what?'

'Let's get down to business,' Tony said. 'These aren't Cornell and Spencer?'

Rick laughed. 'Not them.'

The two black men laughed as well. Roy Farrell exhaled noisily. His cigarette smoke hung in the air.

Tony didn't laugh. 'I said bring 'em with you.'

'I don't take orders.'

Rick was grey and broad, slightly older than Tony Iles, who looked as if a hundred years ago he'd come from Italian stock. But they both had leadership. No one doubted that.

Roy Farrell exhaled more smoke.

Tony said, 'I asked for Spencer. I made that clear.'

Rick eyed him curiously. 'Do you *know* Spencer?'

'He works for you.'

A smile flickered on Rick's face but Tony didn't know what caused it. Rick seemed relaxed now. 'If I phoned you, Mr Iles, and told you to *damn well* do something, would you do it?' Rick was actually smiling. Tony wasn't. 'For instance, if I told you to *damn well* bring your daughter?'

Tony was too close to Farrell's smoke. 'You know about my daughter?'

'Your wife left you, and took the girl.'

This wasn't the way Tony wanted it. 'Kids go with their mother.'

'Emma, isn't it?'

'So what?'

'One of my men has a boy goes to the same school as your little Emma. When she *goes* to school, that is.'

'Small world.'

'Ain't it?' Rick smiled again. 'You fond of the girl?' It was a threat.

Tony pointed at him. 'You know why I'm here.'

The two men stared at each other. Farrell drew on his cigarette and exhaled again. Rick said, 'Sure. Something about Spencer and Cornell.'

In the desolate hall the silence was as if a clock had stopped. Tony glanced at Rick's men: he didn't want to discuss Emma in public. But he was here now. 'Your man was out of order.'

'My man Spencer? He can be headstrong.'

'Is that your word? Tell it to the girl he killed.' Tony saw Rick flinch. 'And if *I* know he killed her, half of London does now.'

Rick frowned. 'Where'd you hear this?'

'Witnesses.'

Tony felt he'd regained advantage. He heard Rick's angry breathing. Everyone could hear it. 'Think about it, Rick. It happened on one of your films. Spencer killed the girl in front of all the technicians and cast.'

'Who told you?'

Tony took a leisurely glance at Rick's stooges, arranged around the empty space like dummies in a shop window. 'That's not all he done.'

Rick waved away some smoke. 'No?'

'My little girl was in that film.'

'Your daughter? She saw this?'

'She was there, Rick.' Tony grimaced. 'And your man Spencer, your fucking headstrong Spencer, he *raped* my Emma in your film. My daughter, Rick.'

Rick gaped at him.

Tony said, 'Spencer kills a porno actress – that's your problem. He kills her in front of a dozen witnesses – that's a bigger problem. But it's still *your* problem, Rick. I don't *give* a damn. But my daughter – that's *our* problem. Your problem, my problem, his problem. I want him punished.'

Rick sounded old. 'It wasn't your daughter he killed?'

'No.'

Rick sighed. 'OK, leave it with me.'

'Can't do that. *I* want him, Rick.'

'He's my man. I'll deal with him.'

'It seems to me this guy does whatever he likes. He kills a girl, rapes another – you don't know *what* he does.'

Rick glared at him. 'You say this to me? You, a man who lets his daughter do porno films? What is she – fourteen, fifteen?'

In the derelict hall the unshaded lamps were cruel.

Rick continued, 'But I *will* speak to Spencer—'

'*Speak* to him?'

'I'll deal with him.'

'I want him punished.'

Rick nodded. 'You deal with your daughter. I'll deal with Spencer.'

'I want him dead.'

Rick met his eyes. 'Spencer is important here.'

'If you don't kill him, I will.'

'That'll put us at war.'

'So?'

'If we're at war,' Rick said, 'I can't let you leave the building.' He stared at Tony through a fog of Farrell's smoke. 'Play a tune on your little pager, but before your friends climb out of their BMW, you and Farrell will be dead.'

'They'll burn your house down.'

'This place?' Rick smiled. 'Those punks in the car?'

Roy chipped in: 'Plus the others at your back door.'

Tony glared at him. 'Roy, shut up. Let's get real here, Rick. Your man Spencer raped my daughter—'

'I heard you. Look, Spencer can be an idiot, I know. What he did was… unforgivable. I'll make that very clear to him.' Tony snorted. 'What d'you expect, Mr Iles? You seriously expect me to kill my… right hand man? You said you want him punished. He will be.'

'How?'

Rick was thinking. 'When I've done it, you will know.'

Tony narrowed his eyes. 'Suppose I go with this – what'll you do to him?'

'I'll tell you when it's done.'

'I don't want you to just smack his hand.'

'I know.'

Tony glanced around him. He should have thought this through. 'Right. You deal with it. I mean *deal* with it.'

'Give me a couple of days—'

'One day.'

'Don't bargain with—'

'It's a matter of honour.'

Rick paused. 'I realise that.'

Tony looked deep in his eyes. 'Two days. Then call me.'

Rick nodded. 'Two days. Agreed. So. We're all done here. I'll have someone show you out. —And Mr Iles?'

'Yeah?'

'I'm truly sorry about your daughter.'

Tony checked for any sign of sarcasm. But Rick seemed genuine. 'Yeah, right, fuck off.'

Rick nodded. 'The terrible fourteens, eh? When your kids don't listen to a word you say.'

Tony glared at him, but Rick smiled like a grandfather.

'Two days,' said Tony Iles as he left.

- 15 -

From an unlit window, Rick watched the BMWs pull away. Across the floor, big Herbie peered down from a rear window so small, so encrusted with grime, it could have been part of the brick wall.

'Van's still there.'

'Anyone in it?'

'Nope.'

Rick inhaled. When he did so he caught a left-over tang of Farrell's smoke, a foetid smell, as if something had died.

Herbie said, 'The back door's opening.'

'*Our* back door?'

'The van.'

The two bodyguards who had been standing vacantly beside their chairs, wondering what to do, went across to peer out the tiny window.

Herbie counted. 'Two, three, four – no, one's got back inside. There's a guy stretching himself. Someone's on the phone.'

Rick stayed at the front window. 'Can they see you watching?'

'Probably. Right, the guy with the phone is getting in the front. The one stretching himself has got in the back.'

'The other bloke?'

'Shutting the door.'

Rick heard it slam. Not a loud noise. Not unusual, but the only sound in the street.

Then another door. An engine fired.

He asked, 'Did they leave anyone?'

'No.'

He heard the van drive away. 'Go down, check outside the building.'

'Packages?' asked Herbie.

'Anything. I'll take the stairs.'

As his three men got on the lift, Rick wandered across the unused printing floor to the seldom-used stone stairs at the side. This darkened, forsaken floor was where Rick staged his deliberately discomforting meetings. Let 'em stand there, he'd say, with their backsides clenched.

He climbed the stairs, panting a little when he reached the top. Getting older. He ought to *always* use the stairs; forget the lift.

Having reached the top floor he entered a security code on the key pad. This was the only internal door which had an electronic lock, he realised, the last defence inside his castle. He went in.

The contrast between the lower floors and Rick's luxurious apartment was one he no longer noticed. He drifted from one plane to the other so often, so unthinkingly, that both seemed natural to him: the grime and semi-darkness of the old printing works, and the richly furnished penthouse above. Business meetings were held in either – but most were held below. Although the apartment was large and obviously expensive, it seemed a point of honour with those invited here *not* to be impressed. It annoyed Rick: he had come a long way and he wanted folks to know it. To show they knew it. But the men Rick dealt with ignored his wife's paintings and furniture, and treated the soft upholstery like benches in a public park. They knew Rick had made it; they expected luxury. What they didn't expect was the cavern he used downstairs.

Rick was used to it down there. He liked it. Downstairs let in more traffic noise, the world outside, while up here was quiet, deadened, and the murmur of continuous soft music masked external sounds. In the apartment, Rick had a rack of MOR CDs on continuous play. He never changed them – though they *were* changed occasionally by the family. Luke and Rinalda thumbed his collection to find a change of beat, and Spencer had twice replaced Rick's bland selection with his own mixture of Hip Hop and Gangsta discs. Only Spencer thought that funny.

Spencer would.

Rick phoned him. Alone in the large flat, Rick stood beside a low dark table, above which was a muted Philip Hughes landscape. It was too abstract for Rick but Rinalda liked it.

Spencer answered his phone. Rick could hear music in the background. Background? It was so loud it put Spencer in the background.

'Yo? Who dat there?'

'Speak English, Spencer.'

'Oh, *hi* there, Dad! How's it hanging?'

'You're not at home?'
'Can't pull anything on you!'
'I told you to stay in your flat till I spoke to you.'
'Got bored, Dad.'
'Tony Iles has been.'
'You said the man was coming.'
'He came about *you*.'
'I'm so famous.'
'Are you alone there?'
'Does it *sound* like it?'
'You're in trouble, Spencer.'
'Wow. Don't ground me, Dad!'
'You didn't tell me about the girl.'
'I did – that bitch reporter—'
'No, Spencer, the girl you raped.'
Spencer missed a beat. His music didn't. 'Say again?'
'You heard me.'
'Hey, Dad, I don't think we should do this on the phone.'
'That's why I told you to stay at home – by yourself.'
'My place is a morgue, Dad.'
'Not the best word.'
'Not the – what? Oh hey, that's funny. That's a neat one, Dad.'
'I'm not in a funny mood.'
'It's a good joke, though.'
'Spencer.'
'Yo?'
'Get over here. Right now.'

*

Kirsty had given up on him. Was he coming or not? Until midnight she had waited around the boat, re-reading the papers scattered across her table, checking files on her PC, making a diagram on her whiteboard showing the links between the characters involved. But she knew too little about them. Half the links were loose ends.

She watched the late news on TV but Zoë wasn't mentioned. Yesterday's news. Kirsty had expected an update from the police, or an appeal for witnesses at least – but not a word. Watching the news programme, waiting for that item, only emphasised how seldom news was news. A politician made a speech, bankers met, the prime minister visited a factory. Was that news? If any of that had *not* occurred, there might have been a story. What, no politician made a speech? Unbelievable. Bankers hadn't met? How else would they get lunch? The prime minister called off a visit? That might be news.

Commercial break: Kirsty made coffee. More news came rolling in. The royal family had had a photo call, an African war was rumbling on, a coach had crashed. That last piece was news – a tragedy for some: so let's all watch, safe behind our glass screen. Then finally, a cheerful piece to close: a cute puppy, lost and found. That was that. That was the news. Now we'll guess how the weather might be tomorrow.

It'd be news if they got it right.

Kirsty checked the programmes scheduled for later in the night. A sit-com, an unpromising B-film, a repeated fly-on-the-wall. They'd be followed by the sex shows: Bangkok by Night, The Blue Review, an exposé on striptease (wasn't that tautology?), sex in advertising, an erotic quiz show, Ibiza Uncovered, Eurotika... On and on – but it was harmless, wasn't it? Since this was mainstream television there would be no carnal penetration, no genuine abuse, no participating children, no animals hurt in the making of this programme. But after a few hours watching, who would notice if the TV company slipped in a film by cult director Neil Garvey? How would *TV Times* describe him? Up and coming, she supposed. And once people had seen some Garvey films, they might be ready for Van Cock. Then... What did they move on to after that? Where did they stop?

After midnight, when Ken obviously wasn't coming, when he'd obviously decided to stay for a *pas de deux* with his ballerina, Kirsty changed her clothes for a full-length nightdress. Just in case he did come she covered the nightie with a long shapeless dressing gown. Warm clothes for a houseboat late at night. Shapeless in case he came.

She sat at her table and stared at the files.

She ought to go to bed.

But she wouldn't sleep.

Around one o'clock she heard a footstep up on deck. Then another. She looked up and watched the door open. It could only be Ken. When he appeared on the stairs he brought with him a sudden gush of cool night air. He skipped down the wooden stairs smiling, as if he'd just dropped in for lunch. He even licked his lips.

Kirsty stayed in her chair: 'Good job we're not married. What time d'you call this.'

He rubbed his hands together. 'It took longer than I thought.'

'Marion wouldn't let you off with a quickie?'

He held up his hands. 'Apologies.'

'That's a first.'

'Do I smell coffee?'

'You know where it is.'

As he moved to the galley, Kirsty said, 'You're looking smart. You've had your hair cut.'

'I found a new stylist. Like it?'

He rattled a cup. Last time she'd seen him, his hair had been medium length and swept back. Now it was attractively spiky on top. —We've both had our hair cut, she thought: cutting off our dead ends. What did Ken think of her own shorter hair?

'I paid a ridiculous amount for this,' he said from the galley. 'But I thought I'd try the place once – just for a restyle – then go back to the place I normally use. But I rather like this now, and I don't want my usual guy to ruin it. What do *you* think?'

'It's only money.'

'That's what Marion said. —Oh sorry, I shouldn't have mentioned her.'

'Be my guest.'

'She's been encouraging me to spend money. Said I wasn't making enough of myself. I should buy myself a suit, she said—'

'A suit?'

'I know – me in a *suit*? But it *is* unstructured. Very cool. And I bought a jacket. —How d'you like this shirt? The collar's button-down with hidden tabs. I bought three. Must be mad.'

'You couldn't resist?'

'Life's too short. Another coffee?'

'I'm fine.'

He emerged with just the one, in the mug he always used. 'I even bought new shoes.'

'Those?'

When Ken glanced down at his feet he held the coffee aloft like the torch of liberty. 'Not these old things – I just threw these on to come over here. I should chuck 'em out.'

'It's so good to have a clear-out.'

He glanced at his watch. 'I knew you'd be up.' He nodded at her paper-strewn table. 'You love your work.'

'You eat and sleep yours.'

'I don't know – it's important to get a balance in life.'
'Sounds as if Marion is good for you.'
'Oh.' He hesitated. 'I think you'd like her.'
'Sure to.'
'I haven't told her about *you*. Yet.'
'Best not. What's past is past.'
'Exactly.'
'Serious about her?'
'Well.' Ken smiled. 'It's early days.'
Kirsty closed a folder on the table. 'How long is that?'
'Oh, it must be... Hey, I wasn't going with Marion when I was with you.'
'You've only just left me.'
'A month ago.'
'Three weeks.'
'Four, surely?'
'Did you bring the Van Cock files?'
He looked at her sideways. 'You're not still mad at me?'
'We weren't married.'
'No promises.'
'No kids,' she said pointedly, but he didn't notice. She added, 'You were always free to go.'
Perhaps he caught something: 'You *are* all right about this, Kirsty?'
'I'm fine.'
He hesitated. 'Well, you're looking good – even in that dressing gown!'
'It's not meant to look sexy.'
'It's certainly not that.'
She stared up at him. 'But I do look 'good' to you?'
Ken stepped back. 'Hey, hey. I'm sorry.'
'You left some things here, in that box.'
'They're not important.'
'How do *I* know what's important?'
Ken sighed. 'Shall I just leave the files and go?'
She paused. 'You'd better talk me through them. Tell me about Luke Miller.'
'Luke – or his brother? Luke couldn't be mixed up with Zoë's death.'
She looked away. Talking earlier on the phone, Ken had seemed to hardly recognise Luke's name. 'Why couldn't he?'

'Luke's a... He's not into that.'

'He doesn't kill people?'

Ken chuckled uneasily, then sat down in his old chair. 'Luke's a computer freak. He runs an internet business – not a very *nice* business, I admit.'

'A sleazeball?'

'You could call him that. Porno sites – films, video snips – lurid but harmless.'

'How do you know him?'

'My programme, of course: *Sex Is Shopping*.'

'Have you met?'

'Once or twice. Charming, really. Surprising. He's more interested in technology than content.'

'You wouldn't put him down for Zoë's murder?'

'Come on!' Ken leant forward in his chair to place the coffee mug by his feet. Just where he used to. He glanced around the familiar cabin to her houseboat. The lights were low. Kirsty was in her dressing gown at the table festooned with work. He smiled at her. 'Just like old times.'

'About this nice techno-freak, Luke Miller.'

Ken shook his head. 'Why him?'

'Why *not* him?'

'Not the type.'

Kirsty gazed into her coffee mug and drained the cold dregs. She couldn't look at Ken while he sat there so close – like old times, as he'd said. But he was with Marion now, while Kirsty was left to carry his baby. She'd have to tell him. Sometime. He glanced at her and frowned. 'Didn't you used to have long hair?'

She opened her eyes mockingly. 'Observant.'

'Hm. Well. Actually... how did Zoë die?'

She stared at him: thanks for saying how much you like it. But she answered his question: 'They set light to her, then dumped her in the Thames. It was on the News.'

'They?'

'Doesn't sound the kind of thing one person would do.'

'Well.' He picked up his mug. 'Spencer might.'

'Spencer?'

'Luke's brother. He'd do anything, I guess.' She watched him. 'He's into gangsta rap and fast cars and...' He put on a deeper voice: 'Fast women.'

'Your kind of man?'

'Back off, Kirsty. Would I like a guy like that?'

Who *do* you like, she wondered. 'What does Spencer do – for a living?'

'He runs Van Cock Films.' Ken hesitated. 'You mentioned them.'

'So I did.'

Ken sipped some coffee, then grimaced at the taste. Kirsty waited for him to continue. 'Their stuff's pretty heavy, you know? Van Cock Films do everything – gangbangs, animal, anal. Black, white and yellow girls. Tall, short, deformed. Straight and gay. They don't fake their stuff – it's what you see is what you get. Or what *they* get. You must have watched that kind of video?'

Kirsty shook her head.

'Spencer would love to be the porn world's number one. He won't be, of course. It's like Luke with his internet product – whatever you do, someone copies it and goes one better. I'll give you an example: have you heard of that film *The World's Biggest Gangbang*?'

'Not before breakfast, if you don't mind.'

'There were versions one, two and three. Starring – who was it? – Jasmin St Claire. Well, of course, as soon as that film appeared in the *Erotic Video Guide*, everyone had to better it. So we got *Even Bigger Gangbangs*, *Gangbangs Non-Stop*, and then Spencer started sticking numbers on his titles – like *27 Hot Tight Asses* and *13 Rectal Riders* and *14 Virgins Lose It*. Other guys hit back with even bigger numbers, so Spencer went one better – you know: he added footage to his earlier films and came out with even higher numbers still. It got like *Rocky One* to *Rocky Five*. Spence did a film recently called *Sixteen Black Bun Busters*.' Ken chuckled. 'Now, someone's *got* to do *Seventeen* or better still, *Twenty-one Black Bun Busters*. That would be better, because it rhymes.'

Kirsty nodded gravely. Don't think about it.

Ken said, 'Spencer gets carried away. He thinks he's Alfred Hitchcock – you know, doing cameo appearances? He first showed up in one of his own films – when was it? – two years ago. Just a cameo, but he obviously enjoyed the thrill of it!' Ken laughed. 'I'll say. Anyway, after this he took a part in half the films he made. Just a little part but—' Ken was enjoying himself. 'That's the joke: Spence only has a 'little part' himself. He's not fantastically endowed, you know? I mean, he probably isn't small compared to normal guys – a bit stubby, shall we say? – but in this kind of movie he is up against – no, rephrase that! – he is in competition with the world's top-line mega studs. And Kirsty, I don't know how many of these videos you've seen, but these mega studs are *huge*. I mean, their cocks stand out like truncheons. In these movies there are guys with twelve inch, fourteen inch – I kid you not.'

Kirsty studied him. He was like a reel of film that had snapped and was spilling out on the floor. He didn't stop.

'There's a stud called Randy Archer who has a dong that has been independently verified as measuring *fifteen* and a half inches. Imperial. There's another hose monster called Marc Wallice who has a kind of hook-shaped dick that is absolutely perfect for shoving up a girl's arse. Being hook-shaped, you see, it follows the shape of the anal track.'

Ken sniggered but then stopped. He glanced at her warily, then said, 'It makes it easier for the woman, you see?'

'Snug as a bug in a rug.'

Ken shrugged uneasily. 'These girls are used to it, of course. Look at Brooke Ashley – I mean, she's famous.'

'Dare I ask what for?'

'Oh, she did this anal extravaganza where she took thirty-two guys, one after the other, all through the back door.'

'*Thirty-two?*'

'Genuine. So Spencer did a film, *Fifty-two Off The Bottom* – but his was faked, of course. Took him a week to film it.'

It seemed to Kirsty that the cabin lamps were growing dimmer. The boat rocked a little, as if disturbed by a tide. The air shimmered.

She shook her head to clear it. 'But thirty-two *wasn't* faked?'

'No, Ashley really did do it. That was the point – to prove that she could. She'd already done any number of conventional anal films, so here was her chance to show she could be queen of them all. It took its toll on her, though.'

'Don't tell me.'

'She said afterwards that she was so bruised she couldn't have sex with her regular boyfriend for weeks.'

'Shame. He must have been longing to reclaim his property.'

Ken sighed. 'The bad news now is that she's HIV positive.'

Kirsty watched him. The same man, in the same chair, at the same time of night they'd often chatted. But he had a modern hairstyle now.

'You must have watched a lot of this?'
'Research.'
He had been away from her less than a month.
'Do you watch with Marion?'
'Back off!' He laughed. 'She wouldn't watch that kind of stuff.'
'But she knows *you* watch it?'
He paused. 'She has *her* job, I have mine.'
Kirsty nodded. 'So you've met the Miller brothers? I thought you were only monitoring their web sites?'
'That wouldn't make much of a programme, would it? Their sites seem pretty graphic the first time you tune in to them, but you soon lose interest.'
'And want something stronger?'
He looked at her, empty-eyed. 'They say the net is a virtual reality – but it's nowhere near reality. You're just an observer – you can't actually take part. You can choose what to watch – and there's a massive choice, believe me – but in the end you're only watching. You get a bit closer in chat rooms and news groups – you know, a real conversation? But to get closer, you have to break the anonymity.'
'You did that?'
He hesitated, but only because he was thinking back. In the dim light, the wooden walls of the cabin formed a soft barrier that held off the outside world. Two empty coffee mugs sat between them like carefully placed art objects. Her littered table could have won the Turner Prize.
He said, 'A web persona is worse than anonymous: you assume that what you see on screen must in some way reflect who you are talking to – like those old-fashioned chat lines where you talked dirty down the phone. She told you she was a twelve year old schoolgirl but she was probably a grandmother.'
'Well, well,' she said. 'Hello, dark horse.'
He grinned again. 'You know, it's rather nice in here. Brings everything back. Though in the old days we didn't used to talk like this. Maybe...'
'Maybe what?'
He was still grinning. 'You're looking good, Kirsty.'
'In this old dressing gown? The one you said did not look sexy?'
He paused. 'You could take it off.'
She stared at him. He stared back. 'You walked out on me,' she said.

'Now I've come back.'

She stayed in her chair. 'You've seen too many stud movies, Ken. First Marion, then me – all in one night? What happens then – you go back to bed with Marion?'

'I could stay here.'

'As in *stay* here?'

'Well...'

'I don't mean for one night.'

He tilted his head towards his shoulder: one of his more attractive gestures. 'How many nights had you in mind?'

'How about twenty years? We could have some kids. Watch them grow up.'

'You're joking! That's the last thing we need, Kirsty.'

'Is it?'

'You don't want kids, Kirsty.'

'*You* don't.'

He breathed out. 'Wow! It *must* be late.'

'So,' she said, with hardly a break in stride. 'There are these two brothers: Luke the nice guy – though he is a 'charming sleazeball', and Spencer the terrible, who runs Van Cock Films. The company Zoë was investigating.'

'Right. – Oh, *right*! Zoë was investigating Spencer?'

'The management.'

'What?'

'Management. That's who Cassie said killed her.'

'Who's Cassie?'

It was as if a stone had lodged in her throat. She looked at Ken, the cheerful, faintly amorous, porno-watching father to her unborn baby. She couldn't tell him she was pregnant. She ploughed on.

'You've met Spencer – you know him?'

'Met him. Nothing more.'

'How would *I* meet him?'

'You wouldn't want to.'

'I'm a journalist.'

Ken looked grave. 'So was Zoë.'

- 16 -

When Spencer arrived at the Printing Works his bleeper let him in. He parked his TVR in the centre of the ground floor car park, leaving it slewed across the floor. As soon as he and Cornell climbed out they found Herbie Tripp waiting. Nothing unusual in that – Herbie kept an eye on who arrived: the gatekeeper.

Spencer grinned. 'Dad not in bed yet?'
'Wants you alone.'
'And what's Cornell supposed to do?'
'Go for a walk.'
'At *this* time of night?'
Cornell joined in: 'Yeah man, you aware it's one o'clock?'
'Go home, Cornell.'
'And hello to *you*.'
Herbie ignored him. 'Spencer, I have to take you up myself. OK? Come on, Cornell.'
He began leading Cornell to the door. Spencer watched a moment: 'What you mean, you have to *take* me up?' His words echoed in the car park. 'What am I – a guest?' His laugh echoed as well.

The door creaked open. Cornell, complaining, stepped outside. The door shut. Herbie made for the lift. He didn't have to avoid cars on the floor, since there was plenty of empty space. Spencer followed reluctantly, stood on the lift platform and glared at Herbie. But when the lift juddered to a halt one floor up, Spencer spun on him: 'You stopping at all stations? Take me to the top.'

Then he saw Rick waiting. Rick alone. The dirty scuffed floor, the bare bulbs, the old partitions and gloom behind.

Spencer stepped out with a grin. 'You got friends upstairs I am not supposed to meet?'
'OK, Herbie.'
Spencer sighed. Herbie pressed the button and the industrial lift continued up. While the mechanism trundled, Spencer wandered to

the back of the barren floor. He didn't look out of the windows: they looked onto darkness. The lift noise stopped. They heard the trellis open, then re-close.

Spencer sighed again. 'What happens now – Daddy smacks his little boy?'

Rick waited for Spencer to finish his pantomime. They stared at each other. Rick said, 'This isn't a joke.'

Spencer shrugged and came closer: 'You know who that girl was?'

'Which one?'

'For Christ's sake, Dad – the girl in the river.'

'Oh, that one.'

'She was a journalist – a spy.'

'For that you killed her?'

Spencer tried to meet his gaze. Rick stood stock still in the centre of the disused printing floor, solid as an old press. 'OK, Spencer – how did I find out?'

'Who knows – Luke told you? Thanks, bro!'

'It wasn't Luke.'

Spencer shrugged. 'Someone else.' He stared at Rick to no response. 'Someone working on the film?' He stared again, then shouted, 'Am I supposed to *guess*?'

'How many witnesses were there?'

'Who told you?' No answer. 'Listen. I told those people: one word, I cut their throat.' Rick raised an eyebrow. 'One of they mothers is seriously out of order, man!'

'You're supposed to be a white man – talk like one.'

Spencer exhaled. He glanced at the lamps, which tonight seemed less bright than usual. Not that he came to this floor often. He stepped forward. 'Look, Dad, I appreciate you worrying about this and all, but no one's gonna pin that crap on me—'

'You don't think?'

They were so close now they stood like boxers at the shake.

Spencer tried a grin. 'Look, a girl dies. Well, shit happens, you know? We're not kids, Dad.'

'Aren't you?'

Spencer snorted and moved away – but Rick grabbed his arm. 'Who was the girl?'

'For Christ's sake! I *said*. Some reporter.'

'Why was she there?'

Rick's grip was tighter than it ought to be, a man his age.

'She wanted to get the dirt on us. —Will you stop that?'

The grip tightened. 'Why was she there?'

'I told you. I —Look Dad, that hurts.'

'Why?'

'Will you *stop* that? I don't know why she—'

'Did you ask – before you killed her?'

Spencer glared at him. Rick relaxed his grip. Spencer's eyes watered, but he would not rub that arm. 'Look, she's dead, yeah? I'm sorry.'

'When a reporter dies, it gets on the News. What do the others do?'

'What others?'

'Reporters, dick-head! You killed one of their own. That's like killing a cop. They don't rest till they track you down.'

'No chance!'

'How did *I* hear? Who told *me*?'

Spencer's face was white. 'I'll kill the bitch. Just tell me who it was.'

The lift suddenly thumped into life. The chains and blocks went up, then the heavy lift came down. Two people on it: Herbie and Rinalda. Herbie concentrated on the door button. The trellis opened, and she stepped out.

At first sight she looked in her thirties – even in this unflattering light – but Rick's wife was forty-six. Her true age had been a surprise three years earlier when he married her and saw her birth date on the certificate. But even though she was older than he'd expected she was still ten years younger than he was – and a looker. Rinalda had a mane of thick cropped blonde hair and the body of an athlete. Her skin was taut and she had the blue eyes of a natural blonde.

She stood beside the lift. 'Herbie told me Spencer killed a girl.'

Herbie stayed on the lift platform looking at no one. Rick and Spencer looked at *her*. 'Well,' she said, throwing her hands wide. 'It happens. So?'

'I'm dealing with it.'

'Did you bring the body here?'

'No, it's—'

'Why is everyone down here? Come up to the flat.'

Spencer felt stronger with Rinalda there. 'Dad was, like, underlining his point. Keeping me in the cold.'

'Oh, for Goodness sake!' she snapped. 'Spencer is your son, Rick. He is not impressed by this inquisition chamber.'

'He killed a journalist.'

'Is that what she was?'

'And who d'you think told me?'

'Herbie?' She turned to the lift.

He shuffled his feet and muttered, 'I heard about it from Rick,'

Rinalda turned back. 'So who did tell you?'

'Tony Iles.'

'Who?'

Spencer knew: '*The* Tony Iles? That's what the man wanted?' He explained to Rinalda: 'Tony Iles runs a load of gambling clubs.'

Rick nodded grimly. 'He runs a whole lot else.'

Rinalda sighed. 'One of your gangster friends?'

Spencer quipped, 'No, *I* have the gangsta friends. Dad has criminal friends.'

He laughed but no one else did. Rinalda said, 'It's filthy down here.'

Rick persisted: 'First, Tony Iles, who wasn't even *there*, knows Spencer killed her – so how many other people know?'

No answer.

'Second, why was this journalist prying into *our* business?'

'We make good copy?'

'Third—'

'Third*ly*,' she interrupted. 'You really should learn to speak your language.'

She loved correcting him. Her own accent was almost undetectable.

'Third*ly*,' continued Rick, 'why d'you think Tony Iles told *me*?'

They waited for him to answer his own question. He turned to Spencer: 'Because that wasn't the only girl you attacked, son, was it?'

'What am I – Jack the Ripper? Hey, I was there, man. You think I wouldn't notice I did someone else? Like I kill two or three a week?'

'You raped a girl.'

Spencer gaped at him. 'What's that to do with anything?'

Rinalda protested: 'Oh no, I don't think he would do that, Rick. Why should Spencer rape a girl? He can have any girl he likes.'

She smiled at him – but before Spencer could smile back, Rick snapped, 'His daughter!'

Wife and son stared dumbly. Then Rinalda asked, 'What is this about? And can we please go upstairs?'

'You didn't hear me. Spencer raped Tony Iles's daughter.'

'That's a mother-fucking lie!'

'I don't like your tone, Rick,' complained Rinalda. 'Explain yourself.'

'Explain *my*self? *He* raped the girl.'

Rinalda turned towards the lift. 'Always arguing. Well, he's *your* son.'

'Exactly. Wait upstairs.'

She spun as if to slap him down. For a moment her eyes blazed – then she switched them back to Spencer: 'It's late and I need my beauty sleep. Tell me, Spencer, did you really kill this... girl reporter?'

'Afraid so.'

'And did you rape her first?'

'No way!'

'That was the other girl,' said Rick. 'Iles's daughter – a girl in the film.'

'I didn't rape *no* one in the film.'

'She says you did.'

'Look, I...' Spencer suddenly looked uncomfortable. 'Hey, Rinalda, you go on up. Me and Dad can sort this out.'

She didn't move. 'I hope this is not true?'

'It's late, Rinalda.'

'Tell me.'

Spencer couldn't hold her gaze. 'I didn't rape nobody—'

'*Any*body,' said Rinalda.

'Any*body*. Whatever you like. Any*one*, anybody. Some *body*. Yeah.'

In the silence of the dimly lit printing floor they could almost hear Spencer's brain working. Rick and Rinalda watched him. Herbie lurked by the lift.

'Sometimes in these films, you know, I... well, hey, sometimes I join in. But that isn't rape! These are actresses – it's why they're there. Yeah? I join in sometimes to liven things up.'

He tried to pretend they weren't all watching him. But even Herbie was.

'Look, it's different when you're there. Everyone screws every motherfucker – what, I'm supposed to just stand and watch?'

Rinalda said, 'I don't like the word motherfucker.'

His voice rose: 'Don't pretend if was different in *your* films, Rinalda.'

Rick punched his arm. It was not a friendly punch: he hit the place he had gripped before. 'Don't be rude about your mother.'

'She's not my mother – she's your wife.'

Rinalda cut in: 'Fine! Why *not* be rude to me, Spencer? You rape one girl, you kill another – why *not* be rude to your father's wife?'

'I didn't rape the girl.'

Rick said, 'She was a child, fourteen years old.'

'That one? No way, man, she wasn't no child. She loved it. *Every*one was fucking her.'

Rinalda snorted: 'Oh! So that's all right? You fucked her after everyone else had had their turn? That's disgusting – you realise you might catch something?'

'We were making a gangbang scene, that's all. You've done gangbang scenes, Rinalda, scores of 'em. We've all seen your films. Let's get real here, shall we?'

For a moment no one spoke. Then Rick said, 'I don't want another word about Rinalda.'

'Yeah, OK, I went too far.'

'*Now* he tells us! Tell me, Spencer, who arranges your auditions? Christ, you hire a journalist, you hire Tony Iles's daughter – anyone can walk in.'

'I can't hardly remember his sodding daughter.'

'Well, she remembers *you*. First she remembers you killing the journalist, then she remembers you raping her. I think she found it a memorable evening.'

'No, it was the other way round—'

'Then she told her dad. And we all know who *he* is.'

Spencer mumbled something.

Rick said, 'We run a peaceful business here. We do not cross swords with villains like Tony Iles. But you did, Spencer – and now Tony Iles has threatened me. Can you guess what he wants from us?' Rick held the pause. 'He wants you dead.'

Reel Four:

PENETRATION

- 17 -

Ken's flat in The Barbican was near to the Isle of Dogs – so it was easier for Kirsty to collect him there, rather than for him to come to her houseboat.

'You're mad to bring the car.'

His voice was distorted on the entry phone. She stood on the stained concrete outside his block, bright sun sparkling on the grit, and tried not to listen for other sounds behind his voice. Was Marion in the flat? Did it matter?

His block of flats, early Eighties but Sixties in its style, was too white for this sunny day. The concrete reinforced the heat. When she returned to the Clio she found it trembling softly on its double yellow, its metal hot to touch. She stood by the car door and checked the street for traffic wardens.

When Ken appeared – his new haircut gelled and his face freshly shaved – he gave off a faint aroma of soap and citrus. He was in a sharply-cut loose jacket over an open-neck shirt with treble-buttoned throat.

'Very Barbican,' she commented.

'I have to look the part. It's expected.'

In the car beside him she felt dowdy, despite her own dark city jacket and matching trousers. He looked every bit the entrepreneur.

'Nice sunglasses,' she said.

He warmed at that, taking them off to show the spring hinges and gold plated rims. 'Optical glass,' he said. 'Gucci frames.'

As she drove along London Wall he explained his relationship with Luke: 'Remember we are internet entrepreneurs.'

'You and Luke?'

'You and me. In theory. Luke thinks I'm a start-up web business.'

'How big is *his* business?'

Ken chuckled. 'I doubt *he* knows. He's more interested in technology than the balance sheet.'

'So *he* says.'

'Anyway, I've half convinced him I can help.'

She drove via Houndsditch and Minories, then through Smithfield and The Highway. After West India Dock Road she let Ken navigate.

'Luke majors on ActiveX and streaming video – even Flash, for God's sake. I mean! But his scripts are basic CGI.'

'Translation?'

'He'll expect you to know the lingo. Anyway – um – don't be surprised if his conversation gets a bit ripe.'

She sighed. 'He *is* a porno king.'

'A techie – I told you. He's not that interested in the content.'

'Oh, he *forces* himself to look at it? Right. And what exactly does he think *you* are?'

'Pretty much what I am.' She shot him a startled look. 'I'm an interactive whiz – so-called,' Ken said with a laugh. 'Great cover for the story. While we concentrate on the technical side he hardly notices the amazing porn he's showing me. I'm talking Java X and all the while there are these Asian Babes and College Girls and… cum cameras and all that stuff. Try not to look too shocked.'

*

Luke Miller's South Quay offices were in a block which looked as if it had been moulded out of plastic, a cuboid honeycomb. Ken and Kirsty ascended to the ninth floor of the atrium in a silent-running glass box that lifted them above a huge encapsulated acer towards the sky. At the ninth floor they got out into an empty hallway – marble effect vinyl floor, plain vinyl walls – to face a metal and glass door bearing the legend *Apuleius Productions*.

The door swung open as they approached.

The man behind it was tall, blond, good-looking – but the first thing Kirsty noticed was his jacket: sharp and loose, the prototype for Ken's. She glanced at his shirt, to see if *his* collar also had three buttons, but no: perhaps he wasn't wearing his today.

She hardly needed the introduction: 'Luke Miller. I don't believe we've met?'

His hand felt firm. Dry. Warm.

'You can call me Kay.'

'I'd be happy to.'

He had an amused look, as if he already knew her real name – but it was surely the easy tolerance of a man who knew he was taller, better looking and wealthier than most. No sign of vice, she thought. No dirt beneath those fingernails.

As he led them along a ten-yard corridor she had time to notice that although the reception desk was unattended, the open plan area beyond housed ten to a dozen staff at VDUs. Young mostly. Clean fingers again. She noticed several anonymous computer units and a tall communications rack. Boys' toys or contempo corporate? The screens showed boys' toys also: girls alone, girls in pairs, girls with men, girls topless or entirely nude. One of the girls fingered a computer keyboard. Hardly a fetish object, Kirsty thought.

Luke led them into a smallish office, the only closed area in the open plan, a supervisor's cubicle. Its exterior wall was glass and looked down to an Isle of Dogs blue sparkling waterside. 'Business booming?' Luke asked Ken.

'We're optimistic, Mr Miller. We've had another positive response to our development plan.'

'Promises.' Luke smiled at Kirsty. 'But no hard cash?'

'Liquidity is not the problem,' Ken declared. 'Our game-plan presupposes an initial twelve months of negative in-flow, and we have in-house resources already to cover that.'

'How far are you into those twelve months?'

'Oh, a year's hypothetical. I'm confident we can wait out the launch period with minimal operational expense.'

'Coffee?' Luke moved to a Cona on the windowsill. 'I love you start-ups. You're so full of... vigour.' He poured three cups. 'But you're looking for money?'

'There's an investment opportunity—' Ken began.

'Exactly – you need money.'

When Luke brought the coffees his hand was steady – while Ken was acting so hard that his coffee slurped in his saucer. Kirsty put her cup down. Nothing spilt. She could be cool.

Luke smiled at her. 'Ken is getting me terribly excited.'

'That's good.'

'I'm not so sure about his Harvard speak—' Luke switched his smile to Ken. 'But I *have* been impressed by the techno services your company can offer.' He glanced back to her. 'What exactly do *you* do?'

'I'm still learning.'

'You don't look like a techno nerd.'

She gave a fetching giggle. 'One of your screens out there featured a nude with keyboard. Is *she* a techno nerd?'

'All our girls have keyboards. How else would they talk to customers?' Luke glanced at Ken. 'You told her about our Pay To View? No? Well – Kay, was it? – those are live feeds to our Amsterdam studios. Chat rooms with live pictures. Customers like to see who they are chatting to, and being on-line allows them to key instructions, telling the girls what they want them to do.'

'By keyboard? Why not just talk?'

Luke's accent had slipped a little, but he still tried to sound the gentleman: 'OK, it's a little old-fashioned – but keying keeps our customers on-line longer.'

'Certainly keeps their fingers busy.'

'These girls, English is not their first language – or if it is, they're from the English gutter. Keying hides their accent. You didn't tell me – what exactly do you do?'

Ken cut in before she could reply: 'Kirsty – Kay – handles public relations.'

Luke nodded slowly. 'An independent?'

She began to play her part: 'Yes, Ken is a major client for us.' She smiled up at Luke. 'But I'm always looking for new business.'

'Aren't we all?' He studied Kirsty. 'So you don't make films for Ken?'

She laughed lightly. 'Ken doesn't make films.'

'No?'

Whoops, she thought: surely Ken hadn't said he did?

Luke still seemed interested in her: 'Public relations – does that include sourcing actors and actresses?'

She shook her head. 'Nothing so exciting. PR in the normal sense. What do *you* do, Mr Miller – do you run the company, or have a more specific role?'

'We all play roles,' he said. 'Does Ken know the role you're playing at this moment?'

She looked blank. Ken said, 'Excuse me?'

'Kirsty,' said Luke Miller slowly. 'Not Kay. That's Kirsty Rice?' He glanced at Ken. 'DarkAlley Films?'

Ken said, 'I'm not sure what you're talking about.'

'*She* knows. And do you really *not*?'

In the tiny pause that followed, Kirsty could see Ken about to bluster. She had to save him: 'OK guys. Luke's right – I am a journalist. Sorry, Ken, I've been kidding you.'

Luke was watching Ken. '*Was* she kidding you?'

It was each one for themselves. Ken said, 'What's going on – what journalist?'

She was amused to see Ken lie, but she went straight for Luke: 'You know there have been accusations against your company?'

'Oh, really?'

'You remember Zoë Rand?'

'I remember what happened to her.'

Ken looked increasingly uncomfortable. 'Mr Miller, I really had no idea. Perhaps we should call off this meeting so you and I can reconvene at a more convenient future date?'

'Which of you is wearing the microphone?'

She said, 'Neither of us.'

'Your colleague had one.'

So he did know about Zoë. 'What can you tell us about Zoë's death?'

'Us?'

'When you and I spoke before—'

'Are you wearing a microphone, Miss Rice?'

'No, you're quite safe, Mr Miller. Why did Zoë die?'

'I have an irresistible urge to... satisfy myself.'

Luke stepped forward and before she could stop him he reached out and grabbed her shirt.

'Stop that!'

When she tried to step away she found his other hand firm behind her back.

'Ken!'

'Stay where you are, Ken.' Luke stared into her face. 'I'm sure Ken is as concerned as I am to discover whether you're wearing a hidden mike.' He glanced towards him. 'Isn't that right?'

Ken spluttered something.

'Let's find out.'

Luke moved his hand to Kirsty's buttons. She raised a foot to kick him. But there was no point – he'd only rip her shirt.

Luke undid her top button. 'Anything to declare, ma'am?' He undid some more. 'Only your talent.'

He gazed at her brassiere, then slipped his hands inside her loosened shirt, round to her back.

'No!'

'Oh Kirsty, the mike could be anywhere!'

One hand was pressed against her spine, the other reaching for the bra fastening.

She kicked him. Luke Miller smiled. As the strap sprung free she saw Ken dithering by the window. Beneath her loosened bra Luke brought his hands swiftly to her front. She kicked again, tried to pull herself away, but he was stroking both her breasts.

'Investigative journalism,' he said. 'Someone has to do it.'

When she jerked away he didn't follow. As she quickly reclipped her bra, Luke smiled mockingly: 'Ken, shouldn't you check her over for yourself?'

Kirsty started refastening her shirt buttons. Her face was hot. 'Did your people kill Zoë?'

Luke leant his head as if to hear. 'Definitely no mike?'

'Did *you* kill her?'

'Me? Good God, no.'

'Did Spencer – your brother?'

'Ah, no pretences now. Have you met Spencer?'

'No. Do you *know* who killed her?'

'I'd tell you, naturally.'

'Was it him?'

Luke shook his head. 'Interview suspended at – what? – ten forty hours.'

'Was it Neil Garvey?'

'Why, you do know a lot of people. Who else, I wonder? Might *Ken* have done it?'

Ken said, 'That's ridiculous!'

'Hello, Ken, welcome back. Kirsty suspects everyone, you see. I think you should take her home.'

Ken stammered, 'She's nothing to do with me—'

Kirsty concentrated on Luke: 'I want to meet your brother.'

'I wouldn't advise it.'

'What do you know about Van Cock Films?'

He reached out to touch her. She stepped away.

'I'm trying to be friendly.' He smiled ruefully. 'But you'd better leave now – before I do something we'd both hate.'

- 18 -

The police, in traditional fashion, arrived simultaneously at the front and back doors of the Printing Works. A cursory glance at the viewer showed they'd break the door in if they had to, so Rick sent Herbie down to let them in. Herbie tried to stonewall but wasn't good at it. Jennifer Gillett led a three-man squad in through the front door, and an officer immediately began taking details of parked cars. There were only two, as Spencer had taken his TVR away. In the flat upstairs Rick decided that rather than let the police upstairs he would go down. He summoned the lift and arrived on the ground floor looking crumpled, old and harmless.

Could he help them?

Yes, he said, he did recognise the name Van Cock Films.

Yes, he'd be pleased to accompany them to the police station – though they must understand that, in the circumstances, he would insist on being joined as soon as possible by his solicitor.

*

One thing Luke had in common with his brother was that they both drove a TVR – but where Spencer's was acid yellow, Luke's was gunmetal blue. When he pulled to a halt inside the Clerkenwell ground floor he saw his brother's car returned. The place was fuller than usual: half a dozen cars, parked untidily.

In the luxurious top floor flat he found the meeting underway. Rinalda had summoned them, and was pacing the floor smoking a Dutch black-paper cigarette. From the state of her nerves she might have done better with the spliff Holland was famous for.

Spencer was lying across a pale pastel armchair, cocktail in hand, while his friend Cornell sat more primly in a high-sided chair, clutching another lime-green drink. Herbie stood by the drinks bar as if guarding it. Spencer had been doing his best to calm his stepmother, although Spencer's best did not stretch to his getting up from the chair.

Rinalda said, 'The police are not the problem. Rick can handle them – and anyway, Thane is there to help him.'

Spencer said, 'We pay Thane too much.'

Rinalda spun on him: 'Rick shouldn't *be* in a police station.'

Spencer laughed. 'He'll be back.'

Rinalda stamped her foot. 'What are we going to do about Tony Iles?'

'He should learn to look after his daughter—'

'Don't start that again. Of all the girls to choose!'

'You're right, you know. Hot damn.' Spencer put on a bad American accent: 'Of all the gin joints in the world she had to walk into mine.'

'Iles wants to kill you.'

Spencer cackled. But this time he did drag himself up from the pastel armchair. He lumbered across to his step-mother and threw an arm around her shoulder. Luke was at the drinks bar, where Herbie was looking glum. Luke asked what he knew of Tony Iles.

Herbie poured Luke's Scotch. 'Only time I saw him is when he came here.'

Luke called to Spencer: 'You haven't met him yet?'

'Pleasure to come, bro!'

'You've only hit on London's toughest gang leader.'

Spencer and Cornell hooted. Cornell clearly found it so funny that he would have laughed all day unless Spencer told him to stop. They would have laughed like kids forever if Rinalda had not slapped Spencer's face. 'You're a spoilt boy. Just a boy.'

'Rinalda?'

He looked at her, concerned, as if she'd complained of something in her eye. She glared at him in despair: 'You do not understand the trouble you're in.'

'Sure I do. Iles says I raped his daughter. That is bullshit.'

'Bull*shit*!' echoed Cornell.

Luke said, 'At least his daughter had better luck than the journalist.'

Rinalda cut him off: 'We are talking about Tony Iles. This *child* you raped, Spencer—'

'Rape? Come on. You know what happens, Rinalda – you were an actress. If anyone knows how—'

'Oh yes, tell everyone.'

'We already know, Rinalda.'

She patted her magnificent hair. Forty-six she might be, but she could still hold the room. Spencer put a hand on her soft shoulder. 'You were the greatest—'

'Once upon a—'

'Still are,' agreed Cornell.

'Absolutely.' Spencer drew her to him. 'Abso-bloody-lutely. You *are* the greatest.'

'Iles will kill you, Spencer – that's what he said.'

'Talks big, don't he?' Spencer chuckled. 'But I'll speak to the man.'

That made Luke chuckle. 'Out of which hole?'

Rinalda tutted. Spencer's hand dropped from her shoulder. 'What does that mean, bro?'

'Out of your mouth, your backside, or the bullet hole in your chest?'

'Oh, man,' chuckled Cornell.

Spencer wasn't chuckling. 'Hey bro, don't try to act tough.'

Although Spence looked menacing, Luke was taller and unperturbed. 'You play at violence, Spencer – Iles is for real.'

'I play at it, do I?'

Cornell slurped loudly on his cocktail, then looked up sheepishly and laughed. No one else laughed. Cornell looked down and muttered, 'Shit.'

Rinalda took a breath. 'Your father will deal with Tony Iles.'

'I fight my own battles.'

She stood firm: 'Tony Iles would not give you time to open your mouth. You raped his *daughter*.'

'A fucking actress! Getting fucked is the job. Right? Am I right?'

She turned away. But he wouldn't drop it: 'His daughter wants to be an actress – in *our* films. That means we fuck her, yeah? That's the deal. I mean, Christ, Rinalda, how many movies did you make?'

'Spencer—'

'OK, sorry, but you remember those gangbang movies—'

'Stop it.'

'No.' Spencer raised a commanding hand. 'I am making a point here. In your career *you* could've fucked two hundred guys—'

'Leave it!' said Luke sharply.

But Spencer turned on him: 'The point is this, bro: Rinalda – our beautiful mother here – did things in her movies that those *wankers* in what you call the real world think should kill a woman, yeah? But did it? No. She fucked some guys – so what? It was nothing. No more than having a crap.'

'Oh, thank you,' sniffed Rinalda – but Spencer grabbed her arm: 'We love you, Rinalda. Really. You're a gorgeous woman – that's the point. You did all that and not only are you still beautiful—' He was holding her with both hands and staring into her face. 'Not only are you drop dead gorgeous, but you are *rich*. A successful businesswoman. A walking advert for what we do.' He planted a kiss upon her forehead. 'Tony's daughter would like to be like you.'

Rinalda looked confused.

Luke said, 'I doubt her dad sees it that way.'

'I'll talk to him.'

'What'll you do – offer the girl a starring role in your next film?'

Spence chuckled. 'Is that what she wants? I don't even remember what she looks like.'

Rinalda touched his arm. 'We must apologise to him properly.'

He looked back at her and smiled. They could have been talking to each other alone. 'Well, it don't cost nothing.'

Cornell chuckled uneasily. Luke asked, 'Why did the police come?'

'About the other girl.'

'The one you murdered.' Spencer stared at him. 'How did they connect you to her?'

'Me?'

'Dad's at the cop station.'

Spencer glanced warily around the room – so elegantly furnished, secure and safe. He muttered, 'She was a journalist, bro. Maybe she... told someone in the office.'

'The whole cast saw you kill her, and her employers must have known where she was. They're called DarkAlley Films, by the way, and they've been on to me.' Luke paused for emphasis. 'They phoned me. At my office. Now, remind me: Tony Iles – did *he* know anything about the reporter?'

Spencer didn't reply. Rinalda frowned. Then from over beside the bar, Herbie cleared his throat. 'It was Mr Iles first told the boss that Spencer killed the girl.'

*

There was nothing left to say. Kirsty glanced at Ken, but he seemed as altered as his flat. There was a new box on his PC and she could hear the disk whirring. Around the flat were tiny imprints from the invisible Marion: a vase of long-stemmed freesias, and beneath the coffee table, a large book of ballet photos. The furniture had been subtly rearranged. Kirsty wasn't sure what had moved, but it wasn't a layout she remembered clearly. The flat was fashionably minimal, and compared to the snug disorder of her houseboat, Ken's spartan high-rise had never welcomed her. The flat was neatly furnished but had little to indicate who had bought the pieces. She drank a last sip of coffee – even that was different: Marion had definitely made an impact.

She stood up. 'I guess this is the last time I'll see this flat.'

He was sitting by his PC. 'No, any time you want to pop round or anything...'

'Yeah, ditto.'

He smiled. 'At least we'll still be friends.'

She chuckled wryly. 'Old mates.'

As she made for the door Ken said, 'Look, I'm sorry, you know?'

'About Marion or...?'

'No, sorry I let Luke... fondle you like that.'

'Enough already.'

Her hand was on the door. His hand strayed to his mouse. He said, 'I couldn't let him know...'

'We're more than colleagues? Well, we're not, Ken. That's all dead.'

He lifted his hand. 'You see, I wasn't supposed to know you were a journalist.'

Kirsty opened the door.

'I felt so feeble, you know?'

'It was a defining moment.'

He sat perched on his swivel chair. 'Hardly.'

'Good luck with Marion.'

'Oh, thanks. I'm not sure about her, actually.'

She didn't want this conversation – yet perhaps this was the best time: she had opened the door, and had one foot in the outside world.

He said, 'Marion's great, but we don't have a lot in common. She doesn't understand my work.'

'Does anyone?'

'She doesn't understand why I'm doing this.'

'Forgive me, but I don't want to talk about you and Marion.'

'Oh?' He looked mildly surprised.

'I suppose I should tell you,' Kirsty said, half through the open door. 'I'm pregnant.'

'Who's the father?'

He gazed across at her from his work station. She paused, then chuckled ruefully. 'How long ago did you leave me?'

He took a moment. 'No, it can't be.'

'If your PC was this slow, you'd upgrade it.'

He half stood up and then sat down. 'You're certain?'

'Every detail.'

'That's terrible.'

'Is it?'

Ken was thinking. 'How far are you... how many weeks?'

'Four. Five?'

His face cleared. 'So there's plenty of time. Do you know someone?'

She moved her head ambiguously. He said, 'I'd be happy to help out, of course. Assuming it's my – yes, it must be.'

'You think I should abort it?'

Ken flustered. 'Well, you and I are – I mean, what do *you* think?'

'I'm asking you. It's your baby too.'

'Right. Well...'

Ken glanced at his PC screen as if the answer might be there. Kirsty watched him. Then her phone rang.

The atmosphere changed immediately. Kirsty took out the phone, glanced at the display, and said, 'Kirsty Rice.'

She was watching Ken as she listened. But his mind was elsewhere.

'Give me that address again.' She nodded. 'I'll meet you there.'

- 19 -

'Inspector Gillett has entered the room.'

She had, in fact, been watching through the one-way. The sergeant who had handled the questioning had been deliberately pedantic, taking Rick right back to the origins of his business – when the group was formed, its subsidiaries, its customers, its banking arrangements, the members of its board – and wearisome as this was, his questions gave few grounds for Rick to refuse to co-operate. Whenever Thane did object the sergeant would pause – insulted, almost – and would repeat for the tape-recorder that Mr Thane, representing Mr Miller, wished to object *again*. To perfectly normal questions. To unobjectionable questions. Perhaps Mr Thane didn't want his client to co-operate at all?

It was a neat trick, which Gillett had suggested because the word on Thane was that he was a stonewalling block-out solicitor who defended his clients as if they had been entrusted with state secrets. He thought villains should never have lost the right to silence. If someone *had* to speak, he preferred it to be him.

But Jennifer also observed that Rick was playing his own game. Quite frequently he would interrupt Thane, over-rule him, stressing – for the tape recorder – that he was only too willing to co-operate. Could he have that question once again?

Jennifer reckoned she was still ahead. The investigation appeared to be about the deceptive nature of Rick's business – dubious film product equals dubious business practice – while the real reason for dragging him in – investigations into the disappearance of an actress – had been forgotten. Hopefully, Rick had forgotten too.

The sergeant looked back through his notes. 'I still don't know if I've untangled this.'

'There's nothing tangled about it,' Thane cut in. 'Mr Miller's various businesses are amalgamated into a group which he controls.'

'But the group itself is owned by a Panamanian company—'

'Cayman Islands.'

'Much the same, isn't it?' Thane held his tongue. 'An enigma wrapped in a riddle wrapped in an enigma.'

Thane glared at him. The sergeant wanted him to object again; he was keeping score. 'Now, this Cayman Island company doesn't actually do anything—'

'It's an international group—'

'Oh, another group?'

'Is it under investigation? No. Let's move on.'

Rick leant forward. 'I'm happy to answer this.' His eyes – hurt, weary, trustworthy – were on Jennifer, the inspector. 'I could write to the Cayman Islands – I'd be happy to – and get all the clarification you need, assuming you think it necessary to your... investigation.' He frowned, as if trying to work out what the investigation was about. 'But you must realise that I'm not a director of the holding company. I'm at their beck and call.'

'As your subsidiaries are at *your* beck and call?'

'I wouldn't say that.'

Jennifer asked, 'Which of these companies do you have an active role in, Mr Miller?'

'I'm not really active in any of them.'

'You're hands off?'

'The light touch.'

'Who runs Van Cock Films?'

'It's not really a company,' Rick said calmly. 'It's a brand.'

'A phantom company?'

'I object to that,' said Thane. 'My client said it *wasn't* a company.'

'Yet I could buy a Van Cock film?'

Rick smiled. 'I hope you'd enjoy it.'

'I've seen a couple,' Jennifer said. Rick kept no more than a half smile on his face. She said, 'I studied the title sequences, which say, a Van Cock Film.'

'You can buy a Kodachrome film, but there's no such company.'

'Who's in charge of it?'

'I guess the Kodak corporation—'

'Van Cock Films.'

'Van Cock's a brand. No one runs it.'

'It runs itself?'

Rick sighed. 'Each film is its own profit centre.'

She waited for more, but he gazed back as if he'd explained everything. He waited for *her*.

'So if I wanted details on a particular Van Cock film – who was in it, how long it took, where it was filmed – who would I ask?'

'The director. We have several.'

'Who directed the one on which the girl was killed?'

Rick was prepared for this. He looked puzzled. Thane looked tense.

Rick asked, 'Which girl?'

'There's been more than one?'

Silence.

'You know the one, Mr Miller – when the reporter was burned to death.'

'I don't recall that script—'

'Then dumped on the river bank.'

'It doesn't sound our sort of movie.'

Thane said, 'Inspector, do you seriously believe that my client knows anything about this?'

'He was there.'

Silence.

Rick said, 'This wasn't a movie, then?'

Thane leant forward. 'If you have any evidence for this incredible—'

'Tuesday evening, Mr Miller – where were you?'

'Tuesday? I'm not sure what I was—'

'Let me remind you. You were on the set of a film—'

'No.'

'A Van Cock film. A costume drama.'

'Certainly not.'

'There was an orgy scene.'

'Quite likely. But I wasn't there.'

'Where *were* you?'

'I expect I was at home.'

'You joined in the orgy scene.'

'At *my* age?'

'And had sex with one of the actresses.'

'I wish.'

'Then you discovered the hidden camera.'

Gillett leant across the table, her face close to Rick's: 'You also found her hair lacquer. You sprayed her with it. Then set light to her. Didn't you?'

'Not me.'

Thane's hand was on Rick's arm: 'Do you have any evidence for this?'

'We have a witness,' Gillett said. 'Which must be obvious to your client by now, since we know *exactly* how he killed Miss Rand.'

She stared at him. Rick looked serious but unconcerned. 'This is total rubbish. I was nowhere near that film.'

'Who was?'

'Who was what?'

'At the film.'

'Which film?'

Thane cut in again: 'My client knows nothing about whatever film you are talking about. He knows nothing about whatever *incident* you are talking about. He will produce an alibi for Tuesday evening. My client is innocent of any charge.'

'Who else was on the film set?'

Thane answered: 'What is your charge? What is my client accused of?'

'This is a murder investigation, Mr Thane. Your client is helping with our enquiries. So, Mr Miller, at what time did you arrive on set?'

'I was never *on* set.'

'Was it before or after the murder?'

'I wasn't there.'

'Who directed the film?'

Thane said, 'My client—' as Rick asked, 'What film?'

'The one where the murder took place.'

'You've lost me.'

'How many films do you make in a week?'

'I'm not sure—'

'You run the company.'

Thane said, 'My client runs the UK *group*. He is not concerned with—'

'Who made this particular film?'

Rick said, 'I'll try to find out.'

'Do you need a telephone? You can do it now.'

Thane stood up. 'This is harassment.'

'Who directed the film?'

'I don't know which—'

'How many directors do you employ?'

'They're freelance.'

'Why did you kill the girl?'

'I didn't.'

'But you had sex with one?'

'No way.'

Thane said, 'You've no grounds for these—'

'According to our witness, Mr Miller, you first had sex with an actress, then when you discovered an undercover journalist was on set, secretly filming what was happening, you set light to her and killed her.'

'Unbelievable.'

'You then threatened the cast and technicians, saying that if anyone revealed what had happened you would kill them.'

'What d'you read in bed – fairy stories?'

'But your threats didn't work, did they? We have a witness.'

Rick pursed his lips. 'We could employ you as a script writer—'

'Perhaps it was an accident – you didn't mean to kill her?'

'I wasn't there.'

'Who *was* there?'

Thane said, 'This is pointless.'

'This is murder.'

'You're making unfounded allegations against my client about something which you *say* happened on a film you cannot even name.'

'A film he *won't* name.'

Thane sneered. 'Didn't your so-called witness name it?'

'She didn't know the exact title—'

'She?' queried Rick with a benevolent smile. 'What was her name?'

Gillett shook her head. Thane said, 'I think we've been as helpful as we can, inspector. But if you've no further questions—'

'We have plenty.'

Rick smiled again. 'You see, if you tell me the name of the actress, I might be able to find out the film she was working on.'

She gave him a pitying look. Thane said, 'You have no grounds on which to hold my client—'

'Withholding evidence?'

Thane looked at her. She said, 'This Tuesday, on the set of a nasty little sex film made by Van Cock Films, which is a company controlled by your client—'

'He doesn't—'

'A young woman was viciously murdered in front of the entire cast by a member of the management—'

'Supposition.'

'Fact. Fully supported, Mr Thane, by a signed witness statement.'

'We'd like to see that.'

'Oh, you will.'

Thane remained standing, ready to leave. 'A 'member of the management', you say? Yet you can't name the person, you can't name the film—'

'Your client can.'

'He can't.'

'He must.'

*

Over in Clerkenwell the Millers had broken for lunch. The apartment was large enough to have a separate dining room, so some months ago Rinalda had imported a dark oak dining suite from Holland, and had had the walls panelled with dark wood. She had used so much dark wood that even though the room was on the top floor it was gloomy in daylight. Rinalda had fitted a chandelier.

Herbie acted like their butler. In the giant American fridge were enough left-overs for him to create a cold platter of turkey slices, smoked salmon and slightly suspect gravadlax. While he attended to this, Cornell sat in the kitchen to watch. Herbie set out the bowl of five-leaf salad and a dish of baby tomatoes, cucumber and gherkins, then found jars of condiment. He cut some bread – with additional slices for Spencer – but given the occasion, decided against champagne and laid out canned beer instead: Holstein for Rinalda, Mexican for Spencer. He opened some pizza-flavoured crisps.

When he wheeled it into the dining room he found Spencer and Rinalda at the table, with Luke standing by the window. Luke had his back to the room. Spencer was stroking Rinalda's hand. 'Don't worry, they can't hold Dad for long. So we better save him some lunch.'

'You should be there.'

'He's got Thane with him.' Spence passed a critical eye over Herbie's food. 'Hey, nothing hot?'

'You want *my* cooking?'

'For you that's a joke.'

'Enjoy. I'll bring coffee.'

As Herbie slouched out, Luke turned from the window. 'So, Spencer, you're not worried?'

Spencer sucked some gravadlax. 'Nope, why should I be? They got the wrong guy. Which *proves* they don't know nothing.'

'In a city with eight million people they pick the father of the man who killed her. Sounds close enough to me.'

'Coincidence.'

'Van Cock Films.'

'Could be any reason.' Spencer licked gravadlax from his fingers. 'Hmm. I knew a woman once, tasted like this.' He laughed.

Rinalda chuckled indulgently. 'You're such a boy.'

'I hope so.'

Luke sighed. 'Who told the cops?'

'Told 'em what?'

'She said you were a boy, not an idiot.'

'Sit down, bro. You're blocking the light.'

'And you can't see what's happening.'

Rinalda raised her hands. 'Boys! Don't squabble. What do you say in this country? Little birdies in their nest should not fall out. Sit down, Lucas, please.'

'I'm not hungry.'

'Oh, *sulky*,' sniggered Spencer, his mouth full of gravadlax and gherkin.

'Dad could be facing a murder charge and you sit there stuffing yourself as if it has nothing to do with you.'

Spencer nudged Rinalda. 'Help me, Mummy, Luke is picking on me.'

'Everyone behave,' she said. 'Lucas is right, Spencer. You've brought dishonour on a decent family.'

Spence made a choking noise.

Luke said, 'This was hardly the perfect murder, Spence. Everyone on the film knows you did it—'

'Oh, sit down!'

'Cornell knows—'

'Of course he does. Cornell poked the girl as well.'

'He poked the journalist?'

'The other one – Tony Iles's virgin daughter – not!'

'OK. Tony Iles knows.'

'I've heard this track. Fast forward.'

'Who *doesn't* know?'

Spencer pointed his fork. 'The cops, that's who. They don't know shit about it.'

'So why did they come for Dad?'

'To put you off your lunch. Listen, Luke baby, no one on that film would *dare* open their frightened little mouth. I told 'em: talk, and I cut your tongue out and ram it up your arse. Talk? No way. No one's gonna say nothing.'

'They told Tony.'

Spencer waved the fork. 'No, they didn't. *They* didn't tell nobody. Think about it, dickhead: his daughter told him. It's obvious.'

'Great. First she told him you raped her, then that you killed the journalist?'

'I guess so. You see, Luke baby, I am not her cuddly little friend any more. So she ran home and cried on Daddy's shoulder.'

'Tony Iles wants you dead. If he can't kill you himself he can tell the police you killed the journalist. Maybe he's already told them. He's got you, Spencer – he can do what he likes with you. Enjoy your lunch.'

'Tony Iles tells the police? Do me a favour! He's a gangster. We're all gangsters. We sort *ourselves* out.'

· 20 ·

Becky Phelps had known it would happen – it was bound to – but not today. She wasn't ready for it. She had filled a whole basket at the supermarket but when they swiped her credit card it was 'declined'. The girl was nice about it. Happens all the time. It can happen to anyone – a glitch on the computer. Can you pay cash? No. Do you have a Switch card? No – they stopped it weeks ago. It's amazing the credit card lasted this long.

Becky had to leave the basket beside the till and walk out of the shop empty-handed, head held high, as if it were no problem, an inconvenience. At the inconvenience store.

She had put some good things in that basket – useful things. She had *nothing* now. The fridge at home was empty – and knowing her luck, she'd get home to find they'd cut off the electricity. She'd already had a red demand.

Becky chewed her lip. She was in the High Street, shops crammed with stuff, but she had less than ten quid in her purse. No credit card. No bank account. What could she do?

Ten quid. Not even that. But she could chance a couple of quid on scratch cards. If there was any justice she'd win today.

*

Perversion: the turning of a thing or person away from its proper use or nature; leading astray from right conduct; preference for or practice of an abnormal form of sexual activity; persistence in error; misapplication; corruption. *Perversion of justice*: tampering with testimony or evidence to produce an unfair verdict.

How far should Kirsty help the police? What could be legitimately withheld?

Zoë was dead, to begin with. There was no doubt whatever about that. The register of her burial was signed. She was as dead as a doornail.

Kirsty's mind was racing; she felt feverish. Strange phrases jostled in her head. Till now she had not had to face the fact – the minor reality, hardly important at all – that she might be withholding evidence. Journalists did that all the time; they did not reveal their sources, they respected confidences, they followed independent enquiries. And what had Kirsty held back? Hardly anything. She had told the police about Van Cock – she had at least given them the name. But everything else – the tiny scraps of background information which she'd withheld – had been on Zoë's PC, which the police had taken away. If they looked, they could find for themselves the name Luke Miller, and his phone number.

But they hadn't phoned him. That was obvious from her visit, when Luke had been far too confident. *Far* too confident. Should she have given the police his name? Was it relevant? Well, of course it was. Luke Miller. His brother Spence.

'Miss Rice? Please come this way.'

In her early days as a cub journalist, Kirsty had visited half the police stations in London. Each one was different, yet there was a sameness to them, a timeless quality. This one was large, quite busy, yet it had that familiar smell of old damp cloth. It could be reassuring or unnerving.

She followed the WPC along the undecorated corridor to an interview room. Inside, although Kirsty would not have known it, Inspector Gillett had rearranged the furniture to be a little less intimidating: the chairs had been shifted sideways to allow interviewer and interviewees to sit indirectly from each other across the table; a fluorescent tube had been switched off; an electric fan had been switched on.

Gillett stood up when Kirsty came in, but Rosa merely half turned and gave a tired smile. The WPC returned to a seat at the side, away from the table. Unthreatening. The woman's room.

Gillett smiled, waited for Kirsty to sit down next to Rosa, then sat herself.

'Good of you to come in.'

'My pleasure.'

Ritual words.

'We're checking details on Van Cock Films – you remember? The people Zoë was investigating the night she died.'

Kirsty nodded.

'We've been in touch with the company,' Gillett continued. 'In fact, we have their managing director with us now. Have you met him?'

'I don't think so.'

'Mr Rick Miller?'

Rick – which one was that? Kirsty's face showed the name was new to her.

'Have you met *anyone* from the company?'

'Not really.' Gillett raised her head for more. 'I met a Luke Miller – but he denied having anything to do with them.'

'Luke Miller – where was this?'

Kirsty gave the address and Rosa shot her a look – Kirsty hadn't told her about Luke yet.

'Describe him.'

'Mid-twenties. Tall. Fair hair. Quite good looking. But arrogant.'

Gillett smiled. 'Rick Miller's son.'

'He has a brother. Spencer. I've not met him, but apparently he's not so nice.'

'Luke Miller's *nice*? Well, so is Rick. They may smile and smile and be a villain, I suppose. You know Cassie Nelson?'

'Yes, she phoned me.'

Gillett cocked a brow. Kirsty spoke in a rush: 'I phoned her mother. She wasn't in – I mean, Cassie wasn't.'

'You know Cassie?'

'We only spoke on the phone. She... wouldn't speak.'

'I don't understand.'

'She only phoned to tell me she wouldn't speak. She was returning my call, was all she said.'

'She wouldn't speak about *what*?'

Kirsty mumbled, 'A story I'm working on.'

Gillett looked less friendly now. 'Cassie was there when Zoë died, wasn't she? Did she tell you about that?'

'I didn't know you knew about that.'

Rosa snorted. Gillett leant forward: 'She's our principal witness – our only witness. And although you knew she was a witness, Miss Rice, you didn't tell us you had spoken to her.'

Kirsty felt humiliated. 'It was stupid of me. I'm sorry.'

'What else have you not told us?'

'Nothing.'

Gillett glared at her. 'I *had* assumed you were a friendly witness.'

'I am.'

'I'm not sure I can take your word for that. We'd better start again at square one.'

*

Rosa was sent away. As she left the room she gave Kirsty a look so black it could have raised a bruise. Gillett's manner had hardened too. She escorted Rosa off the premises, leaving Kirsty alone with the WPC for what seemed thirty minutes, though Kirsty's watch told her it was only ten. The WPC said nothing. Kirsty wondered if she ought to speak, but guessed that was how she was meant to feel.

A brusque Gillett returned. 'Come with me, please.'

Kirsty was startled. Even the policewoman raised an eyebrow. Where were they taking her? She had done nothing seriously wrong. Gillett led her along the corridor a few yards, then paused beside a door. 'After you.'

She pushed the door to let Kirsty inside.

Two men sat facing her, while across the table from them, his back to the door, sat a uniformed policeman. He didn't turn round. The two men glanced at Kirsty, then concentrated on Gillett.

—Who said, 'Right, we all know each other.'

The two men looked as blank as Kirsty did. The thinner one said, 'Are you going to give us her name for the tape?'

'It's not running. For the moment.'

Kirsty saw Gillett intent on the men's faces. She didn't know whether to continue into the room or not.

Gillett said, 'We'll find somewhere else,' and pushed Kirsty back into the corridor. As she was closing the door the thin man called, 'If you've no charge against my client—' But the door cut off his words.

Gillett marched Kirsty back to the first interview room. 'Sit down.' She walked round the table so fast she was in her seat before Kirsty sat down.

'You didn't expect to see *him*.'

'Who was he?'

Gillett studied her. 'OK, you've never met.' But she watched Kirsty's face for any sign of relief.

'I've never met who?'

'Whom, isn't it? You're the journalist. When did you meet Cassie?'

This was the pattern: as Kirsty stumbled through each answer the inspector cut across her with the next question. When had she met Cassie? Where had she found her phone number? Why had Cassie phoned *her*? What did she say? What had Luke said? Who was Ken

Lawrence? How had she heard about Spencer? Had she heard of Rick?

Kirsty knew that Gillett wasn't giving her time to think. Questions rained in like blows. Like an out-manoeuvred boxer, Kirsty could neither defend nor cover up. Questions jabbed in to every vulnerable spot.

Suddenly Gillett changed tack. She leant forward, her voice softened, and she almost grabbed hold of Kirsty's hand: 'I do understand, Kirsty, I can see the plight you're in. You didn't think you were doing harm. You're a journalist – young and ambitious – but this time you went too far.' Kirsty was nodding. 'You thought you had stumbled on a scoop. And when Luke spoke to you he told you things you thought you could use. I understand. But if you don't tell us everything, Kirsty, you'll be withholding evidence – in a murder case. Right? Not even a journalist can do that. So will you help us?'

Kirsty nodded dumbly. She felt hypnotised.

'Who else have you met, Kirsty? What else have you learned? Anything, Kirsty, anything that can help us find the man who killed your friend. Have you seen Rick Miller before? Have you heard of him? You know he runs the film company? He is management, Kirsty, and 'management' killed Zoë. Management. That's what Cassie Nelson said. Did Rick Miller kill your friend? Help us, Kirsty. You want to help us. *Please* help us. Please help me now.'

There were tears in Kirsty's eyes. Suddenly, unaccountably, she began to cry.

The inspector patted Kirsty's hand. 'That's better. You can help us. You can help Zoë.'

- 21 -

Spencer was on the phone. He stood in the steel kitchen of Rick's flat beside the window where, in Spencer's opinion, reception was clearer. Cornell sat at Rick's kitchen table, acting as if he couldn't overhear. Luke and Rinalda were in the dining room, and Herbie had skulked off to who knows where.

'Gordon? You carry a phone, you ought to answer it. I don't *care* what you were doing, bro. The film can wait. Now, the one you were doing Tuesday: I want the cast list. The names of everyone on set. *Yes*, the cameraman. Yes, everybody. No, Gordon, I want it today. That means *now*. I'll send Cornell round to pick it up.'

Cornell woke from his nap.

'And Gordon – don't give me that, I am *talking* to you. Gordon, I said shut up. I want the names, I want everyone's address. They must have agents or something – where d'you send their cheques? Gordon, let me explain this to you. I am sending Cornell, who is leaving this place *now*. And when he arrives you will give him a sheet of paper with every mother's personal name and address. *Capisce?* Do you fucking understand? That's ten minutes, Gordon. And Gordon – have a nice day now, understand?'

*

When Inspector Gillett returned to the interview room, Thane went on the attack. 'Was that your witness, Inspector Gillett? She knew nothing. She didn't even recognise my client.'

'I noticed that.'

Thane stood up. 'So we can go now? Mr Miller is—'

'That wasn't the witness.'

Thane paused. 'Then why did you bring her here?'

Gillett smiled.

Thane said, 'Confrontation? Putting her face to face with my client? Well, it didn't work, inspector—'

'On the contrary. I wanted to be sure she *didn't* know your client.'

Rick said, 'A good looking girl.'

He looked tired but chipper, and stayed in his seat.

Thane asked, 'Who *is* your witness?'

Gillett chuckled confidently. 'In due course we shall reveal that to the defence.'

Thane nodded wryly. 'One dubious witness – that's all you have. This is outrageous, inspector.'

She ignored him and turned to Rick: 'I believe you *hire* the costumes for your films?'

'My girls don't usually *wear* costumes.'

'It was a costume drama, wasn't it?' Both men waited for what she'd say. 'Miss Rand was wearing her costume when you set light to her.'

Thane expostulated. Rick shook his head. Thane said, 'You must withdraw that unwarranted accusation.'

'This is not a courtroom – yet. But let me reveal something else to the defence: yesterday we contacted every costume hire shop in London. It was so *nice* of you to hire from a legitimate company.' She paused for six long silent seconds. 'One dozen assorted eighteenth century gowns. Hired to Van Cock Films – which is just a brand, of course. So will you be returning a dozen costumes, Mr Miller, or only eleven?'

*

Kirsty wasn't released till evening, by which time it was too late – or she could persuade herself it was too late – to go back to the office, and by which time anyway she had an over-riding desire for a drink. Make that two drinks. If she hadn't been pregnant she might have drunk a damn sight more.

She was finishing her second when her phone rang. Someone, at least, wanted to speak to her. Unexpectedly, it was Ken, who started by saying, 'Thank you very much.'

'Excuse me?'

'For fouling up my life.'

'Oh, has Marion left?'

'I expect you're working on it.'

'I've had a hard day, Ken—'

'*You've* had a hard day? Luke Miller has been to see me. He accused me of planting you deliberately.'

'Which is *true*.'

'But he and I were *close*, Kirsty.'

'Close?'

'Commercially. I was cutting a fantastic deal with him.'

'I thought you were *investigating* him?'

'But the deal got me in with him – right in. Now he wants your address.'

'You didn't give it him?'

'Credit me with *some* sense. He'd have given it to Spencer – who is storming around on some kind of damage limitation exercise. That'll be about Zoë, right?'

'Spencer was involved with Zoë?'

'Then the police came.'

'To *your* place?'

'They've just left. Wanted to know what I knew about the story she was working on – what I knew about Luke and Spencer and Van Cock Films. I said I didn't know *anything* about any of it. But I didn't know you'd told them half our life story.'

'Not exactly.'

'Which half did you leave out? They knew about us seeing Luke; they knew I'd been working with him; they even asked about his family.'

'And you said?'

'Oh Hell, I didn't know *what* to say. The woman from the police said you'd already told them everything. I thought they'd *arrested* you.'

'What on earth for?'

'I don't *know*. You've been lying to *everybody*, Kirsty. That woman got me so confused.'

'Poor you.'

'Then to cap it all she said she knew that you and I had a secret but it was all right now because you'd told her.'

'And?'

'Well, I thought she meant the secret about the baby, so of course I made a complete *fool* of myself—'

'You told her I was *pregnant*?'

'I thought she knew.'

'Oh, thank you!'

'Where's the big deal? It's not *your* problem, is it?'

'Not *my* problem?'

'I was half way through telling her when *Marion* walked in!'

'Oh, dear.'

'Now Marion's not talking to me. She saw me being interviewed by the *police*. She didn't see *my* point of view at all.'

'Poor Ken.'

He sighed. 'It's no use feeling sorry for me now. What am I supposed to do?'

'About Marion?'

'Help me, Kirsty – you got me into this.'

She paused. 'Why don't you make *Marion* pregnant? That should make things crystal clear to her.'

*

They didn't release Rick till dark, by which time he thought they were going to keep him in all night. On the way home Thane grumbled that they had never had enough to hold him. Rick said, 'The inspector fancied me, that's all.'

He invited Thane up for supper. Earlier, at the police station, Rick had refused to eat a thing, but now he didn't feel hungry, he just felt tired. Rinalda fussed around him, suggesting all kinds of exotic food, but Rick said he'd make do with a sandwich. Thane looked disappointed and Rinalda suggested a restaurant, but Rick still refused to shift. Even when Spencer confessed he'd eaten all the gravadlax, Rick still would not eat out.

Thane said, 'Give me some bread and cheese. Anything. I'll faint if I don't eat.'

Rick asked where Herbie was.

'Spencer sent him and Cornell on a job.'

Spencer glanced up at his name. 'Oh, *sorry*,' he said defensively. 'Is Herbie the only one can cut a slice of bread?'

Rick asked what job Herbie was on. Spencer glanced at Thane: 'Should you be hearing this?'

'You want to confess something?'

'It's about a witness.'

'Spencer, Spencer... You think a brief shouldn't hear his client admit guilt? You watch too many movies.'

Spencer grinned. 'Your client,' said Rinalda pointedly, 'is not guilty.'

'They never are.'

'Rick did not kill this wretched girl.'

'Not my problem,' Spencer said.

Rinalda turned on him. 'Your father spent all day in the police station.'

'But they had to send him home.'

'They have a witness to the murder,' Thane murmured.

Rinalda looked at him. He looked at Spencer – who said, 'I don't *think* so.'

Thane said, 'A female witness.'

'Well, bro, they won't have after tonight.'

'Don't tell me,' sighed Rick.

Rinalda laughed. 'Perhaps Spencer is going to *kill* all the witnesses!'

'If I have to,' said Spencer. It made them all laugh.

- 22 -

Cassie had had another row with Ma. She should never have told her she had gone to the police. Tell Ma about the filming, about foreign studs, about English actors trying to keep up ('keep up' made Ferdie cackle); tell her, as Cassie had done, about her early days, when model photography turned to glamour, when glamour turned to porn – and Ferdie would listen avidly, encourage her, ask for details of the naughty bits. But to admit she had been to the police was unthinkable. No one does that. Not even about a murder. Keep your head down. Stay out of it.

The fact that Cassie, like most of the cast, had been stunned and terrified – ripped from the bizarre fantasy of the film into the blazing horror of real life – was something Ferdie could not see. It's a hard world, she said dismissively. They're dangerous characters. If you don't like it, go back to modelling. Then came the words which sent Cassie storming to her room: 'If you can't stand the heat of the fire…'

Cassie couldn't sleep. She lay in her room – a kid's room, teenage magazines, three racks of juvenile CDs – and asked herself why she was still there. She was grown up. She stayed out many a night and if any of her men lasted she would stay out forever, she really would. Her mother was ancient, thirty-six, and had lost her figure. It was only cigarettes that stopped her blowing up – like a balloon, thought Cassie suddenly: not a fully stretched balloon but one of those half-deflated, obscenely soft wrinkled blobs that hung around after a party for weeks and weeks. Ferdie should be taken down, pricked and thrown away. Cassie snorted: Ferdie *was* pricked and thrown away. Often. The fat old cow.

Lying in the dark, raging silently at her Ma, improved Cassie's mood. She could hear Ferdie snoring in her bedroom. She was getting worse: on a night like this when she had supped a few, Ferdie snored so loud you could hardly miss it. Outside was quiet. Apart from Ferdie's racket there was an odd car passing, a distant voice, a faraway siren, a burglar alarm. There's always one somewhere. Part of London life. —What's that?

She listened.

Nothing.

The thing about noises late at night is that the lack of other sound makes them seem close. You hear a car door and it could be the front door to your house. You hear a footstep in the street and someone could be walking up your stairs.

That, for instance. That creak, just like a footstep. She heard another – a two-beat groan, like when a plank of wood rubs against another. What *was* that?

It must be Ferdie. Someone in the street. Perhaps Ferdie had shifted in her bed. Her bed was not the quietest—

That! Another squeak. The bedroom door was opening. It couldn't be—

Cassie sat up, terrified, as the man stepped in. She opened her mouth to shout – but he was across the room, the tiny bedroom. His hands shot out and cut her scream. He had one hand across her mouth, one behind her head, and he pulled Cassie close to him, her face to his chest as he whispered fiercely in her ear: 'Shut up, you hear?'

She struggled and tried to bite his hand – but he whipped it away, and with his other hand pulled her face into the rough material of his jerkin. She could have screamed then, but the man hit her, a stinging punch against her ear.

He whispered furiously, 'Shut up, I'll kill you. Keep your mouth shut.' She struggled again. He grabbed her ear. Her sore ear. 'Want another? Keep your mouth *shut* and you'll be OK. Hear me, *Cassie*? Keep your mouth shut.'

He knew her name. He used it again: 'You're Cassie, right? I got a message for you. Keep quiet and you'll be all right.'

She stopped struggling. But she was ready to scream.

He said, 'Don't make a sound, girl, I'll punch your head off. Understand?'

She quivered.

'Right?'

She nodded.

'Now, *Cassie*, I'll give you one chance. You scream or make one single sound... Right?'

Cassie nodded again. He relaxed his hold. But not completely: with one hand behind her head, he squatted so their faces became level. He didn't wear a mask. He didn't hide himself. He was a black man. He grinned at her. 'You couldn't sleep?'

She shook her head. She recognised him now, although she had seen him only once. He had been there that terrible night. The killer had already come here. Now this one. 'Why me?' Cassie whispered.

He raised a finger. Put it on her lips. In the gloomy room, Cassie and Cornell stared at each other. Did he know she had told the police? Was that why he'd come here? In the silence, Ferdie snored.

Cornell smiled slightly. 'I tried her room first. Your mother?'

Cassie nodded.

'Out like a light. Smelt like she'd been on the bevy. So, Cassie.' He moved back slightly and glanced up and down her body. She had a nightie on but Cornell grinned as if she were nude. 'We met before.'

She stared back but didn't answer. She must keep calm. This was not the killer, this was the man who'd been *with* the killer.

'Remember?'

She nodded.

'No, you don't,' Cornell said softly. 'You don't remember nothing about it. Like it never happened. Did it?'

She shook her head.

'You made the film, Cassie, you were on the set. We got no problem with that. But nothing else happened. No one got hurt.'

'All right.'

But she had already told the police.

'If the filth come, Cassie – like they might, they just might – you know nothing. You were there, but you didn't see nothing. No reporter. No little accident. Right? Everything else you can tell like it happened. What you done in the film, that's all right. Who was there, *that's* all right. Except I wasn't there. And *he* wasn't there. And that girl, she wasn't there. No way. Absolutely. Got that?'

'Yes,' she whispered.

'Tonight we're telling everyone, Cassie, that nothing happened. And remember.' He stared at her. 'I know where you live. I am sitting here in your bedroom.' Cornell put his hand on her breast and fondled it through her nightie. 'And very nice it is here. Are you going to tell someone?'

'No.'

Cornell smiled, and as he removed his hand he shrugged reluctantly. 'Nice little room here. You and me. No problem.'

She stared at him. Did he want sex?

But he took a step towards the door. 'You be a good girl, Cassie. *Save* yourself for me.'

He blew a kiss, then he was gone.

*

Late night. The phone rang – that irritating warble. The pearl coloured, delicate little phone that *she* had chosen. A woman's phone. Still on *her* side of the bed. One day he'd—

Tony Iles crashed across the mattress for it.

'What you want?'

'Mr Iles? I'm sorry – you're not in bed?'

'What's the time?'

'It's Wayland.'

'Who?'

'The Blue Mingo Club?'

'For Christ's sake. Where's Tucker?'

'With *Mrs* Iles. She's in a state.'

'So?'

'She's sounding off. Slagging *you* off. To be honest, Mr Iles—'

'Is she drunk?'

'Well yes, you could say that.'

'What d'you want *me* to do? Call a taxi. Send her home.'

'She won't go.'

'Make her. Christ, I—'

'Everyone knows that she's your wife.'

'She *was* my wife.'

'Mr Tucker said he thought you'd want to know.'

'At this hour? What's he thinking of?'

'The state of her, Mr Iles. What she's saying. She's not fit to be let out.'

'She never is.'

'Mr Tucker says she could ruin your reputation. We can't trust her in a taxi. That's why he thought you should know.'

'Put her in the office. I'll come down.'

*

Two o'clock. In the western edges of London beyond Teddington the Thames ceases to be tidal. Yet in the long curve of river that sweeps around Hampton Court and beyond – out in the tideless stretches of West Molesey and Sunbury – people on houseboats say you feel the swell. Late at night, they say, when there is no river traffic, when the pace of life has slowed and you lie in your bunk feeling that you and your wooden craft are a part of the black water which bobs gently to the shore, then, in those quiet hours, you feel each tremor of the tide.

Across the river from Hampton Court, in Thames Ditton, when the tide turns, tiny backwaters slurp to a different rhythm. The shift at Teddington makes the houseboats gently rock. In daytime you'd not feel it, but in the dark lonely hours when noises normally unnoticed swirl like eddies in the silent air, those who cannot sleep feel every movement of their boat.

A drag in the water. A step on deck.

Kirsty would not normally have noticed. Half an hour ago, awake in bed, her head muffled against the pillow, she would not have heard that gentle step. She would not have felt the boat shift slightly. But awake and out of bed, sitting in her dressing gown at the littered table, Kirsty heard the footstep. Then the next. Someone on deck. She watched her stairway as whoever was up there paused at her door.

Strangers rarely came on board. At moorings further into town, unwanted visits were more frequent: a late-night drunk, kid on a dare, potential burglar. Kirsty watched the door which she had locked. As usual.

Then the scratching noise. Someone fumbling at the door. Trying to pick the lock—

The door swung open. Against the outer darkness she could make out only the man's shadow, but at the littered table with its single lamp he couldn't fail to see her.

'Still awake?'

Closing the door behind him, picking his way carefully as if unfamiliar with the companionway, Ken descended into the light. 'I thought you'd be asleep.'

She breathed out. 'Come to give my key back?'

Opposite her at the table he grinned stupidly. 'Hello again. D'you want a coffee?'

'Are you drunk?'

'I *have* drunk, but I am not,' he announced. Then he lurched towards the galley.

'Do make yourself at home.'

'It feels like home,' he said expansively. He threw a hand out and banged it against her timber wall. 'Ouch.'

'Strong and black,' she muttered. 'Two cups.'

While Ken made coffee, Kirsty sat at the table feeling numb. It was too late at night for deep emotions. Ken clattered around the galley and there was no room for Kirsty in there as well. When he returned he sat opposite her, and she studied him across her coffee cup, his face wavering in the steam. He tried to meet her gaze. 'Nothing lasts,' he said eventually. 'Marion has finally walked out.'

'She's allergic to police?'

'I don't know why she was so horrified.'

'Till now she thought you were a nice boy, like those dancers she spends all day with.'

He stared at the steam rising from his cup. 'Can I get a Scotch to go with this?'

'Have some water.'

'Far too wholesome.'

But he lumbered to the galley and poured a glass. 'Get you some?'

'No, thanks.'

He downed the first glass, poured a second and returned. He said, 'Your fault, of course. I've been meaning to have a go at you.'

'Don't bother.'

'You're right – it's too late for that. Apologies accepted.'

Kirsty shrugged.

He ran a hand through his new haircut. 'But it wasn't fair, was it?'

'Who are we talking about?'

'Marion.'

'Let's not.'

He looked surprised. 'I was hoping you would...'

'Lend a sympathetic shoulder?'

He inhaled some steam. 'Bed for the night?'

'Go home, Ken.'

When he exhaled he created a minor squall across the meniscus of his coffee. He looked at his watch. Focussed on it. 'Come on, Kirsty – it's a long way back.'

'You can say that again.'

He grinned sadly. 'Listen. You smashed my contract with Luke, you sent the cops round to interrogate me, you chased Marion away.'

'I didn't smash any 'contract' you had with her.'

He reached across the pull-down table. 'She and I didn't have one.'

She ignored his hand. '*We* did.'

'That's not broken.'

She gave a wry look. 'Whereas the party of the first part, aforementioned, did knowingly walk out—'

'No, Kirsty, come on.'

'And the party of the second part, never mentioned, did find herself left holding the baby...'

She stopped and watched him.

'So 'the second part' is—' He frowned. 'Oh, the baby! How is that?'

'That? Ex*cuse* me?'

'You're pregnant. I forgot.'

She sat back. 'Have you finished that coffee? I'm washing up.'

He looked at her, bemused. 'Did I say something?'

'No, Ken. That's the point.'

He sniffed. The low light in the boat was cosy. 'Maybe I *have* had too much to drink.'

'Go home and sleep it off.'

'I can't drive in this state. I'll get stopped.'

'You drove *here*.'

He paused, remembering. 'So I did.' He shook his head as if to clear it. 'Christ, you blew me out, Kirsty. Luke knows nothing about internet technology. I could have transformed his cruddy sites.'

'Nothing else is bothering you?'

He snorted sarcastically. 'Well, apart from Marion, who is now not *speaking* to me.'

'I'm so interested.'

'Show some pity, Kirsty. You can be really hard, you know?'

'A mother's prerogative.'

He stared at her as his mind cleared. 'Right. Let's talk about this baby. It's definitely... all there?'

'Oh, she's all there – a bright kid. Just passed her first test.'

Ken raised his fingers to his forehead. 'It's a girl?'

'It's a baby.'

He nodded. 'This is kind of sudden, isn't it?'

'That's how they come.'

He continued nodding. 'What are you going to do?'

'What am *I* going to do?'

He stretched his face to help himself wake up. 'This is a bit above my head, Kirsty. Are you going to... should we get rid of the baby? I suppose that would be best.'

'Best?'

Ken sighed. 'No, no, you're right.'

'About what?'

'Well, I'm sorry about this, Kirsty. I mean, it's bound to cost something, so if you need money, you know, obviously... You know.'

'You'll pay maintenance?'

He gaped at her. 'You're not going to keep it?'

She spoke carefully: '*It* is a baby.'

Dangerous waters. 'Right. Your decision. I respect that.' He nodded approvingly. 'Up to you. Wow, what a day.'

'Life goes on.'

'Absolutely. Hey, look, I didn't know her well, but Christ, it's terrible about Zoë. You don't really think Luke had anything to do with that?'

She blinked at the change of subject. 'I *know* he did. He told me on the phone.'

Ken stared at his coffee. 'He couldn't have been there.'

'You're his alibi?'

'No, it's... He's not that involved with the films. He *shows* them, but he doesn't make them. He's a techie.'

'You told me he knew nothing about technology.'

'Ah, but he's a techno *fan*. Doesn't know how technology works but loves what it can do. You know, like driving a car but you can't fix it?'

The boat seemed to shift again: a change in the tide.

'This 'contract' you had with him – you don't think doing that was outside your brief?'

'Not exactly. I needed an excuse to get inside – and it's not as if I was giving him something unique. He can buy it anywhere.'

'If you didn't sell it him, someone else would?'

'Precisely.'

'Like selling bombs to a third world dictator?'

'Be fair, Kirsty – it was... a ruse to get me inside his organisation. It's brilliant for my film.'

'That was your only objective?'

Ken sat back. 'Oh, that's nice! What are you saying – I sold out?'

'Convince me.'

'Wow, heavy! Heav*ee*! Look, Kirsty, just because I make money on the side does not compromise my film. Though I could make more *on* the side than I'll ever make from the film.'

'That doesn't compromise you?'

'Absolutely no way. I *had* to get in there. Do you *know* about my films?'

'Sex on the internet.'

'I'm working on two films, *Sex Is Shopping* and *Why Hackers Hack*. And I'll contribute a bit into Rosa's *Real Net Millionaires*. The Millers are millionaires from sex'n'shopping, yeah? But *I'm* the hacker!' He chuckled.

'Does Luke know?'

'He doesn't even know I'm a journalist. I hope he doesn't.'

She raised a hand: 'OK, I'm sorry about what happened. I thought you were selling out.'

'Not me, babe.' He looked at her. 'Can I say something?'

'Can I stop you?'

'Huh!' He drained his coffee. Whenever he stopped talking, the boat fell absolutely silent. But he carried on. 'In this series, you've had the easier assignments. —No, listen: you weren't even underground, were you? Zoë was under cover, and look what happened to her.'

'That's not fair.'

'Well, I'm under cover too. In *Sex Is Shopping* I get right behind the web sites – the streaming videos, the interactives, the chat rooms and visual one-to-ones. Telephone sex. That stuff you saw at Luke's – punters telling girls what to do—'

'Peep-hole sex. You can buy that in Soho.'

'Ah, but that's just peep, not communication. You see, Kirsty, what the modern world wants is one to one communication.'

'Virtual sex.'

'It's better than some anonymous voice breathing down your voice line, *pretending* she's doing things. Here you can *see* her, watch her, *talk* to her. Ask her and she plays.'

'Wind her up and watch her go.'

'Your cyber slave. High-ticket. But if you can't afford it you can always come down a price level and look at photos or video.'

Ken waved his coffee cup in the air. She hoped it was empty.

'Amazing world. Manning the lines and pumping back material is this weird mixture of telesales girls who've moved on, and lifetime hookers who are getting old. They're the real face of Sexy Susan.'

'Surprise, surprise.'

'You've been following *amateurs*, Kirsty. These are the pros.'

'They're pros, all right.'

'Don't come high and mighty, Kirsty, just because you don't buy the stuff. You're so prudish. You're so straight.'

She looked astonished but he carried on.

'So, I hear you ask, if Luke Miller has all this, why does he need *me*? To exploit technology.' Ken thumped the table with his cup. 'Every time you click on a site you leave an electronic fingerprint, showing who you are, where you are, the exact details of your PC, the details you keyed in when you first bought it – remember, when you registered the operating system? Every marketing company you contact on the net leaves cookies on your machine, yeah? What do you think those cookies do – sit there? They are clocking you.'

'Big Brother.'

'Microsoft's not the only company people register with. Whenever folk buy things on the net they register again. People register with the sex industry. They might use false names but to actually buy anything they have to give their credit card number – which is checked on-line. That's like handing the key of your bank vault to a guy you daren't tell anyone about because he knows all your dirty secrets. You lay yourself open to someone where the only thing you know about him is that his business is prostitutes and paedophiles and drug pushers. You see what's happening here, Kirsty? Customers are hypnotised by the screen.'

'But *you're* OK?'

'Oh, it can't harm *me*. I know what I'm doing. This series will *make* me, Kirsty. When I saw all this – which I bet is a damn sight more riveting than your material—'

'Thanks—'

'I knew I had to star in the film myself.'

'What?'

'I'm going to break into Luke's sites and bring them down.'

'Yeah, right.'

'His sites are primitive – flashy but primitive. Internet sex companies are not like banks. They may be *richer* than banks but they're *not* banks. They don't have money you can steal, so their security is lower. It's not impossible for a hacker to break in and access their customer account files. It has been done.'

She looked at him with new eyes. 'You mean to do this?'

'Too right. On-line. Bring the whole lot tumbling down.'

'And you'll film yourself doing it?'

'That's the point. I'll be a star.'
'You'll be dead.'

*

Two forty-five. When Tony swept into the Blue Mingo Club the doorman, half asleep, had time only to say 'Evenin', Tony,' before Iles was in. He strode across the bar-room as if nobody was there. If the doorman was half asleep, the customers were awake. A busy night. Music and mobile lighting gave the place a restless, churning atmosphere. Baccarat, Blackjack and Roulette. Croupiers in evening dress, girls in undress, customers in any kind of dress. Stunted souls who preferred to play alone sat at a chattering bank of slot machines. There was a sparkling cocktails bar, there were girls with trays, the scent of burgers and perfume.

All of which Iles ignored.

He slammed through into the office. His ex-wife glanced up and it was as if two rival dogs had met. Two steps inside the room and they were at it.

'The hell you drag me out of bed?'
'How dare you lock me up?'
'The state of you.'
'If *you'd* sat here—'
'Drunk—'
'Treated like I was some kind of—'
'Tart—'
'I'm nothing to do with you—'
'People know you were my wife—'
'You've no *right*.'
'Where's Emma?'

They were still squabbling when Tony dragged his ex-wife out through the rear fire door. He opened his car.

'I'm not getting in *there*!'

He pushed her in. As she sprawled across the seat he leant close enough to say, 'Do anything stupid I'll rip your face off.'

She knew he meant it. Lisanne had lived with him twelve years. Drunk as she'd been earlier, the dreary wait had brought her down. Not sober, perhaps, but tearful and morose. When he climbed in his own side she managed, 'We're not married now. You can't do this.'

But he turned the key and drove her home.

- 23 -

Rick was keen on breakfast meetings. Maybe he'd read a book on interview psychology; maybe he'd written it. People he wanted to threaten he met on the disused printing floor – preferably at dawn. Rick thought dawn meant six o'clock in overcoats, collars raised against cold air – and although he could force that through with strangers, his family refused. For them, dawn meant breakfast, nine o'clock.

Rick had showered, been for a walk, but Spencer looked as if he'd stayed up all night. Luke was calm and unreadable; Rinalda alert, if over-decorated. Mornings were not her best time, but she never missed a meeting. No one suggested that she should.

Herbie Tripp was there too. Like Luke he never altered – where Luke kept his unstructured business look, Herbie mooched about silently like an old family retainer, a slippered butler. He drifted from kitchen to dining room, replacing food. For a man who seldom moved fast, Herbie had a lot to do. Rick had fried breakfast: bacon, mushrooms, sausage – and always two crispy eggs. Rinalda ate yoghurt and a brioche. Spence had leant across to sample Rinalda's brioche but he was a toast man really, slice after slice. Luke was the difficult one, because he always had something different: tomatoes on toast one day, muesli the next – and back in the days when he'd lived at home Luke occasionally infuriated the whole family by filling the room with the smell of boiled kipper or grilled haddock. (Herbie drew the line at kedgeree.) But today Luke ate scrambled eggs.

Spencer said, 'We've seen most of them.'

'Most?'

'Kurt's in Germany – or Belgium. Someplace abroad. Where Berenice is I don't know – but if *we* can't find her the cops won't.'

Rick was chewing sausage. 'Anyone else you couldn't get to?'

'Well, obviously we didn't get to the Iles girl.'

'You try?'

'You serious?'

Rinalda asked, 'Does she live with Tony Iles?'

'With her Ma. They got divorced.'

Luke laid down his fork. 'Her mother's bringing her up so delicate and refined.'

Rinalda bristled at the gibe. 'Nice girls appear in movies too.'

Spence reached across and touched her hand. 'None nicer than you, Rinalda.'

Rick cut in: 'Any more you missed, apart from two girls and a stud?'

'The two abroad can't say nothing, and the Iles girl, she won't talk.'

'She already did.'

'Only to her Dad.'

'You hope.'

Spencer shrugged. 'Hey, Herbie, how about another stack of toast, bro?'

Luke picked up his fork. 'Tony Iles holds the high cards. He can tell the police who killed the journalist.'

'He'd cut his tongue off first.'

'He'd cut off *your* tongue, or something else you can't control.'

'Boys!' chuckled Rinalda.

Luke said, 'Iles doesn't have to tell the cops himself – nor does his daughter.'

Spencer laughed. 'That man wouldn't give Babylon his *spit*.'

Rick dropped his cutlery. 'Will you drop that coon talk, Spencer? Do you realise what you've done? Here we are, an ordinary family trying to run a decent business—'

Luke hooted. But Rick turned on *him*: 'What, our business isn't decent? Listen, we supply things people like to spend their money on. We don't force nobody. We don't use violence like Tony Iles.'

'Much,' sneered Spencer.

'You know what he *might* do? Tell a journalist.'

'Like they'd print it in the papers? I'd sue the mothers.'

'A journalist prints half the story then slips the rest of it to the cops. You killed one of theirs, Spencer. That makes it serious to them.'

'Personal,' smiled Luke.

'What I think,' declared Spencer, waving a freshly buttered piece of toast, 'Tony Iles don't got the intelligence. The man's a bruiser.'

'Talking of journalists,' began Rinalda.

'They don't know nothing,' insisted Spencer. 'I kept her video tape.'

'One of the tapes,' muttered Luke.

'Meaning?'

Rick explained: 'She could have been filming us for months. She could have been one of a dozen journalists—'

'Come on!'

'Could have a hundred hours of tape.'

'So what, Dad? All she had on that tape of hers was a duller version of our film.'

'You look at it?'

'Sure. It was a mess.'

'She hadn't edited it,' said Luke. 'She might have only wanted thirty seconds – on top of all the stuff she'd shot before.'

'I never *saw* the girl before.'

Rinalda asked, 'What *was* on her tape – what had she concentrated on?'

'Dunno. As far as I could see she left it running.' Spence was buttering his seventh slice of toast. 'She had loads of stuff on the Iles girl.' He took a bite. 'Hey, maybe she was working for Tony Iles – you know, making a home movie for his birthday!'

'Don't be stupid,' growled his father. Having finished his fry-up, Rick had lost interest in the meal. 'If Iles had any inkling his daughter was on set he'd have sent someone with a Kalashnikov, not a camera.'

'How old is she?' asked Luke. 'Fourteen?'

'Says Iles.'

'That could be the story the journalist was working on: underage sex, paedophiles.'

'I am not a fucking paedophile!'

'You know a paedophile who *doesn't* fuck?'

Spence pointed his slice of toast. 'Stay out of this, bro.'

'You're dripping jam.'

'*Marmalade*, not jam.'

'That's something to make an issue of?'

Spence bit a double-size chunk of toast. Rinalda rapped her spoon: 'This journalist?'

Luke said, 'She worked for a company called DarkAlley Films – remember them? They phoned me the day she died. And came to see me yesterday.'

Rinalda frowned. Herbie paused at the door. Luke smiled and added, 'They asked after *you*, Spence.'

Spencer stared at him. Luke said, 'Because you run Van Cock Films.'

'You told them that?'

'They knew.'

A pause. 'What else did they know?'

'That's the sixty-four thousand dollar question.'

Another pause. Till Spence said, 'I ought to bust their offices.'

Rick pointed a knife at him. 'Give your mouth a rest.' He turned back to Luke: 'This DarkAlley mob – you think they talked to the police?'

'The dead girl worked for DarkAlley, so the police will have talked to *them*.'

Rick nodded. Spence exhaled.

A phone rang. Rick's phone. They watched him answer it: 'Oh, hello, Thane.'

While Rick was on the phone, Spence leant across the table and muttered to the other two: 'Whatever material DarkAlley has, they can't have nothing that'll hurt us. Just some porno, which they'll water down for TV. They do a story about how disgusting it is, and the viewers nod their stupid heads and call out, 'Hey, look at the tits on her'. Could be good for us – people ringing in to ask where they can buy the uncut video!'

Spencer laughed.

Rick clicked off the phone and glared at him. 'You say your boys got round everyone last night?'

Spencer's face went still. 'Yeah, any mother who ain't gone abroad.'

Rick nodded. 'Thane has been talking to the cops – and they say they got a witness. Some girl called Cassie Nelson.'

*

'Spencer Miller,' explained Tony Iles, 'turns out to be the youngest son of *Rick* Miller.'

Roy Farrell nodded. 'Must be the *prodigal* son.'

They were in Tony's L-shaped dining room with its great view of Turner's Dock. Since Tony didn't often eat at home, this room functioned as his office. Only half the L was used. The other half, left bare, gave the room a fashionably spartan look – or it would have done, if Tony had not piled his luggage at one end. There was nowhere else to store it: the tiny bedroom struggled to take a bed.

Tony said, 'So when we met Rick Miller, I was saying I wanted his *son* dead.'

'He didn't look too keen.'

'He didn't tell us Spencer was his son. So he ain't gonna kill him, is he?'

Roy glanced at the ceiling, then looked down. Up there in the living room the *cause* of all this, Tony's Emma, was watching TV. Loud. She'd moved back home. Roy wondered how long *that* would last.

'Nevertheless,' continued Tony. 'Someone has to kill the bastard. You saw the film.'

'That was Spencer?'

'No, some actor. Some *acting*. Faking or not, I should cut his cock off. But Spencer *raped* my daughter, Roy, and he killed some girl as well.'

'The boy sure does get carried away.' Roy saw Tony's face. 'Right, you want Spencer dead. Is that dead so his family knows we killed him?'

'As long as Spencer knows.'

'He'll die knowing.'

Tony grimaced. 'Leaving Rick Miller with a grievance. I don't like someone to have a grudge against me.'

Farrell shrugged. 'I can think of a dozen who do.'

'Not like I killed their sons.'

'Their sons didn't rape your daughter.' Today Roy couldn't say anything right. 'Ah shit, maybe we should take out Rick as well.'

'He's got another son – and the porno empire. We could have a gang war on our hands.'

'Empire! They make *porno* films. The only guns they know are props.'

'They're a powerful family, Roy.'

Farrell thought a moment. But every time they stopped talking they heard the pounding from upstairs. Pop video. 'We could kill Spencer in an accident.'

'Might be best.'

The music stopped. Tony added, 'Listen, Roy, between you and me – should I go through with this? I mean, he raped her, sure, but no one knows about it. Apart from you.'

'Hey, you're Tony Iles. You'd sweep this under the carpet because nobody *knows*?'

The door opened. Emma appeared. 'You want coffee? I'm making some.'

Tony raised a hand to silence Farrell's next gaffe. 'Thanks, darling. That would be great. You know Roy Farrell?'

'Hi, Emma.'

'Emma*line*.' She studied him. 'Hi, Roy.'

Farrell smiled back, remembering. She looked younger than in the film, but he'd seen her naked. He knew what she could do. What she *would* do.

She was staring at him. 'D'you like sugar?'

'I like it hot.'

'Should I... add some milk?'

The little strumpet licked her lips.

'Oh, I'd like that.'

She flounced off to the kitchen. Roy tried to keep his face straight.

Tony sounded tired. 'You could be right, Roy. You and I know. *Craddock* knows. Who else?'

'Craddock? He knows numbers.'

'He still knows. And Rick Miller knows. Spencer knows. Those two black guys Rick had with him. And the actors and the film crew. Half of London knows.' Tony gazed sadly through his window at the peaceful Turner's Dock. 'Everyone's waiting to see what I do.'

*

Cornell was on Tower Bridge Approach. When he saw Spencer's TVR he vaulted a railing and stood in the road. Spencer hardly slowed. He had the soft top down, so Cornell hopped over the door and grabbed the screen.

'Whoops!'

Spencer carried on. 'Got the address, bro?'

'Been there already.'

'We do it right this time.'

The sports car blended with traffic going south over Tower Bridge.

*

Rosa sat on the empty desk. It was as if Zoë had never been there – till Kirsty asked about the episode Zoë had been working on.

'We'll cobble it together from material she left us. Most of the good stuff is in the bag.'

Ken was reading an internet magazine: 'If we need porno snippets I can find a million out there.'

Rosa pushed herself off her perch and began walking around the office. She was never comfortable sitting down. 'You've got my material from the King's Cross arches – ex-porn queens reduced to prostitution. You've got my crack cocaine sequence – and the whore in the cardboard box: 'Please help me get off these drugs.' We'll use the King's Cross material in tiny fragments throughout to undermine the so-called glamour.'

'What about your stuff on Czech and Yugoslavian girls?'

'We may have to bin that. Zoë did the model agencies, glamour photographers and movie auditions – all young and hopeful. Zoë concentrated on one girl to show how easily they can be exploited.'

'Which one was that?'

'They all have made-up names. This one called herself Emmaline.'

'How old?' asked Ken.

'Thirteen? Fourteen?'

'Oh, that's not young.'

Rosa gave him a look, but he was still skimming his magazine. She said, 'It would be better if we had a clip of Emmaline in a porno film, but Zoë didn't get that. Unless it was on her last film. We'll never know.'

Kirsty looked up. 'That's an angle we could take: stay with the girl till she gets sucked into the industry and then, just as you think you're going to see what happens, she disappears. Drops from sight.'

'Just fades away? It'll have to do – we're up against a deadline.' Rosa glanced at Kirsty. 'Finished?'

'Practically. I'm still editing.'

'Let it go, then. Move forward. Are *you* done, Ken?'

'Sorry, no.' He put down his magazine. 'One film is – the *Sex Is Shopping* thing, but I have to do another sequence on *Why Hackers Hack*.'

'And *Real Net Millionaires*?'

'I've got most of it. Another week and I'll be done.'

'Can't give you a week. We can stretch to three days at most. That's three days for finished material, fully edited – so that means no more filming after tomorrow.'

'You're such a dominatrix,' laughed Ken. 'Well, if that's it, ladies, I'm on my way.'

He folded his magazine and left. Rosa waited till he'd gone. 'Ladies!'

'He's unreconstituted.'

Rosa dropped her voice. 'So you two are talking again?'

'Hmm?'

'Is that a blush I see before me?'

'Come on, Rosa.'

Kirsty's phone rang. Rosa smiled: 'Saved by the bell.'

Kirsty wandered off to stand beneath DarkAlley's digital clock. A husky voice in her ear: 'This is Mrs Nelson.'

Which meant nothing to Kirsty. 'Who did you want to speak to?'

'I'm Cassie's mum. You phoned me.'

'Oh, Cassie, yes.'

'She's gone away. So you can stop looking for her now.'

'I'm not—'

'I told 'em she'd gone.'

'Told *who* she'd gone?'

'Those men you sent. That was disgusting, you.'

'Ex*cuse* me?'

'She's gone, you hear?'

'Gone where?'

'I'm not telling *you*! You're from that film company, right?'

'Yes, I work for—'

'You sent those heavies round.'

'I did what?'

'Let me tell you something, Miss Rice or whatever your real name is – like I told your men: I don't know where my Cassie is but I'm *glad* she's gone – 'cos she's safe. And I can't tell you where she's gone – 'cos I don't bloody know.'

'Calm down a—'

'She should never have got mixed up with dirty sods like you. So piss off, Miss high and mighty, and *stay away from us*!'

- 24 -

At his senior rank, Inspector Damon Wright should have eaten regular meals, but he had never lost his taste for burgers. Often he would eat them out but when his casebook was overloaded – and when wasn't it? – he would have his secretary bring a burger in. Seated behind his executive desk – office door closed – he would lean back in his chair beside the window and chomp into the swollen hunk of carbohydrate. He liked the relishes. He liked the meat to be on the fat side so he could taste and *feel* its flavour. He liked to fill his mouth with warm chewy food and let droplets of juice seep through his lips. It was like oral sex.

The only drawback was the smell. Onions, relish and the ineradicable aroma of charred meat could hang around his office half the day. He'd leave the window open, spray air freshener, but it wouldn't go. And he hated air freshener. The fact was, he realised, that he enjoyed the burger smell. It was a comfort: he had been fed. Burgers had a warm, fuggy, companionable smell, while some offices in the station smelt of smoke. Cigarettes were banned, officially, but then so was drinking on duty.

What Damon didn't realise was that, like cigarette smoke, the burger smell stuck to his clothes. He could open the window, turn on the fan, waft like Canute against the smell, but it had become a part of him. Pass Damon Wright in the corridor and you knew whether or not he had dined today. Damon didn't know that: he thought his was a secret vice.

As soon as Jennifer Gillett asked if she could come up and speak to him, Wright threw open the window and switched on the fan. He considered reaching into his trash basket and hurling the carton out into the air. But instead he dropped a phone directory across the basket.

She looked harassed, as if she hadn't eaten. Wright suppressed a belch.

Jennifer said, 'The Miller case is falling apart.'

'Thane's speciality.'

'We've lost the witness.'

'*Lost* her?'

'Cassie Nelson has disappeared. Her mother is acting stupid but it's obvious what has happened: she's been scared off.'

'Can't the mother help us?'

'Anything she told us would be hearsay. We need the daughter – she was there.'

'We have her statement.'

'She won't back it up in court.'

Wright stood up behind his desk. This wasn't Gillett's fault. 'We'll find her, Jennifer. Any idea where she might be?'

'I wish. We've no mention of a boyfriend or father.'

'Cassie must have sprung from *someone*'s loins.'

'Her mother's not the type for virgin birth. But they lost contact with the father long ago.'

'Kids sometimes try to track them down.'

'Cassie has not gone looking for her roots, Damon. She's the key witness in a murder case. She knows that.'

Wright walked to his window. It wasn't a great view but it sometimes helped. 'What else do we have on Rick Miller?'

'Not enough to charge him. There's the girl's costume – we can pretty well tie that to Van Cock Films. But so what? It doesn't mean *he* did it. Cassie didn't even name Rick Miller. "Management" is what she said.'

'He's management.'

'Not really – nobody is. There's no such company. It's a brand, owned by the Jolly Miller Group.'

'He owns *that*, I guess?'

Jennifer gave a weary chuckle. 'A closed trust in the Cayman Islands. We're working on it.'

'But it *is* his?'

'I assume so. The trust owns his film company, his internet sites, his trading company. It doesn't mean he killed the girl.'

Wright continued staring out the window. 'Who else is "management"?'

'Officially? We don't know. Unofficially, the word is that *he* runs the trading company, his son Luke the internet side, and the other son Spencer is deeply involved in Van Cock Films.'

'Involved in – means he runs it?'

'Is he 'management'? We don't know. But he's very young. Rick used to run it himself, but he may have gifted it to his son.'

'Why not to his wife? Wasn't she...'

'A princess of cyber-porn?' Jennifer smiled. 'Oh yes. I'm sure the lads downstairs have several films of Rinalda in her prime – that sort of material never gets destroyed. But she went on to found her own company.'

'Ah!'

'In Holland. It's still there, I think. Live sex films, blue cabaret acts. She probably runs a donkey sanctuary too!'

Wright chuckled. 'A Home of Rest for retired studs.'

'Some actresses get worked up about animal rights.'

'They *give* 'em their rights, from what I hear.'

Jennifer had joined him at the window. 'It's easy to laugh at her, but it could be Rinalda who runs the company.'

Damon coughed. 'Of course. It doesn't *have* to be a man.'

'In the porn business men don't always call the shots.'

'Women wear the trousers?'

'Cue for a string of feeble jokes.'

'From a 'stand-up' comedian.'

'But seriously, sir—'

'That's what they all say – but *seriously*, folks!'

'Seriously, sir – what are we going to do about Cassie Nelson?'

'Put out a call. *Find* the girl.'

'She's a witness, not a perp.'

'If the girl obstructs the course of justice—'

'She thinks that if she *helps* it, she'll be dead.'

*

In the closed waters of Turner's Dock the motorboat had looked smart and powerful, but on the river it looked too white, too clean. Although shipping traffic had long since quit the river and the vast old docks had been repopulated by commerce and designer living, the Thames itself was still a working channel, with dredgers and barges, police launches and pleasure cruisers. The water was muddy with estuarial silt, yet riding out on it they smelt an unexpected trace of sea salt. The tide was turning, and opposing currents brought choppy waves and swirling eddies. Gulls shrieked around Tony's boat as he held his spray-soaked course mid-river. Tony liked the spray. He liked to wet his girlfriends in it and today, for the first time in two years, he risked putting an arm around his daughter's waist. She didn't shy away or stiffen, and when she leant closer to him Tony felt an unfamiliar surge of fatherhood.

It was noisy in the boat and he nuzzled her hair before shouting, 'This beats school. Beats everything.'

'Right,' she shouted back. It was not a big speech but her cheeks glistened, her eyes sparkled. She was enjoying this.

'I could teach you how to drive this thing.'

'That'd be good.'

He shouted, 'You could stay at my place a while. Centre of town.'

'Cool.'

'We'd have fun.'

She was watching passing buildings. From down here, practically *in* the water, the river banks looked high and the City buildings towered above them. To slip beneath a bridge was truly scary. After Blackfriars he reduced speed to let them cruise past the moored ships on the north shore beneath Temple skyline.

He didn't have to shout now. 'Emma, I got to ask you something. But if you don't want to talk about it, that's OK.'

'Is that why we're out here?'

He smiled encouragingly but she looked nervous. He said, 'That guy in the film, you know, the one who...'

She stared at the water.

'The one who raped you – then killed that girl. You want me to deal with him?'

She shrugged her childlike shoulders. He battled on: 'I could have him punished.'

'Right.'

They were approaching Waterloo. The bridge looked huge as Tony manoeuvred his little boat beneath it. At the side of the river, a few people stood on the steps and watched – but they weren't watching the boat, they were gazing at the river.

'If I punish him there could be consequences. His dad's a powerful man.'

She sighed. 'So you're saying you should ignore it? OK, that's cool.'

'I didn't say that.'

She stared at the South Bank as if she'd suddenly noticed the Festival Hall.

He asked, 'D'you know where I'd find this Spencer character?'

She glanced at him once, then looked away. 'I could ask.'

'Ask who?'

She shrugged. 'The film company. The director. They're filming today – they're always filming. Coining it in.'

'Do you know where they work?'

*

Kirsty glanced at the walls. Now Marion had gone, Ken's flat looked especially spartan. Brutalist, almost. And Marion *had* gone. No more ballet photos. No vase of freesias. She had appeared on stage, pirouetted and slipped away. Exit right.

Kirsty stood at her ex-lover's shoulder as he logged on and entered Luke Miller's internet theatre. If she thought she'd seen pornography in Neil Garvey's films, these images were beyond pornography – the films, dialogues and one-to-one exchanges were obscene. The sex was violent and triumphalist, the bodies dirty, and the close-ups were so anatomical she was surprised that anyone would be aroused by them at all. Kirsty was repelled. Her stomach tightened.

'Young boys watch this?'

'This is sex to them.'

In practically no sequence did a normal couple have normal sex. They buggered, fisted, had oral sex, squirted sperm and licked it up. They took children, animals and rubber toys. They raped and battered, tortured, cut and killed. Kirsty assumed that what she was watching had been simulated. Some sequences may have been. Some were dreadfully made. But not all: there were acts she found so depraved, so physically extraordinary that she had to force herself to watch.

Ken said, 'You've been viewing for twenty minutes.'

'Have I?'

'For the first few minutes you kept looking away.'

Her face was grim. 'I must be getting used to it.'

'That's what happens.'

Ken began to zap rapidly between sex photos, sex films, live sex, hidden camera sex—

'What's that?'

'You're so naïve, Kirsty.'

The so-called hidden cameras were in shower rooms, locker rooms, bedrooms and lavatories. The most popular camera position seemed to be from inside a lavatory pan looking up. Being splashed on. Golden rain. You could phone to be chatted up, phone to be visited—

'That's an escort service, surely?'

'Not everyone likes Do It Yourself. Look, the site is regionalised – all major cities.'

'You can buy a prostitute on-line?'

'Where better? When you see a card in a public phone box you've no idea *what* you'll get. Here on screen you see her photo, a strip of film. Maybe you've already used the girl as your cyber-slave. Maybe you've already watched her in a video. Now you can buy the girl for real.'

'Look at the prices!'

'Quality does not come cheap.'

Ken explained that it was common for porn stars, male and female, to offer a personal service too. French or straight, front or rear, male or female. Sado-masochist. Animal.

'Kids?'

'Not so easy. You find them mainly in chat rooms – though there *are* sites. Look.'

He showed sites baldly labelled 'under-age', 'kiddieporn', 'barely legal', 'men with animals'. Entry pages were not too revealing. Tiny 'censored' stickers were overlaid on blatantly obscene photos, while other shots were shown thumbnail size: click here for the full-size image.

'Which is where the fun starts. You can see this much without a credit card—'

'So any kid can log on to what we're seeing from his bedroom—'

'Or from hers. Why stop at corrupting *boys*? I'm using this as the opening sequence to my *Sex Is Shopping* film. We'll see an ordinary boy and girl, about eight and ten – could be brother and sister, could be friends – in his bedroom at night, watching the internet. Then we'll see what *they're* watching. We'll follow a series of web links just like this, and maybe we'll forget the kids are watching – until we'll pause on one of those nasty little thumbnails and hear the boy say, 'd*amn*, I *wish* we had a credit card'. Then *she* says, 'I can borrow Mummy's from her bag'. Then we'll see how easy it is to get in.'

Kirsty said, 'I don't want to look at kiddie stuff.'

'Too grown up? Here's one for teenagers.'

'I've seen enough.'

'Really?'

Ken clicked his mouse – and Kirsty hesitated. She found something cloyingly compulsive about the brightly coloured up-front images and their cheerfully coarse text. She watched: it was her job, after all.

Ken had accessed eastendsex.com. The entry screen displayed a selection of photos of different girls. None of the shots were obscene and to Kirsty the pictures seemed reasonably tempting – surely tempting to teenage boys – these were sexy girls, not scary women.

'Choose one,' Ken invited, passing the mouse. 'Pick any one.'

She clicked a photo and it linked immediately to the girl's own personal site. Here the sell was more obvious – three more photos, explicit text, and an invitation to 'make a reservation'.

'That's prostitution.'

Ken stretched lazily in his chair. 'Where's the harm? The customer knows who he's buying and the girl's paid in advance. Everybody's happy.'

'How many sites are a front for prostitution?'

'Who knows – thousands, I expect. There's money there. People get tired of shelling out for dirty pictures on screen. They ask for more. And they can *get* more. Believe me.'

Kirsty stared at the selection of girls on this one page. She pointed to one. 'I recognise her.'

'Oh, she's famous. She's an actress—'

'She can't be a prostitute!'

'It's a con. The site pinched her photo to display it here. When a punter clicks on her he'll either be told she's away just now but here's an excellent alternative, or he'll be sent the alternative anyway. Maybe a look-alike, maybe not. What's he going to do – complain to the authorities?'

'That's mean.'

'She's standing on his doorstep. He's hungry for it. He'll invite her in, like as not. Look at this.'

Two clicks to start a video sequence.

'Meet the world famous Jasmin St Clair – with her notorious party trick.'

The girl on film bent over, gave the camera an 'up you' look, then belched a jet of fire from her backside.

'How on earth?'

'That's a classic sequence.'

'One for the collection.'

Ken nodded as if that kind of collection was a normal thing to own. Perhaps it *was*, she thought – compared to sequences of Asian girls being raped, children sodomised, animals and humans in sexual congress, and the clips she knew that Ken had spared her: mutilations, torture, sado-masochistic blood-bursters, dwarves and cripples misused for sex.

Ken chuckled again at the St Clair sequence. 'She has another where she takes the top off a champagne bottle with her arse. Pop! Exploding foam. The cork shoots right up inside her. I'll find it for you – the clip, I mean – not the cork!'

'Don't bother.'

'They had to send a search party to find it!'

Ken laughed. But Kirsty was sad. 'I suppose I *am* naïve.'

'You keep watching till you hit your own personal shock barrier – but each time you watch, you find your barrier has shifted further on.' He turned to her in his chair. 'It's like when you're a novice learning how to use your PC. At first it's overwhelming, but after a while, when you've got the hang of it, you find *you* can teach the novices. Now it's your turn. You see them fumbling around, not knowing what to do, and you think, God, where has this person *been*?'

Kirsty had left the screen. 'How much of this stuff have you watched?'

'Call of duty, ma'am. But it's harmless. It soon wears off.'

She wandered to his high window, then turned to say, 'Your film isn't going to *say* it's harmless?'

'Of course not. But because we can't show this stuff on terrestrial TV I've prepared an alternative climax. Every sex film needs a climax.'

He grinned wickedly. She said, 'Go on, don't keep a girl waiting.'

'I thought that was what you liked? Right, I'm hacking into their web sites, yeah? I'll bring them down. OK, the sites will be up again within a day, but it'll make good television.'

'Sounds techie.'

'I'll keep it human – I'll be the star.'

She frowned. 'Is this wise?'

'Oh, come *on*. Live a little. I'm going to persuade Rosa to let me do my sequence live – literally live, an insert to the programme when it's on air.'

'But if you show yourself – your face, your name... You're not really going to take down Luke Miller's web sites?'

'His are easiest. He's already let me work on them, so getting in again is a piece of cake.'

'But if you take their sites down, what will the Millers do to *you*?'

- 25 -

Becky found it hard to talk to Melanie as if nothing unusual had happened and as if what they were talking about was normal. Perhaps it was normal for Melanie; perhaps she was used to being beaten up by her boyfriend and sitting in the flat with one eye blackened. Perhaps she was used to her boyfriend coming back unexpectedly, taking a final swipe at her, then scarpering with her TV. Or whoever's TV it was. Whoever's *flat* it was.

Melanie said, 'I'm skint now. I can't hang about.'

'I'm not hanging about.'

'I don't mean *you* – you'd take a job if you could find one. I mean *me*. I got kids to feed.'

'You get money from the Social.'

Melanie sneered – not at Becky but at the pittance from the State. With that black eye, a sneer from Melanie was not a pretty sight. 'We're both on the Social, Becks. I get more than you but I've got kids. They eat it up.'

The little boy looked as if he was eating fluff from the carpet – but it was probably a half-chewed biscuit dropped by his younger sister. Both kids looked reasonably content at present, though how long *that* would last with no TV…

Melanie said, 'That's why I was interested in Gina's proposition.'

Which was the other thing, Becky thought. Melanie was sitting with a black eye, her flat half stripped, two little kids scuffling around the carpet – and she was talking about going on the game.

'We could rent those rooms above the bike shop for a song. *They* don't use them and they're knocking the whole row of shops down soon. That's why they're so cheap.'

'Yes, but would the bike shop let you… You know.'

'It's money, innit? They should care.'

Becky shook her head. 'It's tatty, though. Who'd come there?'

'Blokes don't come to look at your wallpaper! Anyway, it's a good High Street address – we'll call ourselves the Deptford Bikes! Easy to find, too.'

'Easy to ride.'

'Sniff my saddle.'

'Pump my tyre.'

The two girls giggled, and the kids laughed too. They didn't know why, but it was good to see Mummy laughing.

Melanie winced and touched her painful eye. 'That bloody Gary. He made sure I don't forget him. Well, what about it, Becks – d'you want to come in with us?'

'I don't know,' muttered Becky, with a slight smile to show Mel that she wasn't shocked. 'I've not done that sort of thing before.'

'One bloke is like another.'

'Hmm.'

'It's not as if you've got a regular boyfriend, is it?'

'Thanks.'

Melanie smiled and grabbed Becky's hand. '*I've* not done it before neither. But I reckon it'll be just like when I made them films: it seemed odd before I done them, but once I started there was nothing to it.'

'I don't know.'

'The advantage of this is you get paid immediate. They walk in the door and the first thing happens is they pay you – cash.'

'Well, my card's been stopped...'

'Exactly. Look, I don't want to press you into this.'

'I've still got these last six lottery tickets—'

'No, Becky, no. It's them lottery tickets as got you into this mess—'

'Them and the betting shop.'

'Gambling's a mug's game.'

Becky shrugged. Melanie still held her hand. 'It don't mean you have to do what *I'm* doing. Me and Gina, well, we're kind of used to it.'

'Gina maybe. She always was a tart.'

'No, be fair – I did the films, Becky. Fucking some guy I never met for a couple of hundred quid. Where's the difference? It's still sex for money.'

'Films pay more.'

'But you only do one film a day. Some days. This you can do every day.'

Becky shuddered.

'Well, every day you *feel* like it. Be your own boss.'

Becky nodded reluctantly. 'But who will organise us?'

'We will.'

'Oh great. Come on, Mel – there's the shop and rent, and there's furniture and advertising and… looking after ourselves. We'd need a man for that.'

'Why? Furniture is just curtains and a bed. Gina's got a spare, and we can scrounge another bed off the Furniture Project.'

'That's for the homeless!'

'If you're homeless you don't *want* furniture. Stands to reason. No, we'll take it; we're entitled. We'll shift our beds out to the shop, then go down the Project and say we've got nothing to sleep on. They'll give us one – they've got dozens. No one wants their second hand beds.'

'What about advertising?'

'We'll put cards in phone boxes. They're cheap to print.'

'And rent?'

'We only need some key money.'

'Where's that coming from?'

Mel studied her. 'Me and Gina saw the landlord.'

'Obviously.'

'He'll take payment in kind.'

- 26 -

The hospital ward is quiet. From the night sky glimpsed through the windows a blue light floods the room. Beds are lined either side beneath the dark windows and in each neatly-made bed a man lies sleeping. At the end of the ward, in the corridor between the beds, the double doors swing open. A nurse enters. She is a good-looking woman but her hair is up beneath her cap and her normally voluptuous form is trapped inside her uniform, which is immaculate. Glancing briefly to either side, the nurse begins slowly down the ward. Her high-heeled but sensible shoes clack along the floor. She carries a clipboard and as she walks she taps a pencil against her teeth.

When she is about a third of the way down the ward there is a movement behind her, but she doesn't notice. From the farthest beds – the first she walked past – two men slip silently from beneath the blankets and step out into the corridor. They wear striped pyjamas. Their feet are bare. Almost immediately, two men slip from the next beds along. Four men now trail the nurse down the ward. She pauses, frowns prettily, but carries on. When the next two men slip out, only one wears striped pyjamas. The other, a tall and well-built black man, is naked. He leads the pack as they close in on her. She stops again, and this time surely must hear their shuffling feet – because she turns warily to find herself confronted by six gleefully determined men, one of them naked, and that man's member is like a lance.

Frightened, the nurse turns away from them. She takes one step, but before she can start to run she realises that her way ahead is blocked. Other men have climbed out of bed. Surrounded by these men she begins to panic. But they are on to her. She screams now, but they are laughing. Taunting. They pull at her clothes. One man wraps his hand across her mouth. The group bustle her from the corridor into a space between two beds. The ward is full of noise – men laughing, calling, the nurse occasionally letting out a yelp. Her cap is off, and her long blonde hair is streaming free. Her blouse has been ripped open and she is wearing a surprisingly sexy bra. Someone is clutching at her waistband and suddenly, as if fixed by Velcro, the skirt falls away, leaving the nurse clad from the waist down in black g-string panties and stockings – not tights – black shapely stockings held taut on her young legs by the skimpiest of suspender belts.

Her blouse is ripped away – and now, feebly protected by sexy underclothes, the nurse tries to laugh the young men out of it. She pretends to share the joke: 'No, boys, stop it. No, boys, please!'

But a man has unclipped her brassiere, and once those large breasts have bounced into view, there is no way these men will stop. She pleads with them ineffectively: 'Oh, don't. Don't hurt me, boys!'

The black man is on his knees before her, sliding her stockings down her legs. She tries to kick against him but that only helps her stockings come off. The man's black hands clasp her g-string panties and pull them down.

She is naked, and for a moment the men in front of her move aside. She is held arms akimbo, a white man at each arm till she is exposed to every watcher. With hearty laughs the men drag her backwards onto the bed. Her legs kick, but two men grab them and pull those legs apart. Then the naked black man steps between the nurse's lovely legs, leans forward, tugs her forward to adjust her position on the bed. To a universal sigh from the other patients, he plunges into her. She cries aloud.

As the director cries, 'Cut!'

*

Gordon was immediately on his feet. 'Ten minutes tea break, boys and girls, then the gangbangs from boy thirteen.'

He looked at his watch. Only a little behind schedule: he should still be able to finish today. How awkward these gangbangs were! Not for the woman, he thought – she only had to lie there – but men were disadvantaged by the lack of foreplay; they had to stand around waiting their turn until suddenly, just as if they'd been waiting offstage at an audition, they had to step into the limelight and perform. One or two men always went limp. Gordon's usual remedy was to have one of the girls effect a timely oral but if that didn't work he'd have the next man jump the queue. This was the trouble with amateurs: they weren't used to it. Gordon thought that for most heterosexual men the chance of free sex with an attractive woman should arouse them, but it was surprising what delicate flowers they could be. Gordon had to live with it: for gangbang scenes Van Cock preferred to use amateurs because they were cheaper than professionals. Most of these men, plucked from a pub or the community service scheme, weren't paid at all. They took part solely for the sex. Yet when their moment came they were not up to it.

Susie Souxx could take two dozen grinding amateurs lying down. A professional. Nevertheless, Gordon made the day as easy for her as he could: several tea breaks, no more than six men at a time, and for today's film he'd hit upon the idea of breaking up the endless gangbang by filming half the encounters first, then pausing to film the less exhausting opening sequence. After tea, Gordon would shoot another half dozen encounters, break again to shoot the closing sequence – men back in bed, the nurse agreeing she wouldn't tell if they didn't ('You naughty boys!') – and then he would close the day with the final half dozen gangbangs.

Straightforward. Or it should have been. Except, he noticed, something had disturbed their precious tea break. He looked up from his notes to see intruders on set. It happened sometimes, because Van Cock wouldn't pay for security.

Four men strode across to him. Presumably one of the cast had pointed him out. Gordon drew himself to his feet. 'Did you want something? We're working. If you'd like to come back at—'

Wham! One of the men thumped him in the face. Gordon felt the shock more than the pain. He sat on the floor, rubbed his jaw, and wondered how on *earth* he'd landed there.

The man dragged him to his feet. Gordon raised his arms to shield his head. He glanced beyond the man to his large cast of lustful actors. Two dozen sturdy young men. Who backed away from him.

Between Gordon and his cast stood three intruders, their backs to Gordon as they dared his actors to intrude. The fourth shouted in Gordon's ear: 'Where's Spencer?'

'Who?'

Smack. 'Spence Miller. You heard me. Is he here?'

'No.' His head rang.

'You're lying.'

As the man dragged Gordon to a small table at the corner of the studio he heard the cast and technicians being swept away. Wouldn't *anybody* help him?

'Dirty little film, this.'

'Why are you here?'

'You should be grateful, mate – we waited till the scene ended. Where's Spencer?'

'I don't know—'

Whack. 'Where's he now?'

'I *don't* know.'

'Phone him up.' The man pushed a phone into his hand. 'Phone him.'

Gordon shot a glance across the makeshift studio. Everyone had crowded into the far corner, and one of the intruders was now crossing the floor towards them.

'I don't know Spencer's number—'

'He's your *boss*, fuckhead.'

'But… Oh, my God.'

The new man said, 'Don't piss about.'

'What d'you want with Spencer?'

The first man, ominously close, stared at Gordon incredulously. Without warning, his head shot forward and cracked against Gordon's nose. The pain was unbelievable. Gordon reeled back, clutching his face, blood streaming between his fingers. The small table tumbled to the ground. The man grabbed Gordon's collar. 'Give me the number!'

Gordon gasped, jabbered and told him.

The other man keyed it in but didn't press the Call button. He stood the table upright and placed the phone on it. 'Give me your hand.'

Gordon stared as if he were deaf. As if the man spoke a foreign language. And when the man saw he'd not been understood he seized Gordon's hand and dragged it down onto the table. Gordon was aware only that his face was a ball of pain. He barely noticed as the man changed his grip and transferred his hold to Gordon's wrist. He only began to realise – his brain reacting slowly – when the first man placed the point of a flooring nail against his hand. The man had a hammer. Gordon suddenly flinched. Tried to pull away. But the metal hammer came thumping down.

In pain already, Gordon screamed before the shock-wave hit. The two men held his hand down. The hammer flashed again, driving the four-inch nail further through his flesh, deeper into the table, and Gordon saw his hand pinned against the wood like a grotesque medical specimen. He continued screaming. The man shouted in his ear.

The other man took the phone some paces away. Gordon's shrieks had fallen into a dreadful rhythm synchronised with each outgoing breath. The man made his call.

'Spencer? Sorry about the noise, but we've got Gordon for you. He's a bit excited.'

The man smiled grimly and began walking around the table, speaking into the phone. 'We're at the studio. Gordon wants you to come down here. Tell him, Gordon.'

The man offered the phone but Gordon, huddled across his pinioned hand and screaming with each breath, made no move to take it.

So the man said, 'Get down here, Spencer.'

Gordon felt himself nudged heavily by the one with the hammer: 'Take the bloody phone or I'll bash another nail through your hand.'

To demonstrate his point the man tapped against the floor-nail. 'I'll bend it over, so you'll *never* pull it out.' He tapped again.

Gordon tried to blink away his tears. Blood had spread across his hand. Blood from his face dripped onto the table. Blood was in his eyes. He gave one sad rasping breath and reached with his free hand for the phone.

He heard Spencer's voice. Spencer asking something. Spencer demanding. Gordon yelled, 'Get down here quickly, Spencer! *Please*, they're hurting me.'

'Who is? What's going on, bro?'

'Spencer! They've nailed my hand to the *table*.'

'Who's done *what*?'

Gordon stared wildly at his assailants and asked, 'Who *are* you?'

'Tell him you're speaking to Tony Iles.'

Gordon repeated the name into the phone. When he heard Spencer's reply he began to sob. 'Please, Spencer. Please. *You* tell him.'

He offered the phone to Iles, who took it and barked, 'You coming, Spencer? You know who I am.'

'Go fuck your daughter,' Spencer jeered as he cut the call.

Reel Five:

INTIMACY

- 27 -

Two TVRs stood cooling in the ground floor car park – Spencer's acid yellow outshining Luke's gun-metal blue. Rick's Merc was there, stone cold, beside Rinalda's Lotus and Herbie's beat-up van. There was also Cornell's Mazda Sport, standing apart.

He and three other black men were one floor up, on the printing floor. They'd been there less than half an hour and were just about remaining interested. Two of the gangstas stood by the window at the rear, Cornell and the other man at the front. One at the rear spoke: 'We staying here all evening? I need a chair.'

'You don't be going to sleep now, man.'

Their voices echoed.

'Shit. Nothing gonna happen.'

'I want to be a sentry I work down Whitehall.'

'Your face under a busby helmet? I *like* it!'

'Who is this man we look for, anyway?'

'Big Tony Iles.'

'White trash.'

'Hey, Cornell?'

'Yo?'

'This a serious mother warfare 'tween Rick and Tony Iles?'

'Go for it, bro.'

'We all think we on the winning side?'

Cornell preferred not to answer that directly. 'Won't come to nothing. It's bluster, man. We stand around like motherfucking heroes, they think we indispensable.'

'Whoa! Shit, man. Indie – what you say?'

'Cool it, brother. This look to be a long cold night.'

*

Upstairs on the top floor the atmosphere was less laid back. Arranged around the pastel living room were Rick and Rinalda in enormous armchairs, Luke on a dining chair turned back to front, and Spencer stretched full-length on his step-mother's settee. He was finishing his recap for the sake of Luke who had just come in: 'Table didn't weigh nothing anyway. Gordon could have picked it up and *carried* it home.'

Rinalda shuddered. 'Did *you* pull the nail out, darling?'

'No, someone in the cast. It was all done by the time I got there. Everyone had drifted home, 'cos Gordon said he was too upset to finish filming. This will cost me money, you know?'

Luke asked, 'How quickly did you get there?'

'Well, I didn't go straight away, bro! Could have been a trap. Hell, it *was* a trap. They *called* me there.'

'Exactly. Tony Iles called you – and you refused.'

Rick interrupted before they took off: 'What would *you* have done, Luke – walked in to face a man who wants to kill you? Stop carping, and *help* your brother.'

'It's not *my* affair.'

Rick jumped out of his armchair. 'This is family.'

Luke straightened from the seat-back but did not stand up. 'Did Spencer think of family when he killed that damn reporter?'

Spencer sat up on the settee: 'Fuck the reporter.'

'No, Spencer, you fucked the *actress*. You *killed* the reporter.'

As Spencer shambled to his feet Rinalda shrieked, 'Spencer!'

Rick said, 'Sit down.'

Spencer slumped back on the settee.

Luke scratched his ear. 'I'm just pointing out that the police have questioned Dad, reporters came after *me* – but Spence lies on the sofa and goes to sleep.'

'We deal with this as family,' Rick said. 'United.' He glared at his two sons, then sat back down. 'The cops are going through the motions and the reporters are out of their depth. But Tony Iles… This was a marker he set down.'

'To show he's serious,' Luke agreed.

Rinalda said, 'Let your *father* speak.'

Rick turned to Spencer: 'On the film set this afternoon, how long did Iles wait?'

'Fifteen, twenty minutes? He didn't expect me to go down there.'

'Then he left?' Luke queried. 'He didn't phone again?'

Spencer grunted.

'Well, did he?'

'Leave Spence alone,' pleaded Rinalda. 'He has Tony Iles attacking him already. He doesn't need you to join in.'

'I can deal with Iles,' said Spencer.

Luke laughed. Spencer stared at him, a hurt expression on his big face. 'What? Iles thinks he's tough because he puts a nail through Gordon's hand? I'll show him tough. And it won't be his hand—'

'Grow up, Spencer.' This was Rick. 'Iles isn't one of your dress tough, talk tough gangsta boys. This guy *is* tough.'

Luke looked up. 'You know why he put a nail through Gordon's hand?'

Spencer cut him off: 'Yeah, we got the message – Gordon gets it through the hand; I'll get it through the dick.'

'And then he'll kill you,' Rick continued. 'That's what he said.'

'Man's got to catch me first,' sneered Spencer. He saw their faces. 'What is this – we sit here shaking? That's what he wants.' Spencer plonked his heavy feet onto the floor. 'OK, *you* sit here – it's my battle. I'll get my—'

'You won't!' snapped Rick. 'You'll keep your head down.'

'Ha!'

Rinalda jumped in: 'Spencer, darling, heroes get killed every day. It's best, I think, if you take a holiday. Let this blow over.'

'It won't.'

'Go to Amsterdam,' she insisted. 'Let your father deal with Iles.'

'It's *my* problem—'

'Rinalda's right,' said Rick. 'If Iles sees you, it'll only be to say Goodbye. But I can talk to him. I already did.'

'To say what – hello, goodbye? Some conversation.'

'I'll cut a deal—'

'A deal!'

'What's your alternative? Iles said in *public* that he wants you dead. He can't back down from that – unless I offer him something else.'

'I'll tell you what – I'll marry his daughter!' Spencer laughed. 'A shotgun wedding. What is she – fourteen? She can't be that bad looking – I wouldn't have screwed her else!'

'Spencer!' exclaimed Rinalda.

'No, no, I'm serious. Dad, listen – you tell Iles I'll marry his precious daughter, make an honest woman of her – when she's eighteen, say. Even twenty-one. That gives us several years while everyone forgets all about it. Better still, we *don't* forget it: I marry this chick, whoever she is, and our two families get united. An arranged marriage. Like aristocracy.'

'Are you from planet Earth?' Luke asked.

Rick said, 'Spencer, you'd better disappear—'

'Speak to Iles, Dad – he can fix that for me!'

'No, go to Holland, to Rinalda's family – go to America, whatever. Meanwhile, I'll find something to offer Iles—'

'Some*one* else. How about Gordon? Iles already took his hand in marriage!'

'Shut up,' Rick snapped. 'This isn't just you, Spencer – the whole damn family is involved. And while we clear the shit you left we do not need you sniggering and making jokes.'

'We *could* give him someone else,' Spencer insisted. 'I never met this Tony Iles. He wouldn't know me from Luke. – Hey, there's an idea! Give him Luke.'

'One more word,' warned Rick. 'And I'll save Iles the trouble. I'll *present* you to him.'

Spencer rolled his eyes. Luke said, 'Don't forget the police are sniffing too. A small matter but—'

Spencer clutched his head. 'Oh, now I'm *really* worried! The police. Do me a favour, Luke – they're busy giving parking tickets.'

'You weren't at the pig station,' Rick pointed out. '*I* was.'

'Because they thought you was me!'

'They've got a witness—'

'Not now they haven't.'

'You may have frightened one away—'

'I frightened all of them.'

'But one squawked.'

'And now she's vanished.'

Rick sat forward in his armchair. 'You kill her?'

'What am I – some kind of nutter?'

'No comment,' Luke said.

'Belt up.' Spence stretched again on the settee. 'Cassie Nelson has gone on holiday – like Dad is suggesting *I* should. Maybe I'll go find her – Ibiza maybe.'

Rick asked, 'You *know* where she is?'

'Oh, I'd *let* her go? Of course I don't know. The cops don't know either – that's the main thing.'

'She could turn up.'

'She won't.'

'What about this DarkAlley mob?'

'What do *they* know?'

'You tell me.'

*

The telephone: a hundred years ago it was a novelty in black ebonite. It stood like a candlestick in the draughty hall: mouthpiece and microphone at the top, earpiece – or receiver – hanging down. Lifting the receiver automatically cut the call bell and connected the mike and receiver to the line. Houses were linked to their local exchange by copper wires, hung overhead in rural areas and underground in towns. Individual wires were separated by wrappings of paper and enclosed in a lead tube inside an earthenware pipe, and each householder's individual line finished at the exchange at its own numbered jack or spring. Jacks were arranged in rows on a board, two hundred to a group, subscribers to the same exchange physically connected by a flexible wire between their jacks. Subscribers at different exchanges were connected by a trunk wire linked to each exchange. Callers would lift the receiver from its hook and *speak* to the operator, asking to be connected to the required number. Only if that line was not in use would the operator insert a calling peg into the recipient's switch spring and use the magneto generator to ring their bell. The internet had not been dreamt of. Neither had mobile phones. The fixed telephone in the hall was a servant that knew its place, while today's mobile is a search engine to track you down.

Wherever you are.

'In the office?'

Kirsty wasn't: 'Who's that?'

'Luke Miller.'

She propped herself upright in Ken's bed.

Luke continued: 'Am I interrupting something?'

She glanced at Ken, no longer asleep but—

'I'm not doing anything.'

Ken purred, 'Not wearing anything either.' He wanted to register his presence.

Luke said, 'If you're in the middle of something—'

'I'm finished.'

'You should get out of the office more, Kirsty. Get a life.'

'You're concerned for my *health*?'

'Look Kirsty, I'm sorry about yesterday.'

'When you gave me that physical examination?'

'I was hoping you'd forgotten.'

'It's not something that happens to me every day.'

'Even *my* days are not that exciting.'

'Lovely to chat with you. *But?*'

'I'd like to meet again. To make amends.'

'Got the *feel* for it, have you? I'm busy this year.'

'Then it'll have to be this evening. Dinner somewhere?'

'I'm busy tonight.'

Ken joined in: 'Absolutely.' He was awake now and smiling pleasantly as he tried to work out who was on the phone.

'What kind of food do you like?'

'Expensive.'

'I can do that.'

'A table for three.' She paused but Luke didn't answer. 'You, me and Ken.'

'So you're more than colleagues?'

'He's my back-up.'

'Yes, he got my back up too.'

'Three seats.'

Ken prodded her and shook his head.

Luke said, 'You and your lap dog – fine, your every wish. Shall I collect you from the office or would you prefer to pop home first and change?'

'Won't they let me in this restaurant without a tie?'

'Where *do* you live?'

She snorted.

'OK, I'll collect you from the office. I know where *that* is.'

'I'll meet you at the restaurant. Which one?'

'Rules, Maiden Lane. Eight o'clock.'

'For three of us.'

'Two and a doggie bowl.' He rang off.

Ken nuzzled her bare back and ran a proprietorial hand beneath her arm. 'Your friend Luke Miller,' she told him.

'He threw us out.'

'Now he's inviting us back in.'

'That's unfortunate.'

'Free meal.' She placed her hand on *his* hand and held it against her breast.

Ken said, 'Best not to go. He's dangerous.'

'In a restaurant?'

'He's from a criminal family.'

She turned her head. Their faces touched. 'This is our job, Ken.'

'You shouldn't go.'

'You want to keep him for yourself?'

Ken dipped his head. 'I can't make it.'

She sat upright. 'I thought we were spending the night together?'

'Did I say that?'

'So what was this – afternoon delight? Nice to see you again but I must fly?'

'I've something on.'

'No, you're naked.' She slipped out of bed and faced him. 'So give me the naked truth.' Her lip trembled as she tried to smile.

'I made arrangements.'

'When?'

'This morning.'

'You were with *me* this morning.'

'Before that.'

He sat up. As the sheet fell away his bare chest looked immaculate. 'I'm sorry, Kirsty.' He blew out his cheeks. 'But Marion rang.'

*

Becky looked at the faded decoration. 'Give it a spot of paint, you could make a decent flat of this.'

'We're not "decent", Becks.'

The rooms above the bike shop had been kicked around through several uses. One room held stock for the shop below, another had been a store room, the other two rooms looked as if decades ago they'd been children's bedrooms: one was papered in whirligigs and swings, the other with farmyard animals.

'Three coats of paint,' Becky decided.

'And keep the lights low,' Mel agreed.

There was a stained and seedy bathroom, shared with the downstairs shop, but at least the taps worked. A small heater produced scalding water, and the lavatory flushed and refilled efficiently, if noisily. The rooms were carpeted in shabby dust-coloured cord.

'All electric,' Mel pointed out.

'Five hundred a month,' said Becky gloomily.

'He thinks we'll make a fortune.'

'I can't afford five hundred quid.'

Mel was pacing the room as if measuring for a refit. 'There's three of us, times four weeks – that comes to only forty-two pounds a week. You'll get that from one trick, Becks.'

'Plus expenses.'

'Four hundred quid should do this up. Then we must think about printing and accessories – say two hundred each to start us.'

'I'm broke.'

Mel gazed appraisingly. 'D'you want to stay broke? Gina says she'll sub us, and we can pay her back in a couple of weeks. Look Becks, a trick a day, you've covered expenses. Two tricks a day and you're earning two hundred quid a week. Gina says four tricks a day is hardly difficult.'

'Is Gina, like, the boss?'

'We're a co-operative. She just isn't as broke as we are.'

'How will men, you know, come for business – they queue on the stairs or what?'

Mel laughed. 'I wish! Queuing. You won't even get a trick an hour. But they can make an appointment. We'll keep an appointments diary.'

'A diary!'

'An appointment book, my dear!'

'How will they phone us?'

'On our mobiles, silly.'

'But mine's... you know, they closed it down.'

Mel shook her head. 'What did you do – bet it on a horse? You can share mine. Look, seriously, by the time a man phones he doesn't want an appointment. It's get straight round here, mister, and pull your trousers down. In, out, thank you very much. And next one, please.'

'Like on the buses.'

'That's the ticket. Sorry sir, this one's full, but there'll be another one along in just a minute.'

'Hold very tight, sir. Away we go.'

*

On the north side of the Strand the theatres, pubs and shops back on to the much quieter Maiden Lane, which is a cut-through from Trafalgar Square to Covent Garden. Rules has been there since the late eighteenth century – a dark, old-fashioned restaurant with prints and playbills that merge into historic wallpaper.

'You're too young for this place,' Kirsty said. They had ascended the old Georgian stairs and taken their seats at a small table where it seemed likely that ghosts would sit alongside.

'My father's favourite.'

'You or the restaurant?'

Luke blinked. 'Sore point.' He straightened his napkin. 'So Ken won't be joining us?'

'He's unpredictable.'

Luke smiled. 'I suppose I should say I'm sorry.'

'To miss him?'

'About yesterday.' He leant forward. The dark atmosphere encouraged intimacy. 'We could *both* apologise.'

'And forget about what happened?'

Luke shook his head. 'It's one moment I won't forget.'

He smiled wickedly across the table, daring her to pretend outrage and storm out in a huff. If she didn't leave now she never would.

'I'm too hungry to take offence.'

Luke handed her the menu. 'So that's apologies for two, and what would you like with the main course?'

'Don't we get a starter?'

She gave a half smile. He was easy to talk to and, although it might have been the subdued light, he seemed surprisingly good looking. Time slipped away. By after-dinner coffee they were murmuring to each other like childhood friends. The restaurant was full – quiet, warm and cosy. Each table was sheltered from its neighbour. In here, Londoners had gossiped and intrigued for two hundred years.

'So,' she said, glancing around the room. 'You come here with your father?'

'Sometimes.'

'And Spencer?'

Luke picked up his coffee and inhaled its aroma as if trying to place the mountain its beans had grown on. 'D'you really believe my brother had any connection with her death? Is that what Cassie told you?'

'It was 'management', she said. Spencer is management. How do you know what Cassie told me?'

'The police say she's a witness.'

'Can't be the only one.'

'The only one who spoke to *them*. That makes her vulnerable, of course.'

'I know. You've already tried to silence her.'

'Me?'

'You sent men to her house – but she'd gone, hadn't she?'

Luke moved his coffee cup on its saucer. He looked regretful. 'I'm sorry you think I have anything to do with this.'

'Meaning it was Spencer on his own?'

'You're fixated on Spencer. Cassie said it was 'management'?'

'She said Zoë was killed by whoever manages the film company – that's your brother. Whoever sent his men round to silence her – that's your brother. Whoever asked *you* to sweet-talk me over dinner.'

Luke showed empty hands. 'You think we're all villains, don't you?'

'Guess.'

He sighed. 'My brother makes mucky films. I run sex sites on the internet. Am I being honest enough now? If you think those things are villainous, then yes, we are guilty – but we're not *murderers*, Kirsty. I'm puzzled as to why you think we are. Is that what Zoë claimed in her film?'

'*Wouldn't* you like to know?'

'What *did* she say?'

'You know already – you or your brother kept her last film.'

'We didn't kill her, Kirsty.'

She finished her coffee. 'You invited me here to tell me that?'

He smiled. 'Not really. To be honest, Kirsty, you're an attractive girl—'

'Drop it, Luke.'

'And I behaved disgracefully.'

'Your *brother* behaved disgracefully.'

'Did Cassie *name* Spence?'

Kirsty pushed her chair back. 'Cassie's in trouble, isn't she?'

'Perhaps she really did see someone kill Zoë, or perhaps... I know you're dubious, Kirsty, but it wasn't my brother, it wasn't me, and like you, we'd like to find out who it was.'

She smiled incredulously. 'And you'd particularly like to speak to Cassie?'

He smiled back. 'You know where she is.'

'You think I'll tell you – if you're nice? Failing that, I suppose you'll send your brother round to persuade me?'

'Are all journalists so cynical?'

'Come on, Luke, you choose the most respectable and reassuring restaurant in London, you play the nice guy all through the meal. This isn't you. What happens next – you offer me money?'

'You wouldn't take it – would you?'

'No.'

'Cassie did. I suppose DarkAlley paid her?'

'DarkAlley? We make documentaries, Luke.'

'And you don't pay people? She was helping you.'

'You're clutching at straws.'

'More coffee?' She didn't answer but he poured some anyway. Kirsty brought her chair back in to the table. He said, 'Cassie helped Zoë with her assignment – she got her the job, for God's sake, pretending Zoë was an actress. Now, why would Cassie do that? She's a so-called model turned so-called actress. She does sex for money. So why did she help Zoë sneak into that film? For money. Cassie is a girl that money can buy.'

'You have a high opinion of your staff.'

For the first time Luke looked irritated. 'They're not *my* staff, not even my brother's staff. She's freelance.' Then he chuckled. 'Oh Kirsty, you have such a low opinion of me that I hardly dare say this.'

'I'm sure you will.'

'Cassie claims she saw what happened.' He raised his hands again. 'No, let's believe her. But if she did see something, and if she did tell the police, she's in mortal danger, Kirsty. Whoever killed Zoë will have to silence Cassie.'

She nodded pointedly. 'She's got that message.'

'Now, my brother is no angel—'

'I've heard.'

'But he can protect her—'

Kirsty laughed. 'Oh, right! Come into my parlour, said the spider to the fly.'

Luke leant forward. He *looked* convincing. 'Spencer wants Cassie alive. She can clear his name.'

'Good try, Luke.'

'He can give her a place to hide—'
'Six feet down—'
'And he'll pay her, of course, to cover expenses.'
'To cover his backside.'
'Ten thousand pounds.'
Kirsty shrugged. 'Sounds cheap, to save his life.'
'He could have her *killed* for less.'
'If he could find her.'
Luke watched her. 'So, you think ten thousand is not enough?'
'She isn't doing this for money.'
'I beg to differ.' He reached out his hand. Kirsty withdrew hers from the table. Luke said, 'Cassie does everything for money.'

The cosiness had ebbed away. There must be a moment like this, thought Kirsty, at many a business meal: the eating and drinking done, the small talk brushed aside, a sudden switch to negotiation. Now's the time, she thought, over a sobering coffee in a darkened restaurant, when we agree the contract.

'What you're saying,' she said carefully, 'is that you and I are negotiators. Cassie can have Spencer's protection if she lets you buy her silence.'

She stood up. Luke stood up also – calmly, as if they were any other couple at the end of a delightful meal. 'Will you ask her?'

'Ten thousand pounds?'
'And guaranteed protection.'
'I'll pass the message on.'
She turned – but he called, 'Kirsty,' softly. 'When can you let us know?'

She was acting now. 'Two or three days.'

'Tomorrow would be better.' He walked round the table. 'One further thought.' He paused, then smiled. 'Since you find it so hard to trust us, how would you like to meet the rest of my family?'

Kirsty laughed as she ran downstairs.

- 28 -

'I'm having lunch today with the man who killed Zoë.'

It was a cheap shock but Kirsty enjoyed the effect. She was with Ken and Rosa in the DarkAlley offices discussing work outstanding.

Rosa said, 'There's no answer to that.'

Ken looked irritated. 'You had dinner with Luke last night.'

'Luke Miller?' asked Rosa.

Kirsty nodded. 'And today I meet the rest of the Miller family.'

'Is this safe?'

'Safe as houses in an earthquake zone.'

'No way,' spluttered Ken. 'Absolutely no way.'

The two women ignored him. Rosa said, 'Presumably you're having lunch with the man who *might* have killed Zoë?'

'Cassie Nelson told me he did – but his brother Luke says he didn't. In fact, he'll pay Cassie ten thousand pounds if she'll testify that he didn't.'

'Sounds like he did,' said Rosa. 'Are you going wired?'

Kirsty chuckled. 'No, they're wise to that. And this time I won't have Ken there to protect me.'

Rosa frowned. Ken said, 'Come on, there was nothing I could do.'

Kirsty smiled at Rosa. 'They're a very touchy-feely family.'

Rosa said, 'I think I'm missing something.'

'Private joke.'

'As in funny?'

'As in, Ken, why don't you tell Rosa?'

Rosa glanced at them. 'We were a happy team once. Yesterday I thought you two were back together.' She got no reaction. 'OK, it's not my affair.' She turned back to Kirsty: 'No hidden mike, then?'

'You'll know where I am.'

Ken looked exasperated. 'Look, I know I'm the bad guy here—'

'*They're* the bad guys.'

Ken appealed to Rosa: 'You can't allow this. If the Millers did kill Zoë, what'll they do to Kirsty?'

Rosa glanced at her: 'It isn't worth it.'

'Zoë's death isn't *worth* it?'

Ken leapt in: 'Oh, high ground, high moral ground! Rosa's right, Kirsty – leave the police to sort this.'

'You'll both know where I am. And the Millers will know you know. So I'm perfectly safe.'

'Do you have time for this?' asked Rosa, drawing breath. 'Half a day talking to villains who know you're a journalist, and a deadline staring you in the face?'

'Deadline, breadline. —Yes, Janine?'

The girl looked as pale as when she'd first heard about Zoë's death. Perhaps she was scared to interrupt. 'Excuse me, Kirsty – there was a message on the phone? Cassie Nelson? She said don't try to find her. She's in hiding, she said, because the people who came the first time came back and tried to kill her last night.'

*

Ten minutes walk. According to Luke, the Miller family lived ten minutes' walk from the Victoria offices of DarkAlley Films – in Westminster, he'd said, a quiet lane behind Tate Britain. It was a route Kirsty had taken before on foot. She enjoyed the Tate, and had eaten several times in its crowded but lively basement. She preferred the old Tate to the more startling Tate Modern across the river. Since that had opened the old Tate seemed less crowded but more stimulating. It's paintings, even the modern ones, seemed classics from the past, a civilised inheritance. Even the streets she took to get there were familiar: Greycoat, Marsham, John Islip Street. She had walked them all before. She must have passed the Miller's very door.

Their house was one of a line of three-storey Georgian houses which could turn out to be anything from a fine central family residence to a small embassy or spy nest. People did live around here – there was a children's playground, an estate and Millbank School – but how much did this property cost? Flats on the estate might not be too expensive but to afford a house such as this, one would have to be seriously well off: a banker perhaps, an international businessman. An emperor of porn.

The green door was opened by a uniformed maid. Well, of course, thought Kirsty: seriously well off. An emperor of porn? The maid was classically dressed – black frock, white frilly apron – and it wasn't till Kirsty had stepped inside that she asked herself when she had ever met a maid in uniform in real life. Was this real life?

The maid left her a few minutes in a tiny room on the ground floor, a box room, a panelled cupboard, a room where guests were sat to wait. Small tasteful landscapes. Two dark wooden chairs. A coffee table.

Luke Miller eventually appeared. 'You don't mind eating in?'

Following him up the stairs she admired the half panelling, the sumptuous wallpaper, the soft carpet. Luke opened a door.

The living room was small. As in many Georgian houses, all the rooms were small. But plentiful. This room led to another, from which Kirsty could hear people talking.

Luke said, 'I'm afraid we've already started. I didn't think you'd come.'

'My boss said I *shouldn't*.'

But they were already in the dining room. Small again. Dominated by a gleaming dark wood table and old matching chairs. Two people rose when she came in. The man must be Luke's father – shorter, stockier, with greying hair – a man at ease with himself. Then she realised that she had seen the man before – in the police station, with Inspector Gillett. Yes, of course – Rick Miller. Beside him was a woman who, to Kirsty, looked extraordinary: in her forties perhaps, with vivid blonde hair, strikingly good looking in a handsome and ravaged way.

Luke introduced them as his Mum and Dad. If this is his mother, Kirsty thought, she must have married very young.

The woman said, 'Please excuse us for starting without you. Luke insisted you wouldn't come. He is such a pessimist.'

The woman had a faint foreign accent. Kirsty sat down and smiled at them. Smiles all round.

'Let me help you,' said Rick's father, ladling food onto her plate with a waiter's expertise. He had an accent too – but a London one, half tamed.

'Couldn't Spencer make it?' Kirsty asked. 'I thought he'd be the main course.'

'He's abroad,' purred Mrs Miller.

'Yeah, we know you want to see him,' added her husband. 'But at least the pair of you won't start arguing over lunch!'

The Millers laughed. It cleared the air.

Kirsty nodded at the wall. 'Exciting pictures. Downstairs were tasteful, but...'

'This is where we *live*,' laughed Mrs Miller.

The three 'exciting' pictures were French *déshabille* etchings in which wisps of underwear failed to cover private parts. Two pictures were of a woman in her bedroom. In the third she had been joined by a man – was about to be joined *with* the man. Who did not wear wisps of underwear.

'That's enough food for me, Mr Miller.'

'Call me Rick. You're family here.'

'So soon?' She heard herself sounding nervous.

'Luke brought you.'

'And you must call me Rinalda.' Luke's mother pronounced the 'R' with brilliant sexy clarity. 'You're not married, Kirsty?'

'No, I'm fancy free.' But pregnant, Kirsty thought.

Luke poured some wine. 'Kirsty is beautiful, intelligent – and a demon negotiator!' He smiled across the table.

Rick asked, 'Has Cassie Nelson agreed for you to negotiate on her behalf?'

'Is that what I'm doing?'

Rick's eyebrows flickered. 'I thought so. Didn't you tell Luke you'd talk our offer through with her?'

'Is that what he told you?'

Rick nodded slowly, but Rinalda exclaimed, 'Luke tells us everything!'

'Don't mind mother. She's an awful tease.'

Rick said, 'Famous for it. She *was*.'

Rinalda chuckled, deep in her throat. 'Now, now, we mustn't make family jokes in front of strangers.'

'Kirsty's not a stranger,' Luke said lightly. 'I hope?'

Kirsty toyed with her wine glass. 'As a family you're a class act. They could do a sit-com on you.'

'*The Millers!*' sang Rick, to the tune of *The Simpsons*.

'They've already made *The Sopranos*,' said Luke. 'So we'll have to be *The Mezzos*.'

'*The Altos*,' said Rinalda. 'A purer sound.'

Kirsty smiled. 'A regular wholesome family.'

Rick nodded. 'That's us – plain homely folks.'

'So why did Spencer slip abroad?'

Rick smiled stiffly. 'Straight to the point.'

Rinalda's eyes sparkled. 'You warned us she was a terrier, Lucas.'

He chuckled. 'I said she was a *terror*, not a terrier.'

Kirsty ploughed on: 'Mr Miller, you know your son is accused of murder?'

Rick composed his face to look serious but good-tempered. 'What *is* this, an interview?'

'I'm a reporter.'

'You're not on duty now.'

'Mr Miller—'

'Rick.'

'Let's not play around. I know it would be easier for us to pretend I was Luke's girlfriend, brought around to meet the family—'

'Aren't you?' wailed Rinalda comically. 'We've been getting on so well!'

'But Spencer is accused of murder.'

Rick sighed. 'You wearing a mike by any chance?'

Luke answered. 'No, Dad, we put Kirsty in the waiting room.'

She frowned. Luke explained: 'We have an automatic mike sweep installed in that little room. It told us you were clean.'

She gaped a moment, then collected herself. 'Why don't you install one in your office?' He grinned at her. 'Or *is* there one?' He grinned again. 'You bastard.'

'Made my day.'

Kirsty stood up – but Rick was faster. He put his hand on her shoulder and eased her back onto her chair. 'You don't like our jokes? We could get serious.'

She chilled. She heard Rinalda say, 'I think fun is so much better.'

Rick said, 'D'you want to be a journalist and ask a load of unpleasant questions, or d'you want to negotiate Cassie Nelson's hush money? Ten thousand pounds. Plus your own commission, of course. How much would that be?'

All three watched her. 'Are you trying to buy me, R-Rick?'

'I guess five thousand should be enough for you?'

'For what?' she whispered.

'To persuade Cassie Nelson to shut her mouth.'

An awkward silence fell.

Rinalda broke it. 'You see, Kirsty – and I speak as a mother here—'

'You're not old enough—'

Rinalda smiled. 'You see? The girl can flatter. Yes Kirsty, I am Spencer's step-mother. But step-mothers have feelings too, and I don't like to see my boys unjustly accused. Poor Spencer did not do this.'

'*Poor* Cassie says he did.'

'*Does* she say that?'

'Yes.'

'Excuse me,' parried Luke. 'You told me that Cassie said 'the management' did it – or have you spoken to her since?'

Kirsty hesitated. 'She sent a message this morning.'

She held the pause, wondering how to play it.

Rick asked, 'A message?'

'Telling me not to meet with you. Telling me that Spencer tried to kill her last night.' Kirsty took a breath to cover the approaching lie. 'But I'd already moved her into hiding.'

The silence hummed. Rick nodded. 'So you do know where she is?'

Kirsty nodded back.

'Do the police know?'

She shook her head. It was easier than speaking.

'I guess they wouldn't,' Rick said.

Rinalda leant across the table. 'And this Cassie still insists…'

'She does.'

Luke broke his silence. 'Well, Kirsty, we have a simple question for you: are you with us or against us?'

She hesitated.

'We are honest people,' Rinalda said.

Rick glanced at his wife. 'And we look after our friends.' He reached behind him and pressed a buzzer. Kirsty assumed it was a buzzer, although she didn't hear a sound. She knew that all three were waiting, so she stonewalled with a question: 'What d'you want me to do?'

Rick was brisk. 'Offer her ten thousand to keep her mouth shut. She can go to the police and withdraw what she said – which ain't easy but at least it lets her go back to her normal life – or if she wants, she can stay out of sight. That's up to her. Either way, if the cops do bring the case she'll have to disappear for the duration, for which she'll get another five grand – plus an air ticket, which I'll throw in. And for all of this, if Cassie Nelson stays stumm, then you, Kirsty, get five thou commission. I think that's generous, don't you?'

She was spared from answering because the dining room door opened and the frilly maid popped in. 'Another bottle,' Rick said. 'Then we're done.'

'Oh, make it champagne,' Rinalda pleaded. 'I've been so worried that I really do need cheering up.'

*

Article One of the company's Health and Safety Policy – if they had got one – might have stated: 'Employees too ill to work do not get paid – and may be replaced permanently'. Hence Gordon's punctured hand was not enough to keep him away from work. The wound didn't generate much sympathy anyway: the few people he had mentioned it to found it amusing. At the hospital they'd made cracks about his not being a dab hand at DIY. His friend Peter had asked if he was playing Jesus Christ: a great stigmata, and was it a *riveting* audition? Gordon thought the cracks about as funny as haemorrhoids.

But, bandaged hand and all, he had put in a full day at the studio and had practically finished *Night Nurse* before real life returned. The gangbang stuff was done and all the male actors were in bed for the final scene in which the raped nurse would introduce a new nurse to the ward. Young and sexy – a cameo role in which the new girl did not even strip – the nervous newcomer followed the other along the corridor between the beds. The men watched from beneath their blankets, waiting for the night nurse to declare, 'This is the men's ward. You'll enjoy it here.'

She never said the words. Half way down the ward the nurse stopped. Men sat up in their beds. Someone called out.

Into the studio marched Tony Iles with a dozen men. As they quickly fanned out around the studio, Gordon scrambled from his canvas chair and looked for a place where he could hide. Actors jumped out of bed. Some were naked, some in trousers. But Tony was on set before anyone could find a way out. There wasn't one: he had seen to that.

'Hands off cocks,' he shouted. 'Hands on socks.' He pointed. 'I want everyone in a group – over there.'

There was a scramble. No one disobeyed. Gordon crept in among them, trying to look anonymous – which wasn't easy for him, fully dressed. Tony's men arranged themselves on set. Gordon and his technicians, together with the entire cast in various stages of undress, clustered beside the dummy door.

Tony said, 'It's time to test your fire drill.'

Two of his men strolled between the beds, splashing fuel from five-gallon drums. As they approached the cowering cast, Tony spoke. 'I said I wanted Spencer. So where is the fuck?'

No one replied.

Tony hadn't expected them to. He said, 'I'll send him a smoke signal.'

He gestured to his men. 'Lights.'

Three men grabbed the free-standing lamps and moved them onto set beside the sodden, sharp-smelling beds. 'Camera.'

Another of his men grabbed the camera and pushed it into the ward corridor.

'Action.'

His men stepped sharply back from the set as Tony lit what looked what looked like an old-fashioned washing-up mop, then tossed it onto a bed. There was no explosion, just a whoosh like a collective intake of breath. But when the sheet of flame burst across the beds it was as if a dam had opened to release an unstoppable flood of fire.

*

The police were waiting at DarkAlley Films. Kirsty waltzed in, a little tiddly from champagne, and it was as if she had Fast Forwarded to hangover. Rosa had aged ten years, Ken looked dishevelled, Janine was close to tears. The woman police inspector – Gillett – had a uniformed man in tow.

The inspector spoke immediately, to catch Kirsty unprepared: 'Glad you're back, Miss Rice. How was Cassie Nelson?'

Kirsty looked bemused. She glanced at the others, but Gillett pressed on: 'Where's she hiding?'

'I don't know—'

'You've just seen her.'

Kirsty glanced at the others. 'I've just been out.'

The inspector snorted. 'And you didn't get dumped on by a flying pig? Where's Cassie?'

'If I knew I'd tell you.'

'What's her phone number?'

'I don't... She's left home, I think.'

'And gone where?'

'I don't know.'

Gillett sighed. 'You realise that to withhold her whereabouts is to obstruct the course of justice? Or do you think that as a journalist you're allowed to protect your sources?'

'She phoned *me* – I don't know where she is.'

'Where did she phone from?'
'If I knew that… I'm sorry.'
'This is a murder investigation, Miss Rice. She's a key witness.'
'Have you spoken with Cassie's mother?'
'Yes. She said we should ask you.'

*

They used DarkAlley's meeting room because it was the only place with privacy. Gillett sat opposite Kirsty at the table, while the constable – unnecessarily, Kirsty thought – stood by the door.

'You say she phoned you?'
'Only to tell me to leave her alone.'
'You'd been bothering her?'
Kirsty shrugged helplessly. 'She called *me*.'
'Out of the blue?'
'We've been through this.'
'And we'll go through it again. When she phoned, did she tell you what she'd seen?'
'Not really.'
Gillett closed her eyes in irritation.
'She said she'd told the *police* everything.'
'We know what she told us, Miss Rice. What did she tell *you*?'
'Not to pester her.'
Gillett placed her hands on the table as if about to rise. 'You're not being helpful, Miss Rice. I think a recorded interview at the station would be more fruitful.'
'I'm sorry, I don't know anything.'
'For a journalist you don't know much – yet you're in contact with the missing witness. Why did she phone you?'
'She simply returned my call. I'd phoned her mother.'
'Where'd you get her number?'
'From Zoë's file.'
'Which file?'
Dangerous question. Kirsty licked her lips. 'Her Address Book on PC. We all share each other's files – it's more convenient. I'd been checking Zoë's contacts.'
'After her death? Are you carrying out your own investigation?'
'Just following up.'
'And you phoned Cassie?'
'I got her mother. She gave Cassie my number.'

'Why did she bother to phone you back?'

'To tell me to stop pestering her.'

Gillett sniffed. 'This is where we came in.'

'Cassie sounded frightened on the phone but she didn't really tell me anything.'

'Didn't *really*? What *did* she say?'

'I don't remember her exact words.'

'You're a journalist.'

'She told me Zoë had been murdered... by the management, she said.'

'What else?'

'Well, yesterday her mother phoned and said Cassie had run away. She said some men had come round after her, but by that time Cassie had gone.'

'Then Cassie phoned you again?'

'I didn't take the call. I got a message telling me that she'd rung. It only told me what I already knew – that she was hiding from the men.'

'And who would they be?'

Kirsty took a breath. 'I assumed the killers – or someone acting for them.'

'Killers? Does that mean more than one? What makes you say that?'

'Cassie said "the management", not "the manager". It sounds like more than one.'

'The management of the film company?'

'I assume so.'

'How much are you paying Cassie?'

'Paying?'

'For exclusive rights.'

'We're not—'

'You're journalists.'

'We make documentaries—'

'You have a crucial witness hidden away. How much does she get?'

Kirsty shook her head. 'Everyone thinks she'll do anything for money.'

'Everyone?'

They stared at each other. Gillett asked again: 'Who's everyone?'

Kirsty shrugged. 'Oh, anyone.'

'Who have you been talking to?'

'No one. Well, only the people here. Colleagues. Not even them, really.'

'Yet 'everyone' says Cassie is in this for the money? The film company Cassie was working for – the one where Zoë was killed – does it have a name?'

Kirsty made an apologetic face. 'They call themselves Van Cock.'

'Is that their only name?'

'I doubt it, but…'

'They killed Zoë?'

'I imagine so. But Cassie must have told you this – you interviewed her.'

'She's gone now, and without Cassie, her statement's useless. So it's essential we get in touch with her. You understand that?'

'I can't help you. I don't know—'

'Have you contacted Van Cock?'

Kirsty could barely remember what she had said. What had *Ken* said? She blinked twice. 'Well, I met – he's not really from the film company – I met a man who… runs a series of internet sites.'

'His name?'

She was reluctant to say it. 'Luke Miller.'

Gillett's eyes were on her. 'And his association with Van Cock?'

'Um, his brother, I think, may run it.'

'His brother is 'the management'? His name?'

'Spencer.'

'Did you meet him too?'

'No.'

'But you met Luke Miller – more than once?'

'No.' The lie came so easily she hardly recognised it as a lie.

'Where did you meet him?'

'At his office in South Quay.'

'Why did you meet him?'

'Well, because he's – because we're investigating his company.'

'His as well as his brother's? What have you found?'

'Luke Miller runs porn sites on the internet – soft and hard porn. We're making a series that will expose them.'

'I'm sure they'll hate the free publicity. I hear Luke Miller threw you out?'

So Ken *had* told the inspector about their visit. 'Yes, Miller realised I was a journalist. I was there with a colleague. Miller threw us both out.'

'Was that the end of it?'

What else had Ken admitted? 'No, not quite. I agreed to meet him one more time. At a restaurant.'

'Odd, considering he threw you out.'

Kirsty felt the story dragged from her, piece by piece. 'He had changed his attitude. I suppose he was trying to butter me up.'

Gillett raised an eyebrow.

'Luke knew the police were on to his brother and he wanted to know if we – that's DarkAlley – had told you anything that might affect his case.'

Gillett stared at her incredulously. 'What you're saying does not sound at all believable. I think you're closer to the Millers than you're letting on.'

'No—'

'You say Spencer runs the film company? Not his father?'

'His father? Oh no, he's...'

'He's what?'

Kirsty hesitated. 'I think you should concentrate on Spencer.'

'Is that a *hint*? We're not in the business of taking hints.'

'I don't think their father is involved.'

'So you've met the father too?'

Kirsty tried to slide straight past the question. 'I heard that Spencer left the country. Is that not true?'

'Where did you 'hear' that Spencer went?'

'I don't know—'

'Come *on*!'

'I *don't* know.'

'*When* did he go?'

'I got the impression he'd only just left – but I've no real idea. I've never met Spencer. Honestly.'

'People say 'honestly' when they're lying.'

Kirsty bristled. 'I've never—'

'Who in the family *have* you met?'

She committed herself. 'I've only met his brother Luke.'

- 29 -

Rick said, 'That's enough, Luke.'

'I haven't started.'

'Cut it.'

'I'm not a kid.'

Rick started from his chair but Luke was a man now, twenty-five. Rick was fifty-six.

Rinalda covered the pause. 'No quarrels – my little birdies!'

They were back in Clerkenwell. She was at the cocktail bar fixing drinks. Luke was in an armchair facing Rick, while the cause of the quarrel lay full length on the settee. 'Why should I go?' asked Spencer lazily. 'What would people say?'

'Go to Amsterdam,' she urged.

Spencer stayed on his back. 'Whole lot of people look up to me. If I run they'll think I'm scared.'

Rick leant forward in his chair. 'We had the cops round looking for you.'

'They been here, they been to my place – I've gone away.' Spence laughed. 'The trail is cold, sergeant! Hot damn. It's back to parking tickets.'

Rinalda put a Tequila in his hand. She handed beers to Luke and Rick – who said, 'The cops do not give up—'

'I'm not *wanted* by the cops—'

Luke said, 'If Spence disappears they'll say he ran to hide.'

'You said it, bro. Running away is bad.'

Rick glared at both of them.

'Hey, come on, Dad.' Spencer climbed off the settee. 'I'll get Thane to help me out.'

'To *bail* you out,' Luke laughed.

Spence turned on him. '*Think* about it, bro. They got no witness, so the Babylon can't hold me and they can't charge me neither.'

He looked pleased with himself. Rinalda asked, 'Are you sure they have no witness?'

'Believe me.'

He smiled at her. Rinalda sat on the arm of the settee. He remained standing.

Rick snorted. 'You're not worried about the cops, and you don't care about Tony Iles? He wants you, Spencer.'

'Like I said, man, I'll *marry* his daughter.'

'Let's all laugh,' muttered Luke.

'You're such a geek. You're in the wrong family, bro – you should have been a banker's son.'

'He's your brother,' Rinalda said.

'They tell me.'

Rick leapt to his feet and punched Spence on the arm. 'What's that supposed to mean? Of course he's your brother.'

Spence raised a hand. 'OK, he *is* my brother. Amazing but true.'

Luke was unperturbed. 'Glad that's been sorted out.'

'He's my brother, but he ain't heavy!'

Rinalda sighed. 'You should *never* insult your mother.'

Spencer moved to her: 'Don't be offended, Rinalda – *you're* my mother now.'

Luke said, 'A real mother's boy.'

'Can we get serious?' Rick asked. 'Listen, Spencer, when one of your actresses gets murdered, it is not surprising the cops want to see you.'

'OK, I'll see 'em. Thane can sort them out—'

'He can't handle Tony Iles—'

'I told you, I'll marry his daughter—'

'Will you stop saying that? Iles wants you dead.'

'And I never even met the man!'

'Ha, bloody ha. You met his daughter, right enough.'

'They tell me.'

Rick was angry now. 'Pity they didn't tell you not to rape her.'

Spencer shrugged, but Rinalda moved from the settee back to Rick: 'It wasn't rape, Rick darling. The girl was an actress, so getting fucked is in her contract.' Her hand was on Rick's arm. 'She exaggerated.'

'Yeah, and she exaggerated when she said Spence killed the reporter?'

'That was different.' She turned helplessly to Spencer: 'You must have been provoked, I think?'

'Bitch was a spy.'

Luke laughed. 'Journalists are spies?'

'Sure – when they stick their noses into *our* business.'

Rick approached him: 'You don't understand, do you? The cops want you – that's every London copper. Iles wants you – that's the guy who attacked the film studio *twice*. The guy who set light to it, nailed Gordon's hand to a table, just for fun. He's even been *here* to ask for you.'

'He gets around.'

'When he came here he didn't realise you were my son. But he knows now.'

'You show him a photo?'

'What?'

Spence sniggered. 'He don't know *who* I am. You shoot some guy and give Iles his body and say, 'There you go, Tony, that's my son'. If he's stupid enough to believe his *daughter's* crap he'll believe that too.'

'No,' said Rick. 'What we do is move you out of the way somewhere while we carefully sort this out.'

'No, it's an ace idea,' insisted Spence. 'A stunt double. An *ace* idea.'

'Amsterdam,' Rinalda sighed.

Spence grimaced and turned away. 'I ain't going to Amsterdam. I'm staying here.'

Luke said, 'You see, Rinalda, our Spencer is a film-maker, devoted to his art.'

'Shut up,' snapped Rick. He turned to Spence: 'Just get out of town.'

'The *countryside*? Oh, man.'

'The cat house, then. It's London. But you gotta stay out of sight.'

Rinalda protested. 'Spence cannot go to the cat house. What will the girls do?'

'What they always do.'

Spence laughed. 'Hey, I could buy into that. Hole up in the cat house for a week or so – yeah, I could *hole up*!' He laughed again.

Rinalda became businesslike: 'We can't work the house with Spencer there.'

'Why not?' asked Rick. 'He only needs one room.'

Spencer said, 'I'll be like a little mouse. Hiding in my hole.'

'A room can earn five thousand pounds a week. If we put Spencer in, we'll lose a lot of money.'

'Thanks, Ma!' said Spencer. 'Now I know how much I am worth. Look, if I got to hole up somewhere, and if I got to lie in bed all day...'

'You're impossible!'

'That's what *all* the girls say.'

Rinalda exhaled and went back to the cocktail bar.

Spencer said, 'Hey, come on, family, chill out. I'll go for a week in the cat house. You persuaded me.'

Rinalda said, 'I cannot send my girls on holiday.'

'Who said anything about that? It'll be *my* holiday!'

'Stop it,' she snapped. 'It is not a funny joke. My house can earn twenty thousand a week.'

'Less expenses.'

'Oh, so you'd close down *my* business, while your stupid film company, which *caused* all this trouble—'

'*You* were in the film business—'

'With a *good* company. We made *professional* movies—'

'Porno movies—'

'Which made money—'

'*My* films make—'

'Shut up!' Rick shouted. 'The pair of you.' He glared at Spence. 'See the trouble you caused? And now Luke has got himself involved with this journalist—'

'Hot damn! Another journalist?'

'Some girl from DarkAlley Films—'

'DarkAlley *Films*?'

Luke nodded calmly. 'Guess why, Spence baby? Because she knows where the missing witness is – you know, Cassie Nelson, the girl you silenced? The one who went to the police and told them everything she knew?'

'I cannot believe you spoke to a *journalist*!'

'Her name is Kirsty Rice, and you ought to be nice to her, Spence. She's in touch with Cassie Nelson, and Cassie is the only evidence the police have got.'

'Introduce us,' Spencer said. 'I'll be nice to her. I'm great with journalists.'

- 30 -

Ferdie had the door on a chain – so puny, though: a bolt-cutter would snap it in one easy bite. But it made her feel better. Since Cornell and Spence had called for Cassie, Ferdie had kept the front door bolted and chained, the back door bolted, the windows locked. But she let Kirsty in – and Kirsty could have been anyone. Ferdie took her into a tiny crowded living room that smelt like a pub, where she lit another cigarette without offering one. Perhaps she could tell Kirsty didn't smoke.

Kirsty ignored the clinging tobacco smell, although she knew her clothes would reek all day. She had more important things to worry about than passive smoking. Except she was pregnant. Oh, well.

Ferdie said, 'She's my little girl, so of course I'm worried about her. It's natural, isn't it? But I won't tell you where she is.'

'You know, though.'

Ferdie narrowed her eyes against the smoke. 'No one gets to see my daughter.'

Kirsty leant forward in her chair. 'Cassie's in trouble—'

'She's a good girl. Done nothing wrong.'

'She witnessed—'

'She done them films and that, but they're harmless really. She's not a bad girl. I'm her mum.'

'You want to protect her.'

'It's what mums are for.'

Kirsty nodded: that *was* a mother's role. She said, 'Cassie witnessed a murder.'

'You said you wasn't police.'

'I'm not—'

'Were you a friend of that dead girl, then?'

'We worked for the same company – DarkAlley Films.'

'Films? You said you was a journalist.'

'A video journalist. We make investigative films.'

'Well, look, my Cassie was a model, a proper model – she was a lovely girl.' Ferdie gave a squeak. 'She still *is* a lovely girl. She's alive.'

'My friend is dead.'

Ferdie stared blankly. 'Cassie didn't have nothing to do with that. A mother knows.'

Kirsty licked her lips. 'Like you know where she is—'

'I ain't telling you.'

'But when you see her—'

'I won't be.'

'When you phone her—'

'She'll phone *me*.'

Kirsty let Ferdie take a long drag on her cigarette, then said, 'Someone asked me to give Cassie a message. Will you pass it on?'

'I don't know.' Ferdie started stubbing out her fag. 'No promises, mind.'

'You're concerned for Cassie's safety—'

'She's my daughter! I'd give my life for her.'

Kirsty herself would be protective of her own child when she was born. Whatever the child did. 'No one's saying Cassie did something wrong.'

'She's a good girl.'

'But she was a witness. Now she's in danger.'

'I won't let nothing happen to her.' The mother at bay. 'What's this message, then?'

'It's from Spencer Miller.' Kirsty watched for her reaction, but Ferdie looked blank. 'He says he's prepared to give Cassie his protection.'

'Like in gangster films?'

Kirsty was still watching her. 'You don't recognise his name?'

'Why should I?'

'Cassie told the police he was the murderer.'

'Oh.' No reaction. Ferdie had closed down. But Kirsty waited, and eventually Ferdie asked nonchalantly, 'Are you a friend of his, then?'

'Never met him.'

'Then how…'

Kirsty shouldn't have said she'd never met him. But she'd told the Millers she'd deliver the message and she felt honour bound to play out the farce. 'Spencer's family are concerned for him. They want Cassie to clear his name.'

'But she told the police he was...'

'Yes.'

Ferdie reached for her crumpled cigarette packet. 'I'm not with this.'

'Cassie can't stay in hiding forever. Look, Mrs Nelson, what Cassie should do is go to the police and explain that because she's a principal witness her life's in danger, and she should ask them to give her round the clock protection.'

'Yeah, like they *would*!'

'She's important to them. The police could hide Cassie properly, and give her a new identity.'

Ferdie shook out her cigarette. 'What about me?'

'Perhaps they'd hide you as well.'

'Get real, love, will you? What about this Spencer – what protection would *he* give?'

'He's the killer.'

'Oh, you *know* that, do you?'

'Cassie said as much. She's hiding from him.'

Ferdie concentrated on lighting the cigarette. 'So he's going to protect her from himself?'

'That's what he says.'

'It don't make sense.'

'He's even prepared to *buy* Cassie off.'

Ferdie inhaled and held the smoke. 'How much?'

'You wouldn't sell your daughter?'

'Course not. How much is he offering?'

'Ten thousand.'

'Is that his first offer?'

Ferdie had created a smoke-filled room.

'Ten thousand pounds. That was his offer.'

'Well, it's not me, is it? It's Cassie as would decide.'

'That's right.'

'Still, I know what I think.' Ferdie drew again on her cigarette. 'It's better than a poke in the eye with a broken beer bottle. Ten grand. Then he wouldn't have to kill her, would he?'

Kirsty stared. 'She couldn't take his money?'

Ferdie stared back. 'Why not?'

'For ten thousand pounds a guilty man walks free.'

'For ten thousand pounds my *daughter* walks free.'

*

Roy Farrell at home: a neat flat in Peckham, end of the block, with excellent views. In the kitchen, beneath the drop-down table, stands a crate of brown ale – a drink increasingly difficult to find nowadays, but one for which Roy Farrell remains fond. He considers it good for his health. He is sitting stretched out in his living/dining room, shoes off, third bottle in hand, watching a game show. The game is silly and the prizes are astonishingly low. It amazes Roy that people can get so excited about such naff prizes. He wouldn't take the things for free – they aren't worth the bother. Watching this sort of programme makes Roy feel superior: the folks on screen are like the folks he went to school with. He sees them around Peckham. But they are dross.

The phone rings, and he puts it to his ear.

'Is that Roy Farrell?'

'Who's that?'

'Herbie Tripp. Remember we met up again?'

'Bloody Herbie – you old dog.'

'How's it going?'

'Not bad. Well, Herbie Tripp! How come you got yourself mixed up with the Millers?'

'I have to eat.'

'Do they feed you?'

'Kitchen scraps.'

'That sounds like you're hungry – my old mate.'

'No, I do the cooking here.'

'You're a *chef*?'

'Among other things.'

'A jack of *all* trades. So Herbie, my old mucker, how can I help?'

- 31 -

Another sunny day.

That the Miller family could afford to live in this quiet elegant street emphasised their wealth. Ten minutes away in Victoria, DarkAlley's rent was sky-high and the building was mean and shabby, but the rent for a better property would have been stratospheric. To Kirsty, the whole West End – Strand to Chelsea – was a business area, not residential, although she was aware that people lived there. How they managed it she didn't know: ordinary families lived in little flats above shops, little doorways in dark courts. How did they afford it? What rent did they pay? She shrugged it aside.

Perhaps people thought her own abode equally strange – a boat on the river. Shouldn't people live on dry land? But to live here in Pimlico – was it Pimlico; wasn't it Westminster? – was easy to comprehend. To live in these fine Georgian terraces you had only to be rich. The Millers *were* rich – but from what? Did their entire fortune come from pornography? Spencer made sexy films, Luke purveyed internet sex – but supposedly was more interested in the technology than in the product that he sold. Rick and Rinalda seemed too urbane to be involved in their sons' businesses. Did they know what their sons did? Who did know? Kirsty only knew what Ken had told her – she remembered the pictures Ken said came from Luke's sites – but she found it hard to associate that sleazy trade with Luke Miller's smart modern offices. And however Rick made his money it seemed unlikely it was only through porn. Rick was in his mid-fifties – he couldn't have spent thirty years in pornography. And to a man of his generation the internet would not be something he felt comfortable with. He'd want tangible assets, things he could put his hands on. Rinalda? Lovely woman but naïve, Kirsty decided: a wealthy mother – better born than Rick, judging from her accent, but an innocent. If Rinalda knew anything of her sons' businesses, she probably assumed only that Spencer's films could get naughty and that some of Luke's sites might dabble in soft porn. Kirsty could see Rinalda creating a family home in Pimlico, bringing up her boys, supervising her household – with a maid, for goodness sake, in black frock and white frilly lace.

Kirsty had reached the front door. Smart but anonymous. It seemed incredible that such a house in such a fashionable street did not have a multitude of doorbells. But this green door had just one. She pressed it.

It would be wonderful if the elusive Spencer *was* in – but the family claimed he'd gone abroad. Were they fobbing her off? If Spencer were still in England she might find him here. Presumably he and Luke lived with Mum and Dad – although it was equally possible they each had their own flat. Perhaps Luke would be here. Perhaps Spencer. It didn't hurt to ask.

When the door opened, the maid smiled pleasantly but did not invite Kirsty in.

'Can I see Spencer please?'

'And you are?'

'Kirsty Rice. I was here yesterday.'

The maid showed no glimmer of recognition, and it seemed to Kirsty that her manner was less welcoming than yesterday. But yesterday she'd been expected.

'Spencer's not in. I'm sorry.'

'Could I wait?'

'Is he expecting you?'

'Of course.' So much for Spencer's being abroad. 'He wants to see me.'

The maid studied her. 'Yes, you were here before, weren't you?'

She let Kirsty in. As she led Kirsty into the small waiting room she said, 'We weren't expecting him till tonight.' She sighed. 'Everyone wants everything *yesterday*.' She stamped out.

Last time Kirsty had waited here there had been two neat landscapes on the wall, but today those two pictures had been replaced by French *déshabille* etchings similar to the ones the Millers had upstairs. On the table were some magazines. Even the covers were explicit. Kirsty was slightly shocked. The etchings were erotic but these... She didn't open them.

The door banged open. 'Are you with Spencer?'

The woman had a mass of tumbling red hair and wore an open silk housecoat over her underclothes. French undies. The kind of undies never seen outside the cinema. They looked as real as the costumed maid.

Kirsty nodded. 'I'm waiting for him.'

'They said this evening.'

The woman glared at Kirsty and her make-up looked like war paint. But she was glamorous – a Titian. 'I'll need another hour to pack.'

'I'm sorry?'

The woman looked Kirsty up and down. 'You know what you're getting into?'

'I'm learning.'

'You're welcome to him. How long are you staying here?'

'It depends.'

The woman sighed. 'It's bloody thoughtless. Inconsiderate. But that's typical. You know it's the *studio* flat?'

'I didn't realise.'

'Oh yes, only the best for his precious lordship. *We'll* have to share now – three of us in two rooms. That won't work. Not for long.' She glared at Kirsty again. 'Anyway, you'll have to wait – I'll be at least an hour.'

She flounced out.

Kirsty glanced at the etchings, the magazines and the door. How had she not realised? This had never felt like a family home. This wasn't where the Millers lived.

The maid entered – and in that costume 'enter' was the word: enter as on stage. A theatrical artifice. She eyed Kirsty differently now. 'I got through to Spencer. He said it's a surprise but he'd love to see you. He asks if you'll wait.'

· 32 ·

Neil Garvey wore black and tan Italian hand-made shoes, his Bruno trousers and a light-weight linen jacket. Although he had thought about a tie he eventually decided on a cream button-down shirt, open necked. He wore expensive cologne. The way Neil saw it, you had to look the part. Rick Miller might not always dress well, but he ran the organisation and had nothing to prove. If Luke was there, though, he'd wear something cool like Ralph Lauren, and Spence always dressed expensively with a flash of gold. Spence was the man for jewellery, so Neil didn't try to compete: no jewellery, just the shoes.

In today's Clerkenwell you had to look good. Although Neil lived south of the river he liked to show the world he'd made it. Approaching fifty, he didn't wear juvenile fashions, but instead wore classics, good labels, understated. He had walked from Farringdon tube, along the dingy side street, through the lively square, past old London buildings. If he'd felt ordinary in the square he felt overdressed in the side street. At the door of the Printing Works he felt nervous.

It creaked open.

As he followed Herbie inside, Neil asked, 'Is that Spencer's car?'

'Spence is away.'

It figured: the blue TVR wasn't gaudy enough for Spence. *He* would have had a brighter colour and go-faster stripes – if he'd *had* to have a blue car he would have decorated it inside. Neil didn't ask about the Merc: that would be Rick's.

Neil had seldom met the Millers. Most of his trade with the family was routine: he delivered films and the Millers paid on time. Rick didn't bother with details. Luke was the details man while Spence, folks said, was an idiot. The men who mattered were Luke and Rick.

Neil was surprised when the old industrial lift stopped almost as soon as it had begun. Last time Neil had come – the *only* time he'd come – he had been taken to the top-most floor, to their comfortable flat. But today he was brought no further than an empty print floor. Disused. Bare light bulbs. Luke and Rick.

Neil's smile tightened. *They* weren't smiling. Behind him, he heard the lift grunt and move away. But Herbie had not gone with it. He pushed Neil in the back – not hard, not enough that he might stumble, but enough to force him to take an unintended step. Enough to unsettle him.

Rick said, 'You've been talking to journalists.'

'Well, I—'

'Telling them what we do.'

'Oh. You mean… I explained already—'

'You said you were making a film.'

'Yeah, a film about the business – *my* business. I didn't say anythin' about yours, obviously.'

'So how come that journalist was onto me?'

'Which journalist?'

Herbie thumped him in the back. Rick must have signalled. 'You mean the Rice girl? I didn't tell her nothin'. Honest.'

'Two days, wasn't it? What did she do, cross-examine you for two whole days?'

'No, she—'

'Tickle your fancy? Ask for your life story?'

Neil felt suddenly annoyed. He had dressed especially for this. 'What's up?'

'You fucked up, that's what's up.'

Neil stared at him. He stared at Luke, but Luke had a faraway look in his eyes, as if he was remembering his breakfast. No point speaking to him.

Neil said, 'The journalist got nothin' out of me. But after she'd shot the film she came back. Funny, I thought, so I phoned *you*. That's all there is.'

Luke *did* speak after all: 'Why did she come back?'

'She asked about Van Cock. That's why I phoned Rick.'

'How did she know the name?'

'I don't know – saw it on a video? Who knows?'

Luke was examining his nails. 'In this two-day interview, you told her all about your films? She must have asked who you sold them to.'

'I didn't tell her.'

'How did she know?'

Neil shrugged. 'She's a journalist.'

'Did she meet any actresses?'

'Well, one or two. But they don't know nothin' about Van Cock.'

'Are you sure?'

'Natch. They work for *me* – not Van Cock. Where's Spencer?'

He felt Herbie move closer to his back. Herbie didn't touch him. He only blew into Neil's ear.

Rick studied him. 'Why d'you ask about Spencer?'

'Well, Spencer runs Van Cock – that's what we're talkin' about. Look Rick, nothin' happened. The girl came back, I thought it strange, I phoned you. I was keepin' you in touch.'

'*She* got in touch as well.'

'I didn't tell her nothin'. She went away. Since then, she's never come back, never even spoke to me. She learnt nothin' from me, Rick – nor from my girls.'

'She learnt something from *some*body.'

Luke asked, 'Do you know a girl called Zoë Rand?'

'No.'

'Too quick, Neil. Think again.'

Neil made an effort. 'I never heard of her.'

'You're lying, Neil.' This was Rick.

'No, Rick, I—'

Thump from Herbie. This time it hurt.

Rick said, 'Everyone's heard of Zoë Rand. She was on the News.'

Neil gaped. His back hurt. 'I must've missed it.'

Rick glared at him. Luke said, 'You haven't been paying attention.'

'I never watch the News. Look, if there's any way I can help—'

'There is, Neil,' replied Rick. 'You can think back and tell us what happened.'

'Nothin' happened—'

'Shut up.' Rick came closer. Neil couldn't step backwards because Herbie was at his heel. Rick said, 'Since you saw this journalist we've had her and the cops crawling all over us. They took me in for questioning. *Me*.'

'I'm sorry, Rick.'

'You're the reason for this.'

'No.'

Rick came closer still. Herbie pressed against Neil's back. Neil felt like meat in a sandwich someone meant to bite.

Rick's breath was moist on Neil's face: 'Here's an *ace* idea – you can stay here till you remember.'

'Here?'

Luke chuckled. '*Ace* idea,' he repeated softly.

Rick nodded. Neil tensed. Rick was close enough to give him a head-butt, and he looked as if he might.

Luke smiled. 'Remember Cassie Nelson?'

'No.' Neil didn't dare to shake his head. 'Sorry.'

Rick said, 'Fuck you,' calmly, then stepped back. Neil felt Herbie stir behind him – but it was Rick's punch that arrived low in Neil's gut. As he lurched forward he felt a hand behind his head, a push, then a fearsome crunch as his face met Miller's knee. Neil crumpled to the floor. He raised both hands to his face, partly to stop the next blow, partly to prevent blood from dropping onto his beautiful linen jacket. He lay gasping on the concrete.

Luke said, 'Cassie worked for you – Cassie Nelson.'

'You even fucked her,' added Rick.

'In a film?'

Rick kicked him. 'Do you forget everything?' He kicked again.

'I haven't seen the girl for years! Cassie Nelson – yes.'

'What about her?'

'I don't know! I haven't seen her!'

'Well, Neil, she's disappeared.'

He was struggling to sound normal. 'Where's she gone?'

Rick stooped and grabbed him by the hair. 'That's what I'm asking *you*, you brainless git!'

'I don't *know*!' Neil was crying now. The injustice. His face felt like it must have split apart. They had ruined his nice shirt and jacket.

Rick was talking again. Neil tried to listen. 'Cassie Nelson. Zoë Rand. Kirsty Rice. All women. All fucking trouble. One's dead, one's a nuisance, and the other one's gone missing. And you, Neil, you are going to tell us where she's gone.'

- 33 -

She wasn't going to but she did. Left for minute after slow, slow minute in the little waiting room, nothing to do but examine the etchings on the walls, think her thoughts, play with her mobile phone – which, because of the mike sweep, she did not dare switch on – examine her fingernails, wonder why she sat there waiting to meet the most likely suspect in Zoë's murder; the tension built and eventually she succumbed. She picked up a magazine and opened it.

The text was minimal and the pictures – though graphic – were less alarming than she'd imagined. Explicit, yes, pornographic – puerile even, in the way they pandered to adolescent male fantasies – yet in one sense, the photos might be called educational: this is what fits where, this is what a woman looks like. This is what a man looks like. Years ago, Kirsty had occasionally played with a mirror to familiarise herself with that sensitive part of her anatomy which she could never really see – but it had never looked as colourful as in these lurid photographs, never so red, so succulent.

She was staring at one of the shots as avidly as if she were a teenage boy, when she heard the street doorbell. It had a homely, respectable ring. That'll be Spencer, she thought, as she quickly returned the glossy magazine to the little table. She heard the maid run down the stairs and open the front door. She heard voices, a man's voice, footsteps along the hall. Then the door swung open and the maid ushered in a stocky, light-haired man wearing a suit. He was older than she'd expected – not Spencer, surely.

Kirsty stood up. The man gazed at her – and the maid said, 'Oh, I'd forgotten you were here.'

The man smiled and asked, 'Christabel?'

'No,' the girls answered.

The man looked anxious. He was a customer, Kirsty realised, but the maid leapt in before Kirsty could say something wrong: 'No, she isn't Christabel. This lady is waiting for a friend.'

'I think we both are,' he said nervously.

'You needn't worry, she's in the picture.'

Far from looking reassured, the man looked ready to scuffle away. So Kirsty said, 'I work here.'

'Ah.' He looked relieved. So did the maid. Clumsily, he said, 'Well, let's hope Christabel is half as pretty as you!'

'She's prettier. You'll see.'

They smiled at each other – each nervous in their own way. The maid said, 'I'll leave you both together—' She glanced at Kirsty: 'Shall I?'

Kirsty sat down. The maid hesitated, then left. The man stood beside the table, rubbed his hands together, then sat carefully on the other chair. 'My first time.'

'Surely not?'

'Well, my first time here.' He chuckled manfully. 'So you do this too? Gosh. What's your name?'

'Sabrina.'

'Lovely name.'

'Isn't it? What's your name – big boy?'

He chuckled again. 'It's David, actually.'

She made her eyes gleam. Did he look a David? He was certainly no Goliath. 'Have you come far?'

'Oh, um...' He coughed conspiratorially. 'Few minutes, you know.'

She nodded. 'Westminster?' He coloured. 'I'm sure Christabel has something special for you.'

'Indeed.' He looked at the floor. 'I hope so.' He looked up again.

'What do you like?'

He continued to blush. 'I discussed it with her on the phone.' He rubbed his hands again. 'What's *your* speciality, as it were?'

He was looking bolder now, and Kirsty smiled back prettily, wondering what to say. 'I let the man decide.'

'You let him dominate?'

'Most men like to.'

'*Some* men. Well. Do *you* ever... dominate?'

'Do I give a man a hard time?'

'Lay into him, you know?'

'I can be hard as nails.'

They stared at each other, and as they did so they fell into their assumed roles: she was scornful of him, and he cowered happily before her. 'You could be my type.'

'Don't be cheeky,' said Kirsty, her face like stone.
'No, miss. No, I mustn't.'
He panted faithfully like a dog.
She whispered, 'Down on your knees, big boy. Kiss the carpet.'
He slithered readily from his chair. 'Let me kiss your feet—'
'The carpet, I said! Grovel at my feet.'
But the maid returned.

*

After another ten minutes the doorbell sounded again, and this time something about the firmness in the man's voice, his quick positive step, told her that he was not another client. She'd have to play a different part this time. She watched the door.

'Spencer?'
'Hey, Miss Kirsty Rice!'

He was a broad-shouldered, tall young man – a bigger, fitter, yet more babyish version of his brother. He had a slacker mouth, an animal quality – and a curious, almost Caribbean accent. He was shrewd, though: 'Meet the man they love to hate.'

'And should they?'
'Oh, I'm a cutie.'
'So I've heard.'
He shrugged modestly. 'Don't believe everything you hear, babe.'
'I *am* a journalist.'
He nodded. 'Come for a scoop?'
'Let's hope so.'
'Let's hope *not*, babe. You coming upstairs with me?'

He stepped out of the room as if it were perfectly natural that she would follow him. They climbed the stairs. Spencer led her past the first floor where she had eaten with his family, on to the upper floors. The same unthreatening wallpaper, the same soft carpet. She noted a lack of pictures, a lack of any suggestion of what the house was for. They crossed a quiet landing and climbed yet another flight of stairs. On the landing was a small square window looking out across the street, the outside world. On the top floor was another window, similarly square, and this looked out to tiled roofs and a streak of sky.

She saw two unlabelled doors. Spencer opened one.
'This is the studio flat. Like a penthouse.'
'Very apt.'

They moved from the tasteful hall into an excess of good taste. The room – it was more a parlour than a living room – was decorated in dark burgundy and gold, pre-Revolutionary French style, Louis the whichever number. A chaise longue, a couple of painted wooden chairs with dripping ormolu, a gold mirror, davenport, moulded cupboard, and three tiny tables with legs so curved they must have bowed beneath the weight. There was a vase of flowers – silk, she guessed – a murky landscape and two oils of Romantic nudes. Even a chandelier.

But she and Spencer were not alone.

An inner door crashed open to deliver the red-headed Titian she had met earlier. Her mood had not improved. 'I'm getting there, for Chrissake! I need another half hour at least.'

Spencer glanced at his gold watch. 'Take a break, Simone.'

The woman spoke through gritted teeth. 'I'm nearly ready.'

Spencer followed Simone into the bedroom but Kirsty stayed where she was. She could see that the heavy French style continued into that room: an enormous bed, gold-framed mirrors, painted wall statues of putti and nymphs.

She heard Simone start up again but Spencer said, 'I'll *help* you.' He said it reasonably, without apparent threat, but his tone did not encourage a refusal. 'A couple of bags is all.'

Kirsty glanced around the parlour. This deep red, perfumed room could only exist in a brothel. She had never *been* in one before. Such a quiet life.

The Titian emerged to grab a riding whip from behind the chaise longue. She shot an angry glance at Kirsty, then darted back inside the boudoir. Kirsty pulled a wry face. Why did the woman wear such heavy make-up? It only emphasised that she'd not see thirty-five again.

Inside two minutes Spencer had bustled Simone away. When he firmly closed the door on her, a chair shook and the red plush quivered as if the apartment were a stage set, not fastened down.

'Powerful woman,' Kirsty commented. 'Is she as strong as Christabel?'

'You been snooping around? Reporters! Damn. Yeah, Christabel's downstairs. The blue room.'

'She had a customer.'

He glanced dead-eyed.

'I didn't tell him anything I shouldn't. He thought I worked here.'

Spencer grinned. 'Could be arranged.'

'I'm far too young.'

'Christabel's your age. So is Lucy. But Simone's the motherly type.'

'For Snow White, maybe. Looked a dominatrix.'

'Hey, don't the girl talk dirty? No, it's Christabel does the dominatrix crap.' He grinned again. 'Simone is pissed we turned her out. She spends all day being nice to guys, so it ain't surprising she's bursting underneath. Why'd you set the cops on me?'

The room was suddenly silent. She wondered if it were soundproofed – she could hear nothing from the outside world. 'I didn't.'

'Cops think I killed your journo friend.'

'Her name was Zoë.'

'Do *you* think so?'

'*Did* you?'

'We going to trade questions all day long?'

'Everyone knows you run Van Cock Films—'

'Everyone?'

'So you're the 'management'. It was management killed Zoë Rand.'

'You've been speaking to Cassie Nelson. Where is she, by the way?'

'In hiding.'

'I know that. But where?'

'Would I tell *you*?'

He stepped closer. 'This is *my* territory you're standing in.'

'You'd kill me too?'

'If I had to.' His eyes were cold. She didn't look away. 'Because I'm a killer, right? That's what you think.'

'I don't know what to think.'

She saw a glint of triumph in his eyes, as if that's what he wanted her to say.

She said, 'Zoë worked on your film.'

He turned his back on her and ran his nails across a low painted table. He had only to press on it to break it.

'Were you on set?' she asked.

He rattled his nails on the painted surface. 'I run the company – I don't get involved with making movies.'

'But you know which film she was working on. So you know who *was* there – all the people who saw what actually happened.'

His fingers rested on the table. 'What name did this reporter work under?'

'I'm not sure – her own name, Zoë?'

He looked up. 'There you go. Some girl worked on some movie. I can't do nothing with that.'

'Come on, Spencer – how many movies can there be? The whole cast must have seen what happened.'

'Cassie tell you that? What did *she* say the film was called?'

'She didn't.'

He shrugged. 'Funny old business.'

Kirsty began walking round the room. 'You could find out if you wanted to.'

'You think?' Suddenly he picked up the table and glanced underneath. It looked so fragile in his hands. 'If I found out, you'd want me to do something about it. Like what – call the cops in, have them crawling through my business? They'd shut me down.'

'They couldn't.'

'Oh, really?' He weighed the table a moment, then put it down. 'Van Cock being so clean and legitimate, they'd recommend us for an arts award?' He chuckled mirthlessly. 'Luke thought of that. We did a couple of Roman orgy movies – he tried for a grant.'

Spencer snorted. She watched him. He *must* have done the murder, yet he wasn't behaving like a killer. Was he? 'Zoë was murdered,' she persisted. 'You can't let that go.'

'I sure can't bring her back.' Spence wandered to the bedroom door. 'Look, Kirsty, we work with some pretty fucked up people here. Things happen. I'm sorry about this Zoë babe, but it's over.' He stared at her. 'This ain't going the way you hoped, right?'

'Right.'

'No, and our movies like a happy ending – but real life ain't like that. There's only one ending, which is you die. Till then, your real life story mooches along with jobs half completed, opportunities missed, avenues unexplored, yeah? Loose ends everywhere.'

'A philosopher.'

'Well, don't tell anyone. It's bad for my image.'

Kirsty moved to the chaise longue. The piece looked genuine.

Spencer said, 'The past is dead but we're still living. You should be grateful for that.'

'I should forget her?'

'Suppose you do find out who did this? Suppose you bring the guy to justice. That'll make a difference?'

'To me.'

'To the rest of your life? Supposing you solve this murder and come out of it unscathed. After all the fuss and hassle is gone, you've got – what, another fifty, sixty years to live? Will clearing this up transform your life?'

'That's not the point.'

'What *is* the point? *Today*'s the point: enjoy today and stay alive tomorrow. Don't let life eat away at you till only death is left.'

'I said you were a philosopher.'

'You're seeing my tender side. Listen, you can mope around for weeks and let your life trickle down the drain, or you can grab hold of it, pack pleasure in.'

She stared at him from behind the chaise longue.

He said, 'Look at this place. See that bedroom? An hour there is an hour *lived*. Sheer pleasure. What's wrong with that?'

'It comes with a price attached.'

He looked at her. 'You can have it for free.'

'No thanks.' She gripped the back of the chaise longue.

He said, 'Trust me a minute. Come and look at the bedroom.'

'No way.'

'I said trust me.' He stepped towards her, hand outstretched.

She wouldn't move, though he was close enough to touch. He asked quietly, 'D'you want to have sex with me?'

'No!'

'Don't I know that? So, if I get you in the bedroom you are not going to change your mind, are you? Come and look at it. Just look.'

They entered the boudoir without touching. He could have been an estate agent, she the client. And for this room, boudoir *was* the word: French rococo meets New Orleans bordello. There was a huge soft looking bed, deep red walls festooned with drapes and gilt mirrors, a pile carpet, and a coved ceiling embedded with a large unframed mirror.

'This is a room to make you happy,' Spencer murmured. 'Feel the bed.' He opened innocent hands: 'It's cool, babe. Don't worry – you and I made a truce here.'

She stooped to touch the soft silk eiderdown. The sheet beneath was silk also. The mattress, pillows, eiderdown – such softness, such slippery silk. Above the padded headboard scampered a chase of nymphs and putti. 'She shall have music,' Spencer said. He pressed a button and released the sound of tinkling harp music, water in a fountain. He said, 'I figured you for the classical type.

But you can have rock if you prefer. —That's a mini bar beside you.'

She smiled. 'Do the drinks get added to your room tab?'

'Too right.'

'Cheapskate.'

'Some of our clients would drink the house dry.' He straightened a pillow. 'But they can if they want to. They're here to enjoy. Whatever they want.'

His hand stayed on the pillow, as if the silk held a fetish attraction. When she went back to the parlour, Spencer seemed reluctant to follow. But he did.

'Yes, this is fantasy,' he said, coming from the boudoir. 'What's wrong with that?'

She sat carefully on a painted wooden chair. Prim and courtly. She felt safer sitting down.

Spencer didn't sit. 'You'd blow this apart?'

'*This* place has nothing to do with it.'

'Still think I killed her?'

'If you didn't, you know who did.'

'I wasn't there, babe.'

He went to the other chair, spun it round and sat on it backwards, facing Kirsty. Who was questioning whom? 'This Nelson girl – you believe her crap?'

'She's a witness.'

'She *says* she's a witness. Now, if you believe that, there's nothing you and I can talk about. But as a journalist – which I *think* you are? – you ought to… look at every reasonable explanation.'

'Name one.'

'Maybe she's protecting whoever did do it. Maybe she doesn't know.'

'Why—'

'She's an actress – or she'd like to be. Here's a chance for her to star. Big court case, sexy subject, lots of media attention. D'you know where Zoë died?'

'On the film set.'

'In front of a load of people – and no one spoke?'

'Except Cassie.'

'But no one else.' He paused a moment. 'No one spoke. I don't think all those witnesses just forgot about it – do you?'

Kirsty hesitated.

He nodded briskly. 'She could have been killed by anyone – even a stranger. There's eight million strangers in London – but let's say it was someone on the film set. Then who?'

'You.'

Spencer, understandably, looked exasperated. 'How about someone else on set.'

'Such as?'

He studied her. 'Can I trust you?'

She was astonished. 'I trusted *you*.'

He sighed. 'A girl dies – OK, a girl is murdered – who do the cops always look for first? The boyfriend. So let's think: who was Zoë fucking – excuse my French?'

'She had broken up with her boyfriend.'

'Hot damn! You kidding me? Put that man top of the list.'

'No way.'

'In my business, babe, you are never surprised, not even when an ordinary girl in an ordinary job – journalist, say – turns out to have a bizarre private life. A weird sex life.'

'What are you doing, Spencer – practising defences on me, ready for when they get you in court?'

'Zoë liked it violent.'

They stared at each other from prim wooden chairs.

'I thought you didn't know her.'

'My people did.'

She shook her head. 'What are you trying now?'

'Ordinary people – don't you just love them? You can work with someone every day, walk by them in the corridor, and there's a part of their life you'll never see.'

'This doesn't wash.'

'Look, Kirsty, I didn't want to show you this.'

Spencer stood up, walked to the French moulded cupboard and flicked open its double doors. Inside stood a TV, video, DVD, two speakers.

'Your clients watch television?'

'Sometimes it livens 'em up. And the girls watch TV, you know, when they're not working? They're only people, like you and me.'

As the monitor warmed up he pulled a video from his pocket, rammed it in the slot, then with the remote clutched in his hand said, 'This may disturb you, I don't know.' He glanced at her. 'Ignore Zoë and concentrate on the man.'

'What is this?'

The remote drooped from Spencer's hand. 'We're not murderers, babe – even if you think we're pretty shabby people. We make mucky movies, yeah, but we don't always use actors. You've heard of hidden cameras, surveillance, that sort of thing?'

'Of course. That's what *we* do.'

'We?'

'DarkAlley Films.'

'Yeah, so you do.' He narrowed his eyes. 'Anyway, sometimes we film people when they don't know we're filming them. It isn't nice but… it's a living, as they say.'

'Are you telling me you filmed Zoë?'

He sighed again. 'Forget the ethics, Kirsty. Concentrate on the man.'

The screen jumped into life. Bright colour. Gaudy. A woman on her back. Was that… ? Of course it was: Zoë, her breasts prominent in the picture, the breasts naked, massaged by the man who was fucking her – a man in a mask, with the face of an animal, like a wolf. Zoë's own hands ran across his torso.

Kirsty said, 'I don't want to—'

'She hasn't started yet.'

There was no proper editing. The film looked as if it might have been taken with a single camera – though the camera seemed too close to have been concealed – and in a crude jump cut she saw another shot, Zoë on hands and knees, the wolf man behind her, and from this side-on angle there was no doubt that the man really was ramming himself inside her. Each thrust of his erect penis was clear to see. And if there had been any doubt that Zoë was enjoying the action – why should there be? – she slipped her hand down between her legs to cup his balls.

'Watch the man,' whispered Spencer. 'Try to see his face.'

But the man wore that wolf mask – and when the camera angle changed, Kirsty couldn't even see the mask, just his chest, and *Zoë*'s chest. His penis, which had discharged. Zoë's hand. Zoë brought her hand from the man's sticky, glistening member and rubbed his sperm across her breasts.

'No,' said Kirsty.

'His face.'

The camera pulled back enough to show Zoë's face alight with apparent ecstasy. The man's head was still encased behind the mask.

Spencer froze the frame. The image quivered as it captured the couple from head to thigh. Zoë's mouth was open, her eyes were closed. Her breasts seemed especially pert, as if refreshed by the fluid she had smeared across them. Between her legs the wolf man's penis dangled as if it had been her own.

'Recognise him?'

'Not through the mask.'

'His body, then.'

'Of course I don't—'

'I think you know him.'

Spencer was staring slack-mouthed at the screen.

'I don't know that man,' she said. 'I don't want to watch.'

'There's someone else.'

The image cut again, jolting to a shot of Zoë and her masked partner in a passionate embrace. The man held some kind of dildo in his hand – a banana, was it – and he was offering to push it into Zoë's backside.

'Stop it,' cried Kirsty. 'I'm not—'

'Wait a moment.'

Spencer pressed Fast Forward, but almost immediately the image changed and he had to change back to normal time. The screen still showed the Wolf Man but he was with a black girl now – and the dildo definitely was a banana because – Kirsty grimaced – it showed more clearly against her dark skin. The Wolf Man eased the banana into her rear.

'Spencer, you may be getting off on this—'

'Who's the black girl?'

The image cut to a three-shot – Zoë and the black girl, the Wolf Man in his mask, all three naked. The man held the banana and was showing it to the girls. Though there was no sound they were obviously talking about it. About what to do with it.

Spencer froze the frame. 'This is surveillance video, taken the day she died.'

Kirsty's throat constricted. She took a deep breath. 'How do I know that?'

'Why else would I show it you? You never met the black girl?'

'Never.'

'People look different with their clothes on.'

Kirsty felt tired. She closed her eyes. 'I don't know that girl.'

'Do you know the man?'

'I can't tell.'

'His body. The general look of him.'

She made herself stare at the screen. The man meant no more to her than the black girl did. Only Zoë was real. Especially in this latest shot: Zoë was naked but instead of contorting herself sexually she was having a conversation with two friends.

Spencer said, 'I think one of those two did it. Most likely the man.'

'It's not what Cassie said.'

'Forget Cassie. She's a compulsive liar. Don't you recognise him?'

'I've told you, no!'

'Man looks familiar to me. Look again.'

'Forget it, Spencer.'

'Ain't that Neil Garvey?'

She stared at the screen. 'I don't think so. The hair's too long.'

'That's a wig. Look at his body.'

'I don't know what Garvey's body looks like.'

'He didn't fuck you, then?' Spencer grinned coldly. 'But I bet he showed you his home videos.'

She bit her bottom lip. 'I don't remember.'

'Unforgettable, I hear.'

'That isn't him.'

'He's the right size—'

'So are a million men.'

'Look at the shape of him, the way he stands – that's Neil Garvey.'

Kirsty exhaled. 'Give the video to the police.' He snorted but she pressed on: 'How do you know it was the day she died?'

'I know, believe me. She was with Neil Garvey. We filmed it. Might not convince a jury, but that's what happened, babe. That man's your killer.'

'No.'

'That is Neil Garvey. The only question is what we should *do* about it. The police won't charge him, natch – but you want revenge, don't you?'

He stared intently. Waiting.

'What are you saying – you'd kill him for me?'

'Kill the man for all of us – you, me and Zoë. Clear everything up.'

She wet her lips. 'The day Zoë died, I was with Neil Garvey. All day long.'

Spencer's eyes flashed. 'She got killed that night.'

'I was with him well into the evening.'

'And he didn't fuck you? Some stud. What did he do *after* that?'

'You said the film was shot that *day*. This is bullshit, Spencer, and you know it.'

His face turned ugly. 'Are you fucking Garvey?'

'He doesn't get every girl he tries.'

'He did try, then?'

'And I'd have him killed for it? No, Spencer, you want him killed to cover *you*.'

He laughed. 'Hey, listen to this girl! She talks about killing like it's no more than slicing meat.' He leant towards her. 'Or are you vegetarian?'

'It was great meeting you, Spencer – a real eye-opener.'

But he grabbed her arm. 'You're going nowhere.' He kept his hold. 'Where's Cassie Nelson?'

'You blew it, Spencer.'

'The hell's that mean?'

'I'm leaving now, so let go of my arm.'

'I'll rip it off.'

He glared in her face. She glared right back. She dared not show weakness.

'*Where's that bitch hiding?*'

'She can't help you.'

He twisted her arm. Kirsty yelped in agony. Suddenly, humiliatingly, he forced her round and twisted her arm up behind her back. 'What you mean I blew it? I'm gonna do you, bitch.'

A door opened. Somebody came in. Kirsty's eyes were smarting and she couldn't see who it was.

But she recognised the voice: 'Now, now, Spencer. Shouldn't you save this for the bedroom?'

- 34 -

The rooms above the bike shop smelled strongly of new paint, but a client was a client and if he could put up with it, so could she. Becky was nervous, of course, but Mel laughed and said, 'Look how long mine lasted. He'd come and gone inside ten minutes.'

'I'll get a slow one.'

'Tickle his balls. That'll speed him up.'

They were opening windows to reduce the smell of paint. Mel said, 'When I was in the movie business I had all sorts.'

'You were acting, though.'

'Same as this. You pretend you're loving it. He's the greatest ever, you know – then he comes quicker and sods off. That's what Gina says.'

Gina wasn't on till evening shift – but day was busier, she said, not like you'd think.

Becky gave a critical glance around the bedroom. So far, this was the only room in a fit state for entertaining – but as Mel said, in her best secretarial voice: 'I'm afraid we're fully booked at present, sir – can I offer you an alternative appointment?'

*

Spence was visibly stronger, but Luke established himself in the red plush parlour as if he'd always been there. He was tall, languid, utterly at ease, while Spence shuffled about like a caged animal, watching his brother from the corner of his eye. Spence ignored Kirsty while Luke tidied the furniture. 'Let's have a drink,' Luke said. 'Sun's past the yardarm.'

Spencer agreed to a rum and Coke.

Kirsty followed Luke to the mini bar in the boudoir, because it seemed safer to be with him than to stay with Spence. But Luke took the drinks back to the parlour. She trailed behind. Handing his brother a drink, Luke murmured, 'Kirsty, you said just now that Spencer blew it. What did he do wrong?'

'Were you listening?' He shrugged disarmingly. She nodded at her own question. 'A hidden mike? No, these fancy mirrors, of course.'

'Antique, aren't they?'

'Everything here is fake.'

She went to a mirror to inspect it. Luke smiled at Spencer: 'She's so sharp.'

Kirsty tapped the mirror. It had a suitably faded gilt surround but was not antique. The glass was spotless. She tried to shift the frame but it was screwed to the wall, a part of it.

'Don't trash the room,' Luke warned lightly.

'Which mirror's false?'

'Can't you tell? That one's two-way, but in the bedroom they all are.'

'Only two,' said Spence. 'Quit showing off.'

Luke smiled. 'I didn't catch the whole of your performance. Did I miss much?'

'Nothing that matters,' Kirsty said airily.

'You haven't explained how Spencer blew it.'

'He pretended he'd filmed Neil Garvey at the very time Neil was out with me.'

Spence cut in: 'I didn't say it *was* Neil Garvey — I said I thought it was. So it was some other guy — it was still the man who killed the girl.'

The brothers watched her. Her lip curled. 'You're both so desperate.'

'Of course we are,' snapped Luke. His vehemence surprised her. 'My brother is accused of murder. Even you believe he's guilty — but the family knows he didn't do it.'

Spencer snorted through his nostrils like a horse.

Kirsty said, 'Cassie Nelson says he did.'

'She didn't say *Spencer* did — didn't she say "the management"?'

Kirsty shrugged.

Luke added, 'Cassie's a kiss'n'tell girl, doing this for money. Her fifteen minutes of fame.'

Spence muttered, 'Give me fifteen minutes with her—'

Luke rounded on him: 'Were you born an idiot or are you trying to learn the part?'

'Shut up.'

'Is being macho so important? Are you so determined to be tough you'd go to jail for a crime you didn't commit?'

Spence was angry. 'I've had enough of pretending, bro.'

'*Are* you pretending?' Kirsty asked.

But Luke kept on: 'Dig your grave, Spence. Tell her you did it. Show her how well you can pretend.'

'I ain't saying another word.'

'The first sensible thing you've said.'

Spence was silently counting to ten.

Luke turned to Kirsty: 'Please help me here. I'm trying to save my idiot brother.'

She took a breath and blinked twice. Luke *looked* convincing, even if his brother didn't. She stared into Luke's eyes. 'D'you really believe he's innocent?'

'Don't mind me,' Spence grumbled.

She gazed at Luke. '*Do* you?'

'I do believe it – not only because he's my brother. I know he's a hot-head, but if Spence did anything as bad as this, he'd tell me.'

'Because he's your *brother*?'

'We're very close.'

She hesitated. 'You told me he'd gone abroad.'

'So I did.' Luke chuckled.

Spencer had held back long enough. 'Oh, that's it, then – big deal: caught out in a lie! I *must* be guilty. What a give-away.'

'Have you finished?'

'Yeah, thanks for asking, I'll have another rum and Coke.'

Spence glared at his brother, then slouched off into the boudoir. Luke smiled at her. 'He's nearly house-trained.'

'But he can't help ripping his toys apart?'

'He didn't kill her, Kirsty.'

She was getting confused. 'You and your parents asked me to... approach Cassie.'

Luke stepped forward. 'Yes?'

'To buy her off for ten thousand pounds. Yet Spencer's *innocent*?'

Luke brushed it aside. 'What did Cassie say?'

'I knew she wouldn't take it.'

'Shame.'

'But I could be wrong.'

Luke was very close to her. He touched her arm. 'You saw her?'

Kirsty looked away. 'We spoke... through an intermediary.'

'But she didn't turn you down? —Hey, Spencer, open some champagne!'

'Hell, bro – I just made a Cuba Libre.'

'Three fresh glasses.' Luke squeezed her arm. 'So Kirsty, could we be doing business?'

'I don't know.' She looked up for his reaction. 'I asked if she'd really let a guilty man walk free.'

Luke waited a second. 'Pushy, aren't you? So what happened? Did she tell you Spence killed her?'

Kirsty spoke quietly now, almost to herself. 'I was sure he'd done it. I was sure Cassie would refuse the money.' She glanced around the red plush room. 'But then, I was sure this was where your parents lived.'

He whispered, 'You were too sure, too soon.'

'I was sure that Zoë was a simple kid. Innocent.' Her eyes dampened as she recalled the film. 'I was sure of Ken. I was sure of everything.'

Luke whipped out a crisp clean handkerchief. She took it. Suddenly she was finding it difficult to speak. 'I was sure there was... no man in the modern world... who still used linen handkerchiefs.'

Unexpected tears ran down her face, and Luke eased forward to comfort her in his arms. 'Let it all come out.'

'Zoë was my friend,' she sobbed. 'I wanted... I was so sure I could be tough.'

He gently stroked her hair. 'You've been very strong.'

She heard Spencer's voice behind her: 'I shouldn't have turned my back – you little rascals! I better open the champagne.'

*

Mel cracked a bottle of Spumante. She had given it a good shaking and froth shot from the bottle to splash across the wooden floor.

'Good job we haven't laid the carpet!'

Becky giggled as they filled plastic glasses. 'What does that froth look like?'

Mel laughed too. 'Celebration! End of day one.'

'Not bad. Not ruddy bad.'

'And that was just the sex!'

They hooted. Mel poured some more. 'Swig it down, Becks. Give your throat a rinse.'

'It could do with a clean!'

They cackled, clutching at each other in the shabby room.

'The stuff I've had down there!'

They hooted again and drank some more.

'Three tricks each is bloody marvellous. First day.'

'Only *half* a day. It was easier than I thought.'

'*And* we got no trouble.'

'Funny, though.'

'What was?'

'Listening to *you*.'

'I was only pretending—'

'I know – but you sounded so bloody *obvious*! 'Oh, give it to me. Oh yes, just there.' I could hear the old fart wheezing.'

'That one – he was about a hundred.'

'I thought one of mine was going to conk out!'

'Have another shamper.'

'I'm still – hang on.' Becky drained her plastic cup. 'Mind you, it *is* easier, knowing *you're* in the next room, listening.'

'Can't be too careful.' Mel refilled their glasses. 'There's not much of this.'

'That's what I was scared of – being alone with a bloke, not being able to *do* something if… you know.'

'We'll be all right if we listen out for each other.'

'Yeah, 'cos we're a co-operative, aren't we? Look Mel, should Gina really be on her own tonight? I know she's experienced, but…'

Mel shuddered. 'It's daft taking risks. We have to stick together.'

'Too right. How's your drink going?'

'Going, going, gone! It's lovely, this stuff, but it won't keep for another day.'

'No. Nothing lasts.'

*

Champagne is easy to drink, yet it can sometimes play havoc with the digestion. Beneath its fizz lies the stale acid of grapes too sour for other wines. Champagne grapes need fizz, they need party food, they need festival and frolic. On a queasy stomach or on a pregnant belly the fermented froth can lie like lees.

Kirsty felt she was drinking a toast to her murdered friend – drinking to Zoë's murder. Spencer downed champagne like lemonade. He grasped the bottle, kept it in his hand, and laughed as he refilled each half-full glass. 'Things looking good,' he said. 'Bring Cassie here.'

'She's too afraid.'

Spencer shook the empty flagon. 'Playing hard to get.'

'She's not playing.'

Kirsty's stomach lurched. She shouldn't drink on an empty – she closed her eyes: she didn't have an empty stomach. She was pregnant. She was drowning her baby in champagne – the same champagne that washed Zoë's death away. Spencer Miller said, 'Bitch saw a chance to earn real money. What did Dad say – ten thousand pounds?'

'And an air ticket.' Kirsty sat down.

'Nice. We pay her off, move her away from the cops—'

'And you walk free.' Kirsty wondered if she'd throw up.

'Well, fuck you, why not? I didn't do it.' Spencer spun the empty like a club. 'There's another of these in the mini bar.'

As he sauntered into the boudoir, Luke asked Kirsty if she was feeling all right. She grunted and refused another drink. Luke watched her. 'Let me tell you about Spence—'

'Forget it.'

'He's proud. He won't beg you to believe he didn't kill your journalist. He won't plead.'

'Because he killed her.'

Luke laid a hand on Kirsty's shoulder. 'He's not a murderer.'

'He damn near killed *me* – if you hadn't come in.'

'He *pretends* to be a tough guy.'

Pop went the flagon in the boudoir. Spencer laughed. As he came out, Kirsty said that she had to leave. Luke continued as if she hadn't spoken – as if Spence had not returned: 'He wouldn't have hurt you. He knew I was watching through the mirror.'

'Like hell.' Spence refilled his glass. 'If I'd known you was watching, I'd have put on a better show.'

Luke stepped towards him: 'You won't do *anything* to help yourself, will you?' Luke looked angry.

Spencer prodded him in the chest. 'I'm not an actor, bro, I don't pretend. I am 'what you see is what you get', bro, like you should be. Who wants a drink?'

No one did. Kirsty asked Luke how long he had been watching.

'They told me you were up here. So I checked first from the viewing room.'

Spencer laughed. 'To see if I was fucking you!'

Kirsty's head was spinning. She had to leave. 'The viewing room?'

A moment's pause as Spencer drank. Luke said, 'All right. I'll show you.'

*

She knew where it would be – behind the other door on the landing: a box room once, but now equipped with control desk, monitors, and a camera aimed through a two-way mirror into the parlour. What they could see through the large mirror was replicated on a monitor. A second camera and monitor showed the red plush boudoir. A third monitor showed the bed from the ceiling. Other screens were dead.

'We have more rooms downstairs – a single camera each. This one's the honeypot.'

She sat down heavily, like a tired studio technician. It felt uncomfortable to stand. Luke said, 'Anyone important we bring up here.'

Spencer had stayed in the parlour to make faces at them. He mouthed something. Kirsty asked if they could hear.

'You really want to?' Luke faded up the sound. 'The dialogue is so banal.'

Spencer was saying, 'Watch this, darlings.'

'Can we speak to him?'

'We're not Big Brother. This is surveillance – he's not supposed to know we're here.'

Spencer marched off to the boudoir. They could see him through the second mirror and on two screens. He called, 'Ta-ra!'

'Who do you get in here – businessmen?'

'We're only ten minutes from Westminster.'

Their conversation paused as Spencer gyrated by the bed and slipped out of his jacket.

'Please, not a striptease,' Kirsty muttered.

'He thinks you'll be impressed.'

'D'you get politicians here?'

Spencer dived on the bed.

'We try, but we can't be too obvious. She hasn't caught a really big name yet.'

Spencer was pretending to hump the mattress.

'Christabel or Simone?'

'Who?'

'You said 'she' hasn't caught a big name yet.'

'No, she will, though.'

'Who will?'

'Rinalda. This is Rinalda's place. Spence probably thinks he's with her now.'

'Spencer – with Rinalda?'

'Forget it. Sorry, a joke – bad taste, the Millers' speciality.'

Spencer was thrashing up and down, singing a song: *Riding Along On The Crest Of A Wave*. Luke twisted to see her face in the tiny studio. 'I thought we'd already told you this was Rinalda's place?'

'You said you *all* lived here.'

'Ah.' Luke thought for a moment, then chuckled. 'Mum doesn't want to pay business rates.'

Spencer called, 'Hello-o? Anybody there?'

'If you net a politician, he goes on video?'

'We video most people. It's easier.'

Spencer let out a piercing whistle. He was standing by the bed. Confident he had their attention, he opened his trouser zip with a flourish.

'Time to get back,' said Kirsty.

'To see Spence in all his glory?'

'To stop him.'

*

As they re-entered the parlour Spence called from the boudoir: 'If you want a drink I've got a stiff one here.'

'Put it away,' called Luke. 'We're leaving now.'

'Oh, *we're* leaving? The two of you. How sweet,' yelled Spence. He came through the door. Fully dressed.

'Kirsty isn't feeling well.'

'Come on, babe, it wasn't *that* bad a performance! What happens next – you'll bring Cassie here or what?'

'Too soon, Spencer.' Kirsty walked into the tiny bathroom and poured a glass of water. She drank it straight down, then came out with the glass refilled. Both men were watching her.

Spencer sneered. 'Cassie wants paying first?'

She sipped some water. 'Might inspire confidence.'

'COD,' said Spence. 'Word of a gentleman. Ha, ha.'

Kirsty shook her head. 'She'd be a fool to come out of hiding yet.' Luke and Spencer sighed. 'You've done nothing to suggest you're innocent. You just want to buy her silence.'

Spence looked sullen. 'Not true,' said Luke.

Spence shrugged. 'The girl is selling and I am buying. Everyone's happy. No one gets hurt.'

Kirsty started a reply but changed her mind. Luke looked at his watch. 'I have a meeting. Can I drop you, Kirsty?'

'From a cliff,' Spence muttered.

'I'll walk.'

Both men were watching her, and she suddenly realised she had more power than she had used. 'I need to be sure before I can let Cassie come here. What else can you tell me?'

Spence snorted. 'What are you – our fucking auditor? Get real.'

'You don't make it easy for me to believe you.'

Spence fell to his knees in mock humility. 'OK, I'm innocent. I humbly beg your majesty to believe in my innocence. I did not kill the girl.'

'Then who did?'

'*You're* the investigative journalist. Can I get up now? My knees are killing me.'

As he clambered up, Luke touched her arm. 'Come on. I'm leaving.'

'Hey, don't you go sleeping with my brother,' Spencer jeered. 'I'll tell your boyfriend.'

'I don't have a—'

'What's his name? Ken.'

She froze at the door. 'You know his name?'

'Oops. Did I touch a tender spot? Never thought I'd get the chance.'

'Come on,' urged Luke.

Kirsty stared at Spence. 'You know each other?'

Spence closed his finger and thumb. 'Me and Ken – just like that. No, that's not right. That's *you* and Ken, ain't it? That's what he says.'

'Has Ken been here?'

'How would I know?'

Luke said, 'He's winding you up. I told him about Ken.'

Spence said, 'That must be right,' and turned away.

Luke broke the silence. 'Coming, Kirsty?'

But Spencer grinned widely. 'Hey, bro, where's that video with Ken in action?'

He wandered across to the TV cabinet and knelt, humming to

himself. Kirsty turned to Luke: 'You go on without me. I'll find my own way back.'

*

Spencer poured two fresh glasses, but Kirsty shook her head: 'I can't drink any more.'

'You're not feeling good. What's wrong?'

He actually sounded as if he cared. He actually *looked* as if he cared.

'Female trouble.'

'Have something else, then —coffee?' She shuddered. 'Milk?'

'Is there some orange juice?'

'Surely.' He waited. 'Tell you what – I'm famous for my Buck's Fizz.'

'Just orange juice.'

'Your command, babe.'

As he went to fetch it she suddenly wondered if there was pineapple juice. She really fancied that. But she couldn't be finicky – she took the orange juice. 'This video?'

He frowned. 'Hm. Couldn't find the mother—'

'Fancy that. You expect me to believe that Ken came here?'

'Well, I can't be sure he *came* – he might have faked it!'

Spencer laughed. Kirsty put down her drink, spilling a little on the painted table. 'I don't believe you.'

'You don't believe anything.' Spencer wandered away from her, sipping his champagne. 'As I understand things, your boyfriend was investigating us?'

'Was?'

'Oh, did I use the past tense? Hot damn!' Spencer grinned at her. She sat down. 'You're *not* feeling good, are you?' She shook her head. 'Bad period?'

'Yes,' she answered bitterly. 'This is a very bad period.'

'In that case I won't try to make you. That settles that.'

Kirsty was hardly listening. She was only five weeks pregnant. Would it continue like this? She pushed the orange juice away.

'I didn't put nothing in your drink – don't worry.'

'No, no, it's me.'

'I could have,' he continued. 'You wouldn't have known.'

She let a silence fall. She could live with silence – but Spencer couldn't: 'No, that's my brother's trick. Did he try it on with you?'

'Try what?' Her mouth was dry.

'Date rape drug. He uses it sometimes.'

She stared at him. 'I don't believe you.'

Spencer shrugged. 'You *never* believe me. Damn journalist. Hey, Luke is not irresistible, babe. He's too – what's the word? – fastidious for rape. Can't stand the violence. So if a girl won't go along with what he wants he gets impatient, you know? Slips her a little roofie or GHB.'

She frowned.

He chuckled. 'Let me get my tongue round this, as the actress said – GHB is gamma hydroxyl butyrate. That's the stuff: GHB.'

'I know what it is,' snapped Kirsty. 'And roofie is Rohypnol. Every girl knows that.' She glanced nervously at her half empty glass. She felt drowsy, yes, but surely not – 'You're making this up.'

'You hope I am.'

'Are you jealous of Luke?'

'Hot damn! I *knew* you fancied him. Hey girl, if you really knew. —So you don't think people use this stuff.'

'I know they do—'

'Everyone uses it. In this business we get these gorgeous little chicks sometimes who won't come across – young ones especially. Slip some roofie or GHB in their drink and they go limp. They're conscious, but they lose the will to resist.'

'You're disgusting,' she muttered.

'*I'm* disgusting? I'm the only one *doesn't* use it. I don't need it, babe.' He pointed at her. 'You fancy my brother, don't you? Just don't accept a drink from him. And don't ever take a drink from my dad.'

'Come on, Spencer, this is plain ridiculous.'

'How old d'you think my father is?' Spencer stared at her. 'Too bloody old. Tell the truth, now, girl – would *you* go to bed with that old man?'

'He's your—'

'No one would, Kirsty – no woman under forty-five.'

'Rinalda does.'

Spencer snorted. 'You reckon? She used to, maybe, but every year my dad gets older she seems to get younger, know what I mean? The man is past it.'

'He's your father.'

'So that's an achievement? A couple of decades ago he had a hot night and squirted out some seed. Don't mean he could do it now. Man's ten years too old for Rinalda, anyway.'

She smiled mirthlessly. 'I see. Roofie's the only way Luke and your dad can score? Pull the other one, Spencer, it's got bells on.'

'OK, Luke only used it once – but Dad uses the stuff all the time.'

'Rubbish.'

'He's an old man in a young man's business.'

Spencer's mouth hung slack. He must be lying, she thought. 'You're the one in the sex business, Spencer – all those eager young actresses—'

'Ask my dad about his hay fever. Which he has never suffered from. Yet he carries that little bottle of anti-histamine he doesn't need. Why? Because it don't have anti-histamine inside.'

'You're a compulsive liar, Spence.'

'And good evening to *you*.'

She had to stand up, but as she did so her legs felt shaky. She said, 'You told me you had nothing to do with Zoë's murder—'

'Because I didn't—'

'And you'd never met Cassie—'

'Did I say that?'

'You said Neil Garvey was in that film—'

'He was—'

'He wasn't—'

'I *thought* he was.'

'You said my boyfriend came to this flat.'

'I'll get the video—'

'Go on, then, get it!'

Spencer hesitated. 'It's around here someplace, but I can't find it. Perhaps he moved it.'

'No way.' She grabbed the chair-back for support. 'They're all lies, Spencer – everything you say. And now you pretend your father uses Rohypnol. You're something else.'

He studied her, then smiled. 'What's a nice girl like you doing in a dirty old world like this?'

'Meaning?'

'You're too innocent—'

He was interrupted by a sudden knock at the door. They glanced at it, waited, but didn't say a word. The door opened.

Rinalda said, 'Oh good. I was afraid I might find you two in bed. I would have been so cross.'

Spencer said, 'That's what the place is for.'

Kirsty stared at her. Rinalda seemed unconcerned. When she slipped out of her light coat she seemed a little breathless and her cheeks glowed as if she had just come from outside.

Kirsty sat down again. 'You could have checked from the viewing room.'

Rinalda wore a green shift dress that clung to her fine body. Few women her age could have worn it. Few would still have had such thick blonde hair. 'You know about that?'

'Luke gave her the guided.'

'And what did *you* give her, Spencer?'

'Nothing, Ma. Scouts' honour.' He raised his fingers in salute, but then wiggled them naughtily. He leered at Kirsty. 'I didn't even give you my phone number, did I, babe? Here.' He fumbled in his pocket and produced a card. 'That's my cell phone. Now, that's what I call *personal*!'

Kirsty half rose to take it, then sat down. Rinalda chuckled uncertainly. 'I *have* interrupted something.'

Spence said, 'Like she says, Ma, you should have watched from the viewing room.' He sucked his breath and rolled his eyes. 'Oh, *Mama*, what we was doing!'

Kirsty said, 'He's kidding.'

Rinalda gazed down at her on the chair. 'He's such a boy.'

'We was watching videos,' Spence said. 'You know that actress who died? We had surveillance of her in an orgy. I thought Kirsty might recognise the guy wearing the mask.'

'And did she?'

'Nope. I was sure he'd be familiar.'

Rinalda nodded. 'So you've finished now? We need this room.'

'Simone's gone.'

'*I* want it. This is not her room.'

He grinned at Kirsty. 'This used to be Rinalda's pad. Fond memories.'

Rinalda added, 'It's a pretty room, yes? Now, Kirsty, you're sure you didn't recognise the man? His *body* was not familiar? Oh, well.'

'I could take the video away with me.'

Spencer laughed. Rinalda shook her head: 'You can *look* at it again.'

'I couldn't bear to. Zoë was my friend.' Her voice quavered.

Rinalda hovered beside Kirsty in the chair. 'Has this upset you?'

She placed a soft hand on Kirsty's arm. Kirsty looked down. She was thirsty again, but dared not touch the orange juice.

Rinalda stroked her gently. 'To see your friend like that – it must have been disturbing. Your friend Zoë.'

'And Ken,' put in Spencer. 'Her boyfriend. I got this video of—'

'Zoë and Kirsty's boyfriend?'

'No, Ma – different videos. I got one of him, but I can't find the thing.'

'Someone has taken it?'

Kirsty stood up. 'Stop the action – I don't believe a word of this. I'm going home.'

Spence said, 'I'll see you out. Need a lift?'

'No, thanks.'

Rinalda laughed. She was close to Spencer now. 'You've frightened her. She wants to run away from you.'

'Oh, you know me, Ma – I'm a pussycat.'

'With such claws!'

Rinalda nudged her stepson fondly. As they stood smiling at Kirsty their eyes were sharp as cats' eyes. Jungle cats, she thought.

'I'll find my own way out,' Kirsty said. 'Straight down the stairs.'

Spencer chuckled. 'I do like to see a girl go down.'

*

Which she would have done. But when she reached the landing outside the dining room she realised that she was alone and unaccompanied in their house. Their cat house, they called it.

Kirsty paused, listened a moment, then began back up the silent stairs. She was struck again by the anonymity of the hallways – good carpet, clean wallpaper, but no pictures. No indication of what really happened here. On the next landing she paused again, listened, then looked at two plain doors. Two other flats, they'd said, a girl in each. She took a step towards them, then thought no, it wasn't why she was here. She continued up the stairs to the top.

It was a surprisingly quiet house, she realised. Spence and Rinalda were behind that door but Kirsty couldn't hear a sound from them. She hadn't heard a sound from the rooms downstairs. Here in the hall the only sound was a muffled hum of traffic, far away. Few cars came along this back street. The hum of traffic came from Millbank beside the Thames.

Kirsty gently opened the other door.

The viewing window looked directly into the parlour, giving so clear a view that it was hard to believe she wasn't looking through plain glass. She was behind a two-way mirror, yet she felt exposed; she hardly dared to move. But they couldn't see her. They were unaware of her.

Spencer was grinning, showing off, gesticulating with the champagne bottle. Rinalda had a glass. They seemed to be toasting each other. There was no sound.

Kirsty moved to the control desk and slid the fader that she'd seen Luke use. As soon as she could hear she took the volume no further, so the sound would not feed back. Spence was saying, '... care *what* she believes. There's no evidence.'

'This Nelson girl?'

'We'll buy her – pay her off.'

'An expensive mistake. You shouldn't touch these girls.'

'Cassie? I didn't – I don't *think* I did. Who knows? Another actress, that's all.'

'With a story to sell.'

He waved the bottle. 'We'll buy the world-wide rights! Another drink? This one's nearly finished.'

'Are you trying to make me tipsy, Spencer?'

'Now, why would I do that?'

He chuckled and emptied the dregs into their glasses. Rinalda leant closer to him: 'You know, you're a very foolish boy.'

'But handsome with it,' Spence laughed.

'I don't know,' she said teasingly. 'Luke is a little more handsome—'

'Now, now.'

Rinalda gripped his biceps muscle. 'But you are stronger, I think.'

'You bet your sweet ass I am.' He patted her backside.

'It's not as sweet as it used to be.'

He opened his hand and felt more of it. 'Feels pretty good to me.'

After a moment, she moved away from him. 'How precious it is to be young.'

'Now, Rinalda, don't go all maudlin.' He put down his drink. His hands hung free. Rinalda gazed around the room: 'This room. There have been some good times here.'

He was staring at her, a loose grin on his face. 'You had the best of them, I bet.'

She spun to face him. 'Did you fuck Simone in here?'

'No, Ma—'

'Don't call me that.'

'Rinalda—'

'I'm not so old, you know.'

He took hold of her arms. 'I wouldn't fuck Simone in here.'

'Where then?'

'Nowhere – I don't want that bitch Simone.' She broke from his grasp. 'This is *your* room, Rinalda – your place.'

'My hideaway,' she muttered. She shivered and looked momentarily sad. 'But it has changed now. That mirror is so gross.'

She stared at it – and it was as if Rinalda was staring into Kirsty's face. But Rinalda was not making eye contact. When Spence approached her from behind, Rinalda's gaze shifted to his reflection in the mirror. 'I can't relax here with that camera.'

He grinned. 'You've done a lot worse in front of cameras.'

'Not now. I don't like it here. Not any more.'

'It isn't on.'

'You turned it off?'

'I didn't go in there. Luke did.'

Rinalda frowned. Kirsty took a breath. Rinalda said, 'So the camera could be running?'

'No, no.'

'I want to make sure that it's off.'

But Kirsty was already out of the viewing room – not even waiting to turn the fader down. She slipped out across the landing, and had barely reached the stairs when she heard a door open behind her. Kirsty stopped on the stairs and pressed herself to the wall. She didn't dare run down in case they heard. Rinalda said, 'I cannot be private even in my own house.'

- 35 -

Roy Farrell's flat in Peckham is untidy, masculine, not at all like the Pimlico residence. Where Pimlico is an anonymous hotel, Roy's place is the saloon bar of a pub. He has just opened a brown ale to wash down a cheese and onion sandwich when his phone rings. He answers it, bottle in hand, and chuckles. 'Herbie, so soon already?'

Herbie is phoning from the street, a pay phone. He prefers them. Having a mobile phone makes it too easy for people to get in touch with him – usually at the one moment he does not want to be pestered. 'Well, Roy, you said your boss didn't want us to hang around.'

'He's like a rat with toothache.'

'And we're his dentist?'

'Yeah! Rip the tooth out, Herbie. When?'

'Tonight.'

Roy puts down his bottle. 'I'm on for that.'

'Got your kit?'

'Don't worry.'

Herbie gazes through the glass screen of the pay phone at traffic passing by. It is mid-evening. The sun is low. Everyone he sees is going somewhere. 'Shame we can't make this look like an accident.'

'You mean tamper with the fuel line, cut the brake cable? That only works in movies, Herbie, when the guy drives off through the mountains. Worst that happens in London is he bumps into the back of a red bus.'

'You know the *Parrot*?'

'He goes *there*? Christ, the man *deserves* to die.'

'He *starts* there. Or he will tonight. You know his car?'

'TVR, you said. Yellow. It'll be outside?'

'In the car park – till about midnight, maybe later.'

'What time does he arrive?'

'Eleven-ish. Gives you an hour at least.'

'I only need five minutes.'

'As the bishop said to the actress. So you'll put a bomb in the car, or what?'

'I'm not giving you a blueprint, Herbie. Will there be anyone with him?'

'Not at that time.'

'Because no one walks away from this.'

*

Rosa said, 'I've had a phone call.' She'd put her head around the door of the editing suite. 'They're happy with it – thank God.'

Ken smiled. 'Great. So we'll get paid.'

Rosa glanced at the screen. 'You're not still working on it?'

Kirsty leant back in her chair and stretched. 'No, it's too late now. We're just scanning each other's stuff.'

'Cosy.'

Rose looked at their two chairs close together: Kirsty and Ken a couple again. She said, 'We've put it to bed. It's finished. New project tomorrow.' She caught Kirsty's eye. 'You *are* going to let it rest?'

'Sure, it's finished. Dead. Goodbye, Zoë. RIP.'

Ken said, 'Apart from my live scene, when the programme actually goes out.'

Rosa shook her head. 'Sorry, Ken, they said they wouldn't risk it live.'

'You're not going to let them cut it?'

'They like the idea but want it pre-recorded. No hurry, they said – it's only one scene. You can have another week.'

As he swivelled in his chair Ken looked angry and defensive. 'It isn't 'only one scene', it's the climax. It's what the whole bloody film's about.'

Kirsty kept her head down and watched the screen.

Rosa asked him, 'Are you so desperate to get a starring role?'

'We don't *have* to be anonymous.'

'They don't see this as the climax to the film.'

'Why not?'

'Hacking into a computer site is hardly rocket science.'

'But I'll freeze it – bring the site down.'

'It's been done before, Ken. Yawn, yawn. They've got good material already from killporn.com—'

'That's archive stuff. Mine will be fresh.'

'But boring television. You know how dull computers are.'

'Everybody uses them!'

'Exactly – it's like filming a washing machine. But they like the rest of your film—'

'That's the build-up. This is the climax!'

'They're the client. They don't see it your way. They like the AIDS angle—'

'Oh, puh-lease!'

'It's a good angle. Porn films rely on unprotected sex, and since half the cast are druggies and—'

'Don't patronise me, Rosa—'

'You show porn stars doing escort work—'

'Prostitution.'

Rosa had reasoned enough. 'It isn't *your* film, Ken, it's theirs. We delivered on time, they're happy with what they got. You can record your scene, fine, but the job is done.'

Kirsty touched Ken's wrist: 'Hey. After the battle the crusader gets on his horse and rides away. End credits. Fade to a golden sunset. Just be grateful we don't have to stay in the swamp forever.'

'That's my girl,' said Rosa. 'We must move on.'

As she left the editing suite Ken called, 'We're just whores, then? Next customer, please. Is that it?'

From outside, Rosa called back, 'Not whores, Ken. Tarts. There's a world of difference.'

Ken sat fuming. He pushed his chair to the far side of the editing suite. It was a small room, so he was still only a few feet away from Kirsty. 'What, it's not cost-effective to carry on?'

She nodded. 'I don't know if I can drop *my* stuff either.'

'We could *both* carry on.'

Kirsty looked at him levelly. Did he mean it, or was it anger talking? She said, 'We'd get no help from Rosa—'

'She can't stop us!'

'We'll have to chase this in our own time—'

'Haven't I been doing that already?'

'How much time *did* you devote to this?' He shrugged. 'Hours and hours in front of your PC?'

'Plus getting out and making contacts—'

'Luke Miller?'

'Yeah.'

'And Spence?'

'I met him once.'

She looked away. 'Did you ever get to see a movie being made?'

He detected her change in tone. 'What are you getting at?'

'I just wondered if you'd ever... been involved in any—'

'Involved?'

'You know, it's easy to get... close to them.' She found herself short of breath. The words bumped against each other in her throat. 'Zoë was involved. You met Spence and Luke.'

'You did too.' He said it flatly, his words more a comment than a defence.

'We both got in. Now we can't leave it alone.'

'That's not what you meant. Kirsty.' They sat like cripples on office chairs. 'Involved, you said – in Zoë's *murder*?'

'No.' Her throat had dried. She swallowed. 'In a film. Cassie Nelson said...'

'What did she say?'

'On Zoë's film, the management – men outside the film – were sometimes allowed to join in.'

His shoulders slumped. Without his anger, Ken shrivelled in his seat. 'You think... I was there – on set?'

'No, not then—'

'You think I was part of the 'management', as you call it?'

'No, some other time—'

'You think I *killed* her?'

'I don't. I don't.' She couldn't look at him. 'I just thought perhaps, some other time, some other film... Spencer had a video. Oh, I don't know what I'm saying. Forget it. Forget I spoke.'

He stood up, not fast, not threateningly, but because he could no longer remain seated. 'I think you're dangerously obsessed with this—'

'Zoë was my friend—'

'You think I was 'involved' in Zoë's... I can't believe this.'

'I didn't mean that.'

'What the hell *did* you mean?'

He stepped towards her, then forced himself to stop. She looked up once, then looked away. 'I only asked if... in another film, you might have...'

'Made a guest appearance?'

'Men wear masks sometimes,' she ploughed on. 'So no one can recognise them.' She made herself watch his face. 'A wolf mask, for instance.'

He stared down at her. She couldn't read his expression, but he looked – what? – incredulous? Astounded that she knew? Ken shook his head. 'What the hell are you rambling about?'

She didn't dare stand up to face him. But she had to ask: 'You know the wolf mask?'

His expression didn't change. But his voice did: 'You really are accusing me. Aren't you?'

She crumpled. 'I don't know what to think.'

'Makes two of us.'

She looked up quickly, tears in her eyes. 'There was a scrap of film. Spencer said... Zoë and some man. I know it's ridiculous, but—'

'In a wolf mask?'

'Yes.'

'Where did you see this – on the internet?'

'No, I – I can't tell you.'

'I see.' He nodded. 'Rosa was right: we *should* move on. But can *you* move on from this quest of yours?'

'It has sucked us both in.'

'You think I murdered her?'

'No, Ken, please – I'm sorry I said that. But this is so poisonous – it infects the way we look at everything. I can't see straight. And you won't leave those internet sites alone.'

'That's different.'

'Everything's different.'

'*We're* different.' He moved past her to leave the room. At the door he said, 'Of course, I forgot – you're pregnant. Maybe that explains it.'

She blinked up at him. 'How – it makes me irrational?'

'Your word,' he said, and left.

- 36 -

Rick Miller must have spent time inside. It wasn't something Neil Garvey knew for a fact but was the only way he could account for his predicament. Only someone who had been there, who had experienced the sapping loneliness of a prison cell, would have known how soon Neil's stay would become unbearable. In a cell there is no contact, no communication, and worst of all, no information. When Herbie threw him into this darkened cubicle he refused to tell Neil how long he would be kept, when he might be fed, when if ever he might get out. What might happen to him if he did get out. And along with his wallet, belt and shoes, Herbie had taken Neil's wristwatch. 'Boss's orders,' he had said.

At first, Neil felt angry. Then afraid. Then angry *and* afraid. He tested the security of the room, but without any expectation he'd find a weakness. Even the internal walls were brick, nineteenth century brick, brick-solid. The door was solid. The window small but solid. There was a bed – solid too – and the mere fact that there was a bed in the cell at all was ominous: it meant a lengthy stay. Yet within half an hour Neil found the worst thing was that he didn't have his wristwatch. Was it half an hour? Two hours? How long had it been?

How long would it be?

No one came to him. There were few sounds. Neil could do little more than muse on his condition – which, as he realised, was the point. Rick wanted information Neil did not have. After an hour or two – who knows how long? – Neil wondered whether he should make something up. He could tell plenty about Kirsty Rice – what they'd talked about, where she was from – and there was that girl Zoë they said had died. He could pretend he'd met her. No – spoken to her on the phone: if he'd met Zoë he'd have to know what she had looked like. And Cassie – he remembered now. Nothing like an hour or two in a darkened room to bring memories back. Was Cassie responsible for his being here? What could he tell them about *her*?

Another hour passed. The world slowed down. Because Neil had no proper track of time he found himself reduced to the traditional pastimes of the prisoner. He knew they were traditional, but he did them all the same. He paced his cell. He used the plastic lidded bucket. He watched the pale light change to darkness in the window. Tomorrow, when the sun appeared again, he'd watch a small rectangle of light creep slowly across the floor. Would he still be here tomorrow? The day after? He didn't know if he wanted to be or not. Was it safer here than outside?

He used the bucket again, and this time he needed more than a pee. But he couldn't bring himself to sit on the thin-rimmed bucket. He'd have to squat above it. If he took the bucket over to the bed he could hold onto the bedrail while he squatted. But Neil wasn't yet ready to pull his trousers down in the darkened room. Though the bucket was lidded, the smell of his earlier piss had leaked out. He didn't want to add to that.

What *was* the time?

Neil sat on the bed. Since there was nothing he could tell Rick, there was no point scratching his head about it. There was no point lying – pretending he knew something in the hope that Rick would let him out. That was a fool's game. Neil wasn't a fool. He was nearly as old as Rick – he was certainly too old for *this*. His anger flared again, then died.

He should concentrate on Rick. Why had he brought him here? Who could have told Rick that Neil had shafted him? They did business together, nothing more. Rick was head of an empire, while Neil was no more than a supplier. A small supplier. He didn't cheat, he was no threat – Rick could use him or not as he chose. Neil was of no consequence to Rick.

That was not a comforting thought.

And then, at a late uncertain hour when few comforting thoughts remained, when light had faded and his bones had turned to ash, there was no comfort in hearing footsteps and the sound of a key turned in the lock.

The door opened onto the dimly lit, yet to Neil the *brightly* lit, corridor leading to the printing floor. Standing in the doorway was the bulky Herbie Tripp.

'Rick wants you.'

Those words brought no comfort either.

*

Irrational? Maybe. But when Kirsty came out of the DarkAlley offices she told herself she could do whatever she liked in her free time. She checked her watch. Gone ten o'clock.

As she passed a pub she felt what she would normally call a tummy rumble – except that her tummy wasn't a normal tummy: she was sharing it now. It was a rumble of communication.

Where could she find a sandwich? She went back to the pub, pushed open the door, recoiled from the beery tobacco smell, but went inside. She would skip alcohol and ask for tomato juice and a sandwich. Try to swallow it.

They had stopped serving food.

In the streets outside she found that even in the centre of a metropolitan city, half past ten at night, she couldn't find a sandwich. The next pub looked as if it served food but was so crowded she had to walk straight past. There was a smell of meat but it didn't come from the pub – it came from the Donner Kebab shop next door. The smell was cloying. She couldn't eat that meat.

Wasn't there a café? They had all closed. Wasn't there a coffee stall? Not since the market had closed. A takeaway? Only Indian or Chinese food, which she couldn't face tonight. A fish and chip shop would have been excellent – the bland, fatty food was exactly what she needed. Solid and nourishing food for the baby. Kirsty used her detective skills: she stood on the pavement and sniffed. But there wasn't a whiff of fish and chips.

Eventually she went into an all-night grocery and bought a chilled, pre-wrapped salmon and cucumber sandwich and a can of Lilt. Dinner for two. The Lilt was too sweet, a kiddie's drink, and the sandwich filling had oozed into the bread and made it sodden, so that it flopped in her hand and let pieces of salmon fall out.

Normally the sandwich would have sustained her till she got home. But she wasn't going home – not yet. So she went back into the shop and bought a Snickers and a Milky Way, kiddie's sweets, while she finished the Lilt. Eating chocolate as she walked down the street seemed strangely indulgent, more reprehensible than drinking alcohol in a pub. Odd really, what people thought socially acceptable.

She licked her fingers in the cool night air. What she was about to do was not in the least acceptable.

*

Rick was waiting for Neil at the end of the print floor. To Neil the drab lighting appeared fierce; the empty floor vast. The air was fresher, as if someone had left a window open. Neil didn't look for it. He knew he couldn't escape.

Rick started: 'How's your memory?'

Neil tried to explain that he never did remember much about his girls. If there was someone particular that Rick—

'Where's Cassie now?'

'I don't know, Rick. I never knew where she was from.'

'That reporter, Kirsty Rice – what did she pay you?'

'Two days' fee.'

'Not much, then?'

'No.'

'So why mention *me*?'

'I didn't, Rick. She took shots of me in action, you know – makin' a film? Girl strips as she drifts down the stairs, girl on a bed, that sort of thing.'

'Which girl?'

'Some actress.' Why bring Trisha into it? 'No one important.'

'She meet some girls?'

'Yeah.'

'Cassie?'

'No, Christ, I don't know Cassie – that was ages ago. Rice met some new girls – you know, replied to my small ad? And I took her out to some slags who'd made films before and still liked doin' it. You know – I tried to show her it's an honest business with friendly people.'

Rick sucked his teeth. Herbie stood behind Neil – who couldn't see Herbie but could feel that he was there.

'You're too friendly, Neil, for your own good. You show off to this pretty young journalist – next thing I know I've got the police and half the world here on my doorstep. You must've told her *something*.'

'I just fed her a load of old toffee I thought she'd want to hear. I didn't say nothin' about *you*.'

'Can I trust you, Neil?'

'Of course.' Neil felt uncomfortable. 'Christ, how do I answer that, Rick?'

'With the truth, Neil. Try the truth.'

'This *is* the truth, Rick. Every word is true.'

'I can't work with a man I can't trust.' Rick sighed. 'Can I trust you or not?'

'Sure you can.'

'Here's what I'll do. It's an ace idea. What I'll do is I'll let you out on a very short leash.'

Neil began sweating with relief.

'But listen, Neil – whatever you do, wherever you go, I'll watch you. My *boys* will watch you. We'll watch you closely. And if you fuck with me, Neil, you will be dead. I guarantee this, Neil – you will be dead. You understand?'

Neil nodded eagerly.

'We have to test you, Neil. You like cars – smart cars?'

'Well, I can take 'em or leave 'em.' Neil frowned anxiously.

'They don't turn you on?'

'Not really.'

'I have a special car I want you to collect for me.'

Neil nodded slowly. 'You want me to steal a car, Rick? Christ, I couldn't even break in through the door.'

'Oh dear, Neil, where was you brung up? Don't worry, I've got the key.'

'Oh, right. Um... Is the owner of this car likely to be around?'

'He'll be close – but he'll be busy. What I want you to do Neil, is pick up the car about midnight tonight and drive it here. Can I trust you with that?'

'Sure, sounds easy – where do I find this car?'

'At a south of the river club called *The Parrot*. Now, this is a nice car, Neil, I don't want it damaged. It's a brand new yellow TVR.'

*

Irrational? Ken's word echoed in her head. Perhaps she *was* irrational – not only about Zoë's murder but about that scrap of video also. As she walked through the quieter streets of Pimlico, Kirsty knew that she had to see that film again. *Could* the man in the mask have been Ken? At the time it had not occurred to her. Spence had suggested the man was Neil Garvey, and it was only afterwards – after Spence had deliberately dropped Ken's name; after Ken had blithely admitted he had met Spence – that Kirsty had replayed the video in her mind and asked herself whether there was any chance it *could* have been Ken. Of course not – had been her immediate reply. Spence was dirtying the water, stirring up the mud, hoping to confuse her. It wouldn't work.

It didn't work.

At the time.

But *could* it have been Ken? As she crossed John Islip Street her footsteps slowed. She needed to see that video. The image replaying in her brain was growing vague, like an ancient worn video, and with each unreliable replay the man looked more and more like Ken. But it couldn't have been him, could it? Surely, when she first saw the film, she would have recognised her lover's body – if she had expected to see it. If she hadn't been told it was Neil. If the whole idea hadn't been so fantastic.

Or was she being irrational?

She was nearly there. As she walked along the silent street she hoped that on the top floor of that quiet-looking house she would find Spencer's video. It was in that New Orleans style parlour. She considered the contrast between the plush red and gold apartment and the sober dining room downstairs where she had first met the Miller family. On that visit she had assumed she was in a pleasant family home. Naïve. How could she be so naïve? On her next she found it was a high class brothel. But had even that been true? Rinalda said there was no privacy in her own house. My hideaway, she called it. And Spencer had taken her in his arms and said, 'This is *your* room, Rinalda.' He and Rinalda had remained in that room. Might they still be there?

Kirsty rang the doorbell.

Why would Rinalda and Spence be there? Spencer was her stepson. Kirsty remembered her last sight of them as they had smiled like cats and wished her goodbye. She remembered sneaking back to peer through the mirror. Rinalda and Spence had seemed... too intimate to be mother and son.

The door opened.

It was the maid again, in her stage uniform. 'Oh, hello.'

'I'm expected.'

The maid let her in. Life can be so simple, Kirsty thought.

'They're upstairs,' the maid said. 'Shall I go up and—'

'I know the way.'

The maid shrugged and disappeared through a small door leading down to the basement. She was tired, thought Kirsty: nearly eleven at night. She had recognised Kirsty and her job as housemaid was to smile pleasantly and not to ask awkward questions of regular visitors.

The stairs were silent, but Kirsty took each flight carefully. There was no sound from intervening rooms. When she reached the top landing it was as quiet as in the rest of the house. The apartment might be empty – but it was soundproofed, wasn't it? Kirsty paused outside the door, then tiptoed to the smaller one. She opened it carefully, before slipping inside the viewing room.

The only illumination came through the two-way mirror. The console deck was off. The viewing room was in semi-darkness, but light from the mirror – dimmer than before – still made her feel exposed, as if she were standing behind a sheet of clear glass. She didn't panic: she knew that no one in the parlour could see her.

There was no one there. A single lamp glowed through a frilly red velvet shade, and the room seemed barely lit at all. Just that single night-light to comfort anyone who woke.

Was someone in the bedroom? This two-way mirror showed only the parlour. To view the bedroom Kirsty had to ease her way along the narrow room to see through the second mirror, into the boudoir. There was hardly any light. A lamp Kirsty couldn't see emitted a glow like a winter sunset, back-lighting the bed. Was somebody in it? Yes, of course. But she could not see who.

Kirsty glanced at the camera. To film capers in bed the Millers had invested in night-vision lenses. She might see better through the camera than with her naked eye. And wasn't there a second camera mounted in the ceiling? With an aerial view.

Kirsty touched the Power button. Across the console deck several small lights immediately came on – and reflected in the window. Again it seemed extraordinary that nothing would be visible from the other side, but Kirsty had been there; she had looked into the mirror from both sides.

The console hummed softly, but no one would hear it. The monitors quickly warmed but for now they showed no picture. She must select a specific camera. When she touched *Boudoir One* a screen changed to the same dark image she could see through the mirror: the side of the bed, dark and indistinct. Not enough light. Neither on screen nor through the mirror could Kirsty make out any detail – just a lumpy silhouette against a dull background glow. She could see the bed but in this feeble light the camera could not process the image. Kirsty adjusted the controls but it didn't help. Kirsty stared at the monitor. There was someone in the bed.

She selected *Boudoir Two*.

The image now came from above the bed, from the camera in the ceiling, and the first, most obvious revelation was that the room was lit by a small lamp placed on the floor, beyond the bed. *Boudoir One* had shown the back-lit image; *Boudoir Two* looked down on a dim but clearer view of the big wide bed. Someone was humped beneath a mound of bedclothes. Someone. Was it one or two people?

Kirsty shook her head: one, two, a *ménage* – did it matter? With *anyone* in the boudoir she didn't dare creep in the parlour to rummage for the video.

One person or two? In the grainy overhead shot Kirsty could see a leg, an arm – and on the pillow a mass of golden curls. Kirsty assumed they were golden: in this light the screen was practically monochrome. But it could only be Rinalda.

Kirsty peered again. Yes, there *was* someone else in the bed. Kirsty sighed: spying like this did not give her a warm feeling – and to see Rinalda in bed with Spencer was as if she herself had been betrayed. Rinalda was cheating on Rick – but worse than that, was cuckolding him with his own son.

The image from above was faint but definitely clearer than that from the side. Kirsty adjusted the contrast again, faded out the colour – yes, that was better: not a sparkling image but a grainy CCTV picture. Clandestine. Now she could clearly see Rinalda, half asleep. Rinalda stirred slightly and draped her bare arm across her stepson lover, buried beneath the bedclothes.

Spencer was betraying his father – almost incest but not quite. Not that Spencer would make the distinction. He had killed Zoë, he had scared Cassie into hiding, and had pretended to Kirsty that Neil Garvey, then Ken, was in Zoë's video. Ken had warned her about Spencer – yet she had doubted Ken and had almost believed Spencer. His own brother had warned against him – what had Luke said in Rules restaurant? 'My brother is no angel. My father's favourite.' Now Spencer lay with his father's wife.

Rinalda stirred again. Kirsty reached across to press Record. The machine made the faintest additional hum, but no one in that room would hear it. Here was a video that should shock even the Miller family. She snorted. Presumably Rick didn't know? With his family swimming in a cesspool of porn, anything was possible. Spencer was Rick's favourite. Rick had married a younger wife. Rinalda had a dark past. Although she seemed a glamorous and amusing step-mother, Rinalda had this 'hideaway' and according to Luke she ran the whole house. She was its madam.

Rinalda moved again, and this time – yes! – the bedclothes shifted and the young man's head finally emerged. Captured on video. Mother and son. Except that it wasn't Spencer.

- 37 -

'One last customer,' said Gina. 'Then we shut up shop.'

It was gone eleven o'clock. She, Becky and Mel were in the furnished room above the bike shop – the room that functioned as bedroom, meeting room and customer care centre – looking back on day one of their new business. Gina was plumping pillows and smoothing the sheet. 'I hate late-nighters – they spend all evening in the pub and think we'll round off their boozy night.'

Mel said, 'If he's drunk he'll stay till midnight. With brewer's droop.'

'Stuck in neutral. Smelly with beer and a gut full of self pity.'

Becky smiled. 'Makes me glad you're on the evening shift.'

'I won't always be.'

'You know, it's funny,' Becky mused. 'This afternoon seems a lifetime ago.'

'No ill effects?'

'It's like nothing happened.'

'Sex gets meaningless,' Mel declared. 'Just a job.'

'Even with your boyfriend – assuming you've got one?'

Mel shrugged. 'You can put on the same act.'

Gina chuckled. 'Worse is you start comparing – saying, oh he's not so big, comparatively.'

All three giggled. Then the front doorbell rang.

'Back to the waiting room, girls,' said Gina. 'Mother's in business.'

'The *staff rest room*, please,' insisted Mel.

While Gina slipped downstairs Mel and Becky sat on the bare floor next door, suppressing their smiles. Becky wouldn't look at Melanie in case it brought her out in giggles. After a while, Gina came back upstairs.

'Bet she was haggling on the doorstep,' Mel whispered.

They heard footsteps. Gina wasn't alone, of course. But Becky frowned: it didn't sound like one man—

Their door opened. The girls looked up. Framed in the doorway were two uniformed policemen.

*

Kirsty stood with her phone outside the eminently respectable Church of Christ Scientist and keyed in the number on the card he had given her.

'Yo! Spence Miller.' There was music in the background.

'Kirsty Rice.'

'My favourite reporter!'

'I want to tell you something—'

'I *know* I'm beautiful—'

'About your brother...' Kirsty hesitated.

'What about the man?' She said nothing. 'This line dead?'

She took a breath. 'I can't tell you on the phone.'

'Why not, babe – even the *calls* have ears? Don't piss me around.'

'I have to tell you face to face – I want to *watch* your face.'

'It's a handsome one, I do admit. So what is this, Kirsty babe – you laying a trap? It sure sound that way to me.'

'Your brother has been cheating on you.'

'Oh. And that is news?' Spence sounded guarded.

'He's been cheating on your father.'

'Now, that *is* news. Listen, Kirsty, it happens I am enjoying a nice little drink here, and I really do not want my evening fucked up with some poncey little game. Understand me?'

'This is not a game, Spence. It's something you have to see.'

She heard him hesitate. 'You in bed with Babylon?'

'No police, Spence – just you and me. Where are you?'

'No, babe. Where are *you*?'

- 38 -

Spencer was grim-faced. He liked action but he also liked to call the shots. What he especially did *not* like was to be taken for a sucker, and he reckoned this interfering girl poking her pretty little nose into *everything* must surely be setting something up. She knew which buttons to press.

Spence came out of the *Parrot* into the car park. It was colder now, and dark, about eleven fifty – time to *arrive* at the club, not to leave it. The car park was half full. No one about – except: was this part of Kirsty's set-up? – some guy was trying to break into his car! A slim white feller with a crew cut, standing beside the open door to Spencer's TVR.

'Hey!'

Spence began to run.

The crew cut glanced at him, then ducked inside the car. Spence was at full pelt now. He saw the man lean down around the steering wheel as if trying to fit a key. If the punk thought he had time to hot-wire it—

Spence was there.

The man was still fumbling at the wheel when Spence reached across and dragged him out. Car owner, car thief: how do you do? Spence pummelled him to the ground, kicked several times, then jumped heavily on his ribs. Neil tried to slide away.

But Spence dropped to his knees and grabbed his short hair. He didn't recognise the man. Christ, the guy was fifty if he was a day – a *car thief*? 'You know who I *am*?'

Perhaps Neil did. But he barely looked. He couldn't look. He couldn't see through tears and blood.

'You'll remember next time.'

Neil tried to turn his head, but couldn't escape the head-butt. He yelled with pain. Spence slammed Neil's head down on the tarmac, punched again, then got up and kicked him. Neil lay whimpering. Spence trod on his head. Then he turned and climbed into his car.

In his anger, his amazement that someone, anyone, an old age *pensioner*, should try to steal his precious car – *his* car, Spence Miller's own TVR – he didn't question why the key was already in the ignition.

Cursing a world of idiots, he reached down and switched it on.

*

Becky Phelps recalled the day – when was it, two weeks ago, or three? – that she'd lain in bed one morning, no reason to get up, and had let her head flicker with waking dreams. Those were always the most unsettling dreams, the ones she remembered. In films, people woke up suddenly in the middle of the night, startled by a nightmare, and sat bolt upright in their bed. But Becky never had nightmares – she only had waking dreams. Some came when she was more awake than asleep, and if she didn't try too hard she found she could direct her dreams, easing them into warm, comfortable, even sexy directions. But often she had worry dreams – she couldn't find something, she couldn't get somewhere – and when she did wake up, the sense of panic could last for hours. Whatever she did, no matter how much she told herself she was back in the real world, some residual niggle chewed at the back of her brain. And one morning – she remembered it now as she sat with the other girls in the neon-lit hallway at the police station – one morning in her waking dream, Becky actually won the Lottery! She remembered the numbers – her *lucky* numbers! – coming up one by incredible one until she finally had all six. All six! She had won a fortune.

And when she awoke she couldn't believe she had not won. Twice she tried to find that ticket with the lucky numbers – she knew where it was; it was where all the tickets were, in her handbag. But where was her handbag? She panicked, thinking she might have misread the numbers, and was fumbling through her bag before she remembered again that it was just a dream. She hadn't won. She was still stuck in her grotty flat – without a job, without enough money to exist on. Still stuck as she was before.

She looked along the corridor of the police station. The dream had gone. Hours ago, it seemed, she had told Gina that it seemed a lifetime since this afternoon. There was a clock ticking. She looked up. Gone midnight. It was now a lifetime since *yesterday* afternoon.

*

Gone midnight. Jennifer Gillett is alone at home. She should be in bed. She sits in her living room, lights low, TV off, reading papers from her dossier. Damon Wright has told her to pay less attention to the Zoë Rand murder: without a witness they have no case. Not only can they not prove the murder was committed on a film set, they can't even prove the girl was there. The only evidence she was there comes from a fellow journalist who took a phone call which *suggested* Rand was there. The Miller family denies everything. Only if the Nelson girl reappears can the police make progress. But what chance is there of that? The film company does not exist. Any actors employed by it do not exist. Perhaps even the Nelson girl does not exist.

Meanwhile, the city must be policed.

*

Gone midnight. In his spartan Barbican flat Ken Lawrence is barely aware that Marion has left him. They've had another row, but it was so one-sided he hardly remembers it – she argued, he switched off. Now, free of all distractions, Ken is able to sit at his powerful PC and log on to Luke Miller's websites. He watches the lurid pictures – in truth, he lingers over some – but that isn't why Ken's eyes are bright. These sites will soon be dead.

Beside him at his desk runs a video camera – not a low-quality web camera but a professional DarkAlley machine. He is recording himself, the crusader against web porn. His right hand drifts from mouse to keyboard. The pictures change on screen. Ken moves to the text behind the pictures. Then he enters a password, and begins.

*

Gone midnight. Near the heart of the city are the mixed developments of the Isle of Dogs – part commercial, part undeveloped, part new residential. In one of the smart residential enclaves near Turners Dock a girl slips out of the front door to her house and crosses the shared piazza which she calls the yard. She lets herself out of the wrought iron security gates into the outside world. She is off to have fun in town. Some people might expect a girl from this expensive development to have a car to take her there. Most would expect a girl of fourteen to be in bed.

But Emmaline is past caring what other people expect.

*

Gone midnight. Kirsty Rice stands on a street corner beneath a lamp post. She walks up and down a little, then stands still – but it seems to her that she must look like a prostitute touting for hire. Indeed, one car does slow momentarily, but Kirsty's frosty glare, then averted gaze, makes it obvious she is not available, and the car – which may have slowed for any reason, officer – picks up speed and disappears. Kirsty feels the cold. She feels nervous for her baby. She is dressed for day and should be at home in her snug safe houseboat. She should not be waiting in Marsham Street alone to meet the man she believes to be a killer, the man she intends to accompany into a nearby house, the man she intends to present with a sight that will make him angry and ashamed.

It seems to Kirsty that Spencer is taking one hell of a time to get here.

Reel Six:

CLIMAX

- 39 -

The city never sleeps. Where had he heard that? Gone midnight, yet as he drove through the West End it seemed no less busy than at lunch. Taxis, private cars, even a bleary bus or two – and those blasted pedestrians, stumbling out onto the tarmac. Spencer cursed them. He wanted to push forward, to cut through the swirling revellers like a boat through foam. But if he smacked a pedestrian he might dent his car. He loved the TVR, its cheeky yellow, its sleek lines. An expensive, low-slung toy. If you owned a car like this you had money and life was a game.

He cut through one last flurry at Victoria, then into the sudden quiet of expensive back streets. There she was.

When he stopped beside her the engine ticked quietly, like a bedside clock.

'You look like a whore, you don't mind me saying.'

She had been shivering beneath a street lamp. Without a word, Kirsty pulled open the door and slipped inside. She was still cold. 'Where'd you come from – Billericay?'

'Traffic. You wouldn't believe, this time of night. Let me warm you up.'

He reached down to turn the heater on full blast. Kirsty leant towards it, letting hot air waft through her chilly clothes. He said, 'Old-fashioned whores wore fur coats. You can see why.'

'Took you half an hour,' she said. 'I hope they're both still there.'

'Both who?'

'Luke and Rinalda, in Rinalda's hideaway.'

'So what?'

'Do they normally sleep together?'

Spencer covered his gasp to make a sound like a chuckle. 'Rinalda – with my brother?'

She nodded. Spence sat patiently in the car as if waiting at traffic lights, his face expressionless, his body still. He began pumping the accelerator. Though they weren't moving, the car snarled like a dog.

'You feeling hot enough?' he asked.

'I'm on defrost.'

'Wanna go to *my* place?'

'That's not why we're here.'

He pumped the car twice more, then suddenly slipped it in gear. When the TVR shot forward it roared like a tiger in the night.

*

Kirsty followed Spencer up the stairs. On the short car journey he had spoken only once: 'You better be right about this.' Now they'd got here he was silent, grim-faced, light on his feet. On the top landing he paused outside the apartment door and waited for Kirsty to catch up.

He whispered, 'For certain sure?'

She nodded and whispered, 'Try the viewing room.'

'You're too cautious,' he whispered back.

'I was filming it,' she whispered. 'To make it real.'

He stared a moment, knowing she was right, then slipped quietly into the viewing room next door. Darkness. In the adjacent parlour no lamps were on. 'Don't touch the light,' he whispered. She wondered if a full light behind the two-way mirror might seep through to the flat.

As Spencer edged through the gap beside the console there was barely light to see. Its twinkling lights were small, and they reflected in the glass like lights at sea. The hum from the console seemed too loud. Spencer reached the second viewing window but the light in the bedroom seemed even dimmer now than it had before. He glanced at the monitors. *Boudoir One* was useless – a black murkiness – while *Boudoir Two* from above showed the large double bed in too little detail. Spence fiddled with the definition: no better. They peered at the two screens. Was someone in the bed? What was real and what imaginary?

'Someone's there,' he said.

When he turned to Kirsty in the darkened viewing room his face looked expressionless and slack, but there was a glint of triumph in his eyes. Or was that imaginary too?

'Leave the camera running.'

As he squeezed back past her she sensed the relaxed state of Spencer's body. Light as a cat. Yet Kirsty, who had brought him here, was rigid with suspense. She watched through the first viewing window and saw the door open to the parlour, letting light in from the hall. Through the two-way mirror she watched Spencer creep across the room, heading for the boudoir. He paused outside the door and Kirsty guessed he was wondering how best to make his entrance – because he knew he'd be on film. When Rick saw it he wouldn't want his son to look triumphant.

Spencer opened the bedroom door softly, like a burglar – and Kirsty's eyes switched immediately to *Boudoir Two* – the image from the camera above the bed. But still there was too little light to give a clear image on screen. Inside the bed, somebody moved.

Spence shouted, 'Camera, lights, action!' and switched on the room lights. He darted to the bed, clutched the bedclothes and heaved them away. The startled couple sat up in bed, shielding their eyes. On the monitor they looked grey and sordid. But startled as *they* were, Spence looked *more* startled. Kirsty felt sick.

Rinalda cried, 'Spencer, what are you doing here?' but beside her, equally naked but far less beautiful, her husband Rick shouted at his son. Spencer stared at him aghast. Kirsty stared at the monitor. Rick clambered from the bed.

Spence dropped the bedclothes and tried to explain. He stammered. Spluttered. How could he tell them what he'd believed? Rinalda stared at the bedroom wall. 'Did you say camera?' She gazed at the mirror: *Boudoir One*. Her eye's met Kirsty's.

For one brief moment.

Kirsty began to fight her way through chairs and equipment. Through the mirror came little light. She heard angry voices. She heard her name. She had to get out of the viewing room.

Fighting her way past the console she tripped against a stool, righted herself, and stumbled to the door. As she blundered out onto the top landing a blur of white appeared at her side. Rick had emerged naked from the flat.

As he tried to grab her, Kirsty ducked and darted for the stairs.

Rick clutched her shoulder. She pulled away. She practically threw herself downstairs. All the way down she expected Rick to grab her. She heard his footsteps close behind – but after the second flight he seemed to stop. Was he too old? Perhaps he'd realised he was naked.

Kirsty scrabbled at the street door, pulled it open, and stumbled out into the street. She had a stabbing pain in her stomach – and it wasn't a stitch. Oh God, she sobbed. Any moment now, one of the Millers would rush out after her into the street. She saw Spencer's car, his bright little TVR, standing at the roadside. If only she could take that. She paused by it, touching the sparkling metal as she glanced inside – no keys, of course. She turned away.

The front door opened.

Spencer came out, saw her, and began to chase. Kirsty was no slouch: she could run but was hampered by her working shoes – sensible flatties, not trainers, not fast enough, no bounce. But she hurtled along the street. It was empty, late at night – empty apart from Kirsty, fleet of foot, and Spencer, pounding up behind. Kirsty ran with all her might – but he was closer, he was fast. He caught her in fifty yards.

He grasped and held her tight as a rabbit in an eagle's claws. She squirmed as a rabbit might. But she didn't squeal. She didn't scream. She couldn't – because at that moment Spencer clamped his big hand across her mouth. His lips spat into her ear: he cursed and railed at her, words streaming like escaping steam. He began to pull her toward the house.

Kirsty bit his hand. But Spence punched her with his other, and she reeled, head spinning, stomach heaving – and if only he'd stop pulling her along the pavement she could fall to her knees and be sick.

At the door he said, '*You* tell my parents.'

His face was so close she couldn't focus. When he spoke again her head felt trapped inside a drum: 'You made me look an *idiot*. They threw me out.'

He pushed her. She didn't know which way to move, and she stumbled to the concrete. He yanked her up. 'No. In the car first, you bitch.'

Everything was a blur. Her head throbbed from Spencer's punch. Colours in the street were bilious. She was bundled into the car and before she could think of jumping out Spencer appeared at the other door.

'Try to get out, I'll flatten you.'

Things were moving at double speed. He jumped in the car,

switched it on and shot away. Kirsty looked helplessly from the window. If she leapt out at a corner he was bound to come after her. But there were other cars here, night-time traffic, other drivers who might see what was happening, who might leap from their own cars to save her...

No.

Late at night, a big angry man? She looked hopefully for a police car. No chance. Never when you need one.

Spencer drove along The Embankment. In the shiny TVR they looked like a courting couple late at night. What a fine pair, Kirsty and Spence. What a fine car. There were so few other vehicles that Spencer could put his foot down and take the yellow sports car faster than normal. She glanced at the dial: forty, forty-five – now fifty. No great speed – because even at this late hour of night Spencer had to brake for traffic lights and corners. He couldn't begin to open up. The needle moved to fifty again, then sank away. Spencer was constrained. But surely at some point on this journey he would be able to push the needle through the fifty barrier and show her what a TVR could do?

*

'Don't worry,' Roy Farrell says. 'It'll be done tonight.'

'It's gone one o'clock,' says Tony. 'Am I supposed to wait all night?'

'You never were an early bird.'

Roy is sprawled in his Peckham flat as if half way to bed, while Tony is prowling around his Docklands pad, phone to ear, wondering where the hell his daughter is and what Farrell has been doing all this time. He says, 'Roy, get over here, so we can get this done. Nothing tricksey. I just want to go to bed and get a good night's sleep, knowing that the guy who raped my daughter has been blown away.'

'It's sorted.'

'He ain't dead yet, Roy. And it's one o'clock.'

'Don't worry, Tony. The boy is not going to wake up in bed tomorrow telling himself what a lovely day it is.'

'Get over here.'

*

Rick Miller returned naked to the red plush parlour, clutching the tell-tale video cassette.

'You were right,' he chuckled. 'Spencer was filming us.'

Rinalda frowned. She had slipped into a black silk dressing gown. Her blonde hair bounced lightly on her shoulders and the gown hung open enough to reveal a swathe of milk white body. She didn't look her age. 'We don't want to watch that, Rick.'

'It'll be a laugh.'

He strolled to the TV monitor. She asked, 'Aren't you cold?'

'This'll warm me up.' He grinned across his shoulder. 'It's been a while since we saw *you* on film. You and me, caught like all those punters.'

'Come back to bed, darling.'

But he had slipped the cassette in the slot. He pressed Rewind.

'Our lights were out,' she said. 'It won't have recorded anything.'

'Who knows? This could be the greatest sex film you ever made.'

*

Kirsty was catatonic. She sat in the car, barely watching where Spencer drove, vaguely aware that they had cut across Holborn towards Clerkenwell. She had lost the will to fight. She was in a car with the man who had killed her friend, yet even when the car paused she made no effort to jump out. She could have been hypnotised or drugged. She wondered how much Spencer's punch had shaken her. She seemed half asleep.

Above Clerkenwell Green when the car paused again, she saw Spencer touch a button on his tiny remote and in the blank dark building ahead a double door swung open to let them inside. As the car passed through, Kirsty suddenly realised she was leaving the outside world. She moved in her seat and turned to look through the doorway to the street outside. She had missed her chance. Those empty streets offered a ray of hope, but in this dark and brooding building, Spencer's lair, there was no hope at all.

Spencer stopped the car. 'Get out.'

They were in a private car park: his yellow TVR, two other cars, lots of gloomy ill-lit space. No sign of life.

'I said get out.'

'No.' Her voice was small.

'Move it.'

'No.'

He stirred beside her, and for a moment she thought he would hit her again, but she would not get out. Spencer cursed, got out of the car, and came briskly to her door. She moved instinctively, cowering aside to avoid his powerful hands. As she slithered across the seat she realised he had left his keys in the ignition. He had not yet parked the car. Her legs tangled with the gear lever as she leant across and turned the key.

Spencer grabbed the door.

As he pulled it open, Kirsty heaved her feet down to the pedals and slammed the car in gear. Spencer was half inside. She tried to release the hand brake but his fist was round it. She revved the car. The engine screamed. She revved again, and with a roar of protest the car jerked forwards – despite its handbrake – and shot towards the opposing wall. Kirsty spun the wheel. The car responded. As she swung the sports car round, Spencer clung to the handbrake and began pulling himself inside. She held the wheel over in a lock and put her foot down. With a squeal of tyres and brakes the sports car gyrated angrily around the garage. She didn't look at Spencer. She concentrated on the car. She took it through several crazy circles – but Spencer kept clinging on. He had too much body inside. She couldn't shake him off.

But he wasn't fully in – barely half of him sprawled across the seat. His hand gripped the brake and as Kirsty held the car in its noisy vortex he shouted at her, hips and legs trailing outside.

The garage, which had looked so empty, now seemed full of cars. The TVR slithered wildly on the concrete floor. At any moment she might hit another vehicle – but with Spencer there it was hard to keep control. And he was *close* – pulling himself further across the seat. His head was level with his hand. He was getting nearer, inch by inch. And the car was getting faster, the brake pad wearing away. Spencer had both hands on the stick.

Now he could pull himself inside. He released a hand, stretched for the steering wheel – and when Kirsty slackened her grip the car spun in a wider circle. It veered towards a van – missed – but Spencer's feet smacked against the metal side. With a yell of outrage he lost the hand brake and was gone.

*

The video rewind slowed and stopped. As Rick reached for the remote, Rinalda made one last attempt to stop him. She swung her legs across his lap and sat across him on the chair, her black dressing gown loose around the two of them, her nipples on his chest, her hands stroking his naked body. When Rinalda kissed him, her face and magnificent head of hair obscured the screen.

'OK, you're gorgeous,' Rick mumbled. 'Let's see the video.'

'Later,' she breathed. 'Take me like this first.'

She had one hand in his lap, the other reaching for the remote. Rick chuckled. 'You wanna fight me for it?'

'I want *you*, not video.'

'I want both.'

He wrestled playfully with her, then touched the button on the remote.

She laughed nervously. 'I don't want that.'

She struggled but Rick held his hand away. She lunged. He laughed. 'My little cat,' he said. 'Here comes—'

She grabbed his head and pulled him down into her breasts. He laughed and nuzzled. 'Let's watch the dirty video—'

She pretended to laugh with him, opening her dressing gown and wrapping his head in black silk. Again she stretched for the remote. But Rick loved this game. With his face tangled in silk and breasts he tried to force himself from the chair. He clutched Rinalda's squirming body and she pulled him sideways. They crashed to the carpet – but before Rick could disentangle himself Rinalda had rolled him on his back. Again she threw her arms wide to enfold him in her silken tent, and as she sank down on him, Rick began fumbling between her legs. He tried to enter her. She opened her thighs – but found herself uncharacteristically dry. He wriggled, pushed, wriggled again, pushed harder. She tried to help him, pulling his willing member up into her dryness. He grunted. Rinalda gasped. Rick had his hands around her hips beneath the dressing gown to help him guide her up and down. She kept the tent wide. The video played. Rick lay on his back on the thick red carpet and stared up adoringly at his wife. So beautifully preserved.

Suddenly he jerked the silk aside and gazed joyfully at the TV screen. He saw them couple.

'Here we go again,' he panted. 'On the screen and on the fl—*Who the hell is that?*'

- 40 -

Where could she go now? In such a conspicuous stolen car Kirsty didn't dare drive all the way through empty night-time streets back to her houseboat. In the houseboat she would be alone. Too dangerous. Better to take the short journey from Clerkenwell to The Barbican.

When she parked the TVR in the yard outside Ken's flat she saw other cars, long-parked and cold, but no people. She sat in the car a full minute, gathering her breath. She felt as if she had run instead of driven. The windscreen misted but she could still see outside. She had to sit a few moments more: the pain was like acid in her stomach. Kirsty took long measured breaths. When finally she eased out of the little car her moves seemed choreographed. She was alone on a big cold stage, ready to begin a solo turn – like a ballet dancer, she thought, like Marion.

Kirsty stepped back from the car and looked up at the dark block of flats. Two lights were on. Two different apartments. Two night owls. Was that Ken's window up there? Was Marion with him? Kirsty shivered with cold.

As she walked across the yard every footstep seemed unnaturally loud. Her sensible flat shoes didn't usually make much sound but tonight, in this inner city dormitory, everywhere about her seemed strangely quiet. Perhaps, she thought, it wasn't strangely quiet at all. Perhaps around here it was always as quiet as this, at 2am.

Before she pressed his bell she glanced out across the residents' car park. Although separated from the empty side street by a low wall with a single rail along the top, the cars parked inside were visible to passers by. Anyone looking for that car couldn't fail to see it – the police, a car thief, one of Spencer's men. The yellow TVR stood out like an apricot in a tray of plums.

She pressed the bell, waited, then heard his voice. She said, 'It's Kirsty. Can I come up?'

'Oh gosh. I'm rather busy just now.'

'Is Marion there?'

'No.'

'Someone else?'

'No, it's just that, you know, I'm up to my eyes—'

'I'm freezing my butt off. Let me in.'

'Look – um – this is not a good time, Kirsty. Perhaps later?'

'Ken, it's two o'clock in the morning and I'm standing on your doorstep. Do I have to huff and puff and *blow* your door down?'

*

Kirsty stepped inside his spartan flat, hunched her shoulders and rubbed her hands as if she had just removed winter gloves. She glanced around quickly: cool furniture, warm air. No one else that she could see.

'Has she been keeping you up late?' Kirsty nodded at the PC screen, from which a lurid blonde stared, frozen mid-pout. Kirsty could hear disks whirring.

Ken nodded. 'That's Kim Massager,' he said proudly, as if it were an album cover from his collection.

Kirsty was glancing around. Marion might be in the bedroom – though Ken was dressed at least. Beside his PC clustered a video camera, a stand and a supplementary floodlight, not switched on. 'Are you filming what's on the internet?'

'I'm filming me.'

'Oh yes, your programme – How Ken Crashed The Porn Site. Huh!'

She stalked around the room, edging toward his bedroom. She was curious, yet disinterested. And she still had that low pain in her stomach. She said, 'I've had a terrifying night.'

'Must get on,' Ken muttered. He touched the keyboard and the screen changed from the lurid blonde to a black DOS screen. Among the small stark white letters a numeric counter was ticking at high speed. It meant nothing to Kirsty and she was in no mood to learn. Nor was Ken in the mood to teach her. He crouched over the keyboard, hitting one key at a time. The screen changed. She saw DOS screens, sex pictures, site welcome screens and CGI forms, each image following the other like slides in an old carousel – though one of the pictures was animated, a strip of video. It seemed to annoy him that it had appeared – because it wasn't technical? Kirsty had time to register that the clip came from a sex orgy: two men and two girls, was it? Three? She didn't care. She was no more aroused than if she were standing in a condom factory.

Ken got back to a DOS screen, scrolling through rows of impenetrable text. He stabbed the screen with his finger, savagely, as if squashing a gnat. He muttered to himself. She wasn't there.

Kirsty pushed the door to his bedroom. No one inside. The room immaculate. Not only had Ken not slept in there tonight, it looked as if he had *never* slept there. Had Marion enjoyed this aseptic environment? Had she herself slept here? It looked like a freshly prepared hotel room. A surgical ward.

She glanced back at Ken, hunched over his keyboard, and suddenly, with him in the room before her, she could visualise him naked. She saw his body, the way his shoulders sloped. Was he the Wolf Man in Spencer's film? Of course he wasn't. Ken wasn't a wolf. He wasn't adventurous. She tried to remember what Ken had looked like asleep: calm, untroubled, no bad dreams. Her own troubled bed had been left unmade this morning, her pull-down table left uncleared. This morning? No, it was yesterday morning. Twenty hours ago.

Ken sang out – but not to her. Somewhere on his scrolling screen he must have found what he was looking for. He began typing. Kirsty needed to sit down. She needed… As she moved forward she felt as unsteady as an old lady. Her stomach twinged again. She said, 'Ken?'

'Hang on.'

Ken's face was so close to the screen that she wondered if he needed glasses. It was as if rather than try to focus on it, he was trying to become a part of what was there.

She said, 'I think I might lose the baby.'

'There it is,' he said, to the computer screen.

Kirsty winced. As she moved carefully towards his bathroom, Ken began clattering across his keyboard. 'Yes, yes!' he said excitedly, and for a moment he turned round. 'You could film me – no, don't worry, I'll do it myself. I'm already set.'

He flicked on the floodlight, a bright exposing light. Then with a schoolboy grin, he turned the camera on.

Her phone rang. Ken's face clouded. 'Don't answer that now.'

She smiled crookedly. 'I'm a journalist. You never know.'

'I've started to film.'

She took the ringing phone from her bag. 'With sound?'

'Of course I'm using sound. Turn that off. You'll have to wait.'

She shook her head. 'This won't wait.'

He threw his hands wide. 'Have you no consideration? Turn that thing off.'

She continued to the bathroom and shut the door. Looking at the phone she felt awfully tired. Two in the morning. To hell with everyone, she thought. She cut the call. She couldn't talk now. The pain dragged at her.

Kirsty placed her bag and phone on the floor beside the lavatory, then pulled down her panties and quickly sat. Oh please, don't let it happen here. Let it not happen at all, but please, if anyone is listening, don't let it happen here.

The bathroom was peaceful and silent, cut off from the outside world. A convent cell. A place of contemplation. If it happens anywhere, it should happen here.

A sudden cramp seized her and she bent forward involuntarily. The seizure passed. She crouched forward, waited, then slowly sat up again to make herself ready for whatever came next. She waited thirty seconds.

The phone rang.

'Why not?' she thought. 'Nothing else is happening.'

Stooping for the phone made her head swim. But she picked it up, closed her eyes, and put the familiar receiver to her ear.

Spencer said, 'Hope you haven't crashed my car yet.'

'I dumped it.'

'Where?'

Another dizzy spell wandered into her head.

'Lost your tongue, bitch?'

'Are you trying to encourage me to chat?'

'Listen, you stuck up bitch, I rang to—'

She cut him off. It was good to be in control. She didn't have to speak to Spencer. Nor for that matter need she speak to Ken – though it would be nice if *Ken* would speak to her. Had he heard when she told him what she feared was going to happen? Here she was in his bathroom, about to lose his child, and he sat outside and played with his computer.

The phone rang again.

She should have switched it off. But she answered: 'Here are the rules, Spencer. You swear at me or threaten, I turn off the phone.'

'I'll get you, bitch. No way you can hide.'

She chuckled wearily. 'Where I am, you'll never find me.'

'I will. Guaranteed.'

She looked around the compact bathroom. 'I'm in a box inside a box, inside a box,' she said. 'A Russian doll. Where I am now, I'm safe.'

But her brave words were answered by another sickening cramp. Fainter perhaps, but serious. Spencer might think he was a threat but he was irrelevant, a ranting voice from another world.

He said, 'Where you are *now* I may not find you – but how long can you stay there, bitch? You got to come out sometime.'

'Yeah, sometime.'

'I want my car back.'

'When I've finished with it I'll tell you where I've left it.'

'With the keys inside – a TVR? No way. You bring it back to me.'

'You're so tedious. Ask nicely.'

'If I got to tell you—'

'Say please, Spencer, for the first time in your life.'

She heard his angry sigh – both nostrils. 'OK Kirsty. *Please* can I have my car back?'

*

It's a fine thing to regain your freedom. But to come out of a police station at 2.30am into a silent, darkened street, nothing moving, the only light from streetlamps and a single all-night corner shop whose fluorescent tubes glare starkly at the corner; your limbs weary, your mind numbed from lack of sleep, your only company the two girls arrested with you – is like awakening suddenly late at night. You wake from a fitful dream into cold reality. Cold but free.

Becky, Mel and Gina were dressed like partygoers returning home. At a casual glance – from that car, say, parked along the street – anyone would think that the girls *were* partygoers, but that wherever they'd been had not been fun. The three girls huddled together as they trudged along. They hardly spoke. It was late; they had talked all evening and were played out.

If they heard the car start they thought nothing of it. When it drifted past they gave it half a glance – but then it stopped. They halted too. A door opened and Gary stepped out.

Mel stared at him blankly, but Becky glanced back towards the police station. A hundred yards. Light spilled from the station doorway but it illuminated empty steps. She and the others had been processed and ejected. Returned to the real world.

Mel said, 'You bastard. You told 'em, didn't you?'

Gary grinned. 'You was breaking the law.'

The other car door opened and a big man climbed out. He walked around the car and came up to them. 'Hello, girls.'

'So what's all *this* about?' asked Gina.

'This was my boyfriend.'

'Was?' he cried in mock amazement. 'Since when did we break up, Mel?'

Becky glanced again towards the police station. Gary could have read her mind: 'Fancy another chat with the filth, Becky? Who'd have thought?'

Gina guessed what had happened. 'How did you know we were here?'

Mel said, 'He told on us – didn't you, you sod?'

'Oh, *very* nice,' jeered Gary.

'The thing is,' explained the big man patiently. 'You're in trouble now. You shouldn't have tried this on your own.' He could have been a school teacher – he was made for it.

'We're not on our own,' said Melanie. 'There's three of us. We're a collective.'

Gary sneered but the big man said, 'Oh, you tried hard, I'll give you that – but a girl can't manage on her own.'

'There's three of us.'

'Been through that. You need a man.'

'What for?' asked Gina.

'This is woman's work,' declared Mel.

Becky watched without speaking – a spectator, no more able to affect what was happening than if she were watching a drama on TV. A fly on the wall.

The man said, 'What would happen if the Yorkshire Ripper wandered in?'

'He's in jail,' said Gina, trying to be smart.

'Every month,' the big man continued, 'a girl gets herself cut, killed or beaten up.'

'We watch out for each other.'

'And the police will watch out for you now, won't they? You can't handle it on your own.'

Gary said, 'You need protection.'

Mel laughed. 'You? Protect me? Get out of here.'

'Listen,' he snapped, taking one step forward. 'I done you once—'

'Oh yeah, go on, beat me up again – some protection, a real man. Not!'

Like a car park barrier, the big man's arm rose between them. 'Keep it quiet now. We're all friends, aren't we?'

'As if!' Mel spat.

He continued: 'We'll put you in a much nicer flat. We'll do the advertising. We'll pay the rent—'

'You and *Gary?*'

'My organisation.'

'Oh, lah-di-dah. I've had enough of this.'

'You've got no choice,' said Gary. The big man said nothing. His expression said it.

Gina muttered, 'We don't need men.'

Becky felt cold. She looked across at the bright light from the corner store. It was a cold light, unwelcoming, but better than here. She hadn't said a word so far and didn't want to. They were an odd number anyway – five: Mel and Gina, Gary and the man. Mel and Gary, Gina and the man. Gary watched Melanie as if he wanted to give her another hiding; the man watched Gina as if he already saw her in bed. Becky was spare.

She stepped into the street and wandered towards the corner store. The man was saying, 'You'd like a better flat and better money—'

'Yeah, yeah,' scoffed Gina.

'You'll be glad we met.'

Becky crossed the white line dividing the road and still nothing happened. When she reached the other side she could hardly hear them. Then Gina laughed: 'Half? Get real!'

Becky was on the pavement. She reckoned she could drift away as if the others were characters in a TV play, as if she had stood up from the couch to leave the room – till Gina called: 'Hey Becky, where are you off to?'

She stood and faced them. 'I want to get some shopping.'

'At *this* time?'

'Why not?'

She felt light and empty, as if she hadn't eaten all day. If one of the men came across the road for her she wouldn't have the strength to run away. She wasn't sure that she could move at all.

But they went back to talking without her. Mel was angry with Gary but Gina seemed to accept that whatever they said would make no difference. She had stopped protesting. She stood with her head down, staring at the gutter. Mel strutted as if in a film.

Becky walked to the corner shop, but instead of going in she continued round the corner and along the empty road. She would not turn round. With every step she was sure someone would call her name – she waited for the shout to hit her like a stone at her back. But nothing came. Perhaps the four of them had finished arguing and were now discussing the new arrangements. Ten to one they had stopped arguing. Ten to one? Becky shook her head: six to one. With every step, the odds fell away. Four to one they'd stopped arguing and Mel had asked what the new flat was like. Two to one Gary would share her bed tonight. Two to one also for the big man and Gina. A crossed double.

Becky reached a corner. She could go straight on, which was the direct way home – but it was even money that someone would call her back.

She turned the corner. Nothing happened. She walked more briskly down a residential street. It seemed uncanny that they had let her walk away. What were the odds on that? Well, whatever you said, she had beaten the odds. *And* she had money in her pocket.

She felt brighter with every step. This was a bit like backing a winner, as if her luck had changed. If it had, this was surely the time to ride it. She had come away with over a hundred quid, so the least she could do was splash – no, *invest* fifty on a couple of horses. Make that forty on horses and ten on the lottery. No, don't be mean about it – do it proper: fifty on the horses and ten on the lottery. Sixty quid invested – who knows? – could earn six *hundred* easily. Things were looking up.

At the next corner Becky took one last look back. Nobody. She felt happier now: set free. She began down a street parallel to the one that could take her straight home. Somewhere behind she had left a whole way of life, an alternative future. It had been a laugh, for a day – but perhaps a day was enough. She could have stayed, of course, and continued working on her back. But she had walked away. Simple as that. Walk away. Becky's tiredness had lifted and she found she was walking with as much enthusiasm as if it were a sunny morning at the start of a brand new day.

- 41 -

Just walk away. Kirsty had been in the bathroom twenty minutes; the twinges had subsided and in the last five minutes nothing had happened at all. She came into the living room to find Ken still performing at his PC – dancing in the floodlight like a savage at a camp fire, tapping his keyboard, staring at his screen, turning to the camera with a triumphant grin. He spoke to the mike – something about site crashes and defacement pages, a sniffer virus for names and passwords. He barely glanced at Kirsty and clearly didn't realise she'd been gone for twenty minutes. Lost in his virtual world, time had no meaning. He was in a parallel universe; he and Kirsty could see each other but not connect. She stood outside the floodlit zone in which he fluttered like a moth. She went to the door, opened it and looked back pointedly. But he was not aware of her. He didn't see her go.

Outside, she realised it was the middle of the night. She glanced at her watch: nearly three o'clock, the city silent. Late-nighters had gone to bed; early risers had not woken up. She looked across the yard and out through the gap between Ken's block and the block of flats next door. The sky was a dense dark orange, as from a distant fire. The street outside was empty. She was the only person out. Yet the yard was lit by a wire-meshed security light, all the streets were lit, and Kirsty realised that, if she wanted, she could walk the whole way home – twelve miles, was it? – under electric light. The whole of London was lit for her.

But she wasn't walking. In the quiet yard, Spencer's yellow TVR sulked beside its sober neighbours. It was the kind of car that anyone passing couldn't fail to notice – kids, car thieves, joy-riders. Was she a joy-rider or a thief? She looked in her bag for Spencer's key. This wasn't a theft that would come to court. Spencer wouldn't press charges. But she couldn't keep his car. Didn't *want* to keep it.

The key dangled from her hand as she pondered where to take his TVR. Somehow tonight she had got to get to her houseboat, and it was far too late for public transport. But to drive this garish car through empty night-time streets all the way home would have her glancing in the mirror at each cruising vehicle. So conspicuous. The police would wonder, 'Why is that expensive car out so late?' They'd speak to the driver: 'Excuse me, ma'am. Are you the rightful owner?'

And where could she leave it in Thames Ditton? Certainly not beside the houseboat. She jangled the keys. There was only one place she could take this car.

*

The Barbican to Clerkenwell was so short a drive she could have walked it, and at three in the morning she was re-parking before the engine had properly warmed up. She stopped in the empty street outside the printing works, practically opposite the building. Here as everywhere, the streetlamps bathed the tarmac in soulless light. The street between the high flat-fronted buildings was like a corridor in an institutional basement. She sat in the car and glanced up at the Clerkenwell Printing Works, in darkness save for one lit window at the top. She leant over in her seat and peered up at that lit window. No one moving. No one looking out.

She removed the keys from the ignition, hesitated, then pushed them underneath the seat. The car should be safe. No passer-by would dream that this car at the roadside was a TVR to go. When she got out she eased the door back in place. If anyone *were* awake she didn't want them to hear it slam.

She began walking down the road. Two men stepped from the shadows. Three in the morning, an empty street: no way these were casual strollers. She could turn and run, but there were two of them. She was weak. Run from a dog and it will chase you. Your only chance is to stare it down.

One of them spoke: 'Just leaving it? Not going inside?'

Kirsty shook her head.

'Give us the keys.'

'I don't have them.'

The man snorted. His companion stared. Kirsty said, 'They're in the car. You can take it – I don't care.'

'As long as *you* don't get hurt?'

She nodded. 'I don't advise you to steal that car.'

'It's Spencer's, right?'

Her heart sank. 'You know him?'

He nodded imperceptibly. 'You his girlfriend?'

'No chance.'

'But he lets you drive his car.'

'I stole it. Borrowed it.'

They studied her. She realised that they, like her, were speaking quietly, as if they didn't want anyone to hear.

One said, 'What happened – you went out, had an argument?'

'Something like that.'

'What exactly.'

'Forget it, Roy,' cut in the other. He stared at Kirsty. 'Do what I say and you won't get hurt. Go over to the printing works, ring the bell, wake Spencer up. Tell him his car's in the street with the keys in the ignition. Tell him, if he wants to see it again he'd better come down and put it away.'

Kirsty knew that whatever else happened she would have to do what these two men said. 'I guess this isn't Spencer's lucky night?'

'You could say that.'

'Shall I say you told me to ring his bell?'

The men glanced at each other. One asked, 'Are you fond of Spencer?'

'No way.'

'Still pissed at him, huh? OK, get on the buzzer, tell him you're *still* pissed at him and you're going home, but make him come down and get the car. Got that?'

She nodded and half turned away. The man touched her arm. 'What's Spencer to you?'

'I hate him.'

'You brought his car back.'

'I had a choice?'

He chuckled. 'That Spencer – ain't he a sweetie?'

The other man told her, 'Go to the door. Do what we said. Then go home. But this is the important part: forget every word of what we said. You never saw us.'

She nodded. 'You don't exist.'

Kirsty started across the road, detached and light-headed as if she were observing the world through an alcoholic haze. At Ken's flat *he* had seemed in a parallel universe. Ken was in his cyber world, Spence and his family were in their world of porn, these two men had stepped briefly into her life from their own world of violence and shadow. She rang the bell and knew that when she looked back across the street the men would be gone. They were not part of her world.

She buzzed the speaker-phone again, but to her horror the wooden door creaked open. The man before her was not Spencer. He was big, and before she could speak he yanked her inside and closed the door. She was in the car park. There was hardly any light.

'What the hell are you—'

'Shut up. You're Kirsty Rice?'

Her shoulders slumped. 'I've left his car outside—'

'Keep your mouth shut.'

She felt doubly trapped – he knew her name. This was where she had escaped from Spencer, and now she had walked back inside. Who was this man – and why was he fully dressed at this hour? A parallel universe.

'What did those fellers say to you?'

'Oh.' He'd seen them. She felt empty. This was a drama she could only watch. 'They told me to have Spencer come down for his car.'

He nodded. 'Then you better tell him that.'

He led her across the concrete floor. When they reached the industrial lift he added, 'Probably better for you if you don't tell him they're waiting.'

She tried to read his face, but saw nothing. He pulled her onto the waiting platform. As they ascended through the darkened empty building he said, 'Just tell him to go down and move the car. You can tell them I brought you in.'

'Them? Who else is there?'

The man didn't answer. When they reached the top floor it was another parallel universe: soft lights, a carpeted floor – a comfortable flat. As her feet sank into the soft floor covering Kirsty wanted to melt into a dreamless sleep. The man prodded her and they walked a short stretch of corridor into a large pastel living room. She saw paintings on the walls, soft beige furniture, dark Dutch oak.

In the centre of the spotless carpet stood Spencer and Rick Miller. They both looked tired, but Kirsty was beyond tiredness.

Spencer murmured, 'Hello again, bitch,' and Rick said, 'Thanks, Herbie. You can go to bed.'

'I was on my way.'

Rick asked, 'She didn't bring no cops?'

'The street's empty. Take a look.'

When Herbie had gone, Rick and Spencer stared at her silently. She still felt detached. 'I brought your car back.'

'Keys?'

'In the car.'

'Stupid bitch.'

They made no move but Kirsty couldn't stay on her feet much longer. 'What happens now – you give me a ticking off or I call a taxi home?'

'I'll drive you.'

Their drama had become a tableau. Kirsty broke it by walking past the Millers, further into the room. They let her. From behind, she heard Rick ask, 'So you went back again to Pimlico?'

'What?' She was too tired to remember.

'You shot that video, then invited Spencer to see a preview. Right?'

'Oh, that.' She remembered Luke in Rinalda's bed. It seemed so long ago. Another universe. 'Will this take long? I have to sit down.'

Kirsty sank into a wonderfully soft armchair. The arms were high, almost to her head. She felt protected by them.

'Just as a matter of interest,' Rick continued in a strangely level tone, 'what time was it when you shot that video?'

'Which one?'

'The Luke one.' His voice tightened.

Kirsty shrugged. 'Half an hour... no – an hour before Spencer and I arrived.'

Rick sighed. 'Only an hour?' He seemed to age.

'Spencer was late, but he said he'd had trouble with his car.'

She smiled. Enthroned in the huge soft armchair she felt like a queen. Then she remembered the men down in the street. 'You ought to bring that car inside.'

'It'll wait.'

She perused Spencer coolly, but it seemed to annoy him, because he added, 'I tell you one thing, bitch – the night is young. Lots of time ahead of us.'

Rick raised a placatory hand. 'Kirsty – I suppose that *is* your name? Well, Kirsty, you're a journalist, right?' He moved past Spencer across the living room. 'And you think you got yourself one hell of a juicy story.'

'Well, you ain't going to tell it,' Spencer said. He stepped forward and loomed in front of her in the armchair. As she began to adjust her feet he leant down, grabbed her by the front of her shirt and heaved her to her feet.

'Strong material,' he jeered, tugging again at the crisp shirt fabric. 'We'll soon have these off you.'

'Cut it out,' Rick snapped.

'I want to see what this girl's made of.'

'Leave her alone!'

Spencer turned incredulously. 'She's a fucking spy, Dad, nosing about our business, making videos – she could be wearing a mike.'

'You were with her half the night.'

'She's just come in!'

Spencer reached for her again but she stepped aside. As he grabbed her arm Rick shouted, 'Leave her!'

'Don't tell me what to do!'

Spencer glared at Kirsty, his face inches away. She tried to free her arm – but it only made him angrier. With a curse he punched her in the stomach. As she buckled over he punched her head. Kirsty fell to the floor. She lay in agony, expecting a kick, but Rick leapt between them, roaring at his son. 'You killed one already – grow up!'

As they struggled above her, Kirsty crawled away on the floor. Then Rick knelt beside her, saying, 'It's all right, I'm sorry. I'll help you.'

She glanced up fearfully to see Spencer chewing his thumbnail like a chastened child. Rick comforted Kirsty like a caring father. 'He's impulsive. The boy sometimes gets carried away.'

'He should be.'

Rick helped her to her feet. She took a couple of steps, then folded in sudden abdominal pain. She remained stooped, collecting her breath, while Rick supported her steadily by both arms. The wave of pain passed and she straightened up.

Rick said, 'Better now? Sit down.'

'N-not there.'

She knew that if she sunk into that soft high-backed armchair she would never be able to get up. With Rick supporting her she moved to an upright wooden chair and sat on that.

'Are you all right, Miss Rice?'

'Miss Rice, is it? What did I do?'

'Kirsty. I'm sorry. And Spencer's sorry too.'

Spencer didn't say anything.

Rick said, 'I think we could all do with a drink.'

Kirsty waved him away. 'Just water for me.'

'I'll get you something stronger than that.' Rick left her. 'What do *you* want, Spencer?'

'I don't want a fucking drink, all right?'

Rick enunciated: 'I said we could all do with a *drink*.' He stepped into the dining room. 'All *right*, Spencer? Now, what would we like?'

'Water,' she said.

'Oh, right!' said Spencer suddenly, and Kirsty glanced at him. 'I'll have something long, a beer or something.' He smiled at Kirsty as if nothing had happened. 'What do *you* drink – vodka and orange? Rum and Coke?'

'Water.'

'No, babe, have something sensible – something to pick you up.'

Rick called, 'How about an orange juice and lemonade?'

Kirsty stiffened – but tried to look relaxed. What had Spencer said about Rick and his date rape drug? No, surely not. Rick was just being nice.

'What are *you* having?' she stalled.

'I don't know – a beer?'

'I'll have a beer too.'

'Three beers,' he said.

Why would he want to use a date rape drug? Not for that. Rohypnol and GHB were potent sedatives, she knew, but were sometimes used as truth drugs: patients became so relaxed they couldn't prevent themselves telling the truth. They couldn't prevent anything.

Rick and Spencer thought she knew where Cassie was.

While Rick was in the dining room pouring drinks, Spencer wandered away from Kirsty. He didn't look at her. On an impulse he crossed to the window and peered down to the street below.

'See anything?' asked Kirsty anxiously.

'Yeah. The car's still there and it's started raining.'

Rick emerged with three beers on a tray. He offered the first glass to his son. 'That's yours, Spence.'

Spence took the one proffered and Rick used his free hand to remove another for himself, which he placed on a low dark table. He brought Kirsty's on the tray.

'It's so late,' she said kittenishly. 'I don't know whether I ought.'

As Rick bent towards her, Kirsty suddenly stood up and collided with the tray. The glass went flying. Rick tried to catch it but it fell and spilt across the carpet.

'I'm sorry!' she cried, hand to mouth. Before stooping to pick up the glass she had a moment to gauge Rick's reaction. He was furious – but was that because of the wet on his pastel carpet or because she'd wasted a carefully spiked drink?

'I'll get another,' he said testily.

Kirsty knelt on the carpet and her head swam as if she had already been drugged. She had a dragging sickness in her stomach. She closed her eyes. Even if she'd not been suspicious about the drink she could not touch alcohol, not now. She abandoned the beer stain and returned carefully to the upright dining chair. A wave of warmth swept across her face. She felt sick. Sitting on the wooden chair, she licked her lips and swallowed several times. She gave a tiny heave. She was going to throw up, any moment.

Rick returned with a beer.

'I'm going to be sick,' she said. 'I need to get to the bathroom.'

'This'll do you good.'

She waved her hand angrily – almost knocking the second glass from Rick's hand. 'I can't drink that.'

'You're pissing me about.'

Spencer chuckled smugly.

'I'm serious,' she said. She tried to get up and move past Rick but he placed the beer glass in her hand. A telephone rang. They each looked at each other. Then Rick reached inside his jacket. 'Yes?'

Spencer glared at Kirsty. She looked away. The glass in her hand felt cold and wet.

Rick muttered to the phone: 'I thought we had a firewall?'

Spencer frowned. Rick exclaimed and put down his glass. 'How many web sites did they hit?'

He listened a moment before explaining to Spencer: 'Some bastard has taken out our web sites.'

Spencer chortled but Rick raised a hand. 'Reload the security files, that's all you need to – what? Jesus, Luke, this is serious!' He stomped across to Spencer. 'Listen to this!'

As Spencer inclined his head to the phone Kirsty leant forward and exchanged Rick's beer for her own. Every movement made her dizzy. She eased back again on the wooden chair.

Spencer said, 'What?' because Rick had kept the phone and was cursing into it. 'The fuck long will that take?' Rick cursed again. 'Luke, get over here.' He cut the phone.

Spencer said, 'I didn't catch every word of that.'

'One of those fucking anti-porn crusader groups. Not only they got inside our web sites and shut 'em down, but the bastards copied all our customer names and credit card files—'

'What for – to rip off the card companies?'

'Worse. *Think* for once in your life, Spencer. They'll post the whole lot across the net: every customer's name and – Jesus! – their credit card details and the stuff they've bought.'

'I told you, Dad – Luke couldn't run a piss-up in a brewery.'

'We'll lose all our—' Rick threw the phone onto the floor. 'Luke! What the hell have you done?'

As the full impact hit him, Rick spun round on Kirsty. 'Are you a part of this?'

'Not my bag.'

'Luke!' Rick's face crumpled. 'Luke?' When he looked up his eyes were damp with tears. 'First my wife – his mother! – then he fucks our internet business.'

Spencer nodded. 'That man is way off beam.'

Rick grabbed his glass and swallowed some down. 'Luke, my *boy!* I don't believe it.' He drank another draught. Kirsty tried not to watch. Had the beer been drugged? How quickly would it work?

Rick's face was aflame with anger. He glared at Kirsty. 'Oh, for fuck's take, girl – take a drink.'

Obediently, she raised the glass and pretended to take a sip. This had been Rick's glass: it wouldn't be spiked, but the way her stomach was she couldn't let anything past her lips.

'You're so fucking prissy,' he said, as he drank again.

Spencer took a swallow of his. 'I think I'll go move my car. Hey bitch, where'd you put the keys?'

'Underneath the seat.'

'First place any child would look! And it's raining. Damn. I'll freeze to death.'

Spencer strode across the room. She and Rick watched him leave, and without Spencer it was as if the volume had been turned down. They heard the industrial lift shudder, then groan up from whichever floor Herbie had left it at. The lift halted, paused, then began again. In silence, Kirsty and Rick heard it reach the ground floor. Then came a faint sound which must have been Spencer getting off.

Kirsty heard Rick sigh.

If his beer had been spiked he showed no sign of it. He drained his glass, stared at Kirsty briefly but seemed barely aware of her – then turned and wandered over to Spencer's half-full glass. 'Here's to family life. Some family.'

He glanced at Kirsty. 'Well, you've seen it all now. You've seen our high class honey trap in Pimlico; you've seen Luke's internet business and Spencer's films; you got yourself in here; you got into Pimlico's – Rinalda.' He frowned. 'What? Yeah, you got into Pimlico. Got into the s-studio. Film. You filmed my wife. My s-son.'

He frowned again. Exhaled. 'My son and my wife. Blue movie.' He seemed to sway slightly – or did she imagine it? Perhaps he did – it was well past three in the morning and Rick was by no means young. He muttered, 'Mood indigo,' as he trudged across the room. 'Moody movie.'

Facing Kirsty was a companion armchair to the one she had sunk into before. Rick flopped down in it, and as he landed – a little heavily – his hand banged against the high arm and knocked his beer glass to the floor. Spencer's glass, she thought. He has already drunk mine.

Rick edged forward in the chair and peered blearily at the beer-stained carpet. 'Oops,' he chuckled. 'Another—' He looked across at Kirsty. 'Finish it… Drink is beer.'

It *was* spiked, Kirsty thought.

Rick closed his eyes a moment, then re-opened them. 'I'm too old for this.' He paused several seconds. 'Tall me…' He stopped, then stretched his mouth wide as if to shake off the numbness of a dental anaesthetic. '*Tell* me…' He paused to reshape his lips. 'Where… she… is.'

Each word came on a deeper note. She continued to watch him but Rick said nothing more. He didn't pass into unconsciousness, he didn't do anything remarkable. He simply sat in his chair and daydreamed like an old man by the fire.

Kirsty didn't feel too good herself. She had a dull ache in her stomach. From time to time it clenched and each time it did so she sweated through another painful warm flush. She looked at Rick, who stared at the carpet. She sat through two more waves of nausea, then carefully stood up. It shouldn't be hard, she thought, to find the bathroom.

- 42 -

When Spencer reached the street his toy car gleamed at the roadside like the last present on a tree. Soft rain glistened on the yellow paintwork and the car looked fresh and new. It cheered him up to look at it: his pretty car. A big boy's toy. He trotted across the wet tarmac, pulled open the door and slipped easily into the leather seat. He and the car fitted together like two parts of a machine. He smiled to himself, then reached down below the seat to find the keys. The keys were there, all right – the bitch hadn't tried another trick. He squeezed the key fob in his palm: chunky, masculine, a comfortable feel at this late hour.

Then he slid the key in its slot.

Two hands gripped around his neck. Tight. Powerful. From behind. Spencer let go of the key, struggled, but even as he got his hands to those around his neck the driver's door opened, a man appeared, and the man punched him on the nose. Spencer's fists flailed in the air. The man hit him again. Spencer tried to ward off the blows – but he had to loosen those grasping fingers. He couldn't breathe. The man punched again. Spencer tried to swing his head. He tried to squirm sideways in his seat but the man behind squeezed harder and at the same time pulled him against the chair. He took another punch. He freed his legs and tried to kick the man standing outside – but was hampered by confined space. His throat was agony. The man outside slipped between his legs and rammed two more blows into his face. Spencer was losing consciousness. He heard the man behind: 'You hit him again, or shall I finish him off?'

'Keep hold of him.'

The man's grip relaxed a touch and Spencer rasped desperately, trying to snatch a breath. His hands were on those fingers but he hadn't the strength to pull them free. His face raged with pain. He choked. Faster than seemed possible the man outside came round the car and moved into the passenger seat. He pulled Spencer round as if to look at him. The man behind tightened his grip. Spence had to rip away those strangling hands. He tried – but got punched again.

The man in the front seat spoke. Spence struggled. The man punched again and split his nose. As Spencer's head drooped the man in the back relaxed his grip, and when Spencer gasped it was as painful as not being able to breathe at all. The man beside him was still speaking. Spence was meant to listen. He couldn't. But in the tiny car the man's voice cut through his roaring brain. 'You hear me? Hear what I say?'

For the first time, Spencer met his eyes. He didn't recognise the man.

'I'm Tony Iles.'

The other man kept his hands around his throat. Not so tight now. The man beside him was close enough to get at. When he said, 'My name means something?' Spencer hit him.

But he was far too weak. His blow was nothing. When Tony Iles head-butted back, Spencer thought his face had cracked apart. There was blood everywhere. He could hardly see. As he squirmed in his leather seat Iles said, 'You raped my daughter, Spencer. I've come to pay you back.'

Spence was slipping. His strength gushed away like blood from a knife wound. He couldn't sit upright. 'You're a dead man,' Iles said.

The man behind squeezed his throat again and said, 'Blame your Dad for this. We asked *him* to sort you.'

'Didn't have the balls,' sneered Iles. 'Told us to blow your car up – with you inside it.'

Spencer's eyes were bulging.

'We're not the IRA,' said Farrell. 'You'll get nothing fancy.'

'You raped my daughter.'

Iles was gearing up for the kill – but the TVR suddenly filled with light. Another car had entered the street. It pulled into the kerb a few yards behind.

'Get down!' snapped Iles. He pulled Spencer's head into his lap and stooped over him, pressing Spencer down. Roy ducked into the tiny seat-well behind. Spencer huddled in darkness. He was desperately weak and in a lot of pain. But there were no fingers around his throat.

*

Luke Miller switched off his car. He sat for a moment, deflated. Somehow he would get his web sites up again, although for the moment they were frozen rigid – no, not frozen: taken over. As far as Luke could tell, the hacker had swamped his site with enough data to create a buffer overflow, before gaining root access and thus complete control of the site server. Luke's computer had then run the hacker's own corrupting programs, which had downloaded finance files and uploaded a BIOS virus and front page defacement. It had been as complete an attack as anyone could hope for. The hacker called his virus Pearl Harbor II.

Now Luke had to explain it to his techno-retard father and his dumb-head brother. When he'd phoned Rick earlier he learned that Spence was there – and sure enough, parked in the street before him was Spencer's acid yellow car. Spencer had not made a tactful exit. He was waiting to gloat. He couldn't wait for Luke to arrive.

Luke climbed out of his smart blue sports car and glanced idly at his brother's more lurid TVR. A forty thousand pound bauble dropped at the roadside. Spencer couldn't be bothered to park indoors. At 3.30am Luke didn't intend to leave *his* car unattended in the street – not when he had a garage waiting opposite.

As he crossed the road he glanced again at Spencer's yellow racer. It was as smart as his own, despite the colour – such beautiful lines that even when parked, the car seemed in motion. Poised for flight. Just now, for instance, Luke could have sworn he had seen it shudder.

But he crossed to the printing works and rang the bell.

*

Kirsty retched again, but nothing came up. Nothing *had* come up. She knelt at the lavatory basin but although her stomach heaved she couldn't vomit. Her muscles clamped but rather than expel anything they clasped her stomach and held everything in.

She heard the doorbell and took it as her cue. Unsteadily she clambered to her feet and lurched back to the Miller's hall. She heard the bell again, louder now. Someone was trying to get in. —Luke, she thought: his father had ordered him to 'get over here'.

His father. She had left Rick sitting in his armchair. As she pushed the door she felt her head swim. She was dizzy. But when she stepped inside the living room Rick looked even weaker than she was. Still in the armchair – not slumped exactly, but too relaxed – he was like a large rag doll propped in a seat and forgotten. If he'd heard the doorbell he had not reacted. Yet he was not unaware of what was happening: his head lolled around to face her. His lips twitched in an attempt to speak or smile.

She asked pointlessly, 'Who's that at the door?'

His face changed and he made a slurred sound, something like 'look'.

'Luke?'

Rick tried to nod but his head slumped sideways. He looked so helpless that Kirsty stepped forward, paused, then took his heavy head in her hands and raised it upright again. 'You drank the GHB,' she told him. 'Or was it roofie?' He didn't say anything. He couldn't. But deep in his eyes he might have smiled.

She heard a sound from the hall – the lift mechanism. Luke Miller was coming up.

*

Tony sat upright in the car and peered out the rear window. The double doors to the printing works had scraped open and after a moment, Herbie Tripp appeared. He paused at the entrance, frowned at Spencer's TVR, then shrugged and crossed carefully to Luke's. It was hard to tell whether he had seen Tony Iles or not. As Herbie reached Luke's TVR Spencer made his move. He reared up, slammed a fist in Tony's face, then turned and pushed his car door open. He was half out the car as Tony began hauling him back in. Spencer yelled to Herbie – but at that moment Herbie keyed the ignition in his brother's car. The noise of the engine must have drowned the shout, because Herbie began backing the blue car away. And Spencer had no chance to shout again. Tony heaved him by the collar, pulling so hard that Spencer cracked his head against the door sill. Roy was up now too. He leant across the front seat and pulled the door shut. Spencer was struggling but Tony slapped his hand across his painful and bloody mouth and dragged him across the seat. Roy leant over and put three fast jabs on Spencer's pulpy nose. The pain was indescribable.

'Let's finish this.'

'Hang on.'

Behind them, Herbie had reversed Luke's TVR and was now driving it into the printing works. The double doors hung open.

'Will he be coming out again?'

'Wait.'

Spencer tried weakly to break free. Roy glared at him, then

smacked him hard on what remained of his nose. Spence slumped and whimpered in Tony's grasp.

After a few moments Herbie wandered out through the entrance. He glanced at the yellow sports car, then began shutting up. Spencer was in no state to notice him. Tony clasped him tight while they watched Herbie close the large double doors.

'That's better,' Roy said. 'Everything's nice and peaceful again.'

*

Kirsty didn't wait for Luke to come upstairs. She wasn't sure how much he knew: she had filmed him having sex with his glamorous step-mother, she had drugged his father, and she had watched her boyfriend bring down his web sites. Luke liked to hide behind an urbane mask – he would not do so now.

She ran to the end of the hall, opened the door and passed onto the old concrete stairs, a dismal relic from the original printing works. Not daring to switch on a light, Kirsty began to feel her way downstairs. She could hear the mechanism of the lift as it trundled up – and for a moment she wondered whether Luke could see the stairs. Of course not. They were enclosed.

It was dark, but on every landing was a small uncurtained window. The light from each one was faint – but she could see her way. She heard the mechanism stop. He had reached the top. He would be getting out.

She was breathing harder than if she had been climbing up. As she continued down she heard Luke Miller call out – a faint shout which echoed from the top floor down through the stairwell. He shouted, 'Dad?'

Kirsty crept on downward. She felt sick and frightened. Here on the stairs she was hidden from the world – no one knew she was here. Perhaps she could rest a little – she needed to rest. When she reached the final landing she paused. Her stomach was throbbing, her breath was short, and it was surely sensible for her to sit down and wait. She could not keep running. She could barely stand. If she waited till the fuss in the house abated, she could sneak out later and take a taxi home.

If only. To be outside in the street, to hail a taxi, seemed a bizarre concept, an impossibility. The world outside was unreal. Squatting inside here was real. She stretched out a hand and ran her fingers down the old stone wall. Stone walls and a concrete floor, like a prison cell. She must not stay here.

On the last flight of stairs she could hardly walk. She held on to the metal banister and crept ever more slowly at every step, as if the stairs downward led not to freedom but to a demon's lair.

She was at the bottom.

The door facing her looked old and disused. For a moment she panicked – what if they kept the door locked? But she grasped the handle, twisted it, and pushed the small door open. She was in the ground floor car park. But she wasn't free. A man was there, waiting. It was the big man they called Herbie.

- 43 -

In the armchair, Rick had slumped to one side but was supported by the high arms of the chair. His eyes were open. To a casual glance he looked an old man who had dragged himself out of bed because he couldn't sleep. He should have worn a dressing gown.

Luke was getting his defence in first. He strode about the living room, firing off his speech like an actor on stage. It was a monologue. Rick sat in the armchair, faithfully following with his eyes, but he didn't try to upstage his son. As he expounded on the cyber attack Luke began to realise that he had never spoken to such a docile audience – not within his family. He paused to stare at Rick.

'Are you listening to anything I say?'

Rick glared weakly back.

'You're so superior, aren't you, Dad? I eat dirt and you don't deign to speak.'

Luke shook his head in exasperation, strode to the window and peered outside. 'Still raining,' he said. Spencer's TVR shone in the street light below, but Luke hardly glanced at it. The car irritated him. 'Where *is* Spencer? His car's out there.'

He turned from the window and stared at the back of his father's chair. 'All right, don't speak to me.' As he marched back into the room he noticed a beer glass on a coffee table. One here, one there, a third one – 'Are you drunk?'

He walked around to face his father. 'Enough of this – are you all right?'

Rick didn't say anything but his expression changed. His face sagged. Luke hesitated. He wasn't going to risk touching his father – he didn't want to come close enough to be grabbed.

'Where's Spencer?' he asked again.

*

They had beaten him into unconsciousness. Restricted within the cramped confines of the car, Tony could only punch with half his weight. Roy helped – till Tony told him to leave the punishment to him. Tony needed to do it, while for Roy it was just a job. Each blow helped Tony relieve his anger. He couldn't undo what Spencer had done to his daughter, but the punches helped. Spencer could no longer feel the blows, Tony knew. Roy knew it too, but he didn't say anything. Tony had to work this off.

Suddenly he stopped and sat in the front seat, panting quietly. Spencer's blood was everywhere. Flecks of blood and snot had flown around the tiny car and splattered the windscreen, dash and side window. Tony had blood on his hands, blood up his sleeve. Even Roy had caught a drop or two.

Roy muttered, 'You want we take him somewhere quiet?'

'This is where he lives.'

Not exactly, Roy thought, but he wouldn't quibble. He got out of the car and walked down to the alley where their own car waited. Tony Iles sat with the blood-soaked Spencer. He could hear Spencer's laboured breathing, as if he had a heavy cold – and while he waited for Roy he talked to the man who could not hear: 'If your dad had dealt with you himself it needn't have come to this. But he thought he could get away with it, Spencer, like you did. You people don't know how to behave proper.'

He saw Roy approaching, so he clamped his mouth shut and eased himself into the street, leaving the passenger door open. Roy looked quizzical – asking, me or you? – but Tony nodded wearily and Roy unscrewed the lid of the metal can himself. Roy leant into the car and sloshed petrol across Spencer's slumped and battered body. As the can emptied and the car filled with fumes, Roy withdrew his head and poured more fuel over the passenger seat and into the rear seat-well. But he saved a little so he could soak a rag to toss in later.

When he had finished he glanced at the sky – as if the light rain might look different up there to how it looked below. Then he peered at Tony who stood with his shoulders hunched, scowling at the weather.

'You look cold,' Roy said. 'You need a nice warm fire.'

*

Kirsty had reacted like a startled animal. Confronted by Herbie in the car park, she had turned on her heel and disappeared back up the old stone staircase. But she found it harder than running down. She was too weak. At the first half landing she stumbled and had to use the flat of her hands to break her fall. She heard the door open beneath her, and she scuttled across the tiny landing, gripped the metal banister, and began to pull herself up the stairs. On the first main landing was another door. She fell against it, knowing that if she stayed on the stairs he would surely catch her, whereas behind that door might be a hiding place. But the door was locked. It would not budge. She could hear Herbie climbing up the stairs.

As she began the third flight she was suddenly caught with a violent cramp. One hand went to her stomach, the other to a dirty stone step. She would not give up. Half climbing, half crawling, she pulled herself further up the gloomy stairs. She had a pain in her knee – she must have knocked it – but it was nothing to the ripping sensation in her belly. Her breath came in short dry gasps. Her head swum with pain.

On the next half landing Herbie caught her. She was sitting on the concrete floor, legs apart, both hands splayed behind to prop herself up. Her head was thrown back, because she needed to widen the air passage in her throat. She couldn't run away. She couldn't run anywhere.

'Out of breath?' he asked.

Kirsty groaned with pain. There was no question now – she would miscarry. Her gasps turned to sobs. Herbie stood three steps below in the gloomy stair-well but his head was above her. He stared incredulously. 'You think tears will save you?'

Kirsty howled in anguish and desolation. She shuddered. When she caught her breath she found that she had released a bolt of warm liquid into her lap. 'Oh no,' she cried. He frowned at her. 'I've lost my baby.'

*

Bolder now, Luke reached across to touch his father's face. First, as if afraid Rick might be hot, Luke brushed the tip of his middle finger against his cheek, then quickly pulled away. The next time that he touched his father's cheek he let his fingers rest there while he stared curiously into Rick's eyes. Rick was not immobile but he seemed to have lost every ounce of strength. He didn't speak, but he glared so fiercely that Luke knew he was still conscious.

'Come on, Dad, wake up. It's me.' Luke grinned encouragingly. 'Your favourite son.'

Rick glared some more.

Still wary, unwilling to accept that this normally vigorous man was helpless in his chair, Luke licked his lips nervously and reached forward to loosen his father's tie. Rick grunted but barely moved. Awkwardly, Luke undid the collar button to Rick's shirt. He wasn't sure what else to do. Make him comfortable – but he *was* comfortable, surely, propped in the high-sided armchair.

The phone rang. Rick's phone. Luke stared at him but Rick did not react. He sat in the armchair, his chest warbling, but did not move. Gingerly, Luke reached inside Rick's jacket and found the phone. He pressed the button and put it to his ear.

It was Rinalda's voice: 'Rick? Did I wake you?'

Luke grunted.

'Have you gone to bed yet, Rick? I'm sorry. I cannot sleep, my darling. We must not leave everything like this.'

'Mum, it's not Dad, it's me.'

'Lucas? What are you doing with Rick's phone?'

'I'm in the flat. He can't answer just now.'

'The flat? Oh no! Have you been quarrelling?'

'There's something wrong—'

'He knows about us. What did he say to you?'

'I think he may have had—'

'He saw the video. Oh, Lucas darling, what are we going to do?'

'Video?'

'Someone took a video of – is Rick there? Is he listening to me?'

'He's here, but he can't hear you.'

She paused. 'Does he know I'm on the phone?'

'He doesn't know anything.'

'He knows *everything*. He saw a video – you and me together in the bed. Having sex, my love. Oh God. Where are you now – where is he? You are in the flat? What's happening?'

Luke looked to the window. He had heard a kind of muffled roar, and the light outside looked brighter now. 'Hang on. Mum, I think something's happened in the street. I'll go and—'

'It doesn't matter what's in the street. This is more important.'

'You're right.' He gazed at the window. 'This is family.'

'A tragedy,' she said. 'You know when Rick arrived at the house?'

'Um… yes.' He tried to switch to Rinalda's tack. But it seemed so long ago – before the web sites crashed, before Rick had this heart attack or whatever it was. 'Mum, something bad has happened—'

'Terrible. Rick and I sat down... We thought the video – *he* thought the video would show him and I in bed, but I knew—'

'Dad's not well.'

'The video showed you and I in bed together – having sex! That girl shot it – Kirsty Rice.'

'He may have had a heart attack.'

'A *what?*'

'Things are happening here. Hang on.'

As he carried the phone to the window, Rinalda was saying, 'Who has had a heart attack? Please don't tell me you've been arguing with Rick. You mustn't do that. You should show respect for him.'

Luke stared down through the drizzle to the street below. 'Bloody kids,' he said. 'You wouldn't credit it. They've only set light to Spencer's car.'

'Spencer is there?'

'He'll murder them. His TVR. He'll break—'

He stared in horror as the car door suddenly swung open and a man stumbled out, wreathed in fire. The man managed barely two paces before he stumbled to his knees. His blazing arms flapped uselessly around his body but the flames were everywhere – along his trunk, his arms, his head. He seemed to kneel in a pool of flames.

From three floors up Luke watched aghast. 'Spencer,' he breathed. His hands dropped to his sides and he didn't hear Rinalda saying, 'Children nowadays, there is no controlling them. But where is Rick? Why can't I speak to him?'

Down in the street below, Spencer fell forwards. He tried to crawl, but flames bit into every part of his tortured body. He writhed, squirmed, rolled on the ground. For a moment he lay curled on his side, but then he propped himself up on a blazing arm. He gazed at the TVR – and as he looked at it the engine exploded. The front of the car blew apart and two sheets of metal flew through the air, no longer able to contain the fire within. Spencer rocked back, fell to his elbow, tried to look at his car again, but could not support himself. When he slipped back, there was a shower of sparks from beneath his body, and he subsided on glowing embers like a burning log.

*

Kirsty looked as if she had been shot. Blood and fluid puddled her skirt, her face was white, and her hands fumbled helplessly in the mess. Behind her, Herbie knelt holding her up, his chest against her back, his big hands gentle on her arms. She was sobbing. The pain was there but it had diminished and Kirsty was picking at the sodden cloth as if it were a dressing on a wound.

The concrete floor was cold but she couldn't feel it. Neither could she feel the warmth from Herbie's chest. She was barely aware that he was there, although without him she would have collapsed. She sat on the hard concrete floor, stone walls on either side, like a torture victim in a prison cell. And she wept for her lost baby. She lifted her wet skirt and folded it back. Her thighs were red, and although her panties should have formed some kind of barrier they had become a part of her bleeding flesh. Herbie looked away. 'D'you think it's over?' he asked. She didn't reply. 'How far were you gone?'

For the first time, it seemed, she realised he was there. She heard gentleness in his voice. 'Six weeks,' she told him.

He nodded. When he lowered his head it was only so he could murmur in her ear: 'Yes, it's finished.'

She wiped her fingers through the mess. 'Somewhere,' she muttered.

'What?'

'I want to see my baby.'

'There's nothing there.'

'My baby.'

She was picking at the material of her drenched clothes. In the dim light of the old stone landing the blood looked more black than red – a viscous liquid flecked with small dark lumps. 'Is this it?' she whimpered.

'That's a clot of blood.'

'I can't see. Turn on the light.'

'There's nothing—'

'My baby is six weeks old!'

'All you'll see is the placenta. Believe me – what's your name – Kirsty?'

He moved his head forward. He continued to support her but wanted to look into her eyes. At that moment they heard a low whirring noise – not loud, but enough to make them start. 'What's that?' she whispered.

'Just the lift. They don't use the stairs.'

'He'll come looking for me.'

'He won't come here.'

She was scrabbling in the blood. 'I must find my baby.'

'Believe me, Kirsty, there's nothing there.'

'There must be.'

'You won't want to see it.'

She turned so suddenly she nearly banged his head. 'What do *you* know?'

'It's dead, Kirsty. All you'll see is a scrap of tissue, less than an inch long.'

'An inch? Then I'll be able – is this it?'

In the gloom she had found a sliver of grey tissue in a flattened yolk sac that had undeniably been her baby. 'I want to see her properly.'

'Kirsty—'

'It's not *your* baby – you don't understand. I know she's dead. I know there's... hardly anything...'

She held the tissue sac in her palm and touched it gently with one finger. 'This is my baby.'

She was weirdly calm. Neither spoke for half a minute. The lift had stopped.

Herbie said, 'We've got to clean you up.'

'No.' She huddled over the tiny foetus.

'Now, don't worry – I won't give you to the Millers. They'll think you escaped. But you can't stay here.'

She looked at him properly for the first time. He was their man, one of them. Yet he seemed... decent, somehow. 'Where are you—'

'I'll clean this mess up later. Come along.'

'I won't let you clean away my baby.'

'Not the baby. This other mess.' She hid her hand away from him. 'You can keep the baby for a while.'

He shifted behind her back but did not let go of her. She was so light he knew she'd topple. 'Don't try to get up. I'll carry you.'

'Where?'

'I'll hide you in my flat.'

Reel Seven:

PETIT MORT

- 44 -

The car blazed like a dying bonfire on a rainy night. Fingers of flame ran out momentarily along the tarmac before they died. Luke Miller walked quickly past the car towards his brother but in his last few paces he knew he didn't need to hurry. Spencer's body lay charred and smouldering. The smell was of underdone steak, overlaid with a more powerful stink of burnt fuel. There was another, more acrid smell: it could have been burnt rubber but was probably burnt clothes. What told Luke that Spencer was dead was the twisted rigid pose of the blackened body: knees bent, shoulders hunched, fists clenched. Spencer looked as if he had died fighting.

Luke raised his hand above the body, meaning to touch it, but he couldn't bring himself to do so. For a moment his fingers hovered as if giving absolution, and a mist of rain settled on the back of his hand like a sheen of sweat. He looked up and down the rainy street. Where was everybody? Had nobody seen? But it was four in the morning and no one else lived in this little street. No one would help.

He keyed the emergency number and was surprised how quickly they responded. But it was four o'clock, of course – no one else awake. He wondered what he should do about the body – he couldn't leave his brother in the wet street like a sack of rubbish. But should he move it? Wasn't this what the police would call 'the scene of the crime'?

He glanced at the TVR, still burning quietly, lighting up the street. He didn't know what to do next. Then he remembered that Herbie was in the printing works, presumably on his way to bed. He'd know what to do. Herbie always did.

*

Herbie scooped her up and carried her a flight of stairs to the next main landing. She was so light in his arms that when he reached the unlocked door he was able to open it while supporting her along one arm. He kicked the door open and carried her like a bride across the threshold – except that it was not into his flat, it was into a large dark open floor – dusty, uncared for, with boxes and discarded furniture strewn about its vacant space. Beyond the open area stood a partition wall broken by an unlit corridor leading away. Without speaking, Herbie carried her across the space towards it. When Kirsty looked down she saw that he was trudging along a trail through dust from the stair-well to the unlit corridor. There was another trail from the corridor to the lift gate at the rear wall. Two trails through the dust. Nothing else – because nothing happened here. The only disturbance came when Herbie crossed the floor and reinforced these footpaths in the dust.

He took a few steps along the corridor, paused, opened another door and carried her inside. The lights were low, but after so long in the gloom the light seemed intense. She half closed her eyes.

He said, 'I suppose the bathroom would be best.'

He carried her there, switched on the light – but it was so bright that even Herbie flinched. He switched it off again. 'Wait here.'

She sat with the door open, and while he was out of the room she opened her hand and looked at the soft sliver of grey-pink tissue, her unborn child. It didn't look like a child. She had expected to see a foetus – tiny but recognisable, like those full-colour photographs she occasionally saw in magazines – but this looked like a jelly capsule with a distorted bean inside. Could this be life? Was it her baby, or had she picked out the wrong scrap from the fluids she'd lost?

When Herbie reappeared she had withdrawn deep inside herself – but to brighten the dimly lit bathroom Herbie had brought a lighted candle on a saucer. Its flickering flame became a focus in the room. It was too bright to stare at but it cast a soothing light. Shadows on the wall were soft, like scudding rainclouds.

He said, 'You can take a bath. I'll bring a dressing gown and a pair of pyjamas, I suppose. It's all I have.'

He left, and she sat staring at the door. Did he expect her to take her clothes off in his tiny bathroom? He had left the door open against the bath, and she couldn't see if it had a bolt. She remained where she was and opened her hand.

When Herbie came back she showed him the foetus in her palm. 'Where can I put this?'

He sighed. 'You have to let it go.'

She didn't say anything for several seconds. Then she looked up. 'I can't flush my baby down the lavatory.'

'You can't keep it.'

'I need to hold her.'

He looked at her and sighed. 'I'll get you another saucer. You can put it there while you take a bath. We'll think about it later.'

While he was out of the room she didn't move. When he came back he stooped and placed a fresh saucer in her hand, then turned on the bath. 'I'll leave you to check the temperature. Don't let the water run too hot.' He glanced away awkwardly. 'If you put your clothes outside the door I'll stick 'em through the washing machine. They'll be dry by morning.'

She had to raise her voice above the running water: 'You don't think I'm staying here?'

He gazed at her. 'Where'll you go? You couldn't make it to the lift.'

'You can't force me to stay.'

'You're not a prisoner.' His shoulders slumped. 'You're in no state to leave. You need to clean up and go to bed. You can use *my* bed.'

She stared at him. He shook his head. 'What do you think I am, Kirsty?' He turned away. 'Leave your clothes outside the door.'

When he pulled the door to, she saw there was no bolt. It didn't mean anything, she supposed: he lived alone. But because he worked for the Millers she glanced quickly around for a peep-hole or two-way mirror. The only mirror was on the door to the little medicine chest above the basin. The mirror was misted but Kirsty still could not trust it. She opened her hand, slid the little yolk sac onto the saucer that he'd brought, then put it down. Carefully, using both hands for support, she eased herself up and opened the little mirrored door. It wasn't a fake – just a plain medicine chest filled with man's things: shaving equipment, toothpaste, Alka Seltzer. She looked no further but closed the door. The room had filled with steam and the light from the candle had shrunk in on itself. The pale flame shone through the mist like a lamp at sea. Kirsty could sense the bath water running hot, so she took two wavering steps and turned on the cold. Herbie was right: she wasn't strong enough to leave the flat. She was barely able to bathe herself. Did he know that? Did he think she might call him back?

Kirsty had reached the point where she trusted no one. Herbie worked for the Millers – yet from the moment he had seen her condition he had been gentle, decent... She would have to trust him.

Then she heard the doorbell.

*

Herbie had rigged the doorbell from a kit bought at a street market. It was rarely used and on the few occasions it rang he was struck by how inappropriate it sounded: a two-note chime, the old Avon commercial.

He opened the door, knowing it could only be one of the Millers.

Luke said, 'Spencer's been killed.'

'How?'

'Burned.'

'I didn't hear nothing.'

'Let me in, Herbie. We've got to talk.'

'Where *is* Spencer?'

'Outside.'

'Rick with him?'

'No... Rick's not well.'

'So you left Spence in the street – alone?'

Luke looked uncomfortable. 'What else could I do? He's dead. The police are coming.'

Herbie stepped out and closed the door behind him. 'Don't give 'em an excuse to come inside.'

*

Kirsty lay in the bath until the steam had cleared. Moisture clung to the walls, and even the candle flame looked damp. Despite the sodden look of the room the bath water was tepid. Any hotter she would have fainted. But now, lying almost weightless in the bath, thoughts drifting at random through the steam, she began to feel at peace. She had put her clothes outside the door – though Herbie had not returned for them.

On the rim of the bath stood two saucers, one in each corner beyond her toes. The stubby candle had stopped flickering, and its modest flame stood so erect and still that it could have been carved from yellow wax. In the other saucer the blob of tissue looked like a melted sweet: a jelly baby.

*

His first instinct was to stay in the shadows at the side of the street. Herbie avoided the police at any time – but with a dead body outside his home he felt especially uncomfortable. Luke faced them with surprising ease, looking strained, as well he might, and elegantly dishevelled in the rain. He seemed apologetic that he had called them out. But Herbie waited by the wall, hands in pockets, thinking it typical that the cops arrived before the ambulance. Not that Spencer needed an ambulance. His tense charred body lay at the roadside in an oily puddle of black ash, and the police hardly looked at it. They stood in the middle of the narrow street and spoke to Luke as if it wasn't raining. As if it wasn't four o'clock in the morning. Then Herbie heard a policeman: 'Can I ask why everyone is fully dressed?'

*

The water had started tepid, but now was cold. Kirsty lay in it, too tired to move. She was numb, bruised, and waterlogged. A piece of driftwood. The only sounds were the tiny splash when she dropped a hand into the water, and the trickling drips when she slowly lifted it out. No sound from Herbie. Nothing outside. No one there.

No one knew where Kirsty was. No one thought about her. Herbie had left, Ken had abandoned her, and whatever the Millers did took place in some other universe. She was like an actress after a film had been shot – discarded, empty, no role to play. She placed her elbows on the rim of the bath, but even that caused her head to swim. The water was cold and she couldn't stay in it.

When she stood up her knees quivered and she feared that she might fall. But the feeling passed and she was soon able to stand unsteadily in the emptying bath and begin to dry herself. She felt so light that a tug of water might drag her down. She had to hold the rim of the bath while she stepped out to dab her ankles, then her feet.

Beside her, at the corner of the bath, stood the doleful saucer. What ought she to do with this undeveloped baby? As Herbie had said, she couldn't keep her child. But she couldn't flush it down the loo. She couldn't throw it in the trash. Perhaps she could keep the saucer overnight in his fridge while she decided what to do.

Don't be ridiculous. As she reached for Herbie's pyjamas she had a momentary vision of the big man opening his fridge to be confronted with this little saucer and its solitary dead eye. She almost smiled.

She watched the water swirling down the plug-hole. On a sudden impulse she grabbed the damp saucer and tilted it, tipping the blob of tissue like a slip of seafood into the bath-water. It smacked lightly on the surface, bobbed a moment, then was caught by the whirlpool till it disappeared. Kirsty reached out her other hand but it was gone.

She heard the sucking noise as bath water slurped down the hole. She cried out. Her hand stretched towards the plug. Her stomach clenched painfully and she tottered, straightened, then watched the last warm rivulets drain away.

Nothing in the grating of the plug hole. The bath was wet and clean. Everything was washed clean. Along with soapy bath-water, that little scrap of tissue had been sluiced into a maze of pipes and tunnels that led eventually – where? – down to the river, to the sea. Everything, eventually, went to the sea.

It wasn't a baby, it had no life, but she had destroyed something that had once lived inside her. Part of her life had been let go. And it wasn't the Millers who had killed the baby; it wasn't Ken. It wasn't Herbie. It was her. She had driven herself single-mindedly on this quest for a story, for revenge. She had ignored risks, had courted danger, never thinking that she herself could get hurt. Never thinking that her baby could get hurt. Had she thought of her baby at all – had she really sat down to think, or had she pursued her career agenda before all else?

She had killed her baby. Kirsty stood in the humid bathroom and sobbed softly, empty and weak. She shivered. As she struggled into Herbie's far too large pyjamas – arms flapping, legs trailing on the damp floor – she knew she looked a clown. The sad and lonely clown that cried.

- 45 -

Using the Millers' cheapest mugs, Herbie Tripp had made a tray of tea and carried it into their pastel living room. Morning sun shone through the window as if it had never been raining – the only tell-tale being the slight haze of water vapour rising from the sill. Herbie said barely a word to anyone. He was a servant in the background. He wasn't there.

In the room, the police inspector sat on an upright chair while her constable hovered near the door. The Millers sat separately, the last three pieces in an abandoned chess game. Rinalda sat in one high-backed armchair, Rick in the other – the one, in fact, where he had sat somnolent last night. Luke watched from the settee. His father looked tired but seemed to have recovered – except that he claimed he felt sick and couldn't remember much of what had happened. He had been in the flat, he said; Spencer had called round – but after that his mind was blank. He must have gone to sleep.

'So you remember nothing?' Gillett murmured. 'Great timing.'

Herbie was surprised that Luke contradicted his father – saying, of all things, that his father had had a mild heart attack and had been immobile in his chair. Rick glared at him, spitting out his words: 'Some things I won't forget.'

Herbie padded between them, handing out teas. He couldn't fail to see how strained the Millers were, even with each other. They sat in separate chairs, not looking at each other. This is more than grief, he thought: they blame each other for Spencer's death. The inspector seemed to pick up on it: she had a gleam in her eye, a hunter's gleam, and she sat perched at the front of her upright chair watching their taut faces.

Gillett glanced at Herbie: 'Did *you* see or hear anything, Mr Tripp?'

He shook his head with practised ease. 'I was in my room. Mr Miller came up and said there'd been an accident. That's the first I knew.'

He waited till she nodded him away.

As he left he heard Rinalda speak – in a quieter voice than she normally used: 'It was not an accident.'

Herbie paused a moment.

Inspector Gillett said, 'It certainly was not an accident.' She glanced at Luke. 'Nor was it kids trying to vandalise a car. It bears all the hallmarks of a deliberate killing – a grudge killing, perhaps.' She switched her gaze to Rick. 'Who might have wanted to do such a thing?'

Herbie left the room. He could. No one ever thought the butler did it.

*

Tony Iles sat up in bed, feeling better after three hours' sleep than he had for weeks. He leapt out, grabbed a wrap, and went into the hall to knock on his daughter's door. Hopefully she was there. When he'd got in late last night she was home and asleep. She'd looked young and innocent – but as he told himself, she was just a kid.

'Can I come in?'

He hadn't expected her to be awake, but when he entered the room he found her not only out of bed but fully dressed. In school uniform.

'Going to school?'

He got one out of ten for observation. 'It *is* a school day, Dad.'

She sat at a mirror applying make-up. Were school-kids meant to wear make-up? 'I got some news for you. Should cheer you up.' He hesitated. 'Though maybe it's a bit awkward. I shouldn't have brought it up.'

'Your choice.'

'It could upset you.'

She rolled her eyes. Where did parents *come* from?

He watched her in the mirror – his little girl getting ready for school. This wasn't the time to tell her. He turned to go.

'You said it would cheer me up.'

'It's delicate.'

She tensed: 'delicate' sounded like a scolding. Then she relaxed: 'But it should cheer me up?'

'We can talk tonight.'

'I could be dead tonight.'

He sighed. 'Stop me if this is painful for you. You know that man who… you remember his name was Spence Miller?'

Her face set. The girl in the mirror seemed to have aged ten years. 'Well, Miller's dead. He got killed last night.'

'Good.' She applied a touch more lipstick.

'I killed him for you.'

She caught his eyes. They stared at each other in the bedroom mirror. 'You're free of him, Emma.'

She paused. 'Oh, right.'

'Like I've avenged you.'

She frowned – such a young face, trying to look grown-up. Then she burst out laughing. Her laugh was harsh and sounded hostile. 'Oh, so that's all right? That makes it better?' She laughed incredulously. 'You're pathetic, you.'

He saw his daughter's hardened reflection. She didn't bother to meet his eyes. She examined her ageing face in the mirror and applied more make-up.

'Avenged me!' she sneered, and laughed again. 'Wow.' It was a forced laugh, a weapon against him – and Tony turned on his heel and stomped into the hall. Her laugh grew louder and echoed through the house.

Then she shouted, 'It's Emma*line*. Right? I'm not your little Emma any more.'

*

Kirsty opened her eyes. She was in a strange bed, opposite an unfamiliar window, and the sun was shining. Her phone was ringing – and there was a man standing in the room.

It was Herbie. He stood holding the door.

'I heard the phone,' he said. 'I came to turn it off.'

The phone kept ringing. 'D'you want to answer it?'

She nodded.

He lifted her phone from the chest of drawers and handed it across to her. But the call seemed irrelevant. 'How did I get here?'

He mumbled something, but she had already remembered: she had put herself to bed – in his pyjamas? He had told her she could sleep in his bed. 'Where did *you* sleep?'

'Answer the phone or turn it off.'

Her head was swimming. Nothing yet made sense. She clicked the phone and muttered, 'Hello.'

'Hi, Kirsty, I thought you'd never answer.'

Ken. She began waking fast. Yesterday was flooding back.

'Isn't it great? You must have heard.'

'Heard what?'

'I brought down all their porno sites. Fabulous! And that's not all—'

Her hand dropped listlessly to the coverlet. She had lost her baby. Herbie whispered, 'Shall I take the phone?'

'No, I—' Her voice had thickened. Her eyes were damp when she picked it up.

'Wait till you see the film, Kirsty – I look great in it.'

'Don't do it, Ken.'

'I'm the star, you know? Ken defeats the evil empire.'

'They'll kill you—'

'Rosa's seen the rough cut—'

'Don't show yourself on film. Don't even use your name.'

'I blew the accounts files and posted the details on the Killporn web site. The police can get everyone's address!'

'Ken,' she said, but he didn't hear. She lowered the phone.

'Turn it off,' said Herbie. 'Say you'll call back later.'

'I have to tell him.' She lifted the phone and spoke across Ken's chatter. 'Ken, I – Ken, listen.'

Finally he stopped. Perhaps he paused for breath.

'I lost the baby.'

'Oh.' His voice changed gear. 'Oh, that's... Well, that's probably... Well, I suppose it's really for the best.'

'The best?'

'This is no time for you to have a baby. Is it? You've got a career ahead of you.'

'It would have been *our* baby.'

'Exactly. Both of us. But not now, yeah? Listen Kirsty, we've made one hell of a series here. Rosa says—'

She moved the phone away, took a breath, then moved it back. 'Don't you want to ask—'

But he was talking through her. She tried again: 'You haven't even asked—' He wasn't listening She gulped back her tears. As she tried to speak again, Herbie reached across and switched off the phone. 'That was the father?'

She nodded dumbly.

'I thought Spencer was.'

She shook her head. Herbie looked as if he were about to tell her something. 'You're well rid of him,' he said.

'Who?'

Herbie didn't reply directly. 'You should leave the phone switched off a while. Try to sleep. – But you're not a prisoner here.' He shrugged. 'Go any time.'

Kirsty sank into the pillows. 'Perhaps I could sleep a little longer.'

'As long as you like – till you get your strength back. If you're still here tonight I'll take the sofa again, like last night. OK?'

She closed her eyes a moment, then opened them to look at him. 'Thank you.'

He stared back. 'Spencer's dead,' he told her. 'Someone set light to his car last night.'

'He... burned to death?'

She shuddered. Burned to death, like Zoë.

Herbie watched her. 'Things are rough out there. But like I say, you can leave any time – though when you do, you ought to tell me first. I can smuggle you out and drive you home.'

She closed her eyes again. It was as if she were slipping from the real world into a waking dream, in which the events of the last few days jostled for attention like unedited images in a film. She remembered Zoë, who had died; Cassie who had disappeared; the baby...

Kirsty lay in big Herbie's sheltering bed and imagined her baby, small but fully formed in its protective membrane, drifting on an expanse of calm sparkling sea, floating on a scallop shell, pearl white. As Kirsty watched, the yolk sac disappeared and the little girl baby lay naked and smiling in the shell. The child chuckled merrily, and when she raised her hands to the sun she sucked warmth deep down into her body. Fishes leapt, and the sky was blue.

And as Kirsty watched, a peace descended. She knew that the sea would cherish her baby and keep her safe. The bright sun and sea would ensure that, for ever and ever, her child would live.

Also by RUSSELL JAMES, published by THE DO-NOT PRESS

Oh No, Not My Baby

Oh No, Not My Baby is a dark noir mystery set amid the blood and gristle of the meat-processing industry. Musician Nick Chance does an old flame a favour and finds himself sucked into a dangerous world of corporate gangsterism, animal rights terrorism and sudden, brutal death.

> 'A juicy slice of British noir writing, tackling animal liberation taken to its violent extreme.'
> *The Telegraph*

Painting in the Dark

An *Independent on Sunday* Book of the Year – 2000

London, today: An unscrupulous art dealer, the gargantuan Gottfleish, believes that 85-year-old Sidonie Keene is hiding a small hoard of her notorious sister Naomi's valuable paintings.

> ... eclipsing much of contemporary British mystery writing
> *The Guardian*

Pick Any Title

A magnificent crime caper involving sex, humour, sudden death and double-cross.

'Lord Clive' bought his lordship at a 'Lord of the Manor' sale where titles fetch anything from two to two hundred thousand pounds. Why not buy another cheap and sell it high? Why stop at only one customer?

> A brilliant page-turner from 'the best of Britain's darker crime writers'
> *The Times*

The Do-Not Press
Fiercely Independent Publishing

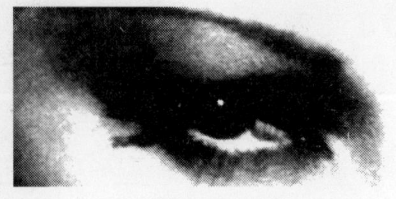

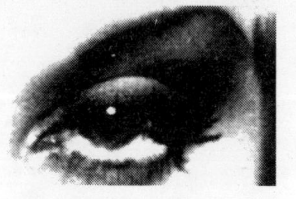

Keep in touch with what's happening at the cutting edge of independent British publishing.

Simply send your name and address to:
The Do-Not Press (Dept. NOGH)
16 The Woodlands, London SE13 6TY (UK)

or email us: nogh@thedonotpress.co.uk

There is no obligation to purchase
(although we'd certainly like you to!)
and no salesman will call.

Visit our regularly-updated web site:

http://www.thedonotpress.co.uk

Mail Order

All our titles are available from good bookshops, or (in case of difficulty) direct from The Do-Not Press at the address above. There is no charge for post and packing for orders to the UK and EU.

(NB: A post-person may call.)